Reviews for 'For the Love of a Man'

"Filled with rich imagery, beautiful prose, and an occasional poem to more fully express overwhelming emotional moments, this is the story of a woman torn between fulfilling the ideals she was raised to believe in and answering an internal need to experience life to greater depth."

"When one is choked of all joy and possibility in life, is it better to grab for the oxygen mask or allow oneself to die? In presenting her story, the narrator here poses these questions without apology or justification."

—Recommended reading by US Review of Books

"Semi-autobiographical, this novel pulls on the author's experiences to build a rich, wholly developed character in Amrita. She is a protagonist we see grow from the start of the novel all the way to the last page. Her journey feels unique to her particular circumstances, but at the same time, there are bits and pieces most women could pull examples from their own lives, understand and relate to and learn from."

"This is a book which will be remembered long after finishing…"

—Pacific Book Review

". . . a heart-rending story of love and strife."

"Bajaj arrestingly evokes the splendors and deprivations of India in the second half of the 20th century, and makes a penetrating case for women forced into marriage and who can't even spend the salary that they earn. Although Rosy too often finds "neither sympathy nor understanding" from the men in her life, including, eventually, her own son, Bajaj all but guarantees that she'll find sympathy from readers as she struggles with both her desires and the potential collapse of her family."

"A passionate, absorbing story of love, rejection, and the burden of tradition."

—*Kirkus Reviews*

"The writer Amrinder Bajaj, takes us on a roller-coaster journey of the typical Indian family and culture system. The book provides fun, drama and satire all at the same time which is bound to keep readers glued. But, after the protagonist is married off to a stranger by her father, the real gist of the story begins. Amrita's life takes a turn from bad to worse. . ."

—*Woman's Era*
(largest selling woman's magazine in India)

"The book 'For the Love of a Man' is a heavily fictionalized account of her life that lays bare taboo subjects like female sexuality, exposing what right-thinking people would carry to their graves with sealed lips."

—*Different Truths*
(e magazine read in over 160 countries)

A tale of triumph

"Advocating feminism, the book revolves around how a woman single handedly takes on worst of the situations head-on and emerges strong enough to raise her children, stay in a muck-like marriage, discharge her responsibilities and simultaneously make a career. These lines of the book speak for themselves:

> *After elusive shadows, long I ran, never again, will I crave the love of a man. From now on it just my dog and me; and a book beneath a shady tree.*

… had she found a shoulder to lean on, this book would have ceased to exist."

—*Dailyexcelsior*
(the largest circulated daily of Jammu and Kashmir)

For the Love of a Man

Books by the author

- *Afternoon Girl – My Khushwant Memoirs*
  publisher – HarperCollins
  A hilarious, salacious, scandalous account of the author's
  interaction with India's most noted (notorious) columnist/writer/
  journalist Khushwant Singh

- *Sailing Smoothly Through Pregnancy*
  publisher – Elsevier
  An easy to understand guide with anecdotes, for pregnant women
  the world over though, chapters like Indian myths, diet and yoga
  pertains specifically to women in the subcontinent.

- *The Adolescent Girl*
  publisher – Books For All
  A wellness book that educates teenagers on reproductive health.

- *Doctor Jokes by a Doctor for the Doctored*
  publisher – Books For All
  Medical jokes arranged subject-wise.

- *Autumn Leaves*
  publisher – Writer's Workshop
  A collection of poems.

For the Love of a Man

Amrinder Bajaj

Library of Congress Control Number:		2016912242
ISBN:	Hardcover	978-1-5245-9353-7
	Softcover	978-1-5245-9352-0
	eBook	978-1-5245-9351-3

Print information available on the last page.

Rev. date: 04/11/2017

To order additional copies of this book, contact:
Xlibris
800-056-3182
www.Xlibrispublishing.co.uk
Orders@Xlibrispublishing.co.uk
736459

All I ask of you is to

Tread the path I travelled

Bear what I have borne

Pass through storms

That passed through me.

Live the lives I've lived,

Before you

Judge me or condemn.

for deep
who did not judge

Vikram Bhattacharya - touching that part of the story of Gautam Buddha that remains largely untouched—that of the wife and child he left behind.

He left her in the middle of the night, the night their son was born. When she heard the news she was devastated. Yet she did not complain though her life lost all meaning. The only reason for her to live now was her son. She wanted him to grow up to be a man the world would look up to.

Her friends and relatives came around and asked her to forget the man who had left her and to start life again but she refused. She was young and beautiful and suitors queued up outside her door, but she refused each of them.

Then one fine day he came back! He stood in front of her and she could hardly remember him as the man who left her.

'They call you the Buddha now,' she asked him gently.

'I hear they do,' he answered in a calm fashion.

'What does it mean?' she further inquired.

'I think it means the enlightened one, a knower,' he informed her. She smiled and then silence.

'I suppose we have both learned something. Your lessons, O Buddha, will make the world richer in spirit, but my lesson will unfortunately remain largely unknown.' She reflected deeply.

'And what lesson is that?' the Buddha probed.

Her eyes sparkled with unshed tears. 'That a courageous woman does not need anyone to complete her . . . SHE IS COMPLETE ON HER OWN.'

Acknowledgments

As an obstetrician and gynecologist
Even my literary analogies cannot but be
Related to my grueling, happy profession
Hence the following:
Can a message forge a friendship between
Two people countries, continents apart?
Can it be cemented by the written word
Like bricks and mortar, to build a house of trust
Into which the two, who have never met,
Move in after a virtual marriage
To beget a brainchild that I conceived and
He, lovingly, selflessly nurtured
Under the expert antenatal care
Of Lloyd Griffith and his team.
When my time came, Jade Allen and Mary Preston
Delivered it in the birthing room of Xlibris and
Handed it over to Edwin Ingram the pediatrician
Whose advise, helped it grow to its full potential.
My heartfelt thanks to all my unseen angels
Who have guided me at every step of the way.

Prologue

I sat on the terrace savouring the most tranquil hour of my day. A mug of tea sent up tendrils of steam. The newspaper lay on the table by my side. My Lhasa pup dozed by my feet. The jamun spread its branches in eternal welcome. A moisture-laden breeze teased its dark green leaves gently swaying bunches of ripening berries. Sparrows and mynahs, bulbuls and babblers, vied for a place in its shade. A pair of crows fiercely guarded the contents of their untidy nest. Besides these old friends, a tiny new bird hovered happily over the monsoon feast. Exquisite green feathers blended harmoniously with the soft yellow of its breast. I did not know its name but how did that matter? It gave me as much pleasure without formal introductions.

Besides the birds, the jamun housed a host of other beings. Wasps industriously built a house of paper on the undersurface of a slender branch. A camouflaged chameleon watched with quiet wisdom the silly scampering of squirrels. I felt a curious bonding with the tree—its stable roots and ever-changing crown. It gave me more joy than the son who planted it years ago did. Karan had been a lovable schoolboy then, fired by the green revolution, not the insufferable, judgemental adult who could not wait to put the distance of the seven seas between us. Human beings were the most ungrateful of all species that inhabit this earth. Why, even the cactus that the gardener had uprooted and I re-planted in a fit of sentimentality had rewarded me with a bouquet of beautiful white blossoms.

The tiny patch of greenery I presumed to call my garden or more fondly, my 'oxygen plant' had, besides the jamun, a neem sapling struggling to assert itself. A row of slender ashokas stood erect as silent sentinels in green uniforms. Succulent, arrow-tipped crotons lined the boundary like soldiers at attention—jasmines and lilies, oleander and hibiscus, myrtle and marigold, added splashes of colour to the green monotone.

With the ripening of jamuns would come the urchins for their undeserved share. I remembered the jamuns of my childhood on Rajpath, the beautiful stretch of road between Rashtrapati Bhawan and India Gate. Flanking the road were verdant lawns with artificial lakes that sparkled like diamonds in green velvet. Around these bodies of water grew shady jamun trees. We lived in an armed forces complex King Edward Mess, (long since demolished) by the side of one of these water bodies. During our morning walks, the boys from our mess would shake jamuns from the branches while the girls picked up the fat berries and ran—the purple juice running down our elbows onto our frocks. The watchman would run after us but the wobble of age was no match for the nimble legs of youth. Storms added to our joy by showering jamuns along with the rain.

'Enough of reminiscing now.' I gave myself a mental shake. I had to put on a brisk manner along with my crisp cotton sari and do the rounds of the hospital. After all, I wasn't just a vulnerable woman coming to terms with the hollowness of her existence. I had a prefix to my name that gave me a lot of respect and responsibility. I had patients who trusted me with their lives. It would not do to let them down, though life had betrayed my trust. I would continue to perform surgeries, deliver babies as before, but something deep within had changed.

Whereas I had swum like a fish within the womb of life, I now emerged from it like a lotus from a pond—attached yet curiously detached. My detachment wasn't the *bairagya* the *sadhus* so extolled. It was a resigned sort of detachment, as if nothing seemed to matter anymore. For long, weary years, I had fought for a place under the sun. It did not seem worth the effort anymore. The sword of resistance clattered to the floor and I wore an armour of indifference over my broken spirit. The mirrors of my past and present juxtaposed and I saw endless Amritas reflected over and over again till eternity. I shuddered involuntarily. The moment passed and my shoulders sagged. Why should it bother me? Life was over and done with.

By worldly standards, my life was a success. I had looks and brains, a roof over my head, and a reasonable bank balance. I had a soft-spoken husband and two lovely children. Who was to see the undercurrents beneath the surface calmness? My husband and lover still fought lethal cold wars over me. My son continued to despise me. Everything was as it was before. It was the battle within that was over. The fire had burnt down, the ash swept out, leaving behind an empty hearth and heart.

For one who believed that to feel was to live, this was akin to death, but it mattered no more. Every single person who had been allowed to enter the sanctum sanctorum had violated it. Barred and bolted now, the 'I' within had become inviolate. Freed of the shackles of hope and expectations, resentment and rancour, desire and disappointments, I felt cleansed; cleansed of love and the hate that love bred over and over again. It would be a joyless existence, but my priorities had changed. No longer did I crave happiness. A healing nothingness, a welcome void was what I wanted at this point of time and for that I would have to look inwards. No one else could give me that.

Father, lover, husband, son,
Have let me down one by one.
Each time I fell on life's terrain
Another's help I sought to gain
Each one jerked his hand away
And, heartlessly walked away.
Each time, something within me died,
As feelings numbed and crystallized.
Each stab, each wound, each little prick,
Scarred and hardened into a brick,
That turned my heart into a fort
Which could now stand, without support.
I have done with sighs and anguished cries,
With love and longing, lust and lies,
After elusive shadows, long I ran,
Never again,
Will I crave the love of a man.
From now on it just my dog and me
And a book beneath a shady tree.

1

I was born in Jalandhar jail. Not because my mother was a convict but because her father happened to be the jail doctor and she had gone to her maternal home to deliver.

Ever since I was apprised of the fact I'd quip, 'I only hope I do not die in jail.' and shudder involuntarily at my morbid witticism.

Besides being born at the wrong place, I belonged to the wrong sex. Under the ancestral *haveli* (mansion) in Jammu was a small airless room called the *kothri*. A large bed dominated the dark precincts of this windowless chamber. It used to be the nuptial bed in days gone by, but ever since its magical properties were discovered, it was reserved for lying in. It was a proven fact that every woman who delivered here begot a son. My father was the first to fly the nest on the wings of the Air Force and hence the retribution of a daughter.

My mother felt that she had let the family down. My father joked that as he was away at the time of delivery, a girl was born; only it wasn't a joke for the next time he made it a point to be with her and was rewarded by a son. My father's sister sent a congratulatory note stating, 'What else can we expect from the daughter of a woman who has borne eight daughters?'

Barring the fact that I was born a girl, my parents could not fault me. I had a crop of crisp black curls and big black button eyes. A rosy baby with rosy cheeks and a rosebud mouth had to be called Rosy. People marvelled at the way I rolled up into a ball, and put my thumbs and big toes in my mouth. I retained

1

both habits for I still often put my foot in my mouth. As for the thumb, it stayed in for long enough to spoil the alignment of my teeth.

The only one who did not hold my being a girl against me was Daadaji (paternal grandfather), perhaps because I resembled his dead wife, Ajit Kaur, who died a few months before I was born. The timing of my birth and an uncanny likeness to her led him to believe that she had reincarnated as me! I felt a sense of deja vu each time I crossed the threshold of our *haveli* in Jammu. The wife who knew no happiness within its confines felt vindicated when treated with love by the same old man as a granddaughter. He *was* partial to me. If the other grandchildren received a paisa each morning, he would put an anna on was my palm and close my fist quickly lest the others saw. I have fond memories of an old man who wore a white turban like a Hindu though he was a Sikh. He dozed whole day in the garden in front of the house and was hardly spoken to. I thought that this was because he was hard of hearing. Much later I learnt that his children despised him, and he deserved their scorn. He was deaf not because of old age but due to an overdose of opium. This attempt at suicide was because his 'mistress' had ditched him for his elder brother!

Daadaji was the typical son of a rich landowner, idle and debauch. Not having done an ounce of work all his life, he sold bits of property to maintain his large family and numerous mistresses. Though his children went hungry to bed, he upheld the tradition of nobility by sending silver plates filled with gold coins to his current favourite's house. Not that he neglected his duty as a husband. Even as he enjoyed the company of other women, he gave his wife a child each year.

As long as the old man—my great-grandfather—was alive, he'd chip in financially. My father Rajinder, was a strapping young lad and there was a mare, eighteen spans high, he had to have. The horse seller boasted that she had a gait so steady that one could hold a bowl of milk in one hand while riding her and not a drop would spill.

The old man walked around the beautiful beast and inquired, 'How much?'

'Rs. 12/-.'

It was a princely sum in those days. Much to Rajinder's disappointment, the deal was called off. Later, the doting grandparent did buy him a horse, that too for Rs. 18. This was puzzling.

'You reject an animal costing Rs. 12 and then buy me one for Rs. 18. Not that I am complaining but . . .?' asked Rajinder.

'It's the pocket my dear child, the pocket. When empty, Rs. 12/- is expensive. When full Rs. 18/- is cheap.'

It was a valuable lesson learnt early in life.

During my childhood, trains would go till Pathankot; a bus journey of six hours would take us to Jammu. Curiosity would pry open eyes bleary with sleep. Happily we'd trot alongside our parents, taking in the sights and smells of the city. Never mind if, at that early hour, the pervading smell was of shit. Never mind if the sights that greeted our eyes were those of children squatting over open gutters. Our shoes clipped-clopped on the cobbled streets as we giggled at the bottoms exposed through *pajamis* peculiar to North India. These were tight flannel pyjamas with a hole in the excretory area. In this way the harried mothers kept their children warm and dry without resorting to a repeated change of clothes.

For the adults, there were open latrines on rooftops. These were door-less, roofless enclosures with parallel wooden planks placed a foot apart at a height of about two feet. On these we had to perch and let fall our droppings like birds. The mound of excreta in various shades of brown and yellow kept piling. If you heard footsteps on the stairs, you had to clear your throat to give a warning of occupancy. Along the staircase rose a jasmine creeper with a profusion of flowers. My most abiding memory of Jammu in early childhood was the fragrance of jasmines mingled with the stench of shit.

Living in sanitary cantonment areas, it was impossible to clear my bowels there. I was in my eighth year, old enough to be over the gutter stage, but too young for the adult latrines. I was in mortal fear of falling into the mess. Moreover, I gagged on the smell. For two days, I enforced constipation upon myself but one could deny nature thus far and no further. On the third day, I waited till the sweeper cleaned the toilets and made Mummy stand on top of the stairs to prevent any inadvertent entry. The formalities complete, I perched precariously on the planks holding onto the wall for support. I hadn't reckoned with visitors from above. Monkeys pried upon my privacy from the overhanging branch of a tree! I was mortified at being caught with my panties down.

Lohri, in mid-January, marked the beginning of the end of winter. The entire clan gathered around a roaring fire in the centre of the courtyard. There was song and dance, revelry and ribald jokes and gourmet delights. Peanuts and popcorn, *rewris,* and *chivda* were offered to the fire god before being consumed by humans. The rich aroma of rice and meat being cooked in clarified butter wafted from the kitchen. Young as I was, I noticed brother flirting outrageously with brother's wife. I also remember the photograph of a foreign girl with a tall Sikh youth displayed in the drawing room. My uncle had met her when he had gone abroad for higher studies. She had fallen desperately in love with him. Though he enjoyed her attentions, he refused to marry her. She was willing to go to the end of the earth with him. He said Jammu would suffice. One look at the toilets killed her love forever.

With a good-for-nothing father, my dad took over the financial burden of his siblings. It was becoming increasingly difficult to do so as he had his own family to raise. The incorrigible old man added insult to injury by stating that he wanted to remarry, as he was lonely!

'I cannot arrange the finance and the bride for you,' fumed Daddy. 'Especially when I know you that you will leave behind another brood for me to look after.'

On this bitter note, father and son parted forever, for soon after, Daadaji died—unloved, unwanted, reaping the just harvest of what he had sowed. Albeit fleetingly, I was perhaps the only one who mourned his death. He had become a toothless tiger by the time I arrived on the scene. Even if the hush-hush stories I heard about him were true, I was too young to understand them. Moreover, even at that age I judged people by the way they treated me rather than by what the world thought of them.

2

My mother's family migrated to Jalandhar after the Partition, where they got a house as 'claim' in lieu of the one they left behind in Pakistan. Here lived Nana (maternal grandfather), Taran Singh, a robust man with a hearty laugh. He was a hefty, hirsute Sikh with a luxuriant salt-and-pepper beard, and a moustache that tickled enormously whenever he kissed me. His heart was as large as his body, so was his family. Eight daughters and two sons were all that were left of the numerous offspring he sired.

The house was full of daughters, for his two surviving sons lived in distant cities. The other two had died unnatural deaths in their youth. One dived into a lake, split his skull on a rock, and did not come up alive. The other, a mere boy of 13, was knocked off his bicycle by a car. He would have survived the fall had not the hooves and wheels of a *tonga* taken along with them whatever vestige of life that remained. Our mother was so shaken by these events that she became paranoid about letting us drive or venture near water.

Naani (maternal grandmother), Manmeet Kaur, was a diminutive woman with flaring nostrils and artificial teeth that clicked interestingly with every morsel she ate. She delivered babies as long as she could, and spent the rest of her life raising them. With such a large family to feed, her natural habitat was the kitchen. Food was eaten by the cosy warmth of the charcoal stove, in which glowed orange embers. The 'baby factory' or the master bedroom was on the ground floor, as was the drawing room where the 'sight-seeing' took place. Prospective bridegrooms were shown marriageable daughters in these exalted premises. The roof of the central courtyard on the first floor had barred rectangular aperture through which people on both floors could communicate. It served another interesting purpose too. The other girls could observe their 'could be' brother-in-law without being seen. Earlier, they would accompany the marriageable sister but when a prospective bridegroom chose the younger sister instead of the one being 'shown', Nani put an end to this practice.

My aunts doted on me. They were enamoured of my vivacity, animation, and intelligence. A girl of 5, who spoke fluent English, was a marvel in Punjab, and I was incessantly put on show. Unselfconsciously, I rattled off poems whenever demanded of me. They loved my rosy cheeks, flashing eyes, and mop of curly hair. I enjoyed the fuss they made over me. They bathed and dried me; powdered and clothed me, and kissed me all over. By 'all over' I mean all over for they found me exceedingly pretty even there! The latent lesbians!

.They took me out turn by turn. I attended an aunt's college one day, and the next day I was singing the national anthem with the youngest one who was in her last year at school. She was a pretty young thing, vain about her looks. An ineligible, young man became obsessed by her and began stalking her. At first, her vanity was flattered. Soon, he became a source of embarrassment, revulsion, and eventually intense fear, for he threatened to throw acid on her face if she did not marry him! No amount of beatings deterred him. A sadhu gave her a charm, which was to be worn over the heart, to ward off evil. In desperation, it was also decided that she be married quickly out of Jalandhar as soon as possible. Innocent were the girls of those days.

As she was tucking the charm in her bra on her wedding day, her married sister admonished, 'Take it off. What will your husband think?'

'How will he know?' she asked, perplexed.

My eldest unmarried aunt was the principal of a village school. The day I accompanied her, a holiday was declared in my honour! The rosy-cheeked village girls gave me their handicrafts and took me to their fields where I gorged on freshly uprooted carrots and radish washed at the pump. Soon, I felt the urge to evacuate and was escorted to the ubiquitous open-air latrines. The heavens opened up along with my bowels and huge drops hit me like pellets. Before I could decide what to make of the situation, an enterprising student rushed in with an umbrella!

I have vague memories of a visit to the jail. Nanaji had long since retired and was running a practice of his own. I was taken there to see the house I was born in, the house in which Nanaji had lived during his tenure as a jail doctor. The prisoners working in the fields looked like ordinary people and held no fear for me. What sent a chill down my spine was the noose—a thick white cord that hung looped and ready for a hapless victim over a raised platform. Below this was a trapdoor that opened into the portals of doom. Nana must have supervised the preparations for the final journey and confirmed the end when it came, I thought with a shudder. Quickly, I put such morbid thoughts from my mind; such a jovial, kindhearted man surely could not perform such a macabre function. He must be looking after the sick and homesick prisoners, I thought loyally.

In Jalandhar, we perceived a strange phenomenon. For the dubious distinction of being our mother's offspring, we were given money. This was a godsend for children whose parents did not believe in pocket money. The only hitch was that Mummy pocketed the money. Soon we devised a plan to beat her to it. We'd station ourselves strategically at the door whenever guests were expected. Before they could cross the threshold we'd inquire, 'Are you our relative?'

If the answer was in the affirmative, we demand an anna as toll tax. Amused and indulgent, they would comply. We collected quite a tidy sum before Mummy caught on!

The very process of spending money was a pleasurable novelty. Balls of candyfloss would melt into sweet nothings in my mouth. Dry fruits were as cheap as peanuts are these days, and were sold by street vendors. I'd buy popcorn for the sheer pleasure of watching it pop. An old hag sat in the open with all the fascinating paraphernalia around her. With her thatch of white hair and toothless smile, she looked like a benevolent witch who magically converted yellow seeds into perfumed flowers with her little broom. On a charcoal fire sat a huge wok, half-filled with sand. Into this was thrust a paisa worth of corn seeds. A short broom was moved briskly in the mixture till the corn began to pop and the hot fragrance wafted to our nostrils. The popped corn was transferred to a massive sieve to sift the sand and handed over to us in huge paper cones. I do miss the traditional way of popping corn in the mechanised world of today.

I was my Nana's first grandchild, and dearly loved. I loved the way he threw me up high even as I gurgled in excitement and fear; the way his moustache tickled when he kissed me, the way he held me tight to his heart and felt the fatigue of his day seep out. It was Nana's earnest wish to see me married before he died, but that was not to be. Like a mighty tree felled, he dropped dead in his clinic after a massive heart attack. With the death of this colossus, an era came to an end. The house was sold off and the family disintegrated. All that remained of Jalandhar and its patriarch were a fistful of memories.

3

The skeletons in my Dada's cupboard were nothing compared to those that tumbled out of my Nana's. If Dada visited other women, it was an accepted way of life amongst the rich. Moreover, the women he frequented were professionals; Nanaji had designs on a married woman, which was unforgivable.

Taran Singh would visit his sister, Ajit Kaur, in Jammu frequently. It wasn't mere brotherly love that drew him to their *haveli*, but the magnetic appeal of a dark-eyed, diminutive beauty, his sister's *devrani* (husband's younger brother's wife) Manmeet Kaur. Despite having a wife and daughter at home, he flirted outrageously with her, though people in Jalandhar vouch vehemently for the fact that it was a misinterpreted platonic relationship. What the truth was, we will never know. What we do know is that two generations ago, segregation of sexes was the practice and the very fact that the two interacted, was cause enough for scandal.

Manmeet remained childless after 8 years of marriage; this when a palmist had told her that she would have a dozen children! I can imagine her look at the lines on her palm and smile wryly. Unable to bear the taunts that a barren woman had to face, she succumbed to the advances of the virile Taran Singh. Soon after a pregnancy ensued which, her husband, with good reason, refused to accept as his own. Secret visits to doctors had revealed that *his* semen had no sperms and therefore *he* could not father a child. It suited him to lay the blame on his wife for he could not have borne a slur on his manhood.

It would have been better for all concerned if he had played along and accepted the child as his own, but his ego got the better of him and he disgraced her publicly. Manmeet's father put his turban at the feet of his son-in-law in supplication, but his broken pride, his abasement came to naught. Manmeet was kicked out of the house along with the turban. To punish her partner in crime, they drove Taran Singh's innocent sister, Ajit Kaur, out of the house! That she was hugely pregnant at that time was a fact of no consequence. That my father, quite like Jesus, was born in a manger, was a happy event that shamed them into taking her back.

Manmeet, however, was not so lucky. They were well rid of a woman who had besmirched their family name. A dishonoured, discarded, married woman had no business staying at her father's place or any place on earth. Anyone else in her place would have had the decency to commit suicide, but not this spunky (shameless) lady. So Manmeet's father took her to Jalandhar and deposited her at the door of the one responsible for her plight. Manmeet and Taran were duly married and together produced the string of children the palmist had promised her.

The first causality of this high drama was Taran's innocent first wife, who moved lock, stock, and daughter to her brother's place. The second was the illegitimate conception that ended in a legitimate delivery. The unfortunate girl, a constant reminder of their disgrace, was uncared for and wasted away to die at the tender age of 3. My mother, Rani, was the first legitimate offspring of this union and her father's favourite.

Time watered down memories of the scandal. Ajit Kaur's family was impoverished by her husband's womanizing; while her brother, who stole their family's honour along with her *devrani*, flourished. Taran would help her out with large sums of money while her husband conveniently looked the other way. All was but forgotten had it not been for my parents who churned the stilled waters into murkiness.

Rani was given an education at a time when girls were barely allowed out of the house. Being the only girl in class, she sat at the master's desk, paid a classmate to do her homework and confessed to her crime only when *she* was to be caned for the sums *he* had done wrong!

When Rani saw her cousin Rajinder for the first time, she was bowled over by his looks, his intelligence, and his sports-toned body. He had a hockey stick in one hand and the flush of success on his cheek. He had won the match and a scholarship! Rajinder was five years older to her and had no use for girls, especially chubby young ones, at that point of time. However, Rani grew up into a beautiful girl and the attraction became mutual. Matters came to a head in Lahore. Rajinder was studying law in Lahore when his uncle Taran Singh came to put Rani in the Girl's College Hostel.

Worried about her being alone in a new city, he told his nephew, *'Beta apni bahen da khayal rakhna* (son, look after your sister).'

Years later after they were married, Daddy would quip, 'I am still looking after her.'

When Daddy was old and Mummy had passed away, he would reminisce about his life with her—61 years post-marriage and 3 years of intense courtship before that. Such was her beauty that a cyclist, unable to take his eyes off her, banged into a car! Besides casual passersby, her looks attracted a host of rivals and Rajinder had a tough job warding off competitors. The two would sneak off to a cemetery to spend time together, where they were sure not to be disturbed by people alive or dead! Later, a friend let them use his vacant house, and still later, they became emboldened enough to go for out station trips. At times, they stayed with Rani's married younger sister, Nimma. Nimma became privy to their secret affair, but jealousy prompted her to stab them in their backs. She had been given in adoption to an aunt, and held a permanent grudge against her parents for abandoning her. Though she lived like a queen in her new home, her adoptive father died when she entered her teens. As women had no personal source of income those days, her mother got her married early and went to live as a poor relation with relatives. Nimma's fortunes turned once again, this time for the worse. Saddled early in life with an obnoxious husband and wailing daughters, Nimma bitterly resented the education and freedom that Rani enjoyed. In order to get even, she broke open Rani's trunk, stole her love letters, and posted them to all their relatives!

One can imagine the havoc wrought. Rani was put under house arrest. There followed days of threatened homicide and suicide, cajoling and scolding, pleadings and beatings. The hurdles against this union seemed insurmountable. Firstly, a love marriage was almost unheard of in those days; secondly, first cousins marrying, was outright incest. Most unacceptable of all was the fact that Rani wanted to become a part of the very family that had thrown her mother out! Through the entire raving and ranting, Rani had but one answer to give. She would not to marry Rajinder on the condition that they would not force her to marry anyone else. It hurt Rani to hurt her beloved father so, but cousin dear had issued an ultimatum—it was either of the two, and she chose him.

Even as war raged between the feuding families, Rajinder set a deadline for the wedding! The audacity of the man! 'How dare he?' fumed Rani's mother, but a shadow of doubt had been cast. What if Rani was pregnant! No worse dishonour could befall parents of eight daughters. Even this disastrous alliance was preferable to a child born out of wedlock, and a marriage was quickly arranged.

Their fears were not entirely unfounded for, at one point of time, desperation had prompted Rani to ask Rajinder to impregnate her so that matters could be settled once and for all. Either her parents would give in or kill her, and she would rather die than live without him.

'And what about the baby?' asked Rajinder.

'We could let it waste away like . . .'

Daddy told me all this when he had sunk into dotage and lost the restrain that had distanced him from his children all his life.

'To think we would have let *you*, my lovely, brilliant daughter die!' he said, drawing me close in a rare show of affection for I was their firstborn.

As of now, it turned out that Rajinder had joined the Air Force and had to report for training in a month's time. He dared not leave affairs in such a volatile state, lest he lose his girl, hence the haste. Naani had been neatly tricked into giving her consent for the marriage.

4

The greatest gift that parents could give their children is a happy childhood. I am grateful to mine for bestowing upon us this priceless gift. There were four of us—Rosy, Romi, Ronnie, and Ruby. Two brothers squashed between two sisters. Though our destinies have separated us, we remain forever united in the memories of a childhood spent together. Being the children of the armed forces, we never struck roots, but when does the wind crave permanency? We wafted from city to city imbibing the fragrance of various cultures, which made us true denizens of India.

Beautiful as a Glaxo calendar baby, Ronnie could walk by the age of 9 months. Disaster struck in the form of poliomyelitis. Though his left leg shrivelled up, polio could not shrivel his spirit. It was heart-rending to watch him struggle to get up. If Robert Bruce learned to try, try again from the spider, I'm sure the spider learnt to do so from Ronnie. A hundred times he fell and a hundred times he rose, willing himself to stand without support. Our hearts bled for him but there was nothing we could do. For months on an end, he was subjected to massages, exercises, and crutches. Children would imitate his gait, beat him, and run away with a cruelty only children are capable; but Ronnie never let his handicap disadvantage him in anyway. The spunky lad took to keeping pebbles in his pockets and many a bleeding scalp had to be stitched on account of his marvellous aim.

My earliest childhood memories are of Poona. I refuse to call it by its new name—Pune, for it was Poona when I lived there. I remember a beautiful house with three gables at Koregan Park. Under the central gable was space enough for a little girl to crawl in with her dolls. It was my favourite haunt. Handsome white pillars supported the porch. On these, climbed creepers with dense green foliage and large yellow flowers. The sun-drenched terrace above the porch overlooked a manicured lawn bordered with a profusion of flowers that vied with butterflies in flaunting their colours. Rangoon creepers, with bunches of small pink flowers, crept over the boundary wall to peer at the world outside.

There was an abundance of fruit-bearing trees in our compound. Boughs laden with plump, juicy mangoes ready to burst out of their skins leaned generously over our balcony. Beside the mango trees, there were custard apples, pomegranates, fig, lime, and guava. There was also a huge banyan tree, our tree. Under its shade, we spent the happiest hour of the week. Every Sunday, we were allowed to cast aside the harness of civilization and give free rein to our natural spirits. Like convicts let out of prison, we'd rush out to swing from the hanging roots like Tarzans and land on a mound of mud underneath it. We'd wet the mound with watering cans and squelch happily, enjoying the feel of slush rise between our toes like toothpaste. A free for all would follow with much mud slinging. Our exuberance spent, we would be washed, dressed, and transformed into disciplined little officer's children all over again.

Speaking of discipline, we chafed against the restrictions imposed upon us by strict parents. What irked particularly was the lack of pocket money. With watering mouths and empty pockets, we'd watch children buy goodies at the school's tuck shop during recess. Desperation once prompted Romi to pick up a wad of chewed up, spat out bubble gum, and put it in his mouth when he thought no one was looking! It also made us decide to generate some pocket money of our own. With this in mind, we committed not one unpardonable sin but a clutch of them. Our parents had gone for their evening stroll and we went across to our neighbour's *through the barbed wire* fence instead of the front gate. *In our nightgowns, bare feet;* that too when they were *entertaining guests*! At home, we weren't allowed in the drawing room when we had visitors. As if this was not enough, we were actually asking them to *buy* old purses, pens, scarves etc.

Before our poor neighbours could decide what to make of our aberrant behaviour, our parents returned! Daddy herded us into a room and gave us a thrashing we never forgot. In those days, people raised their children by following the dictum 'spare the rod and spoil the child'.

Another thrashing that stands out in memory was the one we received on Daddy's birthday. Daddy was inordinately proud of his kitchen garden. Rows of papaya trees lined our backyard, the females heavy with fruit. Whorls upon whorls of upward pointing green baby bananas hung from a banana tree with leaves as huge as elephant ears. The creeper gourd, the ladies fingers, and the brinjals were laden; waiting as it were for harvest in a week or so. The four of us scurried back and forth preparing a surprise birthday present for him. The moment he returned from office, we dragged him into the dining room. Neatly arranged on the table were all the unripe fruits and vegetable from his beloved garden. Months of labour had come to naught. Out came his multipurpose hockey stick (he used it for killing snakes, too) and landed on hands that dared to devastate his garden so.

Daddy wasn't always the tyrant we made him out to be. We had occasion to experience his benign side when Mummy was called away one summer holiday. She received a telegram and began to behave strangely. Banging her head against the wall, she sobbed hysterically, *she,* who always made *us* cry! It was unnerving. Her younger brother had been killed in a road accident and she left for Jalandhar immediately. In her absence, Daddy played both father and mother to us and did we enjoy it! He made French toast for breakfast, took us for long walks that he peppered with nuggets of general knowledge, and bought us black and white striped sweets called Bull's Eye. At night, he told us stories of real inventors and discoverers and we were indeed sorry when Mummy returned.

Our ayah Girija bai kept us company when our parents stayed out late. She would frighten us with tales of a *chudel* (witch) who stalked the neighbourhood on large feet with backwards pointing toes. With matted hair, overgrown incisors, bloodshot eyes, and long flabby breasts flung over her shoulders, she would come in the middle of the night to devour naughty children who did not sleep in time. The very thought would make us cower and cling to each other under our sheets. In the afternoons, when our parents slept, I would play *'ghar ghar* (house house)' with Girija bai's daughters and make tea by melting toffee in water, which we'd consume in dainty toy cups. We'd don saris, stuff a cushion inside, and walk with protruding bellies like Mummy who was expecting Ruby.

I shudder to think that Ruby was almost not born. With three children in four years, my mother seemed to be going her mother's way. Afraid of rearing a brood as big as his father's, Daddy got himself vasectomised. It was almost unheard of in those days, when men set great store by their potency and fecundity and confused the two. He also got drugs for Mummy to get rid of this child, but she flushed them down the toilet. Ruby did have a complex of being the unwanted one, though she got more than her share of affection from all.

My education began in Poona—a violent, messy affair to begin with. Mummy lay in bed while I sat by her feet, counting the numbers. Each time I'd forget what came after 19, 29, and 39 . . . Mummy's patience wore thin at 49 and she kicked me hard. My head banged against the bedpost and bled profusely.

The stitches and shots that followed, taught me as nothing else would, that learning was a painful process indeed!

I was introduced to ballet dancing and Christianity at The Convent of Jesus and Mary. While the former proved to be an insurmountable task for a chubby little girl, the latter was something I wished I were born into. I chafed at being different. My brothers wore their long hair braided and coiled at the back of their heads. This put them to a disadvantage during fights for their opponents used the plaits as handles. It also made them the butt of cruel Sardarji jokes. I even hated my name in those days—Amrita Kaur Arora, which made me stand out like a sore thumb amongst the Brendas and Jennifers. I loved the serenity of the chapel and the kind nuns who encouraged us to do our good deed of the day. The religious backing at home was not strong enough and the cosmopolitan cantonment environment did nothing to expose us to the Sikh way of life. I was not familiar with the humility, valour, equality, and langar (free kitchen)—features unique to my religion. Mummy did *path* morning and evening, but we thought that that was what all mummies did. We also had pictures of Guru Nanak Devji and Guru Gobind Singhji, but that was all. We never stayed in Punjab and therefore did not imbibe its rich culture.

One weekend, Puppy fell ill and there was talk of putting him to sleep. With tears streaming down my cheeks, I held his limp form to my chest and touching his dry nose to the picture of Babaji—the benevolent, white bearded Guru Nanak with a hand raised in eternal blessings and begged for his life. Miraculously, he survived. Our Gurus weren't too bad after all. It wasn't Jesus alone who answered my prayers.

5

Daddy's next posting was at Jalahali, Bangalore, the land of red sand and clement weather, of sandalwood trees and grass snakes, of gigantic dahlias and slender lilies, of red papayas and brown chickoos, of bananas ranging from the size of a finger to that of an arm. Red tiled houses made a U around a central park. The club was situated on the end of the U, and the MI room at the other. Our house was pat in the centre. On our right lived an Anglo-Indian couple with their sons David and Reggie, and very good neighbours they made. Auntie taught me to play the piano and Uncle, ballroom dancing. As they had no daughter of their own, they made much of me. An oft-visualised scene through their window was a bobbed lady at the piano and a middle-aged gentleman dancing with a 9-year-old in pigtails. I was happier in their house than ours.

Those were the days of sputniks and the boys were very much into 'outer space'. In the park lay the broken limb of a see saw. Romi and Reggie carried it up the highest slide and sat astride, holding on to the T handle pretending to be astronauts returning after a sojourn in outer space, and what a landing they made!

'Ouch my balls!' screamed Reggie as he was crushed against the vertical limb of the T. Famous last words of could-have-been astronauts.

On the left hand corner of our garden was a sandalwood tree that fascinated us. It was said that the heady fragrance of sandalwood attracted snakes. Harmless green snakes were battered to death in the hedge, bathroom, on the grass, verandah; in fact, we saw a snake practically everywhere in our premises but on the sandalwood tree.

Pat in the middle of the lawn was a bougainvillea bush. It looked like a green umbrella in winter, and a magenta fountain in summer. Between the stem and the branches was a natural hideout. To this I retreated whenever I wanted to sulk for life wasn't treating me fairly. While my brothers did exciting things like climbing trees and playing cricket, I was being trained to become a lady. Mummy made me sit sedately with needlework or knitting, which I abhorred. The muffler I made had more holes than wool in it on account of the stitches I dropped, distracted as I was by my brothers' affairs, instead of paying attention to mine.

The poet in me (for whatever it is worth) was born in 5th standard, quite by chance. Inattentive as always, I heard but snatches of homework as it was being dictated, and hence ended up writing a poem instead of reciting it! After that, there was no stopping me.

There followed verses like:

'Birds fly

In the sky . . .' as if they could do anything else!

More like 'The Lame Dog', 'The Rag Doll', followed till my brothers began to liken my urge to write to that of going to the loo!

My mother was the dominating influence of my childhood and was not averse to beating us for our 'good'. I would often wet my panties during a spanking! So great was my terror of her that I'd go to any lengths to avoid invoking her wrath. During exam time I feared her cross-examination more than my result. I would learn the right answers from cleverest girl in class on the way back home in the school bus so that when Mummy took *her* test, I would rattle off the correct answers. She could never understand why I got such poor marks in school. No one was more surprised than me when I stood first in the seventh standard! Albeit inadvertent, it was the worst mistake of my life. After that I had a position to maintain and *had* to per force concentrate on my studies.

Ruby and I had an identical pair of pink nylon party frocks that we wore to every birthday party. One evening, as I was being dressed in the same outfit, I blurted out, 'I hate this frock and I hate going to every party in the same stupid dress. The collar hurts and it is much too small for me. Why can't you buy us new . . .' and stopped midway, shocked at my own audacity. I expected a tight slap, but Mummy's gentle manner surprised me. She told us that the entire family depended upon my father's income, half of which he sent to Jammu for his siblings and this was all that we could afford. Young as I was, I understood, and wore our genteel poverty like a medallion.

Our ayah was prone to petty thieving and Mummy made it a point to never leave her alone. One day, there fell upon me the responsibility of keeping an eye on her, as Mummy was entertaining guests. Puffed up with importance, I hovered around.

'Go out and play Rosy,' she cajoled.

'I can't.'

'Why?'

'Because I have to keep a watch on you.'

Infuriated, she threatened to leave. As she marched off in a huff, a packet of rice dropped from the folds of her sari. At being caught red-handed, she fell at Mummy's feet and begged forgiveness. We learnt that the poor woman's salary was spent on the very day she received it, paying last month's dues. With her drunken husband adding nothing to the family kitty, she was forced to steal to feed her family. Instead of throwing her out, Mummy gave her an extra month's salary to even out the backlog and start afresh. At such a small price, Mummy bought eternal loyalty.

Every evening, we would be appropriately dressed and taken to the park. A triangularly-folded handkerchief would be attached to our frocks with a little gold pin as befitting proper young ladies. While the adults played squash and billiards inside, I played with my friend Kavita on the swings. As twilight deepened, we'd retreat to the rock garden to pray. At the age of 10, we were very much into spirituality and even saw a vision once. However, the walk back home was reserved for dirty talk. Just before we parted, one of us would ask,

'Will you marry when you grow up?' and the other, shocked and thrilled at the prospect would say *'No, never!'* with such vehemence, as if it was the ultimate sin.

Autumn break was too short to travel all the way up North to our grandparents. So Daddy got our sturdy little Ford overhauled, packed us in it, and took us on a South tour. We saw the beautiful Brindavan gardens of Mysore with its water canals and musical fountains. Mysore palace was bathed in the golden glow of a million fairy lights during Dusshera. Caparisoned elephants and the sound of trumpets added to the grandeur of the occasion.

Ronnie had just recovered from a bout of measles. Though he seemed fit enough to travel, Mummy worried about his health. It turned out later that he was the least of her worries. We had barely driven out of Bangalore when Romi was covered with spots and I began to feel feverish. In fact Ronnie was the only one, his polio-stricken leg notwithstanding, to accompany our parents up the innumerable steps to the famous rock temple while we stayed in the car.

Our next stop was Rameshwaram, a little island across the sea where the Lord Rama rested on his way to Lanka. A rail bridge across the sea opened up to let ships pass. As we were traversing this remarkable feat of engineering by train (there was no road bridge), I began to shiver. Within minutes, my temperature shot up to 106 degrees Fahrenheit. I was stripped off my clothes and dumped into a tub of ice. Tiny red spots appeared and coalesced to form large weals that itched unbearably. I was the worst afflicted. Hats off to my parents, who completed the trip despite the fact that our little Ford had been converted to a mobile paediatric hospital. It was only after we passed Madurai and its beautiful Meenakshi temple that we were all well again. It was a happy, healthy family that held hands while the waters of the confluence of three seas at Cape Comrin, the southern tip of India, washed our feet.

Ooty, I remember as much for the chicken cut for dinner, that ran around headless for a while, as for the botanical gardens and the lake. The climb up the Nilgiris with its narrow roads and scary bends was an exhilarating experience. Whenever our valiant little vehicle began to huff and pant, we'd stop to let it cool. On the curve of the hill with our food basket open, we'd take in the scenery along with the snacks.

The drive along the seacoast to Cochin was beautiful. We watched fishermen heave in their haul—silvery fish pulled out of a silvery sea, onto silvery sands twitched in silvery nets to be stilled forever. We collected seashells in little reed baskets, and ate steaming idlis with chutney on banana leaves. The boat ride on the backwaters of Kerala, the seventeen-feet-long cobra at Trichur Zoo, we brought them all home as treasured memories along with the seashells.

Soon after our trip, Daddy got his transfer orders again. Life in the armed forces was a series of sorrowful partings and exciting beginnings. As we separated from bosom pals, we vowed eternal friendships. As always, the letters would dwindle and finally stop as new interests and acquaintances took over. As we bundled our belongings for yet another posting, little did we know that we were leaving not only a city but also our childhood behind forever.

6

In Delhi, we had our first brush with cousins, community living, and civilian life. Houses, even for armed forces personnel, were not easy to come by in the capital. Till we were provided with a home of our own, we were to put up with our *bua*, Daddy's sister, and were mighty pleased about it for we would be meeting our cousins Kuku and Harleen for the first time. Naively, we thought that the pleasure was reciprocal and we would stay with them till we got official accommodation. It soon dawned upon us that we had arrived at an inopportune moment and were considered more of an intrusion than welcome relatives. Harleen was my age and we became inseparable within an hour, but her elder brother Kuku was studying for his Higher Secondary board exams and we were a major disturbance. To my parents' surprise, the very next morning, Bua handed us a loaf of bread, a pat of butter, a dozen eggs, and escorted to the temporary accommodations they had arranged for us. I, for one, did not mind. After the sprawling bungalows we had lived in till now, it was strangely exciting to live in a block of identical flats, quite like bees in a hive. Ours was on the second floor and a balcony overlooking a balding park revealed the kaleidoscope of civilian life. Harried mothers, wailing babies, cycling children, teenagers sizing up the opposite sex, gossiping elders interspersed by cats and dogs, dotted the landscape. Most interesting of all were the street hawkers peddling their wares. People residing at our level had a novel way of purchasing goods. A basket on a rope was lowered onto the vegetable/fruit cart in which would be placed the desired quantity of the desired goods and hauled up like a bucket from a well. Money would be lowered in a similar way. We fought over whose turn it was with the basket.

In Delhi, we were also introduced to the 'loo', the hot winds that blew across the plains of Northern India in the summer months. It seemed to be a live thing, whistling and wailing, keening and moaning as the mood overtook it. It slapped you on the face if you dared to confront it, and rattled windowpanes if you did not let it in. It imprisoned us in our homes, raised mud off the earth to whip up frenzied dust storms. After wrecking devastation, it departed, shrouding the city with suspended dust particles that filmed everything in sight. Dust got into our eyes and nostrils, lined our collars and nails, and was coughed out as black phlegm. Nervous irritability and frayed tempers were a natural fallout of such weather. Though the monsoons brought with them their own form of misery—clogged drains and water logged roads— the first few downpours were welcome for they got rid of the omnipresent dust.

After Kuku's exams, I spent a few days at my aunt's place and got a shocking exposure to human sexuality. Harleen was a precocious child and in bad company. With both parents working and her elder brother returning late from tuitions, she was left to her own devices and the corrupting influence of ill-bred girls. A recently married aunt living in the next block was supposed to look after Harleen till her parents returned, but when did newlyweds have time for anyone else? One afternoon, Harleen took me to Aunty's flat saying mysteriously, 'Come, I'll show you something.'

Instead of ringing the doorbell, she peeked through the keyhole and stood glued to it, oblivious to my existence. She seemed awfully interested in what was going on. Curiosity got the better of me and I put a hand on her shoulder. She started and reluctantly gave me my chance. A strange sight met my eyes. Aunty dear was lying on the bed with her large floppy breasts exposed. Her husband was kneading, sucking, and kissing them. He seemed to have some difficulty in breathing. I wondered which of the two was sick. Was something wrong with her chest or did he have asthma?

'What are they doing?' I gasped.

'Making a baby.'

'Don't tell lies!'

'Baby, baby that's what you are.' I was all of 11 years.

That shut me up but set me thinking. Surely my parents hadn't resorted to something as disgusting as this to produce us!

Harleen's paternal cousins were also spending their summer holidays with them. As there was paucity of space, the kids slept on the roof beneath the stars. Beddings were put in a row on the terrace floor. I lay on one side of Harleen, her male cousin Raman, on the other. Sleep came easily to the eyes of the innocent, but Harleen and Raman had better things to do.

The next morning she said, 'I told Raman what I saw through the key hole the afternoon.'

'What did he say?'

'He asked if I would like to experiment.'

'And?'

'I said, why not?'

'What happened?'

'He put his hand inside my frock and squeezed my breasts.'

She hardly seemed to have any. I thought it would be rude to point that out but was shocked nevertheless.

'Now you will have a baby.' I cried aghast.

'No, only married people have babies,' she said mysteriously. There was much I had to learn about the ways of the adult world. What she said was true though. A few months later, our aunt gave birth to a beautiful baby boy. The moment I set eyes on him, I forgave her, her dubious activities.

Soon after, we shifted to our official accommodations away from the damaging influence of Harleen and her questionable friends. We had been allotted a house in KEM—King Edward Mess—on Rajpath. Beyond its walls lay lush green lawns with shallow rectangular artificial lakes, flush with tiny fish. Boating was allowed on another such lake across the road, and we often went there on weekends. Lining Rajpath were flowerbeds, where bright yellow calendulas bobbed their heads in the breeze. The lake was emptied for cleaning once in a year, and many a snail shell we collected from its dry bed. Nostalgia for the happy times we spent at KEM lingers, for it has long since been demolished. It was a self-sufficient enclosure with a club, open-air theatre, a skating rink, and residential blocks that housed families belonging to all the three forces. School too, was within the campus. My best friend took up my sex education from where Harleen had left it, and told me that men and women produced children by drinking each other's urine! Ugh! Between the two of them, I was totally confused. It was best not to have anything to do with boys. In fact, I developed such an aversion for them that I would not let my skirt touch a boy's desk at school.

To my dismay, a fellow called Deepak developed a penchant for me. As if being a boy wasn't bad enough, he came last in class. He read love stories while I subsisted upon a diet of Enid Blyton. There was nothing to endear him to me. I was horrified when he chose me as his wife during a game of 'Farmer in the Den' and burst into tears. During midterm exams he tried to bribe me with seasoned red berries for the correct answers. My chest heaved in outrage and I told him what I thought of cheater cocks like him. Just then the invigilator walked up to my desk and cut ten marks from *my* paper for talking during exams!

I *was* a moral, upright girl who took her scripture classes seriously. Another lesson that went awry was when we were taught to keep smiling in the face of adversity. Now the worst calamity that could befall me was a beating from Mummy, so the next time she hit me, I smiled valiantly through my tears.

At this, she hit me harder screaming, 'How dare you laugh at me, you little bitch?'

There was much backslapping at school in those days and not all of it was due to bonhomie. It was a method devised to discover who wore *'it'*. Every week, we updated our count. My turn came when I had left Delhi far behind. My breast grew late but developed well. I regarded them more as encumbrances than assets and developed a hunch, quite like a tree weighed down with fruit. At that time I was friendly in a tomboyish sort of way with the neighbourhood boys, and anything that made me different was an affront. When Mummy forced a bra and domesticity upon me, I felt like a wild mare harnessed.

Winter holidays at KEM were fun. Excitement built up as truck after truck unloaded multi-tiered green benches on yielding lush lawns on either side of Rajpath. *Chhabees janvery* (26th January) parade, as the Republic day parade was called in local parlance was a good two months away but preparations had already begun. In those days, there was no security, no passes, and India was one happy family. The entire clan collected in our house on the twenty-fifth of January, for a crash tender Daddy had made was to be displayed during the parade that year. As seats were to be got on a first come first served basis, the children were sent early to reserve vantage places. The adults brought breakfast for us later. Till date, I connect the smell of *alloo parathas* and mango pickle with *chhabees janvery parade*.

Holidays were also devoted to learning the art of housekeeping. Though we had servants to look after our needs, Mummy insisted that her daughters learn household chores, which stood us in good stead later on. Our ayah was a beautiful Gurkha woman. Tall and fair, she had knee-length hair, which she wound into a loose bun. Into this she stuck a green chilli that made her look unbearably attractive. One day, she ran away with another man leaving her husband and kids behind. This was my first brush with adulthood vagaries and shook me to the core. It had never occurred to me that a family could break so. Soon after, the scandal of the sixties shook the very foundations of our mess. An officer stabbed his wife to death because she had been two-timing him with his best friend. After avenging the wrong done to him, he slit his wrists with a shaving blade and died! I wasn't sure I wanted to grow up after all this.

7

Once again, it was time to move on and this time we were headed towards Gwalior. In the early sixties, it was a sleepy little town content to bask in its historical past. The fort with its palace dominated the landscape. The only time the city came to life was during the winter cattle fair. All roads leading to Gwalior were clogged with beasts. Camels and cows, goats and sheep, donkeys and buffaloes collected in the largest ever assembly of animals in India. There were all the trappings of a fair to allure customers—giant wheels and merry go-rounds, air gun shooting of balloons, and the hall of mirrors—you had them all. As a wide-eyed 13-year-old, I set out to buy the world with Rs10/- in my pocket. I returned with glass bangles on my wrists, beads around my neck, and my ears red with clip on tops. Narcissism reigned supreme though, the ill-concealed of sniggers my brothers and their friends marred my pleasure. I hated them for laughing at me. In fact, the hating had begun on our first day in Gawalior, six months back. As I was being lifted off a military truck in front of our new home, I heard an unseen voice exclaim, 'Lal frock wali moti (fatso in a red frock).'

I was indeed chubby but it was galling to receive such a horrid welcome. Ignoring the rude remarks, I entered our new house and fell in love with it. It was a yellow single storied 'H' shaped structure with a mehndi-lined lawn in front. The interlocking branches of two neem trees canopied the huge courtyard at the back. Leaves, crisp and curling, crunched underfoot. The roof had neither stairs nor parapet, but that was no deterrent to a bunch of hyperactive children. The neem branches were as good a ladder as any. Squirrels lived by the score on these trees. Up and down they ran in energetic courtship. A particularly adventurous one was inadvertently crushed between a door and the wall. I picked up the limp form and put it in a cardboard box. It stirred after a while and I tended to the little fellow tenderly for a few days, till he was fit enough to be released. The ungrateful wretch scampered up a tree trunk without a backward glance. I yearned for my little friend, but he was indistinguishable from the rest. A few days later, I put some cooked rice in my hand and sat in the middle of the courtyard. There was a joyous singing in my heart as he ventured down to eat the proffered food. Within a matter of days I had the entire clan eating out of my hand!

An ancient peepal tree dominated the garden in front. From this, superb representative of its species an abiding love for trees was born. The beauty of flowers is overrated and tragically transient. They have their moment of glory but all too soon are reduced to drooping caricatures of their former selves. Trees were there for life—permanent yet ever-changing. There were tightly rolled soft brown leaves in spring. As the days grew hotter, these unfurled into sword-tipped leaves of a fresh young green that glinted silver in the sun. Finally, there were the dark green leaves broad as an adult hand that waved the heat away like a myriad little fans. So what if my peepal had no flowers to speak of? Flowers were nothing but pretty little whores. Their flamboyance and fragrance had but one purpose to perform—that of seduction, while an entire world existed in the shade of a tree. Canopied by its love, I felt an incredible peace. The felling of a mighty tree, the killing of a tusker, and the assassination of an emperor were of equal import to me.

In our neighbours' compound was a bearded, old banyan that housed a couple of king cobras. The pair was sacrosanct and no one dared to kill them. According to folklore, the image of the killer was captured in the dead one's eye and its mate would trail the culprit to inject a lethal amount of venom into the hapless being. No one dared find out whether there was any truth in this superstition. Yet, in the three years we lived in Gawalior, though the cobras were sighted regularly, they did not bite anyone.

On our very first day, Mummy sent me next door to inquire about domestic help. I stood on the threshold of our neighbours's backyard, fascinated by the scene enacted in front of my eyes. Children emerged in droves from a side room following a boy of my age. He was supposedly their 'king' and a ludicrous one at that. Clad in khaki shorts and white shirt, he walked as regally as his un-regal attire allowed him to. Handmaidens waved fans of banana leaves. From the rest of the procession, there were chants of '*Maharaj ki jai ho* (long live the king)'.

The procession was headed towards a chair in the centre of the courtyard. As the king lowered his bottom on to his throne, I pulled it from under him! I do not know what devilry prompted Miss Prim and Proper to perform such an uncharacteristic act. Perhaps I was smarting from the remark on my plumpness earlier in the day and wanted to pay them back. There was a moment of stunned silence, as the king lay vanquished on the ground. This was followed by a burst of laughter that dispelled the tension. Little did I know then, that the boy Kamal, who gazed at me with puzzled brown eyes, would be my first love!

I stood on the threshold of womanhood. Hormones were readying my body for love and boys did not seem hateful anymore. Out of the thirteen children in the neighbourhood, Ranjit and Kamal were of my age. The former was an extrovert and professed to be in love with me soon enough. Being an easy conquest, he held no challenge. Kamal, the strong silent type, attracted me. I admired his ability to climb trees, his sixers in cricket, and his bravery in defying parental authority. The fact that he was unwilling to talk with a mere girl intrigued me.

I vowed to show him that I was no less than a boy. Earnestly, I'd take my place at the crease. Never mind if my back-buttons had been ripped off at a previous fight and my frock slipped off my shoulder. All I cared about was making runs. Never mind if the boys cheated blatantly at carom, I took revenge by upsetting the board. As for *antarkshi*, I fancied myself quite a singer of sad film songs. He laughed at my face and received a slap for his effrontery. When Mummy caught me on the highest branch of a tree with the boys peering up my skirt, she decided to rein her unbridled daughter. That was the time she forced domesticity and a bra on me, rubbing in the fact that I could never be a boy. I did not know then that you attracted males by being feminine and not by outdoing them in boyish activities.

School was Carmel Convent, quite some distance away. We passed Gola Ka Mandir daily on our way to school. The black goddess, Kali, with her protruding red tongue, the whites of her eyes stark against her ebony face was the presiding deity. She wore a necklace of severed heads dripping blood. Underfoot, lay her supine husband; one of her numerous hands, poised above him with a glinting sword. To this temple, dacoits of the Chambal valley descended to offer coconuts (golas) and pray for the success of their ventures!

During class, I was entranced by the antics of a couple of birds on a tree branch.

'What is so interesting outside?' asked Sister scathingly.

'Those birds are balancing on top of one another,' I said, unaware of the fact that they were fornicating! Innocent were the adolescents of yesteryears.

My best friends were Summi and Jenny. We quarrelled over our favourite film stars. While Summi drooled over Sunil Dutt, Jenny loved Rajinder Kumar; I thought no one could beat Dev Anand. I had quite a collection of Dev Anand's photographs hidden in my bottom drawer. The fact that Kamal looked a bit like Dev Anand and made a similar puff, was yet another reason for my attachment to him. He had a signed photo of

Dev Anand, which I coveted but he refused to part with it. After all, he wasn't a bona fide lover willing to get the moon for his beloved. He wasn't even an official boyfriend like the one Jenny had. She had even been kissed on the lips. Summi lived in a joint family and her cousin accosted her in dark corridors for a good feel. She so enjoyed these fondling sessions that she literally took to inhabiting dark corridors! And here I was, pursuing a scruffy Dev Anand look-alike for want of anything better. When Jenny's dashing boyfriend wanted to meet Kamal, I had to literally drag him out from behind a curtain by his hair! I almost stopped loving him on this account. I was nearing 15 at that time and unclean tomboys were not high on the list of my priorities. Moreover, he was no match academically for a girl who stood first in her class.

He fell further from my eyes when, along with Ranjit he played a dirty trick on me. To learn whether miss goody two shoes knew a few dirty words too, he pointed towards a bitch on heat with dogs trying to mount her and in my presence said, 'Fucking animals!'

My widened eyes and reddened cheeks revealed all. They knew that I knew. I knew that they knew that I knew. They were horrid boys. I kept away from them and focused my attention on our new Alsatian pup Tojo. When I returned from school, the huge blundering darling would put his front paws on my shoulders and slobber my face with his tongue, while his tail wagged furiously with a life of its own. He was an undisciplined brat and a glutton to boot. Whenever the neighbours heard the sound of banging metal emanating from our verandah, they'd shake their heads and say,

'Tojo must have run away again.' For nothing but the sound of his feeding bowl would induce him to return! Whenever he had been up to mischief, he would crawl under the bed, the whites of his eyes showing and the tip of his tail wagging guiltily. He would bend his front paws inwards for that was where Daddy rapped him with a rolled up newspaper to discipline him. He was lovable, loyal, and decidedly my best friend. Little did I know that he would be snatched from me in but a short while. His gluttony lead to worm infestation and an inadvertent overdose of medicine proved fatal. When we returned from school one day, there was no Tojo waiting at the gate with his customary smooch. He lay convulsing on the floor; his eyes glued to the door, as if for a last glimpse of his loved ones before he breathed his last. I knew intolerable grief for the first time in my life and took a long time to get over it.

While the death of a dog left us desolate, the death of an uncle barely touched us. Due to our nomadic existence, we hardly knew him enough to mourn him. In fact, the holidays in which Daddy's brother died was the nicest we ever had. Our parents left for the funeral and, alone for the first time in our lives, we did, with delicious guilt, all that was forbidden. We climbed the stair-less, parapet-less roof via the neem branches, for carom was best played there. We lit matchstick after matchstick, finishing entire matchboxes for the forbidden pleasure of playing with fire. Best of all, we roamed around in our nightdresses till late afternoon without bathing!

We ate at our neighbours and their children slept with us at night. As we lay under the rustling neem beneath our mosquito nets, one of them farted out aloud. There were whoops of delight. After that, thanks to the gas-inducing dinner of *rajma-chawal(beans and rice)*, in turns and in chorus we all broke wind without the courtesy of a silencer and laughed the night away.

I wore a sari for the first time on my fifteenth birthday. By that time I had gained height and slimmed down considerably. Mummy asked me to take some pieces of cake next door. Kamal couldn't take his eyes off me! Feeling shy and grown up all of a sudden, I wound my sari self-consciously around my chest accentuating my breasts still further. In such attire, it was not easy to resort to our usual teasing banter. Now that I was dressed like a lady, Kamal's mother treated me like one. The three of us sat on cane chairs in the garden. She offered me tea and biscuits like she would have done to a grown up. For one who was brought up on milk, the taste of tea was a novelty.

So what if my parents did not believe in birthday presents? Nature showered her bounties upon me. It was a balmy evening. Twilight fell on my shoulders, light as a cloak. Night presented a star-studded scarf. The moon hung low enough to be plucked from the sky. Peepal leaves rustled silver in the moonlight. The fragrance of mehndi flowers filled the air. There was a glow in the sky, on my cheek, and in my heart. Kamal's eyes were upon me like a caress. To cover my embarrassment, I crushed his baby brother to my breast and kissed him on the cheek. I had no idea how the little fellow landed on my lap. Kamal took the baby from me and put his lips on the very spot my lips had touched. It was the closest we came to kissing each other. A tremor coursed through my form. Overnight childhood playmates grew into adolescent lovers.

My mother's voice from across the fence broke the spell. Suddenly, I was the scared little girl once again who had strayed from home far too long. Forgetful of my newfound adulthood, I ran through the hole in the mehndi hedge and got terribly entangled. If I tore Mummy's favourite georgette sari I had it, birthday or no birthday. Kamal rushed to disentangle me. Painstakingly, he removed my *anachal* (the loose end of my sari) from the thorns, taking care to avoid a rent. Occasionally, he'd look up and smile at me like they did in the movies. It was the most romantic moment of my life.

After that magical evening, we tacitly acknowledged our love for each other. We took to sitting next to each other when our families went to see movies at the Centre in cantonment and held hands surreptitiously. Our romance was destined to be short-lived though, for Daddy had got his posting orders and it was time to move on once again. Hitherto transfers had been fun. New places and new friends were exciting, but transfer from Gwalior was different. I was leaving not only a city but also a part of me behind. The heart wrenching pain of separation from a loved one was intolerable. Not a single eye was dry as we piled into the truck with our luggage. Parting gifts were exchanged. Kamal pressed an envelope in my hand and asked me to open it in the train. It contained his most prized possession, the autographed photo of Dev Anand that I had coveted all along! I began to sob uncontrollably. Each turn of the wheel of this fire-breathing monster was taking me away from my beloved and there was nothing I could do about it.

I never saw Kamal again in my life. From common acquaintances, I learnt that he had become an engineer and joined the army. He had lost his puff and acquired a crew cut, a wife, and two daughters. In short, he was not *my* Kamal anymore. I am glad we never met again for mutual disillusionment would have destroyed fragile memories of an innocent first love.

8

Ganga Tarang—the wave of the Ganges—was the name of our house in Nagpur. It was a beautiful name for a beautiful house, though it looked more like bower, full of flowers and fruit-bearing trees as it were. There were the famed Nagpur oranges with fragrant blossoms. There were drumsticks with tiny white flowers and long green fruit, and a mango tree of the luscious *langda* variety. The fruit was green when ripe and sweet when raw. Hidden in its dark green foliage, a cuckoo called plaintively, striking an answering chord in the hearts of *birhans* (women separated from their lovers) like me. A pleasurable pain would suffuse my heart, rise with my sighs, and spill from my eyes. I'd sit on the swing that hung from its branches thinking of Kamal and sing sorrowful songs, enjoying my role of a tragedy queen.

To the trunk of a guava tree was tethered Gowri, the cow. She was milked at dawn and dusk. As Mummy set great store by feeding pure, fresh milk to her children, it was our duty to keep vigil lest the milkman add water to his bucket. When my turn came, I was clever enough to catch him with a *lota* (round metal vessel) of water concealed within the folds of his dhoti. This, to our embarrassment, turned out to be a hydrocele that he soon got operated. As the thick creamy milk frothed in the bucket, we whiled away our time thrusting guavas in the mouth of Laxmi, Gowri's calf, for the sheer pleasure of watching her crush the fruit between her sideways-moving jaws. Perhaps she was the only calf in the world to develop a taste for guavas. Years later, when a full-grown cow made a beeline for the guava tree, we rightly recognised her to be Laxmi!

Besides the fruit trees, we had an abundance of fragrant herbs and flowers. Basil, *kadi patta*, mint, and coriander perfumed our kitchen garden. The sweet scent of juhi, jasmines, chameli, and haar shringar wafted in from the front. The delicate mauve of the bauhinia and the brilliant yellow of the laburnum caressed the glass wall of the sunroom on the first floor. Most of my free time was spent here drawing caricatures and writing poetry. I had not yet decided whether I wanted to become a famous painter or a poet. Later, I tilted heavily onto the side of poetry though the 'famous' bit has yet to follow.

The Labarnum Tree

My very own patch of sunshine,
Ensnared in my courtyard,
By the wiles of the laburnum tree.
She entangles yarns of sunrays,
In her crown, to dazzle the eye.
Her leaves, unable to compete
With the summer flowering,
Retreat discreetly into winter.
The rain strews petals at her feet
To carpet the earth with gold.
Long brown fruit
Dangle like earrings,
As she shakes her head
In narcissistic delight.
I forgive my beauteous lady
This one fault of vanity
And thank God each morn,
For the gift
Of the laburnum tree.

It is from this room that I sent romantic epistles to Kamal. As nice girls were not supposed to write directly to boys, we'd communicate with each other in the guise of family correspondence. Mummy caught on soon enough and ordered me to correspond via open postcards. I dared not defy her so off went a reluctant postcard. Back came an envelope full of inlands and a stinging letter.

'If you are so hard up that you have been reduced to writing on postcards,' wrote Kamal, 'I am sending you a year's quota.'

This infuriated my mother so, that she put an end to our burgeoning romance. I was 16 years old, supposedly the sweetest year in a girl's life, and I squandered it away pining for a lost love. However I began receiving marriage offers. A cousin's husband wanted me for his brother. An Air Force officer, who had fallen in love with me when I was 5 and promised to wait for me till I grew up, came to claim me! There also arrived a creep from Ludhiana. He was a skinny, birdlike doctor who professed to have fallen in love with me at first sight. I for one could not stand the sight of him. He sounded so phoney. Mummy was so pleased at having the boy beg for her daughter's hand, that she did not bother to ask me what I thought of him. When I told her not to bother with the alluring nightie she had tucked away for my dowry, she got an inkling of the fact that the man repelled me. To her credit, further negotiations were stopped.

Behind the kitchen garden was an outhouse occupied by a girl called Basanti. She was a single workingwoman, an unusual state of affairs in the conservative sixties in Maharashtra. Basanti rectified this social anomaly soon enough. She acquired a boyfriend and a pregnancy. As expected, the boyfriend ditched her but the gutsy woman, ahead of her times, opted for the difficult way out. She gave birth to an illegitimate daughter and brought her up single-handedly. Fearing that illegitimate pregnancies were contagious, Mummy strictly forbade us from playing with the lovely baby.

I had joined first B.Sc. (Bachelor of Science degree course) as a prerequisite for medical college and did not feel squeamish dissecting cockroaches. In fact, I wanted to practice at home. As none were to be found in my house, I got some from a neighbour's manhole in my single-minded pursuit of science! Mummy never forgave me for opening a Pandora's Box, for some of them escaped from the shoe box to infest our house. When someone asked me what I planned to do if I did not get admission in medical college, I was stumped. It had never occurred to me that I would not become a doctor.

Though we changed schools with every transfer, it was not easy to shift to Medical College. When Daddy got his posting orders for Allahabad, Mummy stayed back; lest, given the freedom, her daughters too made unacceptable love matches. It was a sacrifice she never let us forget. When the family was finally united years later, Mummy had got used to total autonomy while Daddy was still under the illusion that he was the head of the household. This resulted in a clash of wills.

9

Mummy was the adult authority that dominated our childhood. Daddy was a distant figure who came home occasionally. Even during the postings Daddy lived with us, he was as remote as the Himalayas and as cold. Handsomely turned out in the Air Force uniform (khaki in summer and navy blue in winter) he'd leave for office early in the morning and return late in the afternoon. He would sleep with the newspaper across his face and not a mouse dares squeak. The four of us would speak in whispers during his siesta time. After his evening walk, he'd spend his time buried in his files. Eight o' clock onwards was silence time again, for Daddy listened to the news in English on the radio and revised it all over again in Hindi.

He subscribed to the school of thought that children should be seen not heard, while Mummy believed in the dictum 'Spare the rod and spoil the child.' Between the two, we stood not a chance. I'm sure my children will fault the way I brought them up, as theirs will fault them. All I can say is that they did what *they* thought was right for us, which did not necessarily coincide with our views on the matter. We were never indulged. No fun or laughter, gossip and banter, lest parental authority be undermined. We ate what they fed us and wore what they chose for us. Time and again we were made to feel appropriately grateful for the wonderful education and upbringing we received. Our needs were satisfied but not our desires; in fact we weren't supposed to have any. Like soldiers, we were not allowed to use our minds—just follow orders—something against which I chafed. Perhaps because I was the first child (experimental child) and that too a girl, they were harsher with me as compared to my siblings. The space available to me was less than the span of my wings and I felt stifled in my invisible cage. Even as an adult, I studied the subject (gynaecology) *they* wanted me to and married the man *they* chose for me. With my spirit crushed, I could never achieve my full potential. They times I tried to rebel were worse. Physical punishment and emotional blackmail broke my will, making me ill-equipped to face the world.

I always had a niggling suspicion that I was the least loved of all four children. Romi was son and heir, Ronnie was physically afflicted therefore doubly dear to Mummy, while Ruby, the youngest, held a special place in Daddy's heart. I yearned for my father's affection and yet did nothing to endear myself to him. I was brash and outspoken, perhaps as an attention-seeking device. I would not take unreasonable commands lying down. Daddy would nip any mutiny in the bud by ordering me to 'shut your bloody trap!' Geysers of frustration would spring from my eyes and I'd rush out crying out, 'It is not fair.'

I did not know then that life was never fair. For all my rebellion, I was extremely sensitive. With no emotional succour from any quarter (my siblings dare not side with me lest they meet my fate), I turned to my diary for solace. On its pages I poured my angst, sublimating my tears into poetry that won me prizes, but not the attention I craved.

I realised that, like dogs, there are two types of people in the world—one that whines and whimpers when hurt and garners sympathy; the other that bites and lashes back on account of which it is shunned. I belonged to the latter category and hence, was always misunderstood and maltreated; this when my pain and that of the 'poor thing' was the same. It is perhaps for this reason that I became a writer. To my diary I would turn as a hurt child to her mother, the guilty to a confessional, the desperate to prayer.

I tried to console myself with the thought that Daddy was not of the type who showed overt affection. This illusion too, was shattered when I saw him with his sister's daughter, Harleen, in Delhi. He doted on her! They laughed and joked and even played pranks on each other. I was devastated for this meant that *I* was not worthy of his love.

When I came to Delhi for my residency, I was subjected solely to Daddy's parenting and found it sadly wanting. Despite being an adult perfectly capable of making decisions, my opinion wasn't sought for matters that concerned me.

My stipend during residency was a mere pittance. Other girls bought chocolates, cosmetics, and pretty clothes. They went to movies and restaurants. They wrote home for more money and got it. I scrimped and saved to buy a transistor but Daddy did not allow me spend my own money. As if this was not bad enough, I got a letter from Mummy stating that Daddy had complained that I was not handing over my measly pay packet to him!

Not that Mummy was any better. When I got my first stipend during internship, I wanted to buy gifts for the entire family. Mummy appropriated the money and insisted that I hide the fact from Daddy lest he deduct that much from her monthly allowance. I longed to see the look of pride on Daddy's face and for the first time in my life I had blatantly disobeyed her.

'I hate you!' she screamed, which stunned me, for I never thought that mothers could hate their children.

With hindsight, I can understand my parents' frustrations. An Air Force officer lived with élan but his pay was nothing to write home about. Mummy scrimped and saved to bring us up as well as she did. With such a meagre amount at her disposal, Mummy started buying my dowry much before she began looking for a match for me! Such are Indian mothers.

As we were travelling by bus to a sari sale one day, she sighed, If only I found a purse full of money I could spend as much as I wish for your wedding.

The conductor came clicking for the tickets. To her horror, Mummy realised that she had lost *her* purse! So much for coveting other people's money! After a frantic hunt, it was discovered under our seat. She did find a purse full of money and was mighty glad about it. It has been rightly said that 'When God wants a man to be happy He makes him lose his donkey and find it again.'

10

Living with Mummy was like growing in the shade of a mighty tree. Stunted and sallow, the very sunshine I got had to be filtered through her branches. I was seed and sapling of the original, yet puny was my development. Mothers are known to be protective of their offspring but not to such a pathological degree. After all, how long did she expect me to stay under her wings? I had to try out my own sooner or later. She gave me neither the freedom nor space to grow into an independent adult, making me ill-equipped to face the world.

I finally got admission in Medical College. Of the hundred odd students who lined up for the interview, I was the only one whose mother tagged along! She carried with her a huge basket filled with food and boiled water! After the interview, we moved from the administrative block to the hospital for our physical examination. Mummy marched along like a schoolmistress. When it began to rain, out came an umbrella to shelter me. I'd rather have caught pneumonia than stand out from the crowd. Worse was to follow. She fished out pair of slippers from her magic basket when mine broke in the slush! This was beyond the diehard advocates of maternal love. It was as if I was taking admission in the kindergarten instead of Medical College!

My first day in the dissection hall was a palpable shock. I had never seen a naked adult before and I had never seen a dead body. To be confronted by twenty-five naked dead men and women with their legs splayed out, was beyond my wildest imagination. For a society that set great store by segregation of sexes, this was something. Twelve students worked on a given body at a time, three on each limb. I was allotted the upper limb of a man. From our Cunninghams, our bibles from henceforth, we learnt how to dissect, with considerable help from our tutors who weaved between dissection tables. Armed with a lot of enthusiasm and very little skill, I marched to 'my man'. The two boys, who were to be my dissection partners for the year it took to dissect a body, were quite willing to let me take the lead. In the beginning, I'd wonder who the wretch was— an unclaimed, un-mourned dead body, broken into bits by indifferent hands before being finally discarded. Later, respect for this lifeless being dawned upon me. He may have been no use to the world alive, but well did he serve humanity in death. Thanks to him, twelve young people would become promising doctors. Whatever qualms I had about defiling a human being were soon quelled in the larger interest of mankind.

Eager to delve into the marvels of the human body, I raced ahead of my classmates. Digging deep into the axilla, I discovered bone, a feat none of the others had accomplished. All crowded around my table to see the glistening white structure. I was the heroine of the moment and my eyes shone in triumph. Alas too soon! Sir took one look at the mutilated armpit and recoiled in horror.

'Who gave you admission in medical college, you butcher! You have hacked through the axillary artery, vein, and nerve, in one callous sweep! You would have killed this man instantaneously, had he been alive! You will not touch the body again till you learn to respect human tissues. Understood?'

To be called a butcher was a fate worse than death to a girl who visualised herself as a future surgeon of renown. If only I could die at that moment. 'Butcher, butcher, butcher' the words reverberated in my mind. Tears gushed out of my eyes. Sympathetic murmurings of my classmates did nothing to stem their flow. I was inconsolable. One by one they left me with my colossal grief except for a girl called Charu. She got me a glass of water and lent me her handkerchief. This sealed a friendship that remained steadfast throughout medical college and beyond. As for my shifting to the abattoir, I soon made Sir eat his words for in due course I became his favourite student.

When we reached the head, we first sawed open the skull, removed the mushy brain, and placed it gently in a jar of formalin to harden—a process that took a month. Meanwhile, we dissected the face. The day we were to begin neuroanatomy, our jar was nowhere to be found! Bemused, I went up to Sir and said, 'I have lost my brain.'

'That I can see!' he said laughing at his own wit.

My friendship with Charu grew day by day. At home and college, even while commuting by bus, we would study together. We had a complete set of human bones at home. Huddled together on a bus seat, we'd fish out a bone from our bags and study it earnestly, oblivious of the shock and disgust of the other passengers. In due course, I became as fond of the skeleton in my cupboard as 'my man' in college.

During physiology practical, I made another friend, Lata, admiring her guts in unabashedly baring her chest for auscultation when no other girl was willing to do so. Another thing we had in common was our buckteeth. While hers spread out like a rake, mine protruded slightly. She induced me to accompany her to the dental department for correction. We sat on adjacent chairs while dentists fiddled with our teeth. My concentration was centred upon the pain in my oral cavity; I did not realise till much later that there was something more than dentistry going on. With his elbow cushioned on my crotch, he moved his arm from the hill of one breast, down the valley in between and up the hill of the other even as he worked with his hands! I was pinned to my seat and dared not squirm. Nor could I scream, lest he poke his lethal instrument elsewhere! Silent tears slid down my cheeks. How could a doctor take such advantage of a patient's trust, and a medical student at that!

When Lata learn of the molestation, she was furious. Feeling somehow responsible, the spunky girl volunteered to sit in my chair at the next appointment to teach him a lesson. I was naturally timid, and abhorred making scenes. When a cyclist pulled the *chunni* off my chest as I was walking to the bus stop, I wore my white coat over *kameez* and cried all the way to college. When a 'gentleman' vacated his seat for me in the bus and rubbed his erect penis against my shoulder, I sobbed silently! It took me years to learn to fend for myself *and* not make a scene. I would thrust my bag between the offending organ and myself, and hope that it got amputated. At other times I would 'accidentally' step on the toes of my tormentor if he were troubling me from behind in the aisle of the bus. Between severe sexual repression at home and exposure to such obscenities outside, it's a wonder that any Indian girl managed to have a normal sex life.

11

Medical college definitely wasn't all work. There was plenty to amuse one, even within the confines of the 'Laxman Rekha' my mother had imposed upon me. We strutted about with white coats draped over our arms and would be thrilled when someone called us doctors. The senior boys would bunk classes to have a look at the new Bhojan (food) as the girls were called. Why, even the girl's common room was called 'Bhojanalaya' where girls had their lunch and the boys feasted with their eyes through the windowpanes.

The boys in our class were ragged real bad. They were forced to wear white, stand in rain puddles, salute their seniors, and then sent home for wearing dirty clothes! They were made to wear pens over their crotches as external representatives of what lay underneath! The hostlers were stripped naked and 'abnormalities' were taken note of. One supposedly had a distorted posterior, which was photographed for posterity. Another was so thin that he was called 'Mr Osteology'. He was made to pose with his scapula and ischial tuberosities jutting, just as a 'He Man' is made to show off his biceps and pectorals!

A third year student took an inordinate liking to me. I would have been flattered had he not been so dark and ugly. The infatuation led him to bunk classes and attend mine! Whether I was fiddling with rabbit intestines during physiology practical, or yawning in the biochemistry class, his face became a permanent fixture at the window. He even managed to take my picture once. The fact that he was the only son of rich parents did nothing to endear him. I wanted a prince charming to sweep me off my feet, and not this ugly toad.

At the Freshers Party—that marked the end of ragging—an exciting game was being played. Girls and boys picked up folded chits from a bowl and those with similar numbers were paired off. They were given five minutes of solitude to get acquainted with each other, after which the boys were asked to fill a questionnaire and read the answers aloud. My partner was a handsome senior and a topper to boot. I was pleasantly surprised to learn that he, too, found me attractive for he wrote:

> Hair – luxuriant, dark, and curly.
> Complexion – flawless.
> Figure – fine.
> Mouth – Cupid's bow!
> Eyes – Beautiful, cannot be described.

It was the best description any girl had got. I was half in love with him by the end of the party. He lived nearby and we went to college in the same bus. He made it a point to sit next to me and I would be acutely aware of his proximity. It would have been easy to convert this infatuation into a full-fledged affair, but I had not the dishonesty and daring that a love affair entailed. A rigid upbringing reined wild yearnings and youthful effervescence fizzled out. The more I was repressed physically, the more my thoughts soared. Thwarted emotions spewed forth a spate of poems that won me accolades, but not my lost love.

Charu Chatopadhay had no such repressions to thwart her desires. She had fallen in love with a classmate solely on the basis of his marks, and the fact that he was the only other Bengali in our class. Though Dipankar Das did not turn out to be the tall dark handsome Mills and Boons hero we dreamt of (in fact he was short, fair with plain features), his intelligence impressed her immensely for he stood 1st in our first exam and all exams hereafter.

Elections loomed ahead and the entire college was in frenzy. Suddenly, freshers were treated as people and not the scum of the earth. After all they had to capture our votes. We were dragged out of class to canvass for whichever candidate managed to reach us first, for college elections were fought with as much zeal as national elections. Fancy cards, scented bookmarks, and key chains were distributed with the names of various candidates printed on them. Charu stood for the post of 1st first year CR (class representative). Das was appalled to see her standing amidst a group of boys who were canvassing loudly for her! He took her aside and took her to task. She returned from the chastisement with shining eyes, pleased with the fact that Dipankar thought that he had the right to scold her! Thereafter, I received a day-to-day account of their affair. Often, I was left to fend for myself when she disappeared for a rendezvous with him. Timid by nature and scared of my stalker, I was unable even to go to the toilet alone and had to per force find stop gap friends.

A peculiar feature of our elections was the Election Devi. The effigy of the most notorious girl of our college was taken in a procession around the campus. This year, it was Bobby, a bobbed Christian girl in a short skirt and obscenely jutting breasts. She held a Lippe's loop in one hand and a *chavvani* (four anna coin) - supposedly her going price, in the other. To protest was to acknowledge, so no girl dared. The Devi was taken around the campus in a chariot by a procession of boys in fancy dress who carried musical instruments and sang bawdy songs. She was installed at the election site to preside over the elections and was burnt after the results.

Vehicles were provided to transport us to college. By then, we knew by rote the names of the entire panel we had to vote for. They prepared us well for a career in politics if one was so inclined. We also learnt that once we had cast our votes, we were as useless as yesterday's newspaper.

The celebrations after elections were grand. It was Holi and Diwali rolled in one. Sounds of crackers filled the air, even as *gulal* coloured it with rainbow hues. Caparisoned elephants and horse-drawn chariots carried the beaming winners. The procession was led by the final year class representative (CR) who sat on a donkey facing its rear end! He was chosen unanimously for being the dunce of the class. A free suit length came with the title. Our batch had the dubious distinction of having competition for this post on account of the prize.

All too soon, play was over and exams loomed large on the horizon. The human body was no longer a miracle that man was trying to unravel since the dawn of medicine. It was one big mass of muscles, bones, blood vessels, and nerves put there specifically to unnerve me. It was impossible to remember everything and I did badly in the first paper; rather, I thought I did badly. Being a perfectionist, every small mistake was magnified ten times over.

'How did it go?' asked Mummy when I reached home.

I kept mum, the old childhood fear resurfacing.

'I asked you how have you done?' she hissed through clenched teeth.

Tears rolled down my cheeks. I looked at her as a goat would at a butcher.

'You cry now! You fool!' she screamed, amazed. 'What were you doing throughout the year? Reading novels and sleeping? Well then, cry properly if you want to.'

She was laying the table and held a steel jug of water in her hands. As I turned to put my bag down, I was conscious first of a thud, then of water trickling down my back. The pain registered last of all! She had banged the jug on my head!

My mother was definitely not one to whom you could turn for solace at times of distress. She was an excellent cook, a wonderful housekeeper, and an economist who managed on limited resources; but a psychologist, she never was. She took upon herself the thankless chores of day-to-day living so that we would not be distracted from our studies. From her, we inherited the legacies of good health and good education that stood us in good stead throughout our lives. That children had emotional needs too, she neither knew nor cared. As for my kids they learnt to answer back the day they learnt to talk. In no way could I make them bend to my will. Life had dealt a raw deal to our generation dominated, as we were both by our parents and children.

12

For a year and a half, we had been entombed with the embalmed. From third year onwards we would be allowed to touch a living patient. Not that 2nd MBBS (Bachelor of Medicine Bachelor of Surgery) per se was concerned with the living. We had pathology, the study of abnormal anatomy; microbiology, that dealt with microbes; and pharmacology, pertaining to drugs—all dry subjects but compulsory nevertheless. Last but not the least was forensic medicine, a subject that fascinated and repelled at the same time.

The day I got my 2nd MBBS course books, I stayed awake all night reading my forensic text from cover to cover. Shocking were the details exposed! I learnt of the different methods one could commit robbery, murder, and suicide. For one not well versed with normal sexuality, the plethora of abnormal sex ranging from rape to sodomy, to bestiality, explicitly detailed in the book were electrifying. There were vivid illustrations and case reports. One such report stands out in memory: A woman had consensual sex with a man but shouted rape the moment they got caught. The man's innocence was proved by an orange pip! He had eaten an orange just before the act. One pip was found stuck between his teeth and another in her vagina!

The first postmortem I attended left a vivid impression on my mind. The pickled specimens in the dissection hall did not look human, while bodies in the mortuary were real. They had died recent deaths due to unknown causes. A fresh, accident victim lay on the cold marble table. Whose husband, whose son, whose father was he? What sort of devastation had he left behind? Did he die immediately or lie on the road, helplessly watching his life's blood ebb away? A thousand questions flooded my mind. I had years to go before I became the dispassionate, competent robot that people call doctors.

The doctor of the dead donned a thick apron and rubber gloves and went about his task with the nonchalance of a butcher. He explained the details of a postmortem as he carved the body expertly. When he palpated the stomach through the open abdomen, a trickle of food emerged from the corner of the dead man's mouth. My eyes were riveted to the mess and there rose in *my* stomach, an uncontrollable desire to retch. To divert my mind, I read at the quotation that hung on the wall beyond, which is still engraved in my mind.

'An operation performed during life is accompanied by pain and is for the benefit of the individual. An operation performed after death is without pain and is for the benefit of mankind.'

It was a relief to move to the clinical side. With admiration, I watched experts do what they were supposed to do—cure patients. The class was divided into tutorial batches of 15-20 students that rotated in all the clinical departments of the hospital. The only other girl with me was Lata. Our first posting was in the surgery department. Each student was allotted a bed and was 'responsible' for the patient on that bed for the eight-week posting.

As the number of students exceeded the number of beds, two of us were given one patient to work up. My partner, a South Indian boy named Reddy, turned to me and said, 'You and I share one bed.'

On account of this stupid sentence I was teased with him for the rest of my college days.

We had to follow a protocol while taking the history of a patient. Besides the details of the present complaints, their duration and severity, one had to ask the past history and family history of the patient. With his poor command over the

Queen's language, Reddy put his foot in his mouth once again. A woman lay on 'our' bed in excruciating pain. Her entire leg was red and swollen with cellulitis, all on account of a small nail prick! When Reddy was asked to take her history he began, 'What is your chief complaint?'

'I have this swelling and pain in my right leg.'

'Since when?'

'Since last week.'

'How did it start?'

'Following a nail prick.'

'Tell me how many pricks have you had before?'

There were sniggers that were quickly suppressed. The woman looked perplexed.

'Never mind, tell me how many pricks are there in your family?'

Enough was enough! Needless to say, Sir banished him from class.

Dr Deshpande delighted in making male students palpate female breasts and girls handle male genitalia. Boys were made to examine breast lumps while I was told to palpate a massive hydrocele. Gingerly, I put my fingertips on the bloated organ.

'Why are you caressing it?' he asked of me, a shy virgin who could not understand why would anyone want to caress something as revolting as an over-blown scrotum?

Acutely embarrassed, I pressed hard.

'What do you think you are doing? Blowing the horn of a truck?'

I recoiled in horror. My eyes filled with tears.

Once you got to know him, Dr Deshpande was not a bad sort at all. An excellent surgeon and teacher, he taught us things that stood me in good stead. There was a patient with cancer penis whose organ had been reduced to a pulpy, foul-smelling mass. Unable to bear the stench, I put my hankie over my nose.

'Take that handkerchief away at once!' he commanded.

I looked at Sir with perplexed eyes.

'Have you ever paused to wonder what it must have cost this man to bare himself in front of half-baked doctors like you? And what does he get in return? Revulsion. If the treating doctor rejects him whom can he turn to?'

It was a lesson I never forgot. Neither did I forget the sickening sweet smell of advanced cancer.

In the minor operation theatre (OT) we learnt to inject piles, apply stitches, and drain abscesses. Major operations were viewed from the student's gallery high up in the main OT. When our surgery posting was over, I was sorry to leave such a dynamic branch of medicine.

During medical posting I developed a massive crush for the head of the department! Of medium height with aristocratic features and slender capable hands, Dr Saxena was my ideal. Wherever he went with his coat tails flapping, his Littman's flung carelessly around his neck, I followed. His mastery over his subject and his juniors was superb. His wards were the cleanest, his interns the sharpest, and his patients were the best looked after. The entire department dreaded his sharp tongue, which fell on the incompetent like a whiplash. Doctors and students alike viewed a posting in his unit akin to a term in the torture chamber. Surprisingly, I thrived on it. Each case was solved with mathematical precision and I enjoyed matching my wits with his.

Dr Saxena, of course, was least interested in me as a person. The only time he took notice of me was during internship. Charu was horrified to learn that she was posted in his unit while I was deeply disappointed at being put in another unit. Mustering courage, we asked him if we could exchange places. Well aware of his reputation, he could understand Charu wanting to run away. What he could not comprehend was my volunteering to enter the lion's den, but enter it I did. And did I work hard? But good performance was the norm in his unit. The day he gave me a lift in his car was the happiest in my life. I remembered vividly every detail of a ride he promptly forgot. The only time he touched me was when I suffered from high fever and went to him for consultation. Soon after, I learnt that he was having an affair with a pretty professor in the pathology department. My heart broke. That the affair lasted longer than most marriages do, did nothing to uplift my spirits. I wrote:

In Love with a Doctor

He took my head in both his hands
And looked deep into my eyes,
He did not see their sparkling beauty
Nor the love in them that lies.
It was for jaundice and pallor
That he observed my eyes and skin!
Trust my fate to make me love
A doctor to my chagrin.
With a look of supreme indifference
His fingers on my pulse he laid,
And for it being fast and bounding
Dearly with a 'disease' I paid.
My heart, he said he would palpate
For signs of a murmur or thrill,
Thrilled I was at the prospect
For he would hear it to his fill.
For my flushed cheek and dry lips,
My unsteady grip and gait,
My rapid breathing, fevered brow,
He said, he'll have to investigate!
He who pretends to know all ills,
And more so their cures;
With no promise of relief
In his trap of love, allures.
But,
Not for all the flattery in the world,
My love for him I'll trade,
Indifferent, serious though he is
I love him as he's made.

Twenty-five years later when I returned to my alma mater for a reunion, I made it a point to meet Dr Saxena. He had long since retired and aged considerably, but his memory was sharp as ever. I was surprised to learn that he remembered me, and the fact that my poems got 1st prize in our college magazine. He also told me that he thought that I was more intelligent than him and would go far! My cup of joy brimmed over. I mustered the courage to tell him of my crush, and I could see that he was mighty pleased.

Paediatrics posting was short and sweet like the professor himself who looked like a pink, overgrown baby. The wards weren't filled with pretty children though. It was more like a veterinary hospital where one had to deal with the dumb and sick. It saddened me to see little ones die of gastroenteritis, tuberculosis, and other preventable causes. Bloated bellies, emaciated limbs, and wizened little monkey faces of malnourished children tugged at my heartstrings. I grieved over the lack of awareness in the people, and the lack of space in the hospital.

The Gynaecology department comprised of a bunch of frustrated females—irritable and irritating beyond measure, and I did not want to end up as one of them. I had a crush on my medicine professor, surgery was such a happening subject, and my heart went out to the paediatric patients. If I had my way, I would have become all three rolled into one, but as for all other things in life, it was not for me to decide. My indomitable mother insisted that I become gynaecologist, and a gynaecologist I became.

Like a first love, no gynaecologist can forget her first delivery. A lady in an advanced stage of labour was wheeled in. It was her fifth child and she was hurling abuses at her husband who took his pleasure, leaving her with the pain. I stood gloved, gowned, and masked between her legs to receive the baby. Even as I contemplated the travails of womanhood, awaiting the flexion, rotation, and extension of the head as described in textbooks, the baby shot out like a bullet! I had to literary raise my knee to prevent it from falling into the bucket!

In the overcrowded wards, women with complicated pregnancies lay two on a bed. Those that had delivered were given floor beds. Such was the crowding during delivery season that we had to jump over one patient on the floor to see the next. During ward rounds, I once chanced upon a hugely pregnant woman who lay with the sheet pulled right up to her chin. To my horror, I saw that she wore no petticoat. Stung by the poverty of the masses, I rushed to my hostel room and got her one of mine. For this altruistic act, I was rewarded by a scolding from my senior! The woman suffered from severe pregnancy induced hypertension that could lead to fits. She was advised complete bed rest but, unable to comprehend the gravity of her situation, she would flit from bed to bed to gossip with the other patients. Her petticoat had been confiscated to ensure that the doctor's orders were followed!

13

We joined Daddy at Allahabad for the summer holidays. The bungalow was beautiful and the neighbours congenial. The sound of airplanes taking off and landing at the airfield nearby deafened us. The Ganges shimmered at a distance. Dark green foliage dotted with light green blobs carpeted its banks. These, as I learnt later, were watermelons that thrived on burning sands; the hotter the summer, the sweeter the red succulent flesh. The harvested melons were brought to the city on camels in quaint, conical jute baskets that hung on either side of its back. A single file of lazy-footed camels carrying these football-sized fruit, filing past on the hot dusty road made an enchanting sight.

Bambrauli, like any other cantonment area, was away from the bustle of the city. Serene and sophisticated, life in the armed forces had a distinct flavour of its own that had nothing to do with the flavour of a particular city. Where else would complete strangers invite you for lunch and dinner on your arrival? Where else would they send you breakfast the next day so that you got ample time to unpack and unwind? We belonged to the fraternity of the forces where friendships were forged instantaneously and lasted for life.

A few days later, our neighbours were planning their marriage anniversary celebrations and Mummy sent Ruby and me to help. Imagine calling fifty odd people to celebrate such a private event. When I got married, I thought it would be just my husband and me, and a romantic weekend spent away from the maddening crowd. A horde of guests to tire you out was definitely not my idea of a celebration. Little did I know that I would marry a man who did not believe in celebrating life. As of now, with the juices of life surging through my body, I was young enough to dream. It was so easy to fall in love with the first presentable male who came my way.

At the party, I met a dashing young pilot who paid me extraordinary attention. He invited me to the airfield the next day to show me the planes. It was a prospect fraught with possibilities. I had not reckoned with my mother who insisted that I take her entire brood along. If he was disappointed at the sight of my bodyguards, he was too much of a gentleman to show it. He took us aboard a Packard. As the cockpit was higher than the body of the aircraft, a small iron ladder led up to it. With a bow and an effusive wave of his hand, he asked the lady to climb up first. I complied. The ladder was loosely hooked and began to wobble. I hung precariously midair for a moment and fell. As I lay sprawled, quite unladylike, on the floor with the ladder over me, my siblings guffawed. The gallant officer untangled me from the iron monster and hauled me to my feet. The romance that had begun promisingly under the moon the night before finished with a bang a mere twelve hours later. It was the shortest love story ever.

No visit to Allahabad can be complete without a visit to the holy Sangam, the confluence of the Ganga, Jamuna, and the mythological subterranean Saraswati. We went for a boat ride on a serene, balmy evening. The sand was cool and silken under my feet. Wooden boats bobbed by the shore. Waves wet their sides with long lazy licks. The clouds were painted orange, pink, and purple by the setting sun. Some of the flush stained my cheeks. A breeze had sprung up as we boarded one of the creaky vessels. It crinkled the surface of the river and teased my curls. Ever the romantic, the song,

Kashti ka kamosh safar hai, shaam bhi hai tanhaee bhi
Door kinare par bajti hai mazil ke shehnai bhi
Aaj mujhe kuch kehna hai . . .
(*On a silent boat journey, in the quiet of the evening*
From the far shore, arises the sound of shehnai (musical intrument)
Today, I would like to say something . . .)

came unbidden to my lips. As I was singing softly to myself, I wished that I was with a lover, instead of admonishing parents and squabbling siblings. Holy thoughts were far from my mind as we rowed towards the confluence.

The water wasn't deep at the Sangam on account of the silt pushed forward by the mighty rivers. It mirrored the sordid face of humanity garbed in the cloak of religion. People threw in coins in reverence that urchins promptly retrieved, with irreverence. *Pundits* haggled over the price of prayers. Ashes of the dead were poured in the sacred waters. A bloated, half-eaten body floated by. I wondered how people found salvation in these waters. It was the same at Haridwar when I went there years later with my in-laws. The Ganga got no breathing spaces whatsoever. There were stairs leading right into the waters at Har Ki Pauri. As omnipresent as God, flies buzzed busily. The unbelievable dirt, the thronging humanity, the rotting flowers, the muddy monsoon waters, made me resolve never to take a 'holy' dip for instead of washing away my sins, I felt I would add on the sins of others. Perhaps I lacked faith, but I had experience to go by. At Ponta Sahib, the historical gurudwara situated on the banks of the Jamuna, the holy waters gave me a taste of after life, for I nearly died of gastroenteritis after taking in a mouthful!

In our backyard, grew a jackfruit tree. The large, prickly fruit stuck out from its tall trunk like so many warts. Being expensive and exotic, Mummy decided that jackfruit would make a good present to take back for our neighbours. Daddy protested, but she was adamant. So the huge, heavy fruits were packed snugly in the holdall and loaded onto the train. We used the bedding at night and re-rolled it hurriedly the next morning before reaching Nagpur. To our dismay, it stuck in the doorway of the train. We hadn't been able to roll it as tightly as Daddy! Time was running short. Our coolie forsook us for more lucrative business elsewhere. We hadn't had the time to 'dejackfruit' the bedding. Stranded passengers were getting belligerent. The train was due to leave any moment. In desperation, Mummy announced a cash prize of Rs 5 to anyone who would push the ungainly bulk out. In a moment, foes turned friends and delivered the bulky bedding. So much for the free gift for our neighbours!

14

Before I knew it, it was examination time once again. Usually, I ran short of time while writing a paper, but I was surprised to find that during pathology theory I had time to revise. The revision was over by the time the first bell rang. Smug at my precision, I began folding the question paper. To my horror, I realised that there was a twenty marks question at the back that I hadn't seen! And I knew the answer! 'A for Amrita' made me roll number 1, and the invigilator came to take my answer sheet first. I snatched it back and tried to explain what had happened. The only way he could help me was to collect my paper last of all. If I wanted more time than that, I would have to ask the head of the department. When I rushed to her, she asked me two questions:

'Do you expect to fail?'

'No, madam.'

'Do you expect to come in the first three?'

'No.' So poor was my sense of self-worth.

'Then what difference will a few marks here and there make?' she said.

It did make a difference. I stood third in the class and the difference between my marks and the one who came second was just four! Such was the lesson I learnt from this incident that even now, whenever I read an important paper, I look at the back first!

It has been rightly said that a medical student is happy only on two days of his life. The day he joins medical college and the day he leaves it. Final MBBS exams were a nightmare. We got a month's preparatory leave. Up and down the terrace, I walked book in hand. When tired, I sat in the balcony learning lessons other than those taught in books. I watched squirrels courting in the day, and geckos at night. The male gecko made strange ticking sounds as he chased the female, till he finally caught up and rode over her. This led me to think of human intercourse. I had got the general idea of how one went about it but I did not know how much time it actually took. There was no one whom I could ask such a question, that too in the thick of my exams! Strangely, poetry flooded my mind during these stressed out days. Though I did jot down a few lines every now and then, I promised myself that I would write reams once the exams were over.

To unwind after hours of studying, Daddy suggested that I read some relaxing literature in between. As luck would have it, the novel I got hold of in those days was 'Gone With The Wind'. It was simply 'unputdownable'. So Mummy took to hiding it. This game of hide and seek went on and on till, in desperation, she hid it in the vegetable drawer of the fridge! I discovered her unusual hiding place and retrieved it at night. Scarlet O' Hara's affairs in far off Atlanta seemed so much more interesting than my final MBBS exams. I wondered how she could be so obtuse to reject Rhett Butler, when she was smart enough in matters pertaining to her beloved home, Tara. *I* for one was totally in love with him. It was 2 a.m. and all I had studied diligently was this blessed novel. Precious time had been squandered irretrievably. Though I had outsmarted Mummy, there was no outsmarting my conscience. My classmates must have mugged up chapters by now. This evoked a surge of guilt and fear that I vent in tears, losing still more time.

Surgery paper was a shock. My mind went totally blank. I would have handed a blank sheet to the invigilator had it not been for Lata. She understood my panic and urged me relax. When I started writing, I realised that I could fill quite a few pages. Practicals went off quite well and the overall marks in surgery were quite good; but people did not let me be.

'You know how girls get good marks?' Someone sniggered behind my back. It was a totally unwarranted barb. Firstly, I was not the sort who made eyes at professors. Secondly, he had been recently transferred to Nagpur Medical College and got no opportunity to judge my mental calibre. Last but not the least was the fact that our Surgery professor was totally pro-Maharashtrian.

There was much discrimination between Maharashtrians and Non-Maharasthrians in Nagpur Medical College, so I stood not a chance. Suddenly, I remembered Charu taking me forcibly to Sir for a painful fissure that made life hell. Surely, a clinical examination of my derrière had nothing to do with my marks!

As for ophthalmology, I did not know that I was shortlisted for the gold medal. The first I learnt of it was during my short case. A dark, cauliflower-like growth arose from one eyeball, obliterating the normal anatomy completely! I had never seen anything quite like this before. Naturally I did not know the answers to any of the questions put to me. The external examiner biased by the fact that he had been told that I was 'exceptional', turned to the internal and taunted, 'So this is your good student?'

Tears sprung to my eyes and I rushed out of the room. By the time I reached my 'long case', I was sobbing uncontrollably. I would surely fail for the long case was no better. He had manganese particles in his eyes! Why couldn't he have iron filings in them instead, or cataract? I felt horrid at letting down Sir when he had so much faith in my ability, but I couldn't see how I could fare better now. What did I know of manganese particles and blindness? I sat on the stool by the patient, with my head bent, to hide my tear-stained face. I felt a hand on my shoulder and heard someone say, 'Don't worry, you'll do better now.'

I looked up to see my 'long case' consoling me! I was thoroughly ashamed of myself. This near blind man who had nothing much to hope for was encouraging a stupid girl who had nothing to lose. He had been the long case for three consecutive days, and knew a smattering of English. He had overheard the questions and answers and apprised me of the fact!

Being roll number 1 had its advantages and disadvantages. The examiners were fresh during viva and practicals, and therefore grilled me more than the others. The best part was that I finished first of all. While the exams of the last batch concluded, a good two days later, I was free!

Free to get up late, laze, watch movies, read novels, embroider, knit, and to write poetry. Now that I had the time, I had no ideas. The exams had taken their toll and I was thin as reed. For a girl who had been teased all her life for her plumpness, this was a novelty. But the world never lets one be. Now the standard refrain was, 'Who will marry this bag of bones? A man does need a wife with some flesh on her.'

As the results drew near I became jittery all over again. Too chicken-hearted to go myself, I sent my brother Romi to look up the results. I prayed that I pass in the first attempt. I couldn't go through another ordeal like this again. Mummy's oft repeated adage, 'Do your best and God will do the rest' would come to my mind, and tears would spring afresh. Well I hadn't done my best so there wasn't much in the rest for God to do. I was undressing for a bath when Romi burst in shouting, 'Rosy, you have come second in class and won a gold medal!'

I couldn't believe my ears. Out I rushed sans my salwar in unmitigated joy! Das stood first while Charu came third. He received seven gold medals and Charu got none. I was happy with my solitary one. That this one medal generated twenty-five others is a different story. My genes carried the gold in them and transferred them to my elder son who did me proud when he passed medical college 25 years later. Though the younger one chose a different profession, he too received a bunch of gold medals for his academic performance.

15

We had to go through a year of rotatory internship for practical training in medicine. With the burden of studies over and the responsibilities of a full-fledged doctor yet to come, this was a period of idyllic bliss. Whether my parents liked it or not, three months of village posting was compulsory. They could not stop me from going with a medical certificate faking illness, as they had done for my NCC (National Cadet Core) camp in 1st year. With a song in my heart, I boarded the bus that sped to freedom. The first half of the posting was in mobile camps. Hospitals were pitched in tents that shifted from village to village every month. We camped in the grounds of an ancient Jain Mandir, situated at the foot of a hill called Ramtek where Lord Rama had rested during his exile. We bathed in the sparkling waters of a shallow stream like village belles. Changing in the open air behind a pile of rocks was an erotic experience. The breeze, sensuous as a lover, licked the water off my naked body.

The weather in February was like that of the desert—sweat-hot in the day, and quilt-cold at night. We lived in tents with a flap door and windows. Food was served on stone tables under shady trees, and crows sometimes added their mite to the fare served. The Out Patient Department (OPD) was a tent the size of a circus. Except for the OT, which was a permanent structure, everything including the wards, was housed in tents. Tubectomies, vasectomies, hernias, hydroceles, cataract operations, and other daycare procedures, were performed by seniors who came every morning from the hospital. We assisted them, took care of the patients post-operatively, and sent them home by two o' clock, after which we were free.

In the hot afternoons, we sought the cool interior of the Jain temple. As the Jains were strict vegetarians and ardent believers of non-violence, we were not allowed to defile the premises with shoes, belts, or purses made of animal hides. We managed to smuggle in a pack of cards with our novels though. Twenty-four naked statues of Mahavira stared disapprovingly down at us as we shuffled cards in delicious guilt. Later, when we got accustomed to their number and nudity, we imagined that their stern countenance had softened to indulgence as if they forgave us our harmless sins.

At dusk, the sweet chimes of the temple bells, the sonorous chanting of hymns, the heron-flecked emerald grass in the shimmering wetlands beyond the temple, filled our souls with tranquillity; but it was at night that we truly came alive. A fun-filled conglomeration huddled around a crackling fire in the middle of nowhere, under a benign February moon. We laughed and sang, cracked jokes and peanuts, and loved every moment of it. I soon realised that Bhaskar, a classmate, made it a point to sit by me whenever he could, be it in the OPD or by the campfire. I was flattered by his attention though his appearance was nothing to write home about. He was so small and wizened that we would call him 'foetus' at college. He certainly was not my idea of a lover, but love was in the air. Like the queen in Midsummer's Night Dream who fell in love with a donkey, I was attracted to this little monkey!

As the camp was some distance away from Nagpur, it was not feasible to return on weekends. All the better as far as I was concerned. For the first time in my life, I was away from the restrictive atmosphere at home and enjoyed myself thoroughly. We spent the time visiting picnic spots around us. One Sunday, we trekked to Ramtek, the hill that dominated the horizon. The higher we climbed, the farther seemed the peak. Barely had we reached the summit when a battalion of monkeys pounced to snatch the offerings we had brought. I barely escaped being bitten myself. After paying obeisance at the shrines of Rama, Sita, and Laxmana, we came upon the altar of Hanuman, the monkey god. Feigning surprise I exclaimed, 'Bhaskar, I didn't know that you were being worshipped here!'

Charu had brought with her a book on human sexual behaviour by Masters and Johnsons. One night, the girls huddled under quilts and took turns to read it aloud. Not even the doleful serenading of the neglected boys could draw us out. This was far too interesting. We learnt of erotic zones and how they could be stimulated. We learnt the right approach to lovemaking and mistakes that should be avoided. We read hypnotised, till the last page. It was an eye-opener and 'tongue loosener'. To think people came to doctors for sexual guidance when most of us were ignorant fools uncomfortable with our own sexuality. The only married girl in our group hadn't been able to achieve an orgasm yet. She was relieved that she could now instruct her ignorant husband. It was strange that, what came instinctively to lesser animals had to be learnt from books by humans. Years later, I learnt that Das had bought this book and had put its teachings to practical use with Charu during our college days. That she had premarital sex in those times was appalling enough, but surprisingly what hurt me now, after all these years was, that she hadn't confided in me then, her best friend.

On Holi Eve, we packed food and utensils, cook and helper in the hospital ambulance and drove off to Khinsi Lake for a midnight feast. Under a yellow moon, we lit the traditional bonfire, recreating the burning of Hola, the sister of the wicked King Harnaksha of ancient India. She had been given a boon in the form of a shawl that would protect her from fire. The king, furious with his child Prahlad for worshipping the true God when he had appointed himself God, made Hola sit with Prahlad in the bonfire till he was burnt alive. A brisk breeze blew off her shawl; Hola perished, while God saved his young devotee's life.

The actual festival of colours was on the morning after; and did the boys take advantage of the licence of the day. Vigorously, they rubbed *gulal* on our cheeks, necks, backs, and rumps. With multicoloured hair and faces, we trooped in the van for yet another picnic!

This time, it was down a narrow path between jutting rocks to a stream in a shady glen. We sat on boulders and dipped our feet in the cool, clear waters. Soon, we found a novel way of whiling away our time. Bhaskar sat cross-legged with eyes closed like a sage in meditation. Idly, I began throwing sand over him. The others joined in the pastime and in a short time he was buried in sand except for the head. He looked like a pyramid with a face; an extremely mobile face at that—showing the white of his eyes, lifting eyebrows one by one, and curling lips in a vicious snarl. In short, it was a face that made faces. It was fun till I felt something squirm under my hand. I screamed only to learn that Bhaskar had managed to expose a foot and was tickling my palm with his toes!

The spell that Bhaskar cast over me worked its magic only at the camp. Back at the hospital when sanity returned, I was astonished at my infatuation with such an unworthy specimen of mankind. I am sure the shock was reciprocated for how could he have even thought of an inter-caste alliance in the conservative Maharashtra of the early seventies. When he eventually married a short and skinny Maharashtrian girl, I was mighty glad it wasn't me.

16

Stark white walls,
Bespattered with blood,
Smiling faces, suddenly
Turn grim,
As anxiety beads
The surgeon's forehead;
A recalcitrant artery
Eludes the forceps,
Merrily spurting,
Sprinkling life.
The pulse ebbs,
The heart beats faster
As,
The sanguine pool expands!
Fear rams its head on
The operator's innards,
Dries his mouth and
Wets his palms. Even
As his hands tremble,
He prays for the
Steadying influence,
On the Unseen hand.
As if on cue, the truant vessel
Is caught and the joke on
The doctor's lip proclaims
The release of tension.

Another patient returns
From no man's land,
Another surgeon
Has made his journey,
To hell and back yet,
To the world outside
It was,
But another day in the OT

After the three months in various villages, we were back at Medical College. I did not realise that I would miss its spittle stained corridors so. The first posting of my tutorial batch was in surgery. The only other girl in my group Lata, was absent on OT day. Excitedly, I entered the operation theatre complex with the boys. Gone were the days of mere gallery viewing. We would now be in the thick of action. Our senior, Dr Patel, was cute looking with absurdly long eyelashes. He asked us to exchange our everyday clothes for OT wear. The boys trooped into the changing room. Feeling rather lost, I followed suit—only to find Dr Patel in a state of undress! The shock was mutual. It was strange how the mere stripping of clothes stripped one of dignity.

'Why have you come here?' he asked embarrassed.

'To . . . to change,' I stammered.

'Don't you know that there is separate changing room for ladies?'

'I thought it was adjacent to the men's room.' I stammered. Forlorn and very much alone, I entered the lady's changing room. I managed to change into an OT maxi but for the life of me could not arrange the head cover over my head. Those were not the days of disposable caps and masks. Timidly, I approached a nurse who was busy soaping her arms.

'How do you expect me to show you how to tie it when I am scrubbing?'

Dr Patel emerged from the changing room with the boys like a mother hen with her brood. Seeing me he taunted, 'You have time to stand and stare like a lady of leisure when we have not a moment to spare.'

Blinking furiously I stretched towards him the triangular piece of green cloth held in my hand.

'Sir, I don't know how to tie this and sister is too busy to teach me.'

He softened at the childlike gesture and selected me as his assistant for his first case. Little did he know that he would live to rue his kindness. I was jubilant! Neither of us realised that I knew not a thing. There was a world of difference between viewing an operation from the student's gallery and actually assisting.

Smilingly, he taught me how to scrub and wear the gown and gloves. Soon, I was standing opposite him with an anesthetised patient between us.

'When I make the incision, wipe the blood with the mop,' he instructed.

Eager to follow his instructions, I rubbed vigorously.

'What do you think you are doing, swabbing a floor? You have to pat the area gently lest you damage the tissues.'

'Yes, sir,' I mumbled from behind my mask.

Eyeless needles were yet to revolutionise surgical techniques. As he was about to take a crucial stitch, the suture came off.

'Thread the needle quickly,' he said.

I raised the bit of catgut to my mouth to wet it as one did during needlework and encountered the mask! My ears reddened with mortification. Dr Patel let out an exasperated sigh and waited patiently till I changed my gloves and threaded a new suture, after discarding the original unsterile one. Each time he took a stitch, I had to pull the suture and hold it taut. Smarting with humiliation at my earlier gaffe, I forgot. His patience finally wore thin and he rapped me smartly on my knuckles with an artery forceps. My degradation was complete!

The tears welled and fell into the open abdomen! Sir had had enough of my 'assistance' and unceremoniously ordered me out.

That I survived this ordeal to perform hydroceles and hernias towards the end of the posting, speaks volumes for my resilience. In the meantime, I drained abscesses, applied stitches, injected piles, and dilated strictures. I had a lot to learn in dealing with patients and often made mistakes, some of them hilarious. I asked a man with acute piles to take a Setz bath by pouring warm water in a basin and sitting in it morning and evening.

He came back the next OPD complaining that he had not been relieved of his symptoms.

'But did you follow my instructions?'

'Yes, doctor. Every morning and evening I put warm water in *basen* (gram flour) and applied it to my bottom.'

Goodness gracious! It was stupid of me to expect an illiterate to understand English. I should have used the Hindi word *chiramchi* instead of basin.

I cut my brother's corns and they grew all over again! Out of fear and affection, I hadn't cut deep enough. This taught me that one must treat relatives dispassionately, like other patients, or hand them over to colleagues.

Posting in the Infectious Diseases Ward was awful. People died terrible deaths due to totally avoidable causes. Typhoid, jaundice, and meningitis—we saw them all. Charu contracted chicken pox and Das diphtheria from these wards (occupational hazards), but survived to become full-fledged doctors. With locked jaws, rigid bodies, racking convulsions, and eyes wet with mute misery, tetanus patients remained painfully conscious till the end. We even saw a 20-year-old with rabies! He was kept behind bars till he died an agonising death.

There was a separate ward for tubercular patients. Only the open cases and terminal ones were admitted. On their thin arms with prominent veins, we learnt to draw blood. Endless rows of skeletal forms with bright, feverish eyes, filled spittoon after spittoon with copious, bloodstained phlegm. There was one with a shy sweet smile on whom I performed pleural tapping to ease his breathing. The next day, he breathed no more. There was an empty space where his bed was.

'Where is my patient?' I asked bewildered.

'Gone up,' said sister with her thumb pointing heavenwards.

'Along with the bed,' I quipped unthinkingly. The truth was that the beds of the dead were disinfected before another occupied it.

Skin department mostly had patients with the itch—scabies, eczema, allergies, and psoriasis. And then there were the lepers. Leprosy was rampant in Maharashtra and they came in hordes. Why, leprosy was less contagious than say, scabies, and treatable, too. It wasn't the disease that ate away the fingers and toes but the lack of sensation that caused painless shedding of the terminal phalanxes after burns or injuries. Yet the flattened noses and finger-less palms robbed them of their place in society, reducing them to beggars who pedalled their sores.

Medicine posting meant detailed history-taking and examination, for a patient with breathlessness could be a case of asthma, pneumonia, rheumatic heart disease, or severe anaemia. Ultrasound had not been invented; kidney, and liver biopsies were done blindly. The only precaution taken for a VIP (very important person) who needed a liver biopsy was that he was entrusted to the care of a senior. I saw a hapless VIP became the victim of 'VIP Syndrome'. The biopsy needle introduced by the unit chief (who usually did far less cases than his residents) entered a blood vessel that resulted in death!

My final posting was in the gynae department. It has been gynae for me ever since, for there was no changing of tracks after that. Pregnant women with ruptured uterus, locked twins, or retained placenta, were brought in bullock carts from remote villages. Eclamptics convulsed and anemics bled. There were hapless unmarrieds with illegitimate pregnancies who had feets of intestines pulled out of their vaginas during clandestine abortions at dubious centres.

The labour room was and still is one of the most stressful places on earth—a battleground where grim, bloody battles are fought. Where life begets life and death is an occasional visitor. It bears mute witness to the dramatic entry of mankind into this world. The walls resounded with the screams of women in labour, the chorus of the attending staff urging her on, and finally, the sweet cry of the newborn. A hundred things could go wrong. At times, the baby's heartbeat drops and the obstetrician's heart sinks with it, the woman bleeds profusely, and the doctor's sweat flowing as freely as her blood. Extensive lacerations can convert the vaginal and anal canal into one! The afterbirth may not deliver and has to be removed manually! Why, even a normal delivery can be called so only in retrospect!

Into this arena, I entered one day as a novice. My seniors had gone for an emergency caesarian and I was asked to hold fort. No one was unduly worried for the only patient in the labour room was a primigravida with very mild contractions. It would be hours before she delivered—so they thought—but unpredictable are the ways of nature. All of a sudden, she began to push. To my horror, a pair of tiny feet peeped out of the vulva instead of the head. I had hardly any practice conducting a normal delivery leave alone a breech. Within minutes the soft buttocks slipped out and the head got stuck! The baby would hang to death from its mother's vagina if I did not act fast, but I stood paralysed. Its chest began to heave with the head still inside! I was sick with fear. What if the infant died on account of my inadequacy or worse still, survived to live the life of a vegetable! I prayed as I had never prayed before. I pledged an offering of Rs. 5 to the gurudwara if the baby survived my ministrations. As if on cue, the baby slipped out with the very next pain! Its lusty cry was the sweetest sound I had ever heard.

When I recounted the tale at the dinner table that night, my brother quipped, 'Sister dear, at this rate, your entire pay will end up in the *gurudwara*!'

Which could be true for we got a mere Rs 150/- as stipend during internship in those days.

17

Two things happened simultaneously. I fell in love and got engaged to, two different people. I was 21 years old and ripe for marriage. My parents were frantic for it was difficult to find an eligible Sikh match for me in the heart of Maharashtra. In all, there were five Sikh boys in Nagpur Medical College. Out of these two were my brothers, two my classmates, and one senior. One classmate and the sole senior were beneath us in the caste hierarchy. A match with either of them was out of question. This left me with only one prospective groom, the other classmate—a handsome enough fellow but one who was scolded so often in my presence that he could earn neither my respect nor my love.

My parents feared that I might run off with a Maharashtrian. I would have, perhaps, if one of them would have me. I subsisted on Hindi films and Mills and Boons novels, and the very thought of a bearded fellow with a turban pawing me was repulsive. Moreover, I had become totally Maharashtranised. I wore cotton saris and flowers in my hair. I made two plaits and put a small black *bindi* on my forehead. I spoke Marathi fluently and fasted on Mondays.

Daddy was stationed at Delhi. He did not believe in consulting his children about their future, and applied on my behalf for a house job in the prestigious All India Institute of Medical Sciences (AIIMS). The first I learnt of it was when I was called over for an interview. Not that I was sorry to leave the pit of venomous, slithering snakes that went by the name of the Gynae Department. The 36-hour shift, the lack of sleep and nourishment, and the environment of animosity had taken their toll. I was more than ready to leave. It was with a gladdened heart that I boarded the train for Delhi. Little did I know that an eligible match, and not superior training, was the objective of this exercise.

Earlier, when talks about marriage cropped up, I had vehemently told Mummy that I would not be displayed to prospective grooms like a mare on sale. It was demeaning to be 'shown' in the traditional way and stand the possibility of a rejection. I understood that, as love marriages were taboo and interaction between the sexes was discouraged, this was the only way parents could arrange a match for their children; but I was horrified at the thought of being humiliated so. She must have conveyed my views to Daddy for he resorted to subterfuge.

He had shortlisted quite a few 'boys' for me without my knowledge. The sifting began on the day I reached Delhi. My uncle, a doctor in Delhi, invited us to a medico's picnic at Vijay Chowk that very evening. Under a moon-lit sky, by the silvery fountain, we gathered. Rashtrapati Bhawan loomed on the horizon. Even as I took in my surroundings, my uncle introduced me to doctor after doctor. Though I smiled politely and made small talk, I promptly forgot their names. After all they were strangers in a strange city. I could not even see them properly in the dim moonlight. I felt uprooted and lonely. I had only a formidable father to call my own, and clung to whatever cold comfort he had to offer.

Uncle invited us over for lunch the next day. Too late I realised that he had invited another couple with an unmarried doctor son. I found him quite handsome and likeable. Later, I learned that he too approved of me, but there was a catch. They needed cash so that their son could start a clinic and expected us to supply it—a not so subtle demand for dowry! I felt as if I had been slapped across the face. Looks, breeding, intelligence, and education, amounted to nothing. It was the first 'failure' in my life and I took it to heart.

The next day, Daddy took me to visit 'friends' at a posh South Delhi locality, GK 2. These people imported gems from Burma and were very rich. Delicacies were served on a trolley. The fish was superb but the family wasn't. The men clipped their beards (a definite no for a true Sikh) and drank even in the daytime. I did not know which of them was the prospective bridegroom but dared not ask. A week passed. When the silence proved too much for my father, he rang them up. I picked up the parallel phone simultanoeuly and to my horror heard him asking what they thought of me! They gave an evasive answer.

'We'll let you know when our son returns from America.' This time it was my father's humiliation I could not bear. I knew what it cost an egoistic man to hard sell a product that had no takers. My self-esteem plummeted still further and I wrote:

The Sale

The girl to womanhood has grown,
Her father's heart is heavy as stone;
It's time for him to arrange a match
And, a dowry for an eligible catch.

She is showcased, put on display,
Bejewelled, bedecked, a statue of clay;
Exposed to buyers, like market-ware,
That she, too, feels; does anyone care?

On her dolled up face a smile is fixed,
Who is to see the humiliation mixed?
The broken pride of a wild mare reined,
The bit in her mouth, her will restrained.

For a prospective groom, she's not tall enough,
From the other she receives another rebuff,
Though her flesh crawls at the indignity,
Who bothers, for she's but a commodity?

Her father, driven to distraction,
Borrows money for added attractions.
With a bride you'll get a colour TV,
A fridge, furniture, and a car free!

At last the speculations come to an end,
Like a cow, she's led from sire to husband,
For milk, for calves, maybe for slaughter,
It's her misfortune, that she is a daughter.

Apparently, the Vijay Chowk suitor, Dr Mohan Singh Anand (MS) had not seen me properly there, so Daddy sent him to meet me. Naturally, I wasn't informed.

By that time, I was ensconced in the girls' hostel at AIIMS. I was fast asleep after a heavy night duty when the hostel ayah informed me that I had a visitor. Since I knew no one in Delhi except Daddy, I went to the guestroom, without bothering to look in the mirror. Bleary-eyed and crumpled, I stumbled in the guestroom with my curls standing out like Medusa's serpents. When I failed to spy my father, I began to retreat. Suddenly, a Sikh gentleman sitting in a corner asked me, 'Are you Miss Amrita Arora?'

'Yes?'

'Your father sent me to meet you.'

I stared at him dumbstruck.

'Would you like to change?' he asked tentatively.

I rushed back to my room shaking with impotent rage. Daddy had played a dirty trick on me. I had no alternative but to return appropriately dressed and talk with MS. He impressed me not at all. My heart had begun to soften towards a paediatrician Dr Rajiv Mehra, and my thoughts were full of him. Barely a month out of my nest and I was already testing my wings. Those were the days when love stories progressed at a slow, shy pace, and mine had yet to ripen.

A few weeks later, MS sent his relatives to see me. I had supposedly won the first round. He had approved and I wasn't even interested. The final approval had to come from the elder brother and his wife who lived in Mussoorie. They came looking for me to the labour room door and stopped a passing doctor to enquire about my whereabouts. As luck would have it, he was Rajiv Mehra, the doctor I was secretly in love with.

'Please send Miss Arora outside.'

'There is no Miss Arora here,' he replied.

'But there is.' They said showing him my photograph. Daddy must have given it to them.

'Oh! You mean Rosy?' he said and came in to call me.

I wonder what they thought of my being on first name basis with boys, but I did not care. My world was full of my job, my heart full of Rajiv and I wanted nothing else from life. I hadn't bothered to find out how far the negotiations had proceeded, not that my father would have told me anything. I had even forgotten the boy's name. That is why when I met his brother I called him 'Voh', which sealed my fate. They thought that I had already accepted MS as my husband, and like a good Indian wife I would not take his name! Because of a stupid slip of memory they approved of me!

Incidentally what the people in GK 2 had said was true. Their son was indeed a doctor in the US and not among the gentlemen who 'saw' me. They contacted me when he returned but it was too late. I was already engaged to MS and felt vindicated when I showed them my ring.

18

.

A mere six months interlude twenty-five years back, has been branded upon my heart with red-hot iron. I have yet to love another with such intensity. As I look back upon that period I wonder what was it that drew me to Rajiv Mehra? It was certainly not his good looks alone. Perhaps it was the old-world courtesy rarely seen in the era of bragging boys and liberated ladies. He belonged to the fast disappearing breed of men called 'gentlemen'. Amidst the jeans-clad, backslapping Delhites, I arrived; a slim, shy girl in a cotton sari with two plaits and flowers in my hair! Timid and self-effacing, I was intimidated by their aggressiveness.

We were in the doctor's room of the Labour Room-cum-Nursery complex, and the gynaecologists and paediatricians were relaxing over cups of coffee. Being the junior-most, I had prepared the beverage. Afterwards, instead of washing their cups themselves, as was the custom, the arrogant group piled the entire lot in the sink for me to wash. My eyes smarted with unshed humiliation as I went about the menial chore. A young, handsome, paediatrician joined me at the sink with the easy familiarity of an old acquaintance. This one act of kindness not only won me over but also succeeded in shaming the others.

If there was one thing I admired in a person, it was excellence in his chosen field. Rajiv was superb. Each time he came to attend a delivery, he taught us something new. At times, the baby arrives before the paediatrician which made it imperative to learn how to resuscitate a newborn. Whenever I had difficulty in finding an intravenous line, I would seek his help for paediatricians were experts in such things, being used to the fine veins of babies. I would revel in his proximity and inhale deeply of his male scent.

The vitality that flowed from him was overpowering. The sad part was that it also overpowered a host of other females. They clung to him like iron filings, helpless against his magnetic appeal. He was truly a ladies man and if I was insane with jealousy, there was nothing I could do about it. The insecurity was a part of his charm. I would pour my heart out in poems, or cry on the shoulder of my friend Shanta. I made her promise never to let him know of my feelings. So she did the next best thing and told him that I wrote poetry.

'Really? I must read them sometime.'

It was a vague statement but I took it literally.

'But I would never allow you to do so.'

My vehemence aroused his interest. It became imperative that he read them. In fact he decided to come to my room that very evening. Elation and apprehension flitted like sun and shade across my face. I began to prepare for his arrival hours in advance. I tidied my room and changed the bedcovers. I bathed and changed into a becoming sari. I put flowers in my hair and fruit in a bowl. Leaning against the pillar of the verandah, I waited . . . and waited. Time ticked inexorably by, but he did not come. The lengthening shadows fell across my heart. I wilted with the flowers in my hair but still no sign of him. I slid onto the floor, my hopes and sari crushed. Naively, I had staked my life on a casual statement. The lump in my throat snowballed to choke me. My eyes smarted with the grit of crystalised pain. Like a statue of sorrow, I would have sat frozen in time had I not heard his laugh; that well-loved hearty laugh emanating from amidst a bevy of girls. My heart broke. The crystals dissolved into tears, and sobs swallowed the lump in my throat. I poured my grief on the cold stone floor. Never would he know of the pain he caused me that day.

I loved him beyond measure and he cared not at all. The situation was hopeless, but I could not help myself. When we met again, a week later, it was on the same easygoing footing as before, as if that agonising evening had never happened. The long winter nights in the labour room would be punctuated with coffee breaks. Though we sat huddled in cosy groups, my eyes sought only his. It was as if the two of us were alone in a roomful of people. So rich was my imagination and so poor my aptitude for turning it into reality, that I could pull my hair in frustration.

To my chagrin, a pair of beautiful sisters Seema and Sunaina flirted outrageously with him. Being bold and modern, they had no qualms about forcing their company on him. One evening, they insisted that he take them to the college cafeteria. As I happened to be in the vicinity, I too, was asked to come. I trotted along happily, content to be near him even though they monopolised the conversation. Just then the hostel ayah came to inform the sisters that they had visitors. That left only him and me! It was a dream come true yet, I was a nervous wreck. I had never gone out alone with a boy. Instead of backing out on some pretext, I clung to Sunaina and begged her to come along. She looked at me amazed, as if I was some medieval maiden. Rajiv leaned against the wall, his arms crossed on his chest, smiling enigmatically. He was enjoying the novel experience immensely.

'I will not eat you up,' he said.

'No, no I did not mean . . .' My voice trailed away. I was in an agony of indecision.

'It will be my pleasure to take you out,' he said with an exaggerated bow. For once, I decided to do follow my heart instead of Mummy's orders and was utterly happy in his company. Later, replete with snacks and *coco-cola*, love and laughter, he walked me to the hostel. The sisters had spread word about the 'sweet little incident', and the girls began teasing me with him.

Though Daddy was negotiating my marriage with the Vijay Chowk suitor, I buried my head in the sand like an ostrich, willing the 'boy' away. My love life was progressing beautifully and that was all I cared about.

The winter of '73 was the happiest I had ever experienced. Little incidents reiterated the love we felt for each other, yet neither confessed to it openly. One Sunday, I was sunning myself with the gorgeous sisters in the hostel verandah when Rajiv and a friend came to meet us. The friend was sweet on Sunaina and though she did not love him, she enjoyed leading him on. Seema was my rival, for she tried to lure Rajiv with her wit and sophistication, and seemed to be succeeding. An impromptu decision was made to go to the movies. I was in a fix. How could I tell them that I had promised Mummy that I would not go out with anyone except with Daddy? They would laugh at me. Sadly, I told them that I had to prepare for a seminar and could not accompany them. It would have been bliss to sit next to Rajiv in the romantic darkness of the cinema hall, but it was not to be. But wait, what was this? Rajiv refused to go despite Seema's urging! Reluctantly, she left leaving us alone. I discovered heaven in a patch of sunshine in the hostel verandah that winter afternoon. The fleeting contact of our fingers as I shelled peanuts and handed them to him, the emotions that spilled from our eyes, the shy, sweet smiles were pearls of joy that I snapped shut in the love-lined shell of my heart.

The next time we were on duty together, he got an emergency call from the casualty. As it was a long, cold way from the centrally heated labour room, he picked up my blue shawl draped on the back of a chair, wrapped it around his shoulders with easy familiarity and walked away. A tremor of ecstasy passed through me. It was as if my arms and not my shawl were wrapped around him. What intrigued was the fact that he did not return it the next day, or the next. Instead he wore it every single day of that wonderful winter wrapped around his throat like a muffler. In retaliation I put *his* stethoscope around *my* neck. Each time our paths crossed, we made a mock hue and cry about wanting our things back.

Rajiv's scooter was the bane of his life. It was proving more and more expensive to maintain with the passage of time. We were walking down the stairs after a night duty. There was a day's stubble on his chin and his eyes were bleary with lack of sleep. I longed to feel the roughness of his cheek against my soft white one, hold him to my breast, and let him sleep his fatigue away. As usual, we talked of things farthermost away from our minds.

'Rosy could you lend me some money?'

'Why, to buy me a New Year present?' I quipped, tongue in cheek.

He smiled in that particularly endearing way of his and said nothing. He needed the money to retrieve his scooter from the mechanic.

'How much do you want?'

'Rs 300.'

'Oh! I only have seventy-five rupees.'

'It's all right. I'll manage somehow,' he said quickly embarrassed at asking money from a girl who earned less than him.

I did not give him the money, but got my New Year gift. This time, everything was unplanned and perfect. There was a knock on my door on New Year's Eve. Rajiv stood on the threshold smiling. I could only gape at him in wonder.

'Won't you ask me to come in?'

'Of course,' I replied, delirious with joy.

He sat on the only armchair in the room while I curled up on the bed. The heater was blazing, the coffee was steaming, and my heart was singing. He had taken my flippant remark seriously and brought me an expensive pen. We talked and talked, at ease with each other, at peace with the world. The night was fraught with possibilities. God knows I was more than willing, but he was too much of a gentleman to take advantage of the situation. Whether it was a compliment or an insult, I have yet to decipher.

A few nights later, we were held up at the hospital on account of an emergency. As it was late by the time everything was in control, Rajiv walked me to the hostel. It was a star-spangled night. The air was heavy with the fragrance of the *raat ki rani*. The breeze played sensuously with my curls, his proximity with my heart. I longed to feel his hand across my shoulder drawing me close but he did no such thing. If only he had declared his love for me at that point of time, I wouldn't be sitting here disgruntled with life, justifying my misdeeds. I would have had something to hold on to; to give me courage to defy my parents when the need arose, to take whatever life had to offer with the quiet strength of love by my side. But it was not to be. That he did love me enough to want to marry me, I learnt too late.

At twenty-two, an extremely sheltered twenty-two at that, I did not know that you had to reach out and grab whatever happiness you could. It did not fall in your lap like a ripe fruit. Life was too short to refrain from living, for the fear of rejection. At that time, I thought that it was a man's prerogative to declare his intentions. It did not occur to me that he might not be able to muster the courage to do so for fear of rejection. Many were the opportunities lost on this account.

A few days later, Sunaina collected the gang together in the common room and publicly imparted an extremely private matter. Rajiv had asked her to ask me if I could wait for him till he finished his post-graduation! Could I? What were two years? I could wait an eternity for him, I loved him so.

Fate and father weren't willing to wait though! Daddy had finalised my match with Dr M. S. Anand, the Vijay Chowk suitor, and did not deem it necessary to inform me. The first I heard of it was on the eve of my engagement!

'But I am on duty, Daddy' was all that I could sputter.

'Get it changed. I'll pick you up at 8 a.m. sharp.' And the line went dead.

I rushed to Shanta's room and poured my heart out. I told her to find Rajiv and apprise him of the situation, but my luck had run out. He had gone home for the weekend and I did not have his address. I never knew such utter despair before or since. On the cold stone floor, I prostrated myself in front of the picture of Guru Nanak and prayed for a miracle. I wept till the early hours of dawn, but no Rajiv came on a white steed (even the battered old scooter would have done) to carry me off. When Daddy came to pick me up, I was resigned to my fate, as a doomed man is to the gallows.

Conditioned to a lifetime of unconditional obedience, I could not contemplate going against my father's wishes especially when I was not sure of the man I loved. Mummy arrived that very morning from Nagpur for the ceremony. Tentatively, I confided in her. After all, she had married for love when love marriages were unheard of. Surely she would understand. She heard me out patiently, more so to glean if there had been any physical involvement. Vastly relieved on that score, she made two bone-chilling statements.

'Your father will never be able to bear the dishonour. He will die of a heart attack. Your uncles will kill you for marrying out of caste.' In my mind's eye there arose the picture of my six paternal uncles brandishing swords even as my father fell clutching his heart.

'How could you forget that you are the eldest? What example will you set for your younger brothers and sister?' She admonished and that was that.

My present, my future, were sacrificed at the altar of family honour. Like a cow, I was led by the nose string from father to fiancé. For a wild moment, I thought of confiding in my fiancé, but I did not know him well enough to gauge his reaction. Moreover, the thought of a scandal scared me. Incidentally, both my brothers married out of caste and *their* brides were welcomed with open arms. *They* had no example to set.

19

I went through the motions of my engagement like a robot. The dumb doll exchanging rings with a stranger couldn't be me. Yet on what basis could I have rebelled? With a bit of a shock, I realised that there was precious little I knew about Rajiv. Such mundane particulars like his upbringing, family, financial status mattered, not a whit. All I knew was that it felt 'right' to be with him and there was no one else I wanted to spend the rest of my life with.

Had it not been for the cold glitter of the diamond on my ring finger, I would have almost wished my engagement away. It was so easy to live in a fool's paradise. Back at the hospital, my ring was being passed around in the coffee room when Rajiv walked in. There was a hush in the room as someone handed the ring to him. Everyone was aware of the high drama being enacted. His beloved had been betrothed to another. What would be his reaction? He gazed at it a long time, smiling wryly. Shanta, fed on a staple of Hindi cinema asked, 'Don't you want to bash him up?' but got no answer.

Unable to bear the tension any longer, I snatched the ring from his palm and defiantly put it back on my finger.

Whenever MS visited, we sat in the common room, stiff and formal, uncomfortable with each other. The conversation was stilted, the pauses prolonged. All I wanted was that the ordeal of his visit end quickly. Once, he asked me to see if he had fever. Dutifully, I counted his pulse though put off by this age-old ploy. The touch did nothing for me at all. Incidentally, that was all the touching we did in the six months of our engagement! I always met him in the common room; though boys were allowed in our rooms. This plus the fact that I never went out with him speaks volumes of my interest in him as a person. He was someone my autocratic father had foisted on me. A repressed childhood that made unquestioning obedience second nature, quelled whatever feeble stirrings of rebellion that arose in my heart.

However, there was no repressing my emotions. They soared like eagles in unfettered skies. Restrictive parents could not restrain them, society could not cage them. My thoughts orbited around the sun called Rajiv. With him, I felt alive and happy. He was so animated, warm, handsome, chivalrous, intelligent, kind, and caring; God I loved him so. Though futility replaced hope, I clung on to this star-crossed love of mine.

Our term was coming to a close, and a farewell party was arranged. I did so want the night to be a memorable one. After all, it was the last opportunity I would get to interact with Rajiv beyond the call of duty. I had worn one of my mother's silks and knew that I looked good. This made me happy not out of any narcissism (vanity was not one of my vices), but because it may please Rajiv. He appraised me appreciatively from top to toe, but said nothing. That one glance was sufficient to quicken my pulse. Suddenly, he knelt at my feet and lifted the hem of my sari and before I could react, snipped off a few loose strands of silk with his teeth. The gesture warmed the very cockles of my heart.

Soon, all of us were packed in a car. I was crushed against Rajiv and wished for nothing more of life. The party however, was an anticlimax. The only time Rajiv looked at me was when he popped an antacid in his mouth. This was because in a wife-like manner, I'd admonish him for drinking too much coffee. After this, he ignored me completely. The sexy sisters flirted with him as usual, but what amazed me was that he flirted right back! An unbearable jealousy lanced through me. Miserable, I watched him laugh at their stupid jokes and felt like wiping the silly grin off by smashing my fist in his face. Yet what right did I have over him? *I* was the one who couldn't wait for him till he earned enough to support a wife!

'Thank God I am not marrying him.' I thought spitefully. I'd have spent the rest of my life worrying about his fidelity. He liked women too much for my liking. Worse still, they liked him right back. I was safer with my MS on this account, at least. He attracted no one romantically—not even me.

Our last working day was over. I sat in the doctor's common room feeling wretched. From now on, I would have no excuse to see Rajiv, hear his voice, and imbibe his presence. Even as I was thinking of him, in he walked.

'Hello, Rosy,' he said cheerfully.

I didn't reply. I couldn't, with the lump in my throat.

'Hello,' he repeated with a bright smile, as if the abominable behaviour at the party hadn't happened.

'Go away. I am not talking to you.'

'Why?' he asked, puzzled.

Why indeed! I asked myself but there was no reasoning with the heart.

'As if to say you do not know?' I said vaguely.

'Do not know what?'

'Nothing.'

'Don't be a spoilsport.'

'So I am being a spoilsport. What about you?'

'What have I done?'

'Nothing.'

I was angry that he was not heartbroken at my engagement. With unseeing eyes, I gazed at a spot on the wall behind his head. He picked up my pen and twirled it playfully. I snatched it from his hand and stuffed it my bag. He stared at me, perplexed by my strange behaviour. How could he guess that all I wanted to do was to lay my head on his chest and cry? No wonder men thought women were unfathomable.

'Are you here for a while?' he asked.

'Yes, why?'

'I have to return something.'

'What?' I thought bitterly as I watched his receding back. 'My heart, my love, my happiness?'

He brought my shawl and laid it gently on my lap. I took out his stethoscope from my bag and handed it to him. Was it that easy to settle accounts?

20

The term over, I shifted to Daddy's place at Subroto Park. One morning, when Daddy was away at the office, MS turned up! It was a bold step for according to tradition, he could come to my house only on the wedding day. For once, I was glad to see him. I was sad, lonely, and bored in the sprawling bungalow. I made omelette and toast for him while he made small talk. He made me promise not to tell my father about his visit as he had come without informing *his* parents. They would not approve. I do not know why but I did exactly what he told me not to. Understandably, MS was annoyed and did not ring up for a number of days. I did not miss him, for I was busy writing sorrowful poetry like the one below.

> *If you had held my hand but once*
> *Drawn me to your breast but once.*
> *Run your fingers through my hair.*
> *And whispered 'I love you' but once.*
> *If my palms had cupped your face but once*
> *And my lips had tasted yours but once*
> *If you had loved me like I love you,*
> *Whatever life had in store for me*
> *I'd have borne with quiet strength.*

Marriage preparations were in full swing. The money Daddy had put by for my marriage fell woefully short of our needs. To top it, the Fiat Daddy had booked a long time back arrived at this inopportune time. After years of driving second-hand cars,

Daddy had bought a gleaming cobalt blue Fiat, which occupied the pride of place in our porch. Daddy wondered if he should sell it to finance my wedding.

'I'd rather not marry!' I said vehemently, surprising him with what he thought was filial love. But Daddy took a loan against his provident fund to see us through.

Meanwhile, Indira Gandhi assumed dictatorial powers, and Emergency had been declared. Gatherings of more than fifty were not permitted. My in-laws wanted to bring a *baraat* (guests from the boy's side) of 350-400 people. Daddy who was Provost Marshall at that time (head of the law and order department of the Indian Air Force), was not going to break laws for their sake, even if they were *ladkewalae (the boy's side)*. I watched the dispute over the number of *baraatis* with avid interest. They insisted on bringing the entire clan.

'Fine, I'll feed fifty. The rest can dine in Dhaula Kuan Jail!' said Daddy.

My would-be mother-in-law was furious. She threatened not to attend her own son's wedding!

Much to my disappointment, the wedding wasn't called off. The dowry or lack of it too, could not severe an alliance stretched to breaking point, for Daddy had told them that I was a milch cow that would provide for life and he was giving nothing else. After the wedding, my father-in-law took great pains to inform me of a businessman who was ready to give them a blank cheque along with his daughter.

'Then why didn't you get your son married to her?' I retorted, stung to the quick.

'Mohan was besotted by you. That's why.' Moreover, she was fat which I learnt later from MS.

I was to be married in a couple of days. The house was full of relatives and ribald jokes. I was told that men from the Northwest frontier Province were very sexy! I shuddered at the thought of being touched by a man other than Rajiv. Sex was the last thing in my mind when marriage was all about legitimate sex. Women sang naughty wedding songs with not too subtle innuendoes during 'ladies sangeet'. Disgusted, I slipped out. Darkness engulfed me from within and without. Huddled on the steps of the back verandah, I let the dense fog of desolation sweep over me. Sorrow welled up and spilled over in torrents. I cried till the last teardrop was wrenched from my eyes; till my heart was emptied of emotion, and my mind of thought. Nothing mattered anymore. If I was condemned to live the rest of my life with a man I did not love, so be it. Paralysed by an extreme lassitude, I curled up in the fetal position as dry sobs wracked my form.

Meanwhile, my absence was noticed. My parents suspected the worst. No wonder people lamented the birth of daughters. They were a potential source of dishonour. At last, they found me fast asleep on the bare floor of the unlit verandah at the back! The flashlight shone on my tear-streaked face and people thought that I was grief-stricken at leaving my parents' place.

I was taken inside for the *mehndi* ceremony. Dressed in old clothes (the bride was purposely made to look plain prior to the wedding so that she sparkled on D day), I sat with my hands spread out. *Suhagins* (married women) gathered around me to apply the auspicious paste on my hands and feet that left behind a brilliant orange colour on being washed away. The next morning, my maternal uncle dipped my *chooda* in milk and slid the deep pink and ivory bangles on my wrists. To these were tied silver *kalires* by various relatives. Had circumstances been different, I would have enjoyed being the centre of attraction. Now, even the beat of the dholak smote my chest like a death knell.

Rajiv attended my wedding with Shanta and the sexy sisters. The only contribution he made was to ask one of the girls to help me with my nose ring, which had slipped off my unpierced nose. 'Damn your misplaced gallantry.' I wanted to scream, but maintained my demure stance and downcast eyes.

There was too much happening in my life for me to sulk for long. MS came astride a white mare to claim his bride. A sheathed sword slung over his side and strands of flowers covered his bespectacled face. We exchanged garlands at the *jaimala* ceremony. The actual marriage took place the following morning. Four perambulations around the *Guru Granth Sahib*, and we were bound for life! I remembered what a college friend of mine had once said about arranged husbands. One automatically fell in love with them during the wedding ceremony. I fervently hoped so. As we bowed in obeisance after the fourth and final perambulation, I vowed that I would let bygones be bygones and be true to my husband, so help me God.

As I crossed the threshold of my maternal home, I scooped handfuls of grain from a plate held in front of me, and threw them back over my head as my mother caught what she could in her *jholi*. It was believed that a woman, as the incarnation of the goddess Laxmi, brought wealth and prosperity to her home. This custom was to ensure that whatever good fortune I had brought to my father's home did not entirely go with me.

As I entered the flower-bedecked car that was to carry me to my new home, not a single eye was dry. *Bidai* was a welcome sorrow that parents of every girl looked forward to. I was at the most vulnerable point of my life. Forsaken by all that was familiar, I was headed for an unknown destination amidst strangers. I wondered what the future held for me, as the life I had known closed its gates upon me forever.

21

I do not know how thousands of virgins all over India allow their bodies to be violated by complete strangers on their wedding night. Much is made of the *Suhaag Raat*. The flower-bedecked bed, the coy bride in red with the *ghunghat* veiling her face and the glass of milk—for enhancement of performance, form an integral part of this night. Grooms that most brides haven't set eyes upon are expected to ravish untouched flesh that night. In fact, if a husband doesn't do so, his potency is suspect. Of course, there are variations depending upon the state. Newlyweds in Maharashtra are wisely prevented from consummating their marriage till the girl's first periods. This ensures that she does not bring another man's bastard along, as a part of her dowry! Orthodox Bengalis display the bloodstained sheet of the wedding night to prove the virginity of the bride!

There were no romantic trappings to my *suhaag raat*. Instead of flowers, the bed was littered with clothes. Instead of the bridal sari, I was clad in a nightie. Instead of my husband, his brother was the first to see me in such flimsy attire! As for the *muh dekhai* (the present given to the bride at the time of unveiling), my husband forgot, and on finding the gold chain in his *kurta's* pocket the next day, gave it to me tamely. Nothing was like it should have been, but I was too disinterested to be disappointed.

By 4 a.m., I was seated by MS in a Jammu-bound bus. A twelve-hour journey in the blistering heat, cramped up in a rattling bus was not my idea of a honeymoon, but there was a train strike. My husband, however, was charmed by the way I slept, unconsciously resting my head on his shoulder. The first thing I did on reaching our hotel was to take a bath. The door wouldn't lock and my husband thought that I left it open on purpose! I was mortified at being thought that brazen.

The flight from Jammu to Srinagar took half an hour. Incredible though it may seem, the distance between heaven and hell was just half an hour. Despite being the daughter of an Air Force officer, I vomited due to air turbulence. My brand new husband did not wrinkle his nose or turn away in disgust. Instead, he wet his handkerchief and wiped my face. I was filled with shame and gratitude.

It has truly been said of Kashmir, 'If there is a paradise on earth it is this, it is this, it is this.' Snow-skinned mountains cupped the jewel of the Dal Lake in the hollow of their palms. Reclining romantically in a brightly hooded shikara, we skimmed the surface of this beautiful stretch of water. The boatman showed us floating fields on its surface, which were called *Chori ke khet*, as they could literally be hauled away by thieves! He stopped every now and then so that we could visit the beautiful Shalimar gardens and Chashme Shahi, and other places of beauty and interest.

Pahalgam, with its transparent streams and polished stones, precarious bridges, pure air, and waterfalls trickling down mountain clefts, was a heady concoction. There was a ride to Gulmerg on horseback. We asked the groom to photograph us. Perhaps he liked the faces of his horses better than ours for when the reel was developed, we found that we had been beheaded! By the time we reached Gulmerg, a fir-fringed grassland on gently undulating hills, it started raining. The other tourists decided to stay put, but I insisted on making the slippery journey to Tunmerg. Our horses skid on the wet narrow paths, and loose pebbles hurtled down ravines, hundreds of feet deep. One false step and we would have followed the stones down to our doom! The rain beat upon us like a thousand needles. My hair fell across my eyes, but I dared not let go of the reins to remove it. My teeth chattered and my feet were numb with cold. I saw snow for the first time in my life, and, slid down its crunchy softness with my husband, on a sledge.

The entire adventure had whipped up an enormous appetite. I never tasted a meal more delicious than the one we ate at a *dhaba* on our return to Gulmerg. Blobs of butter melted rapidly on sizzling *parathas*. There was green almond curry, and omelette, and gallons of *kahva*—Kashmiri tea—to wash it down with. My body temperature was soon restored, though my feet continued to retain the ice. When my husband drew me to him that night, I could not respond on account of my cold feet and asked him to rub them for me.

'How dare you ask *me*, your husband to touch your feet?'

It was as if he had slapped me! Though I did not move an inch, there appeared between us an unfathomable chasm.

Clumsy fumblings went on night after night. I was amazed at his lack of knowledge. Even I knew more, at least theoretically, but was too shy to guide him lest he wonder how *I* knew. We finally managed to lose our virginity after a week. That I had yet to attain an orgasm after the birth of my children spoke volumes about the expertise and concern of my partner.

In a few days, I came down to earth in more ways than one. As my postgraduate entrance exams drew near, I was shocked to learn that I was not to appear. Who were they to decide? My husband was not a specialist, but how should it matter if I became an MD (Doctor of Medicine)? I had yet to understand the fragility of male ego, though I was to spend the rest of my life catering to it. Ironically in those days, the movie *Abhiman* had hit the theatres. The hero Amitabh Bachan, a renowned singer, could not tolerate the fact that his wife became more famous than him, which led to marital discord! Little did I know that this would be *my* story henceforth.

His entire family ganged up against me—a bewildered, defenceless outsider. I was angry with my father for not settling such an important issue; he could have either found a postgraduate match for me or discussed with my in laws the possibility of my doing MD. The interview date drew near and there was no time for a prolonged impasse. I realised that though I belonged to a family of professionals, I had been married into the business community. I tried to speak their language and explained to Papaji, my father-in-law, that the more you invest in a business venture the higher were the returns. MD *was* an investment. Moreover, I would be earning while learning. Finally, I managed to make them agree but there were strings attached. As my brother-in-law and his wife were childless, I was to give the family an heir as soon as possible. I would have preferred waiting till my studies were over but I had no choice.

22

Though they 'allowed' me to appear for the interview, they gave me no time to prepare for it. I was kept busy exhibiting my culinary skills to my new family, but got through despite them. There was a month to go before the session started so Mataji decided to take me with her to Mussoorie. I was keen on seeing my *sasural* and deserted my husband happily.

The early morning ride from Dehradun to Mussoorie was breathtaking. Like a seasoned striptease, the mountain lifted her veil of mist now here, now there, revealing glimpses of unsurpassed beauty. The road snaked through forests of pine and fir, oak and deodar bespattered with lilies and rhododendron. Past terraced fields and moss-clad boulders, we went surrounded by ranges of blue green mountains. The weather changed as quickly as a child's moods. Now fluffs of fog obscured the scenery, now every blade of grass was visible; now the sun smiled, now the sky pelted hail. Finally, we reached the 'Queen of the Hills' as Mussoorie is called. In one of its red tiled houses, perched precariously on a mountainside, lived my in-laws. Veerji and Bhabiji (my husband's elder brother and his wife), made me feel at home. There were the simple pleasures of steaming coffee on misty mornings and of ice cream cones in the afternoon sun. There were visits to Lal Tibba, Kamptee falls, Dhanaulti, and other areas of interest around the hill station. Best of all, was horse riding and walks on Camel Back Road past the cemetery where the British left their dead to rest in peace. At night, there were the lights of Dehradun twinkling like a star-studded sky turned upside down.

Though I had much to occupy my mind, I missed my husband of one month. I had not thought it possible but I found myself writing letters to him. That he too, was as miserable without me, I learnt from the fact that he sent a letter enclosing a false telegram that stated that my MD was to begin in a week's time; he could not overtly ask his newly-wedded wife back from his orthodox family. Gladly, I left the pristine beauty of the hills for the dusty plains of Delhi, for I belonged there.

It was fun playing 'house house' in the cramped two-roomed quarters, though I learnt to my chagrin that my husband was very untidy. Pyjamas, towels, slippers, and combs lay strewn all over the place. Within a few days, I had the place tidied up. MS complained that he could not find anything because everything was in its proper place! It was so much easier in his bachelor days when he could put out a hand to find a comb and stretch a leg to reach for his slippers.

I pined for Rajiv even as I tried to be a good wife. When songs like '*teri duniya me na rakhenge kadam aaj ke baad* (I will not step into your world after today)' or '*zindage ke safar me guzar jaate hai jo makaam voh phir nahin aate (the places we pass through in the journey of life never return)* played on the radio, I would burst out crying. One night, MS casually asked me if I had any affairs before marriage. Now that the situation arose, I decided to get it off my chest. I told him about Rajiv and waited tensely for his reaction. This could very well be the beginning of the end. What if he held it against me for the rest of my married life, but the only question he asked me was, 'How far did you go?'

'What do you mean?'

'Did you both kiss or do anything of that sort.'

'Of course not!' I was indignant. 'We did not even acknowledge our attachment to each other.'

This seemed to satisfy him. Men set such store by physical love, while emotional attachment was far more important to me. However, it was good to live a guilt-free existence. MS rose considerably in my esteem after this. He was so broadminded and gracious, and deserved my loyalty.

Exposure to civilian life was a cultural shock. I had been treated like a lady in the armed forces ever since I was a little girl. Now, instead of having car doors opened for me, I acted as chauffeur till my husband learned to drive years later. Instead of being escorted to the dining table during parties, I was rudely pushed away by male doctors who grabbed the good portions of tandoori chicken, etc. I came back hungry from my first civilian party. Soon, I became adept at their game; forcing my way to the table, I'd load my plate at one go and settle in a corner to devour it! As for my husband, the word 'chivalry' did not exist in his vocabulary. He'd walk a few steps ahead, swinging his hands freely while I trailed behind weighed down by baby and bags.

The gold plating had begun to wear off. I learnt that it was difficult to part MS from his money. My income went directly to the bank as tax paid money, which I could not touch because the 'white money' would come handy later when I needed capital to start my own clinic. As a result, I had to depend on MS for day-to-day expenses. Instead of receiving a monthly allowance, I was forced to ask for paltry sums daily, which was demeaning. He shopped for groceries himself, lest I pocket the loose change left over! I had to beg for bus fare everyday while going to AIIMS for he liked me to be at his mercy. On Daddy's birthday two months after my wedding, I told MS that I wanted to buy a birthday gift for him. He was outraged.

'Yeh kaha ka ulta revaaj shuru karne ke soch rahi ho (what sort of reverse tradition are you thinking of establishing)? Gifts of cash and kind ought to come from the girl's side.' I rushed to the bathroom to give vent to tears of frustration.

A year after the birth of my son, I was going to my parents' place for the first time after marriage. Despite an income of my own (which was more than could be said of his female relatives), I literally had no cash in hand. When I asked for some money, he said, 'I have paid for the ticket from this side, your father will pay for it from that side; you will be living with them and not in a hotel, so why do you want money?' he asked.

'What if an emergency arises? After all I am travelling alone with a child?' I retorted stung to the quick.

Whenever he hurt me, all I did in those days was to lock myself up in the bathroom and cry. I had learnt early in our marriage that I could expect neither sympathy nor understanding from him. The first time I fell sick after marriage, another unsavoury aspect of his nature revealed itself. Instead of looking after me, after all he was husband and doctor rolled into one, he shifted bed and bedding to the other room lest he catch the infection! I wept silently in my pillow, for my heart ached as much with the rejection as my head with fever. What sort of a person had I been married to? I had little time to brood on his callousness for within three months of marriage I realised that I had conceived.

23

The other day, Karan, my elder son, returned from a tiring night at the hospital. As he was dropping off to sleep, I inadvertently switched on the light.

"How dare you disturb me?' he snapped. 'Have you forgotten your residency days?'

Could I forget them? Physically, it was the most harrowing period of my life. Karan had just his duties to manage and his sleep to catch up and yet his irritability was phenomenal. Moreover, the residents have it real easy now—a 24 hours duty, followed by a 24 hours off. We were relieved after 36 hours of gruelling labour, and had to report on duty the very next day. I had to cook food, manage the house, despite the nausea of pregnancy, and the fatigue of a previous night duty. I had seminars and thesis to prepare. There were guests to look after and a husband to satisfy at night. There was overwhelming fatigue, and no help from any quarter. Last but not the least, I had to commute by bus while Karan had a car, and he had the temerity to ask me if I had forgotten my residency days!

In the beginning, MS would gallantly take me to the hospital on his scooter. But Mataji, who spent the winters in Delhi, put an end to such 'nonsense'. Mamma's boy complied readily enough. The overcrowded, smelly bus made me retch. By the time I reached home, my throat was raw and I was ready to faint.

Craving for a word of sympathy, I tried to tell MS about my predicament. He pushed his dinner plate away exclaiming, 'Can't you talk of better things at mealtimes?'

How vulnerable I was in those days. How quickly tears would spring to my eyes, and yet I pulled on with the tenacity of a steel wire.

The nausea decreased considerably by the fourth month. Now that Mataji had come, my physical needs were well looked after. I was fed rich nourishing food. Though my face glowed, I had become quite ungainly. Rajiv and I still worked in the same hospital, but we took care to avoid each other. We met by chance in the lift one day. Giving me a look-over he exclaimed, 'Rosy, you have gone positively fat!'

The fool did not realise that I was pregnant. I wasn't keen on apprising him of the fact and made good my escape as soon as I could.

Finally, on a Sunday morning in late spring, I *felt* the pains I had seen in innumerable patients. I was wheeled into the labour room and experienced hours of wracking pain. Though MS was not allowed in with me, it was reassuring to know that he waited outside. Suddenly, the baby's heart dipped. The membranes were ruptured artificially and the green-tinged fluid that escaped, confirmed that the foetus was distressed. An emergency caesarian had to be performed, but there was no husband to give his signatures! He had gone to attend his morning clinic at the behest of his mother! I could never forgive him for forsaking me in my hour of need. What if the baby's condition deteriorated in the time it took him to reach the hospital? When he finally turned up, he burst out crying. The staff found it quaint, but I was irritated. I ended up consoling him when it should have been the other way round. To compound matters, one of those unbelievable co-incidences that take place in films occurred. Rajiv was on call that afternoon!

I lay on the operation table, my white mound of an abdomen exposed and in he walked! Mortified beyond words, I asked my obstetrician to send him out. As I was going under, I heard her tell him that he was to stay out till I was anaesthetised and return later. There was nothing I could do about it. Thus, it came about that Rajiv was the first to set eyes upon my baby.

On account of the sedation, I saw my son after almost everyone else had seen him. He was pink and white, and bald, and stared at me with wide-open eyes. I kissed his little fingers and crushed him to my heart. An incredible joy suffused my being. I put him to my breast and marvelled at the way he balled his hands into fists, furrowed his brow, and sucked till my nipples were sore.

The next day, we got some shocking news. My son's blood group was O positive while MS and I were both O negative.

'How can that be?' I exclaimed.

'That is exactly what I am asking?' Rajiv had the temerity to cast sly insinuations.

I wanted to slap his face to wipe that wicked grin off his face. If there had to be an illegitimate father for my son, it would have been him and he had the audacity to laugh! But this was no laughing matter. Work in the blood bank and operation theatres came to a standstill till the matter was sorted out. The reagents were checked and rechecked. Their expiry dates were read. Blood samples were drawn again and sent for cross-checking. Finally, it turned out to be a mere clerical error!

To my horror Mataji appropriated my baby! He was her grandson, period. Papaji walked past me, cuddled the baby and said: 'We have got what we wanted of you.'

I was shocked into tears. My stitches hurt, but there was no stopping the torrent. Was I nothing but a baby-producing machine? All the pampering and nourishment had been for their grandchild. Now I was totally redundant for Mataji wouldn't allow me to breast-feed my own baby! It was the bottle, always the bottle. At times, she would put him to her own withered bosom instead of handing him to a mother with full, weeping breasts. How could a woman who had borne four children be so heartless? Later, I learnt that she wanted him for her childless elder son and did not want mother-child bonding to take place! I went berserk and implored MS to make his mother see reason.

'They are our elders; we must do as they say,' was all the support I got from him.

Didn't they realise that I needed the child as much as he needed me? I appealed to the mother in my mother-in-law, but to no avail.

'I gave you my son, you give me yours,' she said. What a barter indeed! She was welcome to take back her spineless son and hand me mine.

I begged and pleaded, but no one paid heed. Taking advantage of the fact that I was still studying for my MD (they were the ones who insisted on a baby before I completed post-graduation), and could not manage the baby alone, they began making preparations to take the baby away. When I suggested that she stay back so that both of us could raise the child together, she retorted, 'Don't expect me to stay in the Delhi heat.' And that was that. She tolerated the heat quite well when she had to stay back for a personal illness later.

Bhabiji had no inkling of the fact that she was getting a ready-made son. Just four years into her marriage, she was being investigated for infertility and hoped for a child of her own. It was preposterous! I wasn't willing to part with my child; Bhabiji didn't want him, so why was Mataji playing God?

In desperation, I asked my mother to intervene.

'Slap her if she disobeys you.' Said my mother to my in-laws to be in their good books. I couldn't believe my ears. Was she the same woman who couldn't snap the umbilical cord of her children, even now?

All I asked for was the right of motherhood that came naturally even to the lowest of low animal, but no one stood by me. Karan's grandmother took him away exactly two months after his birth, leaving me desolate and bereft. I became an emotional wreck. Night after night I cried heartbrokenly. My callous husband would turn the other way and sleep. At times, he'd say *'dramebaazi band kar* (stop this drama)' and put a pillow over his ears to muffle my sobs.

24

I would have suffered a nervous breakdown, had it not been for my kindly seniors at AIIMS. My performance deteriorated; I was taken to task, but couldn't care less. Matters came to a head when I started crying in the middle of a vaginal hysterectomy. I was holding the speculum, but not steadily enough on account of the sobs that shook my body. After the operation, I was summoned by the unit head and questioned. All the pain and deprivation tumbled out. As a postgraduate student, I was on a stipend and therefore not entitled to a three-month maternity leave. The twenty days casual leave I was allowed in these two years had been exhausted post my caesarean section. As a result, I could not even go to visit my baby. My seniors gave me an off every other weekend to see my son. I returned from these visits more depressed than ever. They had taught him to call me Rosy in place of Mummy, and would laugh when I protested. They put *kaajal* in his eyes and stuffed soothers in his mouth. When I objected Mataji taunted, 'You aren't bringing him up, we are.'

During one of these visits, I impulsively picked up Karan and walked out of the door. MS made as if to take the child from me but Mataji stopped him, 'No let her go. What right do we have to detain *her* child?'

'How do you intend looking after him?' asked Papaji sarcastically.

'I'll keep another servant. MS can help, after all Karan is his son, too.'

'My son will not work till I am alive! He has never lifted a towel in his life,' exploded Mataji, which was true, for the wet towel he left on our bed every morning was the bane of my life.

'All the worse for me,' I muttered under my breath.

'Enough is enough, put him down at once,' said Papaji.

'*No!* Let her do as she wishes,' said Mataji. 'Every time she comes, she makes a scene . . . Just wait and see, she'll come back in a week's time, begging me to take him back. Listen woman,' she said, addressing me, 'If you think I'll ever step into your house again you are sadly mistaken.'

Who cared? Triumphantly, I bore my baby back with me. There followed days of sheer hard work and sleepless nights, but all my fatigue would be washed away by a toothless smile from my little tyrant. A month later, I returned from the hospital to find Mataji standing at the gate.

'I wasn't coming,' she began of her own accord. 'But Papaji insisted that I bring Karan back,' not liking the fact that she had to eat her words and come without my begging her to do so.

I bent down to touch her feet, as one is expected to do out of respect. She recoiled as if stung by a scorpion. I rushed inside trembling, for the neighbours had witnessed my humiliation.

Papaji sat in the drawing room holding Karan in his arms.

'What have you done to my grandson? See how weak he is.'

'He's got loose motions,' I replied. 'He'll recover soon enough.'

'We will not allow you to keep him any longer.'

Fed up of his part in child rearing, MS acquiesced readily enough. There was no way I could bring up the baby without his help. Resignedly, I allowed my precious child to be shuttled back.

Against overwhelming odds, I managed to complete my MD. There were no celebrations. By this time, I had got accustomed to my husband's nature. Our first marriage anniversary had come and gone like any other day. I went into a massive sulk. When MS said that he didn't have the money to celebrate, I was naïve enough to believe him. I suggested that we put aside Rs 10 each day, a month prior to our second anniversary (one could buy a lot in those days with Rs 300), but he did nothing of that sort. He just did not have the capacity to enjoy life. It was work and sleep like a clockwork toy day after day.

Almost immediately after my results, we received a telegram stating that Karan was seriously ill! We rushed to Mussoorie to find him in a semi-comatose state, his face blotched, his lips swollen. He had choked on his own vomit during an attack of febrile convulsions. My in-laws went on and on about the wonderful part they played in saving the life of my son. Strange, how he suddenly became *my* son, not *their* grandson. Karan was shifted to the mission hospital in Landour. Innumerable blood and urine tests were carried out and a lumbar puncture was performed on his tiny back.

When he regained consciousness, it was as I had dreaded all along. He refused to come to me! As if being rejected by your own son wasn't painful enough, Mataji rubbed salt over my wounds by tell her cronies, 'Karan doesn't go to her; after all *I* am bringing him up.'

I wanted to push her out of the window into the abyss below, but sanity prevailed. I set about wooing my child back with a vengeance. Every morning, after the doctor's rounds, I would take him up the winding paths on the hillside, crunching pine needles underfoot. We chased butterflies and listened to the song of the birds. In the brooding depths of fir forests, surrounded by undulating blue green hills, we got reacquainted with each other. On misty mornings, with red cheeks and white breaths, our laughter would resound in the veiled mountains. It was, as if there were just the two of us in the universe and needed no other. In a few days, I had won him over completely and not a thousand grandmothers could reclaim him. It was my turn to gloat, but I had won but one round. Ever since I can remember, we fought over Karan. As a result, my insecurity and possessiveness as regards my firstborn verged on the pathological. Perhaps if he had been the usual tiresome brat who got on my nerves, I would I have been only too glad to hand him over to his grandmother and thank her for the reprieve.

When it was time to put him in school, we had a final showdown. I decided that mother and child would be deprived of each other no more. Once he started schooling in Mussoorre, he would be lost to me forever. I was no longer the docile bride who bowed to the wishes of her elders. I was a tigress protecting her young. Having learnt by experience that MS would not stand by me, I took matters in my own hands. This was a Rosy they hadn't seen, and knew instinctively that I could no longer be intimidated. Though I did get my son back, the damage was done for Karan's loyalties remained forever divided.

The birth of my second son Simar, four years later, was an anticlimax. While they overfed me during the first pregnancy, they neglected me in my second. Mataji took one look at Simar's tiny frame, and decided that he was nothing compared to *her* Karan. Boy, was I glad! At last, I had a son wholly to myself. She resented having to stay back in the scorching heat for his sake so, on the ninth postoperative day of my second cesarean, I boarded a train to spend my postpartum period with my parents in Allahabad. It was a risky proposition but did she care?

Mataji gloated over the fact that Simar was a 'weakling' while Karan was so healthy. In fact, Simar was wiry and Karan, positively fat. This bantering between us over 'her son' and 'my son' went on over the years, sometimes in jest, and sometimes in earnest. Every winter, my in laws descended to the plains to avoid the chill of the hills and stayed with us for about four months. During that time, Mataji managed to undo all the right I had done by my children. While she treated Simar in a step grandmotherly fashion, she spoilt Karan rotten. He was a pampered brat who needed a lot of straightening up.

Under her protective cover he would fling shoes, books, and uniforms all over the place, undoing all the good I had done in the intervening months. When I tried to discipline him, Mataji would scold me for scolding him, undermining my authority. Once, in exasperation, I gave him a tight slap. Mataji held him to her bosom and shed tears of her own. It was preposterous. She was the fairy godmother who denied him nothing, and I a controlling witch. As a result, he loved Daadima 51 per cent and me, 49 per cent. The 2 per cent made a world of a difference. She had neatly turned the tables on me, and there was nothing I could do about it.

Simar was different sort altogether. Karan had cried when he was put in school; Simar longed to go where his brother went. He would accompany me to the bus stop when I went to drop Karan each morning. On Simar's first day, the pint-sized fellow rescued his chubby brother from the clutches of the school bully by biting the fellow on his buttocks with his sharp teeth. Caught unawares, he let go of Karan who made good his escape.

Karan was a voracious reader, while Simar hated the sight of books. Karan's classmates complained that he ate up their tiffin after finishing his own; Simar almost always brought back his lunchbox uneaten. After a while, Simar took to showing me an empty tiffin box with as much pride as Karan showed me his good grades. I was happy that my skinny Simar had started eating at last. I caught onto his game when a friend came over to play. During a fight the friend declared, 'Then I won't eat your tiffin in the bus on the way back.'

At home too, I had to cajole him to take a bite during meal times. Once I told him that when you eat, I feel that I have eaten at which he put his hands on his hips, gave me a once over and said, 'No wonder you are so fat!'

The day Simar told me that Madam had punished him, I was worried. Not because of the punishment (he was a veteran at that), but because he complained to me about it.

'So what's so new?' I said.

'She made me stand on a chair.'

'Why? What did you do?'

'Nothing.'

That was impossible but I kept my opinion to myself.

'She also tied my hands.' This was indeed alarming.

I met his teacher and was horrified to learn that Simar was caught examining the private parts of a girl who had lowered her knickers and complied willingly enough!

I was flabbergasted. Worried, whether running a gynae practice at home had anything to do with it, I asked Simar as calmly as I could, the reason for such behaviour.

'I wanted to see her wee wee Mama and you know what,' he continued excitedly.

'What?'

'She didn't have one!' As if it was the discovery of the century! He was 3 years old then.

Having a clinic at home did give rise to certain hilarious situations though. When Karan was small, he saw no difference between guests and patients, and would often offer them sweetmeats from our fridge and make small talk with them.

Once, he stood bare bottomed at the connecting door and announced, 'Mama *potty kar li, dhoi dhoi kar do* (I have finished potty, clean my bottom).'

Time and again I would tell him to keep away during clinic hours. Finally, he paid heed and devised a novel way of obeying me *and* getting his job done. Instead of entering the clinic, he would thrust his foot in for me to tie the laces or a hand with a (inside out) pair of pants that he wanted me to straighten. I did not mind, for at least I was there for my children despite my work. I would have to stay away for long hours if I had a job, leaving them solely at the mercy of an ayah.

When Simar was old enough to use his feet, he was no better. As we lived near an industrial area, besides gynae patients, I would get a lot of accidental injuries; chopped fingers, iron particles in the eye, and would give them first aid before sending them to the hospital. Such patients were often accompanied by horde of other workers, and one of them invariably fainted on seeing the blood and gore. Amidst this motley crowd, I would spy Simar's tiny fair face watching the proceeding avidly without fear or distaste, and shoo him away. He even dressed up as a nurse once during a fancy dress party and got the first prize.

Simar grew up to be a generous and loyal lad. He would be punished trying to save others, but never squealed on them. He took his turtles for a pet show and returned with a prize for best-trained unusual pets!

'What training?' I spluttered.

'Well I put them on their backs and said that they will right themselves when I clap my hands.'

'Even a cockroach would have done that.' I thought, but kept my opinion to myself.

'What else?' I asked.

'I put the two together on the floor and said that they will walk divergently when I stamp my foot between them.' It was his ready wit and his teacher's turtle-sized brains that won him the prize!

It was a marvel to watch the two distinct personalities unfold day by day. I was disappointed, when I did not have a daughter the second time for I was presumptive enough to lump 'boys' together. I now realised that every individual is unique and thanked God humbly for giving me the responsibility of raising such fine specimens of humanity. Everything else was forgotten in my all-encompassing motherhood.

25

Disillusionment had begun to seep in like damp under the carpet. Superficially, matters seemed normal, but the rot had set in. It took me years to acknowledge the fact that our marriage was not what it should be. All that we shared was the roof and two kids. We had separate cupboards and separate bank accounts. We functioned on different wavelengths. I had the responsibilities of a householder without the benefits. There was no satisfaction on any plane be it emotional, physical, financial, or sexual. I did have the social security of being a married woman but that was all.

My husband was totally unaware of the individual who shared his life. I was a robot who had to function as wife and mother according to prescribed norms. That I too needed attention, affection, and companionship, did not occur to him. My welfare was not his concern. I remember the time I had high fever and had neither the strength to cook, nor the desire to eat. Karan was coaxing me to eat last night's leftovers when MS came home. He collected some papers, gave me a cursory glance and left. Hot tears scalded my cheek.

My 7-year-old child wiped them and asked, 'Why are you crying, Mama?'

'My head is aching.' I lied at which he pressed it with his little hands. After a while I dozed off. When I got up, the fever was raging, the door was ajar, and the kids had disappeared! One can imagine my terror. Though giddy and weak, I set out to find them on wobbly feet. After what seemed an eternity, I spied them in the market sliding down the cement slope made on steps for scooters. I almost came under a bus while crossing the road in my hurry to reach them.

Incidents like this kept adding up. We never shared a bank account. It was preposterous as far as married couples went, but he set the rules and I had to abide by them. Now that I had started private practice, I received cash instead of a paycheck. As the amount varied from month to month, he could not glean what I earned. Turning the tables on him, *I* did not hand him whatever I saved. After all, he had divided *our* money into my money and your money. A strange sort of financial equation developed in our household. Though our income wasn't pooled, our expenditures were divided. While I paid my bills immediately, he deferred paying his till the last date. At times, he borrowed from *me* to pay them and took his own sweet time to return my dues. When a neighbour handed me the money he owed MS for house visits, I kept it in lieu of what he owed me. The money had come at an opportune moment, for I was on the verge of buying an expensive piece of medical equipment and needed the cash. Moreover, the money was rightfully mine, but MS wanted it back that very instant. When I refused, he snatched the bunch of keys from my hand, opened my cupboard, and took it!

Barely had I recovered from the shock of such behaviour when my stethoscope broke. I had coveted a Littman's stethoscope all my life and MS had two; one, a gift from my parents. I asked him to give me one but he refused.

'I'll buy one when I go to Daryaganj next week.' He meant the ordinary variety.

'And what do I use in the meantime?' After all, a stethoscope was a necessity and not a luxury for a doctor.

He buried his head in a newspaper without answering. I may have been speaking to a wall for all the response I got. In exasperation, I flung the broken instrument on the paper. This evoked a reaction indeed!

'Don't you know how to behave with a husband?'

'Don't you know how to behave with a lady?'

'Shut up and keep your woman's lib to yourself. The sooner you accept male dominance, the better it will be for you.'

'Is it only dominance you are capable of? Isn't it your duty to provide for those you dominate?'

Little tiffs like these snowballed into unmanageable proportions. It was getting more and more difficult to live in such hostile environments. My clinic was in my residence so that I could manage the house, children, and my practice at the same time. One morning, as I was taking up a patient for an MTP (medical termination of pregnancy), MS knocked on the connecting door. He wanted me to make breakfast as the new help made greasy omelettes.

'You should have told me so earlier. I have already sedated the patient.'

'I don't care!'

With ill grace, I prepared his breakfast. As I was hurrying back inside, he asked me to stitch a button on his shirt. I couldn't believe my ears. He had shirts by the dozen and could easily change into another. Without answering, I shut the door on his face. Needless to say, he left without eating his breakfast.

Over the years, our quarrels became frequent, the silences longer, and the reconciliations incomplete. A little bit of rancour remained and added up with the next quarrel. That he was stingy, selfish, and utterly mean, I had come to know early in my marriage. That I was hot headed, easily provoked to tears and anger, he too learnt soon enough. In those days, his simple goodness, lack of vice, and hardworking nature made up for his deficiencies. Similarly, he found me affectionate, loyal, and efficient. I had the capacity to laugh at myself and we got along fairly well as most married couples go. Our quarrels were like pebbles thrown in water creating the tiniest ripples. Water could not be divided, and all was right with our world again.

The blazing sun of intolerance vapourised the last drop of the moisture. To my dismay, I realised that it was not an ocean of understanding that lay between us, but a tiny lake that dried up in the first fierce summer of marital life. All that remained were jagged rocks that jutted out of its dry bed like caries teeth from a foul-smelling mouth.

We began to bring out the worst in each other. He hated the fact that I was not a docile, obedient *bharatiya naari*, who toed his line for, he diligently followed his father's advice *'aurat nu pair di jutti bana ke rakhna nahin teh sar te chad jayegi* (women should be treated like shoes and kept at your feet otherwise they will sit on your head)'. Spouses, I thought, were wheels that supported the carriage of marriage. Here, I was the beast of burden and his was the hand that wielded the whip.

Late one night, Simar needed to use the toilet. Sleepily, I stood by till he finished, washed his bottom, and took him back to bed. Barely had I closed my eyes when I was rudely awakened by my lord and master.

'Come here!'

'Why, what's the matter?' I asked sleepily.

'I said come here at once.'

Fatigue had almost chained me to the bed. I got up with an effort and went to the toilet.

'Can't you flush the toilet after using it?' he fumed with self-righteous anger.

'Why have you woken me?' I asked.

'To pull the flush,' he said and stood by waiting for me to comply.

Fury flashed through me like a knife. I spun on my heels and went back to bed.

'*I said, pull the flush!*' he raged following me.

I glared at him with ill-concealed hatred.

'Are you human? You know I haven't slept for 24 hours on account of a delivery last night and you wake me up for such a flimsy reason. Simar is your son, too? You will not fall from your pedestal if you pull the chain.'

'*Apne aukaat may rahe samjhee* (remain within your limits understood).'

'MY STATUS!' I fumed, the last vestige of sleep fleeing from my eyes. 'What status do I have in this family? If I recognised my status and lived up to it, instead of consenting to live beneath it, you will be nowhere.'

'Your tongue runs like a pair of scissors.'

'The truth hurts, doesn't it?' I sneered.

'Go to hell.'

'I don't have to,' I flung back. 'I *am* in hell.'

Women

Their comforts halved, their labours doubled,
They sail through life on waters troubled,
Tossed about in the ocean like driftwood,
Atrocities, for ages they have withstood.
In the bargain of life, it's their lot to give,
And asked to be grateful for the right to live;
For female foetuses are aborted before birth
And a girl child simply fades from this earth.
From infancy is conditioned every female,
That she is born solely to serve the male;
As mother, mistress, wife and maid,
For the pleasure of man she's made.
She is used, abused in every way.
And for dowry tortured, every day.
Nourishment of child bearing she needs,
Yet the choicest morsel to her lord she feeds;
God forbid if the marriage is infertile,
She knows that her life isn't worthwhile.
And if daughters are all that she begets
It's a crime she is not allowed to forget.
Shoulder to shoulder with her man she earns,
And yet for spending power she yearns,
When he lies dead on the funeral pyre
She burns with him in the fire.

Widows with children are allowed to live
In a society that will never forgive
Marginalised, deprived, it's her lot to cry
For she is considered a blemish, an evil eye.
What amazes is the meek acceptance of might.
The passivity, the reluctance to put up a fight.
But women by and large have no choice,
For those like me who raise their voice,
And pioneer paths with feet full of blisters,
Fare worse than their submissive sisters.
But the last ounce of strength I will gather,
And flog the horses of my will to a lather.
I'll sow the seed and nourish its roots,
So what if I don't live to reap the fruit?
If my torch kindles light in but one woman,
I'll consider my work on this earth done;
For, when my voice fails, others will be raised,
And the atrocities, the inequality will be erased.

Everything I said or did was wrong. He could not tolerate my calling him 'mean' (which he was), or the fact that I whistled when I was happy. I resented his lack of initiative, drive, and ambition. He was perfectly happy to skim through life while I wanted to dive deep into its waters. So obsessed was he with saving for a rainy day that we could not enjoy the spring of our lives.

I tried to console myself by dwelling on his good points. He had no vices; he did not smoke, drink, or womanize—even with his wife! What rankled was that he did precious little else. I told myself that he was a simple human being with simple tastes. It was too much to expect him to understand my complex personality. Yet a sense of incompleteness prevailed, of life passing me by.

In retrospect, I wondered that if we were sexually compatible, our differences would not have multiplied so. Our libidos were as ill-matched as ice and fire. It was unheard of a woman of a middle class family to acknowledge her sexuality. I despised myself for needing him so. The nights he wanted me were worse. I was made to feel the culprit for our inadequacy. A book on human sexual behaviour awakened me to the fact that I was perfectly normal and the fault lay with him. Yet I dared not castrate my man by making him think less of himself. A tentative hint at seeking medical advice was brushed off, but it mattered no more. I had learnt the art of self-relief.

Even these unsatisfactory moments of togetherness came to an end when we started the construction of our nursing home-cum-residence. Papaji stayed back to supervise the construction. Being an inhabitant of the hills, Delhi summer proved too much for him. There was but one air cooler in the entire house. Instead of buying another one, three generations of the Anand family slept in the same room! This unnatural state of affairs lasted for months. When our marriage anniversary came and went without even an acknowledgement of the fact, the dam burst. I gathered my brood and bedding and shifted to the cooler-less room. The heat was bearable, but not the humiliation. The children thought it was fun. When their father returned that night, they refused to let him enter 'our' room. He thought I had taught them to behave so! As we were arguing, Papaji came to inquire what the matter was.

'Nothing,' I retorted, 'You sleep with your son, I'll sleep with mine.'

26

My self-esteem had sunk to an all-time low. There was nothing but hard work and disharmony at home. In the early years of marriage, the physicality of living— adjustments to a new environment, child bearing and child rearing—had so dominated my existence that I hardly had time for dreams, broken or otherwise. Now, with the children off my hands, time became a commodity that was freely available. I had time for introspection and realised that I was in an extremely unhappy state of mind. Despite putting all I had in the marriage, I got nothing out of it. At the best of times I was taken for granted. More often than not, I was labelled a nag, a shrew, and a feminist who did not know her place.

Once again, my thoughts turned towards Rajiv Mehra. Images of that well-loved face returned. I wondered what life would have been with him. Though we worked in the same institution in the early years of my marriage, I barely met him a couple of times. He had taken me to the cafeteria once again. This time, there was no diffidence for I was a married woman and the mother of a toddler. I had just returned from Mussoorie with photographs of my beloved son. Rajiv selected one, with me holding Karan, and pocketed it. I pleaded with him to return it; for it would not do to jeopardise my marriage for one misplaced photo. But he was only teasing and returned it shortly.

To tide over the awkward silence I asked, 'Why haven't you got married yet?'

'All the pretty girls in college are already married,' he said looking pointedly at me. Finally, when he did marry for love I was unreasonably hurt.

We lost contact after post-graduation. Both of us left AIIMS and shifted to different hospitals. He remained in my mind as a pleasant memory, an unfulfilled dream. I was surprised to run into him one day at my hospital. His left arm was in plaster and on his right hung a pretty girl.

'Ever the ladies' man,' I thought.

'What a pleasant surprise!' he exclaimed.

'Same here. How are you?' I asked, 'Still unmarried?'

'Yes.'

During this exchange, the girl he introduced as Dr Meena spoke not a word. A mutual friend herded us towards the cafeteria. As we drank coffee, she read out a satire I had written on the working conditions in our labour room. It had become so popular that copies were passed around and even put up on the notice board!

After admiring my wit, Rajiv remarked, 'Rosy, I did not know that you wrote poetry.'

I remembered the fruitless wait, the excruciating pain of having been stood up and nodded slowly. Yes, indeed! He did not know that I wrote poetry.

I inquired about the plaster on his arm. He gave me gory details about an accident in which his scooter was caught in the back bumper of a truck! He was dragged along for a furlong and if his head hadn't been protected, the hole in his helmet would have been on his skull! He had been in coma for days afterwards. I shuddered involuntarily. For all the misery he had caused me, I still loved him more than anyone else on this earth. Suddenly, it did not matter whether he loved me or not. All that mattered was that he was alive and well.

As for the Meena, it was a matter of being at the right place at the right time. She was his junior at that time and had taken care of him during those trying times. On that day, Rajiv gave me no hint that she was to be his future wife. I wonder why?

After that, we lost contact. As time went by, I thought of him less and less. After all, how long could a fire last without fuel? I was reconciled to the cage of matrimony and accepted passively whatever life had to offer.

We met again after eight years at a party thrown by a mutual friend and I failed to recognise him! Of all the hundred different ways I visualised our reunion, I never dreamt that I wouldn't recognise him. The constant gaze of an attractive stranger disconcerted me. When realisation dawned, emotions spewed forth like lava from a volcano. He had greyed attractively at the temples, wore spectacles and a moustache. And he smoked. It took all the willpower at my disposal to contain my joy. Carefully, I allowed a rationed response to filter through. We made small talk and I learnt that he worked in a local hospital and lived in the quarters provided to the hospital staff. He had a daughter and his wife was expecting their second child, and therefore had not accompanied him. He still had that ancient scooter with him. Financially, I seemed to have fared better but no amount of material gains could fill the emotional void.

That night, there was no sleep for me. I burned with a fever that set my blood on fire. Feelings fluttered in my breast like wounded birds. Unable to bear it any longer, I crept into the clinic, put my head on the table, and let my tears pool on its polished surface. I realised that,

> *Nothing, but nothing,*
> *Had changed over the years,*
> *Hope, still lingered on my lids*
> *Like tremulous tears.*
> *Desire hovered on my lips,*
> *Like unspoken words,*
> *Memories fluttered in my mind*
> *Like captured birds.*

I still yearned for times
Beyond recall,
And pursued in vain,
Shadows on the wall.
Every bit of the present,
With the past was laced,
It's just that the tumult,
Never surfaced.
The foam, the froth,
Never did subside,
It welled and swelled
And swilled inside.
It took but a look
To burst restrain,
To convert dormant sorrow
Into monstrous pain.
Love I knew was ever,
Present in my heart,
The futility of this love,
Now tore me apart.

Perhaps if I had found fulfilment in marriage, I wouldn't have been so shaken up by Rajiv's reappearance. If MS had taken but a sip of the ocean that swelled in my heart, I would have been content. I had so much to give, but he did not know how to take. Why, I had met Rajiv in the early years of my marriage and he hadn't made such an impact. I had hope in my heart, and dreams in my eyes then. Now all that remained was an emotional desert. Physical abstinence, lack of mental stimulus I could do without, but I was as good as dead if I did not feel. Rajiv made my feelings come alive. Never mind if all that I felt now was hopelessness and despair. If my heart was a wasteland before, it was a devastated bower now, and there was a world of difference between that emptiness and this.

Perhaps it was predestined that we meet again. Though we exchanged telephone numbers, Rajiv did not ring me up. It did not matter for I was not going to make the same mistake again. If I wanted something bad enough, I would have to reach out for it. Yet, I wondered, how could he sleep in peace after consigning me to a bed of coals? How I wished I was like MS—an uncomplicated person with basic needs. All he wanted was food, sleep, and work. Even I was redundant, but that was no excuse for betraying him. Yet I could not bear to stay away from Rajiv. There had to be some way out of the predicament that was tearing me apart.

After giving it much thought, I reached a solution that satisfied both my craving and my morality. Though the bindings of a marriage were inviolate, there was no harm in talking to another man. If talking to this particular one gave me intense pleasure, how could it matter to anyone? When I finally mustered courage to ring up Rajiv, the years of separation fell away like autumn leaves. The easy camaraderie of the early years was re-established. I took to calling him as the paediatric expert for my deliveries. On these innocuous meetings I subsisted, hording precious moments like jewels in the velvet lined box of memory—an inscrutable gaze, a slow sweet smile spreading like sunshine, the joyous ring of his laughter. Once he put his arms around me from behind to help me with a difficult forceps delivery. His proximity overwhelmed and I could barely concentrate on the case at hand. I came out of the labour room with a blood-smattered face. There was no mirror in the bathroom and despite repeated washing, a few bloodstains remained. It would not do to meet the patient's relatives looking like Dracula! He rubbed my eyes, cheek, and forehead gently with wet hands to wipe the stains away.

A particular incident stands out in memory. One night we were free by 2 a.m. after an emergency caesarean section. Reluctant to let me drive alone on deserted Delhi roads at this time of the night, Rajiv followed me on his scooter. On reaching my gate, I thanked him and bade him farewell, but he waited till I was safely inside, which was just as well for no one answered the gate bell despite my constant ringing! This, when the house was full of people for my husband's family had descended from Mussoorie for the winter. In fact, I had asked MS to accompany me as it was dangerous for a woman to go on a night call alone, but his mother stated categorically that she would not put her son's life at risk and Mama's boy acquiesced meekly. Coming to think of it, MS hadn't even phoned to find out if I had reached the hospital safely. As of now, only after Rajiv jumped over the gate to ring the doorbell did someone finally let me in. He was surprised at the lack of concern of my family, but I was resigned to my fate. If they were not bothered whether I lived or died, was abducted, or raped, why should I?

Finally, my own residence cum nursing home was complete. From now on, I'd be conducting cases in my personal premises and would not have to rush elsewhere at odd times. Besides a horde of relatives and friends, I invited Rajiv and his family for the inauguration. His little son walked about the place as if he owned it. I opened my arms and he walked into them as if he belonged. Had circumstances been different, this little boy could have been mine. I kissed him on his cheek. He kissed me right back, making a little game out of it. We would've have kept kissing each other thus interminably had not Rajiv come looking for his son. I do not know how long he stood there watching us with that inscrutable gaze of his.

Though we had made our residence upstairs, we hadn't shifted as yet. The first time I called Rajiv for a delivery at *my* nursing home, I took him to the unfurnished living quarters later, for tea. Sipping the scalding brew, we talked and we talked. I was amazed at how little we really knew about each other. On that mellow afternoon I learned about his family, his boyhood, his likes and dislikes, even as he learnt facts about me. Fat lot of good it would do to me now, nevertheless, I was keenly interested. The shadows lengthened and twilight caught us unawares. As he got up to leave, he gave me a look of pure, unadulterated love. I was completely happy.

What rankled was that I always made the first move. He *did* ask me politely to visit his house and I would reply just as politely that I would come, but I never did go. One day he asked me point blank, 'Why don't you come?'

Unthinkingly I said, 'On what pretext?'

He did not reply but he walked away with a preoccupied look on his face.

A month later, Simar developed fever that lasted for days. All tests proved negative and yet the fever would not subside. MS, as usual, was busy with his clinic and was of no use whatsoever. Rajiv came as often as he could and Simar took a liking for the 'nice uncle' and the palatable medicine he prescribed. One afternoon, Rajiv rang up to say that he had injured his foot and would not be able to come.

'Why don't you bring Simar over?' he said.

'Never mind, look after yourself,' I replied, shyly reluctant.

'You must come. This is as good an excuse as any to visit me.' He had not forgotten. Simar did need a consultation and I knew that I would never get another opportunity to see Rajiv in his habitat.

He lived on the top floor of a building complex. That day, I saw a new facet of his personality—that of a doting father. Meena returned late from work so he managed the kids in the afternoon. His daughter, Kanika, was a thin, intense girl with sharp features. Mayur, the little boy, was chubby and cute. They weren't the slightest bit in awe of their father and climbed all over him. Rajiv examined Simar and gave him a dose of medicine. Gradually, the fever subsided and he slept with his head on my lap.

'Why don't you keep Simar with you till he recovers completely?' I said for want of something to say.

'On the condition that you keep Kanika.'

'I can keep her forever by marrying her off to my elder son.' I said flippantly.

'Good, that will solve the problem of a dowry.' He laughed. 'But you'll have to produce a daughter to marry my son.'

'I can't.' I replied suddenly serious.'

'Why?'

'For three reasons: firstly, if I produce a third child it will be promptly handed over to my brother-in-law. Secondly, there is no guarantee that it will be a daughter. And last but not the least, I gain ten kilos with every pregnancy.'

He laughed and said, 'You were the slimmest girl in your batch. Don't worry, I'll see to it that you don't gain an ounce extra.'

I stared at him in shock. He has spoken to me as if I was his wife! To cover my embarrassment I said, 'I must leave now.'

'No, no don't go. I'll show you some photographs.' Before I could protest, he hobbled out of the room on his plastered toe to fetch them but returned empty-handed. His wife had kept them 'safe' somewhere out of his children's reach.

Desperate for an excuse to retain me, he said, 'Kanika, get your notebooks. Show auntie your grades.'

I was pleased by his persistence. I used to despise myself for wanting to hang on to his company when he came to my place.

After going through the books and duly appreciating the little girl, I made another attempt to leave.

'Stay a little while more,' he pleaded. 'It's almost time for Meena to return. Why don't you meet her before going?'

That was the last thing I wanted to spoil the perfection of the afternoon.

'I really must go,' I said, waking up Simar.

With charming gallantry, Rajiv insisted on seeing me to the parking lot and walked down the stairs, his injured foot notwithstanding. As I was getting into the car, his wife returned. Surprisingly, I felt no animosity, only a strange kinship, united as we were, in the love of the same man. She fussed over his foot and he responded to her concern with warmth. They were lost in a world of their own in which I had no place. A cold loneliness clutched my heart as I watched their receding backs through the rearview mirror.

27

I continued calling Rajiv off and on to feed the hunger of my soul and thought that he derived as much pleasure from our 'professional' visits as I did. It did not occur to me that he was finding them cumbersome. I got a nasty jolt one wet July afternoon. Plagued by the vagaries of a particularly difficult case, I was at the end my tether. The baby's heartbeat dipped and I decided to apply forceps. I called Rajiv as usual to receive the baby and resuscitate it if required.

'Can't you find another paediatrician?' he said on the phone. I couldn't believe my ears. How could he forsake me at a time like this?

'The baby is distressed and I haven't the time to locate another paediatrician. Please come.' I hated myself for begging, but I had no alternative.

I did not know then that he had been toying with the idea of a private practice and, wanted to get a taste of it before he quit his job. Having decided that he wasn't cut out for practice, he did not want to jeopardise his job by attending private calls anymore, hence this rebuff. Little did I know that this was the last case he would attend at my nursing home. Before leaving, he said, 'Dr Anand, could you call another paediatrician for your cases from now on?'.

Each word hit me like a blow from a hammer. Ever since I remembered, he had called me Rosy. The 'Dr Anand' alienated him as no distance of time and space ever could.

'I did not realise that it was a strain on you,' I said woodenly.

'Please do call me if you need me otherwise for Simar or . . .'

'Thank you,' I murmured.

'This is what comes out of throwing yourself at a man.' I thought. Well, now I had a lifetime to wallow in humiliation. With my pen dipped in tears of blood I wrote:

> *Go my estranged love, go,*
> *Without a backward glance*
> *Lest my tears spill,*
> *Before your back is turned.*
> *I would not have you see*
> *My palm pressed against my heart,*
> *To stem the rising tide of pain.*
> *Go before the false façade,*
> *Of valiant silence crumbles*
> *And,*
> *I scream as if mortally struck.*
> *Go before the numbness wears off*
> *And Hysteria takes my head*
> *In both her hands*
> *To break it against the wall.*
> *Farewell my estranged love,*
> *Farewell*
> *God be with you and*
> *May no one ever do to you,*
> *What you have done to me.*

Pathetic had been my dependence on the crumbs he threw my way. As a fitting finale to our association, the baby who made such a tumultuous entry into the world expired. Rejection slips poured in from magazines I had sent my literary efforts to. The saga of my love had ended in a whimper, my clinical acumen was at stake and the talent I had so prided in was non-existent. Life was at its lowest ebb. I thought that no one on this earth was as wretched as I was.

God in His wisdom shook me out of my misery by showing me that there existed a grief far worse than this—that of a mother losing a child, almost! Disaster struck one humid August afternoon. I lay in bed in a cotton gown warding of sleep, till the children returned from school. Simar rushed in to announce, 'Karan has been hit by a car and is lying on the road.'

Without bothering to change my flimsy attire, I rushed out of the house. The crowd parted to let me through. My son lay pale and motionless on the road. My heart stopped for a moment and then began to thud painfully. 'God, let no woman suffer a tragedy of this magnitude.' I begged, yet I could not afford the luxury of being mere mother. I had to be a doctor first and foremost. I lifted a limp hand and felt his pulse. He was alive but barely so.

I picked him up and sped off in a taxi to the nearest hospital. It happened to be the one Rajiv worked in. Halfway to the hospital, Karan regained consciousness and said 'Mamma.' It was the sweetest sound I had heard in my life.

The casualty medical officer gave first aid and suggested that I shift him to another hospital where facilities for a CT scan were available. He was right but in the early eighties, CT scan was done only at select distant places. Moreover, I had phoned MS and he was on his way here. In any case, I'd have to wait till he arrived for those were not the days of cell phones. Meanwhile I rang up Rajiv. He came immediately, his hair tousled, his lids heavy with sleep. I must have woken him from his afternoon nap. Within minutes, he had the necessary machinery moving. MS arrived, took one look at Karan and broke down. That was all he seemed capable of in times of emergency. Time and again I have seen that men are the weaker sex in matters that really mattered. It is only brute strength that they are capable of.

'Shut up.' I hissed. 'This is no time for hysterics.' This shocked him into silence.

The x-ray films arrived. Thankfully, there were no broken bones.

'Karan looks pale; what if there is internal bleeding . . .' I began, apprehensive.

'Rosy, you are paler than him.' said Rajiv. 'Look at your nails.' He made as if to hold my hand, but restrained himself.

'But his pulse . . .'

'Rosy, relax. He will be just fine.' There was a time when 'Dr Anand' hurt terribly. Now the repetitive use of 'Rosy' jarred. Leaving me with Karan, he went with MS to complete the admission formalities. After a while, they returned. Seeing my distraught face he said, 'This is nothing. I was unconscious for 48 hours and here I am in front of you.'

'With all your faculties intact?' I quipped unthinkingly, like a fool.

'That is for you to see.'

For the first time I was aware of my grief-ravaged face, my dishevelled hair, and the fact that I was not wearing a bra under my flimsy attire. Sensing my discomfiture, Rajiv suggested that I go to his house and wear one of his wife's saris but MS said, 'Simar is alone at home. I'll look him up and get your clothes.'

Karan was kept under observation for 24 hours. Blood and urine samples were collected and injections given. Finally, Rajiv and I were alone chatting intimately while Karan slept. It was as if Karan was our son and the accident had served to bring us closer. Suddenly, Karan vomited. I rushed to the nurse's counter to get something to clean him up. When I returned, Rajiv was lovingly wiping Karan's face with his own handkerchief. If I hadn't loved him before, I would have surely fallen in love with him now.

MS returned in a couple of hours. I liked the way Rajiv took charge. We were drained by the ordeal and had as much will power as a pair of rag dolls. He asked MS to sit with Karan while he took me home to freshen up and have dinner. I was painfully shy riding pillion on his scooter and perched myself precariously as far back as possible. Over a speed breaker he went without slowing down. I will never know if it was an act of deliberation or not, but the jolt jerked my body forward in snug proximity with his back; my hand reaching out to clutch his shoulder. It was the closest I would ever get to him. Was there ever such a mother! My son had barely escaped the jaws of death all I could think of was . . .!

'You know,' said his wife conversationally, after we were settled in their drawing room 'a relative met with an accident a few days ago. He was in coma for two days and died yesterday.'

'Meena!' said Rajiv. 'You need not have spoken about it. Can't you see that she is a nervous wreck?'

The last thing I wanted was a quarrel between husband and wife on my account.

'Rajiv has been so kind and helpful.' I put in quickly.

'He's like that with everyone,' said Meena, lest I suffer from any illusion. 'For the last two days, he has been with the relative arranging for a CT scan, etc.'

'That reminds me, isn't a CT scan necessary?'

'No yaar, what's the hurry? He is conscious, talking normally, and moving all his limbs.'

'But . . .'

'Don't worry. We'll get it done later if necessary. Here comes the tea. Now relax and drink it.'

By now, reaction had set in. I pressed my palms between my knees to stop them from trembling. I felt hot and sticky, and asked if I could use their bathroom.

'Of course,' said Meena.

For that short span of time, I was a part of Rajiv's household. I bathed in his bathroom, changed in his bedroom, and tidied my hair at his dressing table. My face looked stark without kaajal, lipstick, and bindi, but I felt refreshed. I had a simple dinner with Meena and the kids. Rajiv would eat later with my husband.

'Is auntie sleeping with us today?' asked Mayur.

'Yes.'

'Where will she sleep?'

'In your bed,' I said playfully.

'But I sleep with Papa!' he said.

Later I sat vigil by Karan, and MS went home to Simar. I touched the face of my sleeping child and shuddered. Little incidents of his past crept into my mind's eye—Karan the chubby, red-cheeked baby; the beautiful child with a golden voice. The bookworm who tried using big words and asked why I was so 'solomon' when I was solemn; the altruistic kid who gave his clothes to the slum kids without telling me. The teacher's pet who did not have to study too hard to do well. I remembered the time he told me that he had been chosen for the school football team and I had remarked, 'As the football?'

'No, Mama, as the fourth extra.'

I could never thank God enough for saving my son, nor could I forget what Rajiv had done for us. He came in the morning to help me with the formalities of discharge. He looked fresh and clean with his wet hair slicked back in place. It curled in such an endearing fashion at the nape of his neck that I had an uncontrollable desire to muss it up.

A few days later, we called the Mehras over for dinner. Perhaps this was the last time I would be meeting him. Lovingly, I cooked every single dish myself and took great pains over my appearance. I wore a white chiffon sari with tiny pink flowers. There were pearls around my throat, and jasmines in my hair. I was glad that I looked good, for I wanted Rajiv to remember me thus, and not in awful state I was at the hospital.

The party was a success. Karan thanked Rajiv formally and presented him a gift and a card. I was surprised at his reaction. Instead of appreciating the present I had chosen with such care, he refused to accept it. He insisted on taking just the card on which I had written:

With gratitude and love.
From,
Karan and family

'Son, where does gratitude come in? Isn't love sufficient?' asked Rajiv.

'But Mamma wrote it,' protested Karan innocently.

Rajiv looked at me in a way that made my heart turn over. He put the card in his breast pocket and said, 'This is all I accept.'

'But why?'

'I have done nothing to deserve the rest.'

'Don't break his heart after mending his head,' I said.

'Leave your poetry for your books.' He laughed.

'Okay, I'll accept; but present will be of my choice,' said Rajiv mysteriously.

'What?'

'A song from Karan.'

Karan was only too willing to oblige. He sang ghazal after ghazal in his mellifluous voice. Rajiv gazed at me across a roomful of people with a look so eloquent that I could have sworn he loved me.

I was glad that our last evening together was a memorable one. My family liked him as much as I liked his. I knew that I looked beautiful for him, because of him. We had a meal together, a meal that I had prepared lovingly with my own hands. I had given my love and he had accepted it graciously through the card. He left me replete with memories—a wealth beyond compare. The aroma of his cigarette still hung in the air, the stub smoking in the ashtray, but he was gone never to return. I picked up the stub of an extinguished love and put it to my lips—a fitting reminder of a glow that was destined for ashes.

28

Happenings of national import in the November of '84 put private problems on the back burner. Indira Gandhi was assassinated by her Sikh bodyguards. It was a dastardly act that deserved to be thoroughly condemned, but the backlash on innocents because they belonged to the same religion was unforgivable.

I remembered the time when Indira Gandhi had tried to convert our democracy into a dictatorship and deservedly lost. Having learnt her lesson, she set out to regain her past glory. She was returning to power after her ignominious defeat. To garner votes, she would give a 'darshan' to her well-wishers, in the compound of her house. My father-in-law, a keen congressman, persuaded me to take him to her premises. Simar was a year old then. As we were leaving, he woke up and began to cry. On an impulse, we took him along. We joined the crowd waiting near the dais upon which 'Madam' was to make an appearance. Finally she arrived, a diminutive lady in pink. Newspaper photographs made her appear larger than life. The rudraksha mala around her neck proclaimed her insecurities louder than words; that she sought such arbitrary aids was pathetic. As I was thinking such unlikely thoughts, my son decided to make his presence felt. He opened his mouth and bawled just when Indira Gandhi opened hers. She took him in her arms. A thousand bulbs flashed, and my little son made headlines the next day.

This was the first time my life touched hers personally. The second time it was in death that she made her presence felt in every Sikh household. The entire community was victimized for the cowardly act of two of her Sikh bodyguards. Though our extended family escaped with their lives, the damage to property was in lakhs. This devastated my father-in-law who was an ardent congressman and had even gone to jail during the freedom struggle for which he got a Tambra Patra.

In our case, the adage 'A clever enemy is better than a foolish friend' proved true. Our landlords were not on speaking terms with us. Though we assured them that we would vacate the premises as soon as ours was ready, they had started acting nasty. When riots broke out, the landlady made her son remove my car from their porch late at night. It would have given us away when the mob that was brutalizing Sikhs arrived, and burned *their* house to kill us! Sure enough, the wild-eyed, bloodthirsty horde surged to our gate the next morning. The landlords informed them that we had fled, saving their home and thereby, our lives.

Meanwhile, I had managed to pass all my money and jewellery to a Hindu friend for safekeeping. MS assured me that he had enough for our immediate needs. As Delhi burnt around us, we stayed entombed alive in our home. The fire station was around the corner, but not a single fire engine came to the rescue the hapless Sikhs from their burning homes. Simar, a tiny kid, watched the carnage through a slit in the curtains and gave in to an attack of hysterics. I had to slap him to shock him into normalcy. For months afterwards, he would be frightened of smoke even if it arose from the chimney of a factory. After days of being holed up like rats, cautiously we emerged. I went to get my car, but it wouldn't start. The mechanic demanded Rs 250 for repairs but MS refused to give me the money! Never again would I depend on any man financially, I vowed to myself. I had to resume my practice and earn the requisite amount to retrieve my car.

Barely had we recovered from one catastrophe when another struck—this time on the personal front. I was woken by a low guttural sound from my husband's bed to find him in the throes of a fit! His head and eyes had turned to one side and he was foaming at the mouth. His limbs were moving in grotesque jerks. After what seemed an eternity, the convulsions stopped and he went into coma. A neurologist was summoned and my worst fears were confirmed. My husband was an epileptic! When he regained consciousness, we learnt that he had dislocated his right shoulder during the fit! I remembered being called back home from duty once by my mother-in-law because MS had dislocated a shoulder. She conveniently forgot to mention that this had been preceded by a fit. From Bhabiji, I learnt that he had similar attacks before marriage, too!

Now began the most trying periods of my married life. MS had been advised to refrain from driving his scooter for at least a year. We were in between servants, and Simar was but a toddler. I got up at dawn to finish the household chores, put up with the tantrums of my father-in-law who demanded fresh food at every meal; acted as chauffeur to MS and continued working. Fatigue seeped into my very bones. To cap it all, MS was a bad patient. When I reached in time and he was delayed, I sat in the car like the driver I was reduced to, feeding Simar (who I had to perforce bring along) a cold lunch. Any delay on my part, he took with ill grace. I put up with his ill humour as long as I could, but when he began scolding me in front of his patients, I could bear it no longer. Couldn't he commute by public transport or hire a driver? *My* practice began to suffer on account of which my income decreased drastically while the petrol bills mounted. The next time we stopped at a pump for petrol, I asked MS to pay. To my utter surprise, he refused.

'How do you expect me to pay the bills which have increased on your account, especially when you give me no time to earn?' I asked.

At this, he got down from the car and walked away. Tears streamed down my face as I watched him stop one three-wheeler after another but none of them were interested in going the distance—too short for a vehicle but far enough for walking. My shoulders sagged with resignation as I drove up and opened the car door to let him in.

With excruciating slowness, these days too passed. The treatment was successful, the attacks were few and far between, and life limped back to normal.

29

It is said that nature abhors a vacuum. Like an unguarded fortress, I was at my vulnerable worst. I ached with loneliness. Anyone could claim me with kindness alone. I did so want to be loved and cherished. I needed a shoulder to cry on, a companion who cared. MS did not bother to know the person he was married to and therefore had no inkling of the gnawing void within. Any attempt to acquaint him with the real me bore no fruit. Passionate by nature, I could not entirely suppress my need for attention, affection, and sometimes, thorough physical sex. It was almost a year since I lived as a married widow and wanted to do something drastic to shake MS out of his complacency.

It wasn't as if I lacked male attention. Being a working woman, and a fairly presentable one at that, I was constantly thrown in the face of temptation. It was my sense of morality that kept the wolves at bay, yet. At least three men professed to be in love with me. It was flattering for a matron on the wrong side of thirty. As long as they remained harmless flirtations, it was all right with me. The moment anyone made a serious pass, I took flight. Certainly not out of marital love. I just did not think that the gratification of vanity was worth the complications that would inevitably arise.

There was Jeeju, my *nanand's* (husband's sister's) husband, twenty years my senior. He lived in Chandigarh but would come to Delhi often for business and stay with us. I remain indebted to him for introducing me to the immortal works of

Ghalib and Faiz, and inculcating in me the love of ghazals. There would be tears in our eyes, as we listened to beautiful words set to beautiful music sung by the likes of Jagjit Singh and Pankaj Udhas. That he was a connoisseur of everything beautiful, including women, I learnt much later. He began to look at me in a manner that did not quite become a gentleman of his stature. When I touched his feet in reverence, the hand that used to pat my head in blessings, now began to slide down my back. He got a silver wristwatch for me from Singapore and told my husband that I had given him money to buy it! It was a blatant lie. As time went by, he became bolder—blowing me a kiss when MS was not looking; asking me to take a sip from his glass of whisky. Once, he pinned me against the wall by placing his hands on either side without touching me, and waxed eloquent on how much he loved me. I ducked and made good my escape. The situation was getting out of control and I did not know how to handle it without dishonouring an esteemed relative.

Matters came to a head one summer afternoon. The children were at school; MS at the clinic, and the servant had taken the day off when Jeeju arrived. He asked for a glass of water. After he finished, I stretched my arm to retrieve the empty glass. He caught hold of my wrist and jerked me towards him. I lost my balance and sprawled over him. I tried to get up but he held me tight by the upper arm. Providence intervened in the form of the doorbell. MS had returned. Never was I happier to see anyone in my life.

As his trips to Delhi were frequent, Jeeju kept a bag of extra clothes in our house. That night, he asked me to take out his night suit for him. As I reached up to get it from the upper shelf, flabby arms encircled my waist. I screamed out aloud. MS came running in.

'What happened?' he asked.

'A mouse frightened her,' lied Jeeju glibly.

I had had enough. When we were alone in bed, I told MS all. After much deliberation, we decided that an open confrontation would be scandalous. After all, Jeeju was his sister's husband and she would die of shame. I was asked to avoid being alone with him, but that was easier said than done. MS left for his clinic and the children for school in the morning, which left me alone at home with Jeeju, as my clinic was in my residence. Now that I had the backing of my husband, I made bold to take Jeeju to task.

'You'll have to stop such disgraceful behaviour otherwise . . .' This was a Rosy he hadn't seen.

'Otherwise what? I'll be barred entrance to your house?'

I maintained a stony silence. Gone was the mousy female who could not stand up for herself.

'I come here only for you. Aren't there enough hotels in the city?' he asked but the new assurance in my demeanour made him wary. The confidence with which he made passes at me earlier began to flounder. After this, though his visits became infrequent and decorous; he professed to be heartbroken.

Sudhir was a medical representative and a friend, or so I thought. He was handsome and young; more importantly, we could relate on the mental level. It was uplifting to talk about the latest book, my poems, and his writings, though he was candid enough to let on that the occasional middle he contributed to a newspaper was on account of contacts and not due to any literary prowess on his part. He was studying for his IAS (Indian Administrative Services) exams and I gave him a lot of encouragement. When his visits became more frequent than necessary, I was vaguely alarmed. That a platonic relationship cannot exist between members of the opposite sex, I learnt on the day he tried to read the lines of my palm. I, for one, read between the lines and pulled my hand away. I let him know in no uncertain terms that he was no longer welcome. He kept away and I wouldn't admit even to myself how much I missed our stimulating conversations.

He turned up six months later on a dull, rainy morning, soaking wet, his blue shirt plastered to his skin, outlining his stunning physique. Raindrops fell like jewels from his curly, brown-black hair. He was like a burst of sunshine on that monsoon morn. Curbing my pleasure, I gave a cautious smile.

'You are not angry with me anymore?' he asked.

'No,' I replied simply.

'I passed my IAS part 1.'

'Congratulations.'

'It was because of you.'

'Me!' I was incredulous.

'I have brought a small gift for you.'

'Why?'

'You were my inspiration.'

'I cannot accept it.'

'Please don't refuse.'

He insisted stubbornly and forced a packet on me. It contained a beautiful rust-coloured silk sari, which was generous of him, considering that he earned less than I did.

'I couldn't possibly take such an expensive present,' I protested.

'I have bought it especially for you,' he pleaded.

I decided to keep it. When I showed it to MS, he was sceptic.

'Why should he give you a sari if he has passed the IAS?'

Words seemed inadequate to explain the peculiarity of our relationship. He insisted that I return it the next time he comes.

'But he'll get hurt.'

'You shouldn't have taken it in the first place.'

'Okay, you return it for me.'

'No. It's your problem.'

So the next time Sudhir came, I handed the packet back to him. The look of pain on his face was exquisite. The dam burst and words came out in a rush. He swore by all that he held sacred, that he worshipped the ground I walked on!

'I have never come across such a rare combination of beauty, innocence, intelligence, and honesty,' he concluded.

'And obesity,' I added flippantly. 'A married woman five years your senior.'

'I wish I had met you earlier.'

'I am sorry, but once again I have to tell you to go away and stay away.'

'But how will I survive?'

'You'll be fine.'

The sun shone like a halo around his brown-black hair as he walked out of my life never to return.

30

Sometime back, a couple began attending my OPD on account of an inability to conceive. The wife, Snehlata, was a mousy nondescript woman with a wheatish complexion, stained teeth, who kept her head covered. Her husband—Mr Rajan Bhardwaj—was tall, dark, with a toned body, startlingly white teeth, and capable hands. He was as voluble as his wife was silent. As the treatment for infertility stretched over prolonged periods, they took to frequenting my place regularly. Investigations revealed that Snehlata was normal while Mr Bhardwaj had a low sperm count. He took this blow to his manhood badly and started coming alone to 'discuss his case'. He tried bribing me with a piece of land (he was a realtor), so that I took special interest. This was preposterous! Though sometimes rewarding, treatment for infertility could be quite frustrating. I explained this to my patients at the outset so that they understand that the time and money invested could be in vain. Mr Bhardwaj had no doubts about the success of my treatment. He had a visitation from the Lord Shiva in a dream one night, who ordained that he would get a child through me! Indeed! I disliked his type intensely.

Insidiously, Rajan Bhardwaj crossed the threshold between our professional and private lives. He wooed my children with chocolates and ice creams. As I hated mixing personal affairs with work, I warned him never to do it again. At this, he shifted his attention to the elders in my family. He would touch Papaji's feet and bring pickles for my mother-in-law. He also helped my husband solve a tricky property matter that had been plaguing him for years. In return, I started treating them for free.

Whenever my ramshackle old Fiat broke down, he would lend me his, taking care to fill the petrol tank. I did not know then that he was a trader of favours. His generosity was a calculated move and he would extract his pound of flesh when the time came. As of now, he pressed presents upon me to try harder? This implied that I did less than my best if I didn't get that bit extra. It was insulting. The man repulsed me. To get him off my back, I tried referring him to my senior at AIIMS, but he said that he was perfectly satisfied with the 'junior'. I was secretly pleased, though I had a niggling doubt that it wasn't solely because of my professional expertise that he wanted me to manage their case.

My attitude bewildered him. I was the first person he couldn't 'buy'. With unlimited resources at his disposal, he had bought land, name, and entry into the upper echelons of society. He kept government officials, the police, and the underworld in his pocket with his 'generosity'. As for women, they tripped over themselves to grab a share, whatever the price. He did have an aura of raw sexuality about him and was a self-confessed womanizer. Considering his extracurricular activities, it was a wonder that he tested negative for venereal diseases. He told me about his indulgence to ascertain if it had anything to do with his low sperm count.

'Would you stop if I said yes?'

'Anything for a child.'

'Then put an end to your excesses at once.'

Meanwhile, the construction of our residence cum nursing home was going on in full swing. Like in any other ambitious project, we fell short of cash and borrowed from friends. Though in dire need of money, Mr Bhardwaj was one person I was never going to ask. I had begun to feel uncomfortable under his gaze. It did not seem right somehow.

One day, of his own accord, he put a packet on my table.

'What is it?' I felt my hackles rise.

'Just a token.' Some people wouldn't take no for an answer.

'Not again!' I flared.

'Accept it as a loan.'

'Loan?'

The packet contained Rs. 20,000/- cash. Conflicting emotions raced through my mind. I knew that we needed the money badly, but I did not like to be beholden to him. God knows what kind of interest I would have to pay on this interest-free loan. He refused to take the money back, even when MS intervened. Finally, I accepted it with an uneasy feeling of having sealed my fate.

Over a period of time, I developed a certain fondness for this intriguing personality. A strange mixture of opposites he was. Beneath his rough exterior lay a soft heart. He was as easily roused to anger as to tears. He was a strict vegetarian who neither smoked nor drank, but had no qualms about infidelity. He earned money with a vengeance and yet was generous to a fault. He spent as lavishly on women as on building temples. He was not particularly handsome, but exuded a sexuality that was overpowering. He was a barely lettered, braggart who made the likes of me feel faintly superior, yet intuitively, I knew that I could depend upon him at times of crisis. He was a lusty male animal who took what he wanted, when he wanted. His body sent me signals I had no business to respond to. Not even Rajiv, whom I loved with all my heart, could evoke such strong physical hungers. While pretty compliments from other men did nothing, a glance from Rajan was enough to strip me. A stern look quelled the amorous advances of others; Rajan let no such impediments come in the way.

He began to look upon me more as a woman than a doctor. The prefix served as a pretext for meeting me. For one who used and discarded women as casually as paper napkins, the pursuit of a doctor was a novelty. He had done everything in his book to seduce me, and I hadn't succumbed. If he only knew how near I was to it on occasion. I longed to rest my weary head on his broad chest and feel those strong brown arms around me. I knew that he would not be gentle in his lovemaking, but I was tired of being handled like a fragile piece of china, or not being handled at all. I would welcome the manhandling and was sorely tempted at times.

Such thoughts left me shocked beyond words. I was sure that I did not love him and in my dictionary, one had to love a person to be sexually inclined towards him. Coming to think of it, I could love Rajiv in a purely romantic way till eternity, and I did have sex with my husband without love. I was thoroughly confused. It took all the willpower at my disposal to prevent my need from overtaking reason. Thank God for my mask of icy aloofness. It would never do to let him know that his tactics were working.

On doing some newer tests, I learnt that Snehlata had anti-sperm antibodies. There was no effective treatment for this condition except corticosteroids or abstinence. Corticosteroids could cause congenital anomalies, so we usually advised abstinence or the use of condoms for a period of three months. The logic was that if the semen did not come in contact with the wife's vagina, the production of antibodies against sperms would decrease. Another couple with a similar problem had followed my advice and conceived, but Rajan was incredulous.

'If you don't want to help us, tell me so. This is a fine way to treat an infertile couple. I can't refrain from sex and I can't wear a condom,' he declared.

'Then go away and don't come back to me,' I said in exasperation. Later when I cooled down, I realised that the treatment did indeed appear paradoxical—avoid intercourse to have a child! How could I forget that we were beholden to him? Rs. 20,000/- was a huge sum in the early eighties. I was bent under the weight of this debt. Returning it became the sole mission of my life.

He returned after a month and boy, was I glad to see him? His sheer sexuality smote me like a whiplash. The first thing I did after the hellos was to return his money. He was reluctant to take it, as he would lose that edge over me. Finally, I persuaded his wife to take the money along with the load off my head. Little did I know that he hadn't finished with me.

31

A patient presented us with a beautiful pup. The children were delighted, so was I. In our enthusiasm, we overlooked the fact that MS hated dogs. Matters came to such a pass that he announced, 'Either the dog stays in the house, or I.'

'In that case,' piped in Simar, 'we'll keep the dog.'

Though he received a slap for his effrontery, there was no denying the fact that their father was a remote figure they could do well without. He left before the kids got up and returned after they had gone to bed.

The family had ceased to function as a unit. With the added burden of construction, MS had no time for us. He did not deem it necessary to tell me about the progress made, though he had no qualms about bleeding me white of my money. Not that I had any reservations on that score. After all, the nursing home was my dream project too, and I had saved expressly for this purpose. When he began cutting down on bare essentials, I protested that this was carrying thrift a bit too far.

'Either the children eat, or we.' He retorted.

'Indeed! Are we in such sorry straits?' His miserliness had deteriorated to pathological proportions, and I was at my wit's end.

There was another niggling worry. MS had received a strange offer to augment his income. An industrialist was willing to pay him Rs. 6000 per month for which he would have to spend an hour each day as medical officer at his factory. A 'friend' was acting as a go between.

'How will the middleman benefit from this deal?'

'Well, if you must know, he will take Rs1000/- of the Rs6000/- from me every month.'

'There has to be a catch somewhere.'

'Keep quiet, woman.' The prospect was too alluring for him to let go.

'But . . .'

'Don't try to meddle in affairs you don't understand.'

'No one will give so much for so little.'

'Shut up, will you?'

MS's ego had been bruised when my income began to soar above his. Perhaps this was the salve he needed. I argued no more.

He began disappearing for prolonged periods without explanations. When I questioned him, he gave evasive answers. Gradually, even these unconvincing explanations stopped. Silence lay between us like an ocean between shores. No two lonelier souls lived together.

I also noticed a suspicious change in his nature. He had a marigold tucked between the folds of his turban every day. Something must be troubling him deeply to warrant a visit the gurudwara daily. I asked him to unburden himself and promised to stand by him.

'Leave me alone,' he said, and that was that.

After that, I avoided communication of any sort with him. I tried to live like a robot, but chronic tension and fatigue were taking their toll. I needed a break, and decided to visit my parents in Jammu.

'How can you even think of going at this time? We are neck deep in the construction work.'

'So?'

'You are essential here.'

I gave a hollow laugh. 'I have been as essential as a piece of furniture. The moment I decide to leave, I become indispensable.'

'You will not go.'

'Every year, we go to your parents in Mussoorie. I haven't seen mine for ages.'.

'How will we manage here?'

'The help is well trained and I will take the children along. I'll be back in no time.'

'Think of the expenditure, of the loss of income.'

'Think of my sanity.'

'You will be going so against my wishes.'

'What have I got for toeing your line?'

At Jammu, I worried about the repercussions of my disobedience and could not enjoy myself. Though I went on a pilgrimage to Vaishno Devi, I did not get the peace of mind I craved. My father was trying to cope with the shock of retirement and words like 'spent force' and 'used up commodity' cropped up in his conversation. I tried to tell him about my husband's strange behaviour, but he wasn't interested. My mother had developed angina recently and I did not want to stress her unduly. It smote me that I was a big girl now who could no longer run to Mamma with her hurt, and make her to kiss it away. I brought my entire bundle of problems back with me.

32

A middle-aged lady came to my clinic one day and said,

'I have come for my money.'

'What *money*!?'

'As if to say you don't know.'

'Who are *you*?'

'I am your husband's patient. He borrowed Rs. 5000/- and refuses to return it."

'I don't know what you are talking about.'

'Don't tell me that *you* do not know that your husband borrowed the money to send *your* brother abroad?'

Smarting with humiliation, I rang up MS. He began a longwinded story, but I cut him short.

'We'll discuss the details later. Just tell me one thing, did you borrow money from this lady or not?'

'Yes.'

'Cheat, borrow, beg, or steal,' I screamed. 'But do not drag my family in your sordid affairs. I am giving her the money, and will deal with you later,' I said, slamming the phone down.

MS would have a lot of explaining to do when he returned. Little did I know then that this was but the tip of the iceberg, an iceberg that would destroy the boat of our marriage, no Titanic to begin with.

Not even the birth of a son could induce MS to shut down his clinic. It would have been commendable if I got to see the proceeds of such earnest endeavour. That day, he closed shop and hurried home. His eyes were blood shot and he was making queer, unintelligible sounds. Tears coursed silently down his cheeks. Then came the sobs, huge heart-rending sobs that shook his entire body. I drew his head to my breast, wrapped my arms around him and waited for him to calm down.

In bits and jerks, the entire story came out. So desperate had he been for that part-time job that he had allowed the middleman to swindle him of 90,000 rupees!

'But how?' I gasped as the magnitude of the amount sank in.

MS wove a long drawn yarn about the middleman needing that amount urgently. In return, he would see to it that MS got precedence over the other doctors vying for the job. MS could deduct it from his monthly commission.

'You give Rs. 90,000/- to get a job of Rs. 6000/-month. I don't understand. More importantly, where did you get the money? I was given to understand that we didn't have enough for basic necessities.'

'Don't ask me, Rosy, don't. I am a very bad man. I am not worthy of you.'

'There, there, don't cry.' I soothed him as I would a baby. 'But I've got to know where the money has come from.'

'I have borrowed right, left, and centre, from everyone we know. What shall I do, God, what shall I do?'

It was as if the ground gave way from under my feet. The shame of being in debt to so many! How would we ever repay them? As it is, the loan for the house was weighing us down.

'It's all right, everything will be all right, don't worry. Now stop crying,' I crooned like a mother to a hurt child. I wiped his tears and gave him water. When he had settled a bit I asked, 'Why didn't you tell me anything? Two minds are better than one.'

'I was afraid that you'd say "I told you".'

'I would have done nothing of that sort.'

The person who had engineered the entire swindle vanished without a trace; MS did not know his address for they met at hotels. The entire story seemed unbelievable!

It was as if the burden of the world was upon me, and I was no female Hercules. After extracting all the money I had, my husband clamped up. Night after night I lay awake, longing for the oblivion that healed, the little death called sleep.

The amount taken for the house paled in comparison to the vast sum thrown down the drain, yet the loss hurt less than the shame of being in debt. MS had spared no one—friends, neighbours, patients, colleagues, and shopkeepers—even his brother's business partners. He had borrowed money from his sister in Chandigarh too, after telling me that she was ill and he was going to look her up. He lost all credence with me.

After giving all I had saved, I bought a piggy bank and told him that each of us would put Rs. 20 in it per day. Even this small amount would accumulate into a tidy amount by the end of the year. After a month or so, MS said that it was foolish to keep the piggy bank on the table with the servant around, and asked if he should keep it in his cupboard. I agreed to my determent; for he broke it, took the money for his nefarious activities, and had the temerity to take Rs. 20 from me daily! Of all the different ways he cheated me, this little one broke my heart.

It was as if my backbone was broken. I could not meet anyone in the eye. I cowered before the very people whom I used to lord over a short while ago. I earned money only to reduce the number of people on the list. Money that could have been put to better use went into repaying worthless loans. Why, we would have been free of our housing loans by this time if my husband had any sense. I remembered one of my mother's favourite quote:

> *'If wealth is lost, nothing is lost,*
> *If health is lost, something is lost,*

If honour is lost, everything is lost.'

We had managed to sink to the lowest level. Veerji was the only other person who knew of this catastrophe. Blinded by love for his brother, he believed that the poor fellow had been hypnotised!

'Goodness gracious,' I thought, but kept my opinion to myself. To his credit, Veerji sent large sums of money and between the two of us we managed to free MS from debt while he got away with that 'poor thing' look of his, and chipped in not a penny.

A year later, Veerji's shop in Mussoorie was ransacked by thieves. Now was the time to repay his kindness, but with what? We barely managed to meet our own expenses. I suddenly remembered a cheque of Rs15000/- I had asked MS to cash. The least we could do was to send Veerji that amount. When I asked him to do so, MS gave evasive answers. He forgot, he did not have the time etc. till I was forced to check for myself. My worst suspicions were confirmed. He had withdrawn the money on the very first day! When I demanded an explanation, he began his bedtime story of 'I am a very bad man . . .'

'Cut the crap and get to the point,' I had retorted. It was as if I had acquired a blood-sucking leech in the garb of a husband.

'Give me time, I'll explain everything.'

'You tell me now, or I'll shout the whole house down.' His father was sleeping in the next room.

'I gave the money to a man who promised to retrieve the stolen money.'

I slapped my forehead in despair.

'Couldn't you pay him from the retrieved money *after* he retrieved the money?'

'I request you with folded hands to keep quiet. If you are fed up of me, I'll leave the house.'

'Why should you leave the house? You are amongst your loved ones. I am the nag who doesn't let their darling live in peace. I'll leave the house and gladly so. I am fed up of your cheating ways.'

'Just give me time till Holi.'

'If you think I believed the previous cock and bull story of yours, you are sadly mistaken. Tell me which person in his senses would give someone Rs. 90,000/- to procure a job of Rs. 6000/-? But everyone is entitled to one mistake, so I forgave you yours. If it's a woman who is blackmailing you, she is welcome to take you, and good riddance. Don't waste *my* hard-earned money in hiding the fact from *me*!'

'There is no woman in my life but you. You know me better than that.'

'That's the point. I don't know you at all.'

'I love you.'

'Shut up. You do not love me at all. You just need me, or rather my money. Now out with the truth.' But he uttered not a word.

That night, I was literally hysterical. The loss of Rs. 90,000/- affected me less than the latest loss of Rs. 15,000/-. Faith in my husband was completely shattered. In a marriage that had no love, understanding, and companionship, trust was the only thing that kept us going. The betrayal of trust was more that I could bear. Something broke inside, never to be mended again.

For the first time in my life I suffered an attack of migraine. It was as if my head was caught in a vice that tightened slowly but surely till my skull was ready to crack, and my brains spill out. I went to the adjoining room, lay down on the floor, and rolled from side to side in sheer agony. I howled and I keened like a wild animal. After what seemed an eternity, the pain became tolerable and I returned to our bedroom to sleep. As I turned off the lights, the bed began to shake as in an earthquake. Another attack of epilepsy was all that I needed now.

33

Unaware as yet of the Rs. 15000/- fraud, I had decided to give my husband a second chance. It was not right to hold that one act of foolishness against him for the rest of his life. I made a serious error in my judgement of human nature. An error that cost me Rs 50 grand as newer facets of the colossal calamity revealed itself. For the first time in our lives, we opened a joint account in which I put the money and he withdrew it to pay the various workers at our construction site. MS did withdraw the money all right, but did not give it to the workers who, to my surprise, came to me, clamouring for their dues. When I questioned him, I learnt that once again we were indebted to every soul we knew!

I was at my wit's end. I lost my peace of mind through no fault of mine. I would get up in the middle of the night with a palpitating heart and a perspiring body. A hundred questions raced through my mind. What would happen to us if this state of affairs continued? Where was all the money going? Why didn't MS come out with the truth? I stopped talking to him completely. Veerji steered clear of us this time so I turned to my father. He did nothing to bail us out.

Besides the marigold from the gurudwara in the folds of his turban, MS started smearing Sai Baba's ash on his forehead. That was all the contribution he made in solving the problem he had landed us in. Of all our acquaintances, I thought that there were two who could be of help—Mr Bhardwaj, with his links with people that mattered, and Mr Saini, an influential exporter.

So I told MS, 'You are in serious trouble. If it's beneath you to confide in me, don't. Why don't you ask Mr Bhardwaj or Mr Saini to help you out?'

I got a phone call from Mr Bharwaj a few days later. Foolishly, I had fallen right into his trap.

'Are you all right?' he asked.

'Yes, what could happen to me?'

'And the children?'

'They are fine, but why do you ask?'

'Your husband has received threats that if he does not pay up in time they will rape his wife and kidnap his children?'

'Who are they, and why would they do such a thing?' I said, trying to swallow the fear that dried my mouth.

'Your husband is contemplating suicide.'

'What are you saying?' I gasped.

'I have already spoken more than I should have. Take care.'

'But how?' I appealed desperately to a dead phone. Before I could dial his number, guests arrived, then patients and finally, MS returned from his clinic. There followed a terror-filled night that refused to end. Each moment, heavy as a boulder, had to be pushed over the cliff of Time.

I rang up Rajan Bhardwaj as soon as MS left the next morning. I pleaded with him to come over and tell me everything. No woman would have waited as impatiently for her lover as I did for that odious man. What a salve it must have been to his ego. All these years I had been the queen, pompous and distant, bestowing or withdrawing favours, as I deemed fit. Here I was, stripped of pride, begging him to meet me. He came—two hours late. He was flirtatious and vivacious. My ill-concealed impatience amused him. When he finally got down to the topic, it was only to inform me that he was sworn to secrecy.

'I only hinted at the matter so that you take care.'

'But how can I keep the children from going to school or MS from killing himself?'

'I realise my mistake. I shouldn't have told you about it.'

I knew it was no mistake. It was an act of deliberation. It would be no use doing my husband a favour without my knowledge. It was from me that he would want to extract payment.

'Mistake or no mistake, now that you have started, it is your duty to tell me everything.'

'Duty?' he drawled with a sarcastic lift of an eyebrow.

'You don't have to help us if you don't want to,' I said, stung to the quick.

'I will help even if I have to put my life in danger.'

The bastard was playing saviour and villain at the same time.

'Why should you put your life in jeopardy for us? We can't repay you in any way.'

'Can't you?' he replied pinning me with a rakish look. 'Do you suspect your husband's fidelity?'

'The wife is always the last to know – as in your case.' I couldn't help adding. He threw back his head and laughed.

'How can he tire of you? If I had a wife like you, I would not look at another woman. With two caesarians, you are as good as new down there.'

It was the utmost liberty a man could take with a lady. He was vile and repulsive.

'If this is the price I have to pay for your information, I am not interested. Just leave.' I said, quivering with rage.

He did not budge.

'I am sorry. I am very sorry,' he said, though he did not look sorry at all. 'Believe me, I really want to help.'

'That's very kind of you,' I murmured sarcastically.

'It isn't out of kindness that I am helping.' Subtlety certainly wasn't one of his virtues.

On one hand, was my mate a weakling and a non-provider; and on the other hand, was this ruthless opportunist, closing in for the kill. The point was how much was I willing to stake to save a marriage that was tottering on its last legs? Why should I give myself to someone I detested to save the life of a husband I loathed? The idea was preposterous, or was it? With sudden insight, I realised that MS was an 11-year-old habit, and man is a creature of habit. I needed him for the sake of our children. Though termites had eaten the edifice hollow, the façade of a married woman was important. I could still get out of the web Rajan had woven if Mr Saini bailed us out. The latter would set no such humiliating preconditions.

The days passed in prolonged agony. Each time the phone rang I'd jump out of my skin. I would get hysterical when the school bus was delayed, or when MS returned late. Over a period of time I learnt that the tangle my husband had got himself into was no small one. He had been enticed into the vice of gambling by a gang of crooks. The sessions took place in five-star hotel rooms and MS was made to sign on the registers. They made him win unbelievable amounts of money, which they kept in 'safe custody'. When he was hooked, good and proper, he began to 'lose'. Thus, he was cheated out of vast sums of money over the period of a year. The amount he owed them was a staggering Rs.1,700,000!

The hounds were now baying for his blood. The tighter they squeezed his balls, the more desperate he became. Forsaking the last vestige of decency, he made the rounds with the begging bowl. Yet all he managed to buy with the borrowing was time. If he did not clear his gambling debts, the repercussions were too horrific to contemplate. Now that he was cornered, he wanted to opt out leaving us to fend for ourselves.

Rajan was a despicable rat, trying to take advantage of my predicament. I had yet to learn that this was the way in which the world functioned. All he lacked was subtlety. Why, even doctors, members of the so-called noble profession, thrived on the misery of others. I was not ready to surrender as yet, but Rajan was not unduly perturbed. The bird was in the net and he could let her think that she had a choice. He had discussed the matter with the Station House officer (SHO) who knew of such a gang that fleeced people by playing upon their greed. He wanted MS to lodge a FIR (first information report), after which they would conduct a police raid and catch the culprits red-handed. MS chickened out, for he was afraid of antagonising them. I agreed with MS, for documented evidence against them would further endanger our lives. Rajan thought otherwise for the police believed, that cheats were just cheats and did not commit murder.

'But they can hire murderers,' I wailed.

'Then the police are helpless. With all the propaganda against police atrocities, they are not willing to act unless they get a written complaint.'

Meanwhile, Mr Saini acted surely and swiftly. All that MS knew was that the second-in-command lived somewhere in Bali Nagar. The goons of that area were contacted, his address located and for a fee, they gave him a thrashing that made him leave the area for good. Bullies are chickens when it comes to their own hides. As for the leader, he landed up in hospital in the terminal stages of liver cirrhosis and died a few days later. The gang broke up and would terrorise us no longer, but how was I to know? MS was too secretive to confide in me and unlike Rajan, Mr Saini was too much of a gentleman to rub it in. I learnt of this, years later (when the damage Rajan could do was already done), during a casual conversation with the Sainis. Mr Saini was surprised that MS had not told me a thing. If I had known, I would not be at the mercy of Rajan and much misery would have been avoided. As of now, he was my only link with the 'case'.

Meanwhile, I was doing that much 'extra' to help them conceive. I was performing artificial insemination husband (AIH) on Snehlata on the day of ovulation. Those were not the days of test tube babies and other elaborate artificial reproductive techniques. The good sperms of a split ejaculate were inserted into the wife's vagina to improve success rates. Rajan brought her to the polyclinic in Cannought Place which I visited on alternate mornings. On account of a bomb scare, there were not many patients; in fact, most of the staff too was absent. While Rajan sized up the situation, I was unaware of the fact.

After the semen insertion, Snehlata lay in the treatment room for half an hour with her hips raised. In the meantime, I took Rajan to my chamber for an update on my husband's activities. He enjoyed playing cat and mouse with me, and was in no hurry to answer my queries. Irrelevantly he asked, 'What are those flowers in your hair?'

'Jasmines,' I said fingering the sprig.

'You like them.'

'Yes,' I replied, resigned to the fact that only after a bit of flirtation would I be able to extract some useful information from him.

'Then I'll send you a basket of jasmines every day all the year around.'

'They grow only in the summer.' It was all I could do to hide my annoyance, but forced myself to humour him. At last, when I could bear it no longer, I asked him to update me on MS's affairs.

'Leave everything to me. You are interested in the results, you'll get them.'

'I'd like to know the details.'

'Doctor Sahib has given in writing that he owes them so much money. With this piece of paper in their custody, we can't register a case against them.'

'O my God!' I exclaimed clasping my head in my hands.

'How you suffer? Now you'll get an inkling of *my* sufferings.'

How detestable could a man get? He had neither tact nor compassion. I got up to leave. In one fluid motion he stationed himself in front of the closed door. Though my heart lurched, I pretended nonchalance.

'I'll repay all your loans for just one . . .' He didn't actually say the word but pursed his lips suggestively.

'You wouldn't dare?' I gasped.

'It has taken me five long years to dare.'

The audacity of the man! Even as I was appalled at the idea, I was unaccountably aroused. Shocked by the betrayal of my body, I tried to flee.

'Let me go or I'll shout for help.'

'You won't.'

'O yes, I will.'

'I'll clamp my hand on your mouth,' he said advancing menacingly.

I did not back away. He had almost reached me when we heard a step in the corridor. At this my tormentor started for he had counted on us being alone. A moment's slack was all that I needed to make good my escape.

That was that. Not a hundred phone calls stating that he was sorry, that he did not know what overcame him (indeed!), not the tears he shed, not the basket of jasmines he sent could appease me. I was done with him and his 'help'.

I told my husband to have no further dealings with Mr Rajan Bhardwaj. He did not bother to ask why. By this time I had realised that it was no use pursuing mirages. Even if we got the crooks booked, we wouldn't recover the money. What was gone was gone. Rajan was only using the situation to his advantage. We should concentrate on repaying the loans and get on with life. This time I pawned my jewellery to repay his debts. Not because I was a devoted wife, but because I could not bear to be beholden to anyone. I told MS that this was the last time I was bailing him out. Once again he repeated his bedtime story of what a bad man he was, and how could he repay what I had done for him? I told him that there was a way. Though the nursing home-cum-residence was built largely on my income, it was in his name; I wanted joint ownership. He agreed readily enough.

This time, whether it embarrassed him or not, I went with MS to return the money to his creditors, warning them that the next time they lent him anything it would be at their own risk. MS stood by shamefacedly taking the insult. Incidentally, after the debts were cleared, MS did not keep his part of the bargain. He had neatly tricked me once again.

34

We finally had a home and a nursing home of our own. An ambitious project had been completed and I was filled with no mean sense of achievement. The house warming, on Guru Nanak's birthday, was a success.

My husband's uncle, Professor Jogi, walked up to my father and said, 'Today my conscience is at rest. I always felt guilty about plucking a hothouse flower and throwing her in the backyard of traders. At last, Rosy will be living in the setting she deserves.' Jogi Mama (as we called him) was responsible for arranging the match from my husband's side.

A few days later, the eunuchs came to demand their due. With painted lips, thrusting breasts, and stubbled chins, they crowded the front verandah swirling their tasselled skirts and clapping their hands in that peculiar manner of theirs. The oldest amongst them settled on a chair, put a bidi between her discoloured lips, and blew the smoke on our faces.

'Pay up,' she demanded. They usually demanded money at the birth of a son, but as the number of children people delivered these days had dwindled, they took to asking money for new buildings too.

'How much?'

'A crisp 500 rupees note or we'll strip naked right here.'

It was an atrocious demand!

Mataji delved into my purse and took out Rs. 50.

'This is all you'll get.'

'Indeed!' said the one in shocking pink. To our horror, she lifted her skirt high and danced round and round, showing us whatever little there was to see.

'We have no penis, no vagina, look, look, look, all of you look,' she chanted. The entire crowd had its eyes riveted to her non-existent private parts. When another loosened the string of her *salwar* and slipped it down her hairy legs, we were truly alarmed.

'How much do you want?' I asked quickly.

'Rs 251/- and not a paisa less,' said the old crone who had been through such bargainings a thousand times before.

'We don't have that much money on us at the moment.'

'We don't have that much money . . .' she mimicked. 'Were you washed ashore on a flood that you have not paisa on you?'

'I really don't . . .'

'If you don't hand over the money right away,' said another, 'I'll bang my head against the wall till it bursts.'

'You won't dare!' I challenged. At this, she laughed and did exactly as she had threatened, her face contorted in masochistic ecstasy. Rivulets of blood ran down the white washed wall. I was horrified. The orgy of blood and exposure of sexless sexual parts was getting on my nerves.

'Please tell us how much do you want?' I beseeched.

'Rs 100/- and a sari.'

Hurriedly, I complied.

Having got their due, they indulged in song and dance, but I was much too shaken to enjoy it. I turned my attention to the quiet one in the corner who intrigued me.

'Is there no way you can earn your living with dignity?' I asked.

'No.'

'Do you remember your natural parents?'

'Yes. I was fortunate or unfortunate (whichever way you look at it) to be "discovered" at 16 years of age. Ten years have passed since then. Now I am a misfit in both worlds.'

My eyes misted over.

'I wish I could help you in some way.'

'You are the only one who has recognised me as a human being. That is more than enough for me. I'll remember you in my prayers,' she said.

I was touched. My problems were nothing compared to hers and yet she had the magnanimity to pray for me.

It took us some time to get adjusted to our new environments. As the colony was not fully developed, civic amenities were poor. It was not easy to locate a plumber or an electrician when needed. Though the houses were few and far, my practice picked up fast due to the paucity of medical facilities in the new area.

We went through a lot of teething troubles though. An incident in those early years left an indelible scar on my psyche. The nursing home was full. A patient, trying to switch on a fan, got an electric shock! She screamed out aloud. Her family, understandably in a state of panic, raised a hue and cry. Other patients collected in the lounge wanting to leave immediately. I got the main switched off and pacified them as best as I could.

'What if such a thing happened in your own home? Would you desert the house?' I asked. 'Bear with me for a while. We'll call the electrician and everything will be sorted out.'

Reluctantly, they went back to their rooms. I rushed upstairs, told MS what had transpired and urged him to look for an electrician immediately. He was getting ready to leave for his clinic which was a good twelve kilometres away, as he had not shifted practice.

'I am already late,' he said.

I glared at him disbelievingly. 'This is an emergency.'

'I don't have the time.'

'If something happens to the patients downstairs, will you have the time to make the rounds of the courtroom? If I die of an electric shock will you have the time to cremate me? Moreover, what's the hurry to rush to those ten-rupee patients of yours?' It was the first time I had taunted him, but I couldn't help myself. I was furious.

He tried to brush past me. I held the lapel of his coat and screamed, 'How can you desert me at a time like this?'

'*Janda marda paya hanh,*' he said.

'*Pher jaldi jaoo maro,*' I said.

At this, he began raining blows upon me! In a state of shock, I stood there taking the beating. After he had expended his fury, he pushed past me and drove off. I was devastated. What had I done to provoke him? I had asked a man to do a man's job. How dare he hit me for that! I wondered why I did not hit him back. Perhaps it was the unexpectedness of it all; perhaps I was all talk and no action.

I desperately wanted to run away but realised with a shock that I had nowhere to go. My parents would not accommodate me. I could not live alone elsewhere for I had no capital to fall back on. I had invested all I had in this building and it was not even on my name. My source of income was in the nursing home downstairs and most important of all, there were the children to consider. Not for anything in the world could I forsake them.

In the evening, I sat watching a movie on TV with my kids. Divorce proceedings were going on in a courtroom scene. I casually asked them if anyone in their class had divorced parents.

'One teacher and one child's parents are divorced,' replied Karan.

'If your parents are divorced, who would you stay with?'

'You Mamma,' said 8-year-old Simar without a moment's hesitation.

Karan, who was 4 years older, was not ready to accept such a situation.

'You wouldn't dare to . . . ?'

'No, but suppose . . .'

'I couldn't hurt any of you. I'll let the court decide.'

'But you have to give preferences.'

'I can't.'

'You'll be better off with your grandmother,' I replied, hurt that he had not chosen me instantly, as his younger brother had.

MS apologised profusely on his return, dramatically offering to cut off his hand if it would appease me. Nothing he said made any difference. Things would never be the same between us ever again. From his one-sided conversation, I gleaned that my saying *jayo maro* had infuriated him so. How could an Indian wife think of telling her lord and master to 'go and die'? Indeed! I could have murdered him myself if I had something handy. Which era was he living in? I was fed up of pampering his eggshell ego.

How long could an emancipated mind remain a slave to traditions made by men to suit men? Why should I bow down to one I did not look up to, just because he was my husband? I refused to become the ideal Indian wife, akin to a blob of dough—fair, soft, malleable, and brainless. Perhaps my concept of a marriage was wrong. I thought it was all about sharing and caring. I knew now that, at best, it was a social anchor, a prerequisite for legitimate sex and parenthood; at worst, a life imprisonment with compromise the key punishment. One by one I had castrated into mules, the horses of my emotions, desires and needs, to no avail. Any attempt to exert my independence gave me nothing but hurt, pain, and now the final ignominy—a beating!

If only I could leave, but we were stuck together like frozen sausages and nothing could pry us apart. With the weight of a dead relationship dragging my feet, I stayed put A sense of bereavement overwhelmed me. For the last time, I cried over the corpse of my marriage., With my individuality buried, my spirit crushed, I sat at the bend of Time, watching the river of Life pass me by.

35

In our perambulations around the newly built colony, we came across an intriguing construction site. A huge house was being built on the lines of a film set. It had a large central hall with a high ceiling that had ostentation written on it in gilt and plaster. From either side at the back, ornate stairs curved to the upper chambers. Curious, we went in to investigate. The house belonged to a Mr Brij Batra. Introductions were made, soft drinks offered, and the premises inspected.

Despite his obvious riches, I did not think much of Mr Batra. He was in his late fifties and ugly as sin. Besides a balding head, he had a forward jutting lower jaw and a mouth full of crooked teeth. His sons were newer editions of him. To ensure a better progeny Mr Batra had, on the strength on his money, acquired good looking wives for them. He also had a grandson of Karan's age.

He returned our call a week later and we passed a pleasant half an hour together. After that, it was a box of sweetmeats and an invitation for their housewarming. Then a servant sustained a minor injury and Mr Brij Batra brought him over for dressing and a shot of tetanus. When he bought us passes for a cine star night, I thought that he wanted to maintain cordial relationship with the local doctor, as people did since my grandfather's time. He also introduced us to Dr Raman, a young physician with a pleasing personality who attended to Uncleji medical needs. Dr Raman began admitting patients in my nursing to our mutual benefit.

Though I called him Uncleji, Mr Batra did not see me quite in the light of a 'niece'. Over the years, he had honed his seduction skills, perfecting them to an art form. He came frequently to get his blood pressure (BP) checked and befriended my nurses. One day, he came with a camera slung over his shoulder and offered to take their pictures. Now, no woman on earth can resist being photographed. As he was clicking, in I walked. One thing led to another and the nurses wanted a photo with their madam. So I got myself photographed with my staff. When the films were developed, he came upstairs to our living quarters to deliver them.

As I was thanking him, Simar rushed in and said, 'Uncleji, tomorrow is my Happy Birthday. You must come with a present.'

'Simar!' I exclaimed, embarrassed. Turning to Uncleji I said, 'We aren't doing anything elaborate. He'll cut the cake in the presence of close relatives that's all.' politely letting him know, that he was not invited.

Despite this not too subtle hint, I was surprised to see Mr Brij Batra at the party. If Simar was disappointed with the lack of a conventional present, the rest of us weren't. Photography was his hobby and he had come with a loaded camera. As he began taking pictures, I was called downstairs for an emergency. By the time I finished, he had already left. I was a wee bit disappointed as I had hardly been photographed. He returned a week later with the pictures. They had come out rather well. I gazed at them wistfully. I was in my early thirties. In a few years, my looks would fade and I had no record for posterity. Except for an occasional picture on Diwali, I had hardly been photographed. With a sigh, I opened my purse to pay Uncleji for his services. He was deeply offended.

'This is my birthday present and I am not a professional photographer. By God's grace I have a flourishing business.'

I thanked him and accepted the gift gracefully.

'You are hardly there in these pictures. I'll come over some day and take a reel especially of you . . .' When I looked up sharply he added, 'With the kids.'

'Please don't bother,' I said, but not vehemently enough for photographs with my children were something I longed for. I did so want to capture their innocence. Uncleji kept his promise and I had my wish. He clicked his first picture as I opened the door. I was acutely embarrassed but gradually I relaxed and posed with narcissistic delight. Thinking that it would be the only time that I would get such an opportunity, I was vain enough to change into various outfits. He asked me undo my hair so that my ringlets cascaded down my back. I complied readily enough. Positioning me in front of the mirror so that the light shone like a halo around my head, he clicked furiously. When the children returned from school, there were pictures with them, too. I was completely satisfied.

A few days later, he returned with the enlarged photos in a golden album. I gasped with pleasure when I saw them, for he had brought out the best in me. Over the months he began to make a habit out of photographing me which alarmed me. The charm had worn off. I no longer hankered for images of myself, but he was like a man possessed.

Besides embarrassing me, Mr Batra spent a lot of effort and money in projecting the right image in our society. He got marble statues of various gods and goddesses for the local mandir and invited the entire colony for *murtisthapna*—the infusion of life in the stone statues of deities by the chanting of Sanskrit slokas and sprinkling of *Gangajal* (holy water from the Ganges) so that they become worthy of worship. This was followed by a sumptuous *langar*, sponsored by him. He was spoken well of and people vied with each other to be counted amongst his friends. We were amongst the few *he* favoured. It was an honour I did not fancy. I did have a penchant for attracting unsuitable men. Was I leading Uncleji on? No. In fact he repelled me, then why this unwarranted attention by a man old enough to be my father? He made it a point to come in my husband's absence till I was forced to remind him about the propriety of such visits. After this, he took to coming in *my* absence and leaving something or the other for me with the nurses. It was preposterous! Why should I take anything from him? How could he even think of having any romantic notions regarding me? When I instructed the nurses not to take anything from him on my behalf, he had the temerity to follow me to the polyclinic where he insisted that I take this last gift.

'*No.*' I was being deliberately rude but there was no other way.

'Give it to your maid if you wish, but please don't refuse.' he beseeched.

'Have you no shame? You have a grandson my son's age and yet . . .'

He told me that I had bewitched him, that I had robbed him of his peace of mind, that though I wasn't his first love, I certainly was his last!

Disgusted, I walked away. I had a battered old Fiat in those days. One of its windows wouldn't close. I kept postponing repairs, joking that whoever robbed this old jalopy would be doing me a favour. When I finished OPD, a good two hours later, I found the present in my car!

I stopped answering his phone calls or acknowledging his presence at colony meetings, but he had not built such a large business by accepting defeat so easily. He rang up my husband and invited us to a party the following Sunday. I told MS that it would be best for all concerned if we had no further contact with him. His intentions were questionable.

'It's your fault. You led him on with your poses and photos.'

'I agree, but I didn't dream that it would come to this. Surely you don't believe that I encouraged him!'

'But I have already accepted.'

'So what? We won't be at home on Sunday. We'll have dinner out and return late.'

We hadn't reckoned with Uncle's perseverance. We returned by 10.30 p.m. I had changed and was lying in bed when the phone rang. It was Uncle. I had stopped suffixing the respectful 'ji' even in my thoughts.

'Why haven't you come till now?'

'I am sorry but my parents called us over. We've had dinner there.'

'Drop in for a while.'

'Sorry, but it's impossible.'

'I have arranged the party specifically for you. I will not start dinner till you come.'

'This is ridiculous. I have told you that we have already had dinner,' I said and put the phone down.

It rang again. This time it was Dr Raman pleading his case. 'We have to stay hungry on your account.' I explained the situation as civilly as I could and hung up.

'You pick up the phone if it rings again.' I told MS. 'Refuse politely. It's different if a man says so.'

Sure enough it rang again. I do not know what transpired between the two, but to my amazement MS said, 'Hurry up and get dressed. We are going.'

What sort of a man was he? Wasn't it his responsibility to protect the honour of his wife? Agreed, vanity made me do things beyond the realms of propriety but when I tried to extricate myself from the morass, MS was pushing me further in it. I was filled with contempt so profound that I could have spat on him.

'You are despicable,' I declared. 'How could you accept the invitation when you know . . .' The humiliation of seeing Uncle gloat over my defeat was more than I could bear.

'I do not want to antagonise Mr Batra. He is a very influential man.'

'So?'

'God knows how he will react if we rebuff him.'

'You are a coward.'

'If I am a coward it is because of you.'

'What do you mean?'

'God knows in what poses you have got yourself photographed. What if he makes them public?'

'You know me better than that,' I said, stung to the core. 'I may have acted foolishly, but I know the distinction between propriety and indecent exposure.'

'Suppose he superimposes your face upon the nude body of another and circulates it in the colony?'

'Why would he do that?'

'Out of spite.'

'As long as I know and you know, it doesn't matter what the rest of the world thinks. Surely you will be able to differentiate my naked body from that of a morphed one.'

What sort of a man was MS? Did he not have one redeeming factor? I had come to terms with the rest, but this—this was the final straw that broke the camel's back.

36

At last it dawned upon me that my husband was neither protector nor provider. He was but a figurehead from whom I could expect nothing. It was a realisation that heralded the end of all quarrels. Expectations ceased, and with them my tears and rancour. I freed myself from my dependence upon him.

Cutting my losses, I decided to go ahead with life. I looked for and found pleasure in simple things. Every Saturday I set out with my sister, her kids, my kids, and a picnic lunch for some historical site in or around Delhi—Jantar Mantar, Birla Mandir, India Gate, Qutub Minar, or Red Fort. The children tread upon the footprints of history and gleaned more about bygone eras than they could from textbooks. Through these excursions, I too acquainted myself with the city I had inhabited but never really known. I was fascinated by the perfect blend of ancient and modern, her multifaceted personality, and was proud to reside in one of the oldest living cities in the world.

At other times, it was in the lap of nature in places like Buddha Jayanti Park where the kids frolicked or climbed trees, while we walked on flower-fringed pavements. After lunch, we'd lie on the soft grass, look up at the cloud-flecked skies, or doze for a while, breathing in the pure fresh air.

We went to Chandigarh to attend the marriage of Jeeju's only daughter, Reena. It was a beautiful city—green and serene. I had long since forgiven him his trespasses for he never crossed the line after that. When Jeeju asked me to leave the congested, polluted capital and start practice here, I laughed.

'I'll have to be a botanist to succeed here. There are more plants than people around.'

It was in Chandigarh that I finally discovered my roots. Though a Sikh, I had no sense of belonging. On account of Daddy's transferable job, we never stayed at one place long enough to strike roots; and Delhi, where I had settled after marriage, was much too cosmopolitan. For the first time I was exposed to the richness of Punjabi culture. There were energetic gidhas by fair-skinned, firm-bodied girls. Naughty songs belittled the mother-in-law and eulogised the flirtatious relationship between *devar* (brother-in-law) and *bhabi* (sister-in-law). The ladies *sangeet* (music) was supposedly an all-women's affair, but we knew that the men were watching us, and the men knew that we knew. In a conservative society where segregation of the sexes is a norm, on occasions such as these, boys and girls of marriageable age could intermingle. Many an alliance was forged during marriages without the demeaning ritual of 'showing' the girl.

Romance was in the soil, in the very air we breathed, but my husband seemed to be immune to it. He preferred sitting with a glass of whisky and tandoori chicken instead of joining in the fun and frolic. I realised with a shock that, despite what had happened, I was totally dependent upon him to satisfy my physical needs. A married Indian woman had hardly any choice.

Reena, all of 19 years, was eager as any youngster for the pleasures of marriage. In the two months of her engagement, and she had often been 'manhandled' by her ardent fiancé.

'There are many a slip between the cup and the lip' I had told her sagaciously. 'Such licence is not becoming for a girl from a respectable family. Before you know it, he'll seduces you then ditch you for being a girl of loose morals.'

She laughed with the recklessness of youth and pestered me for details regarding the facts of life. She wanted to know where the clitoris was situated. I explained as best as I could.

She locked herself in the bathroom and emerged after a while, perplexed.

'Perhaps I don't have one,' she said woefully as I doubled over in mirth.

'Never mind,' I said. 'We'll leave it to your husband to find the hidden jewel.'

It was a joyous gathering. As far as arrangements were concerned, Jeeju surpassed himself. The spread was lavish, as was the dowry. The groom was handsome; the bride radiant. The transformation at the time of *doli* was startling. People who had joked and laughed a moment ago, dissolved into tears as if instant geysers had been turned on. I have yet to see a place more desolate than a house after a daughter's wedding. With red-rimmed eyes, we crept about talking in whispers. Even the children were subdued finding something amiss in the atmosphere. Simar vowed that he would never marry, if it meant leaving his home! The little fellow did not know that *he* would be bringing his bride home.

Soon, we returned to Delhi and drudgery. MS did not know how to drive a car (till his sister forced him to learn eight years later), and upon me fell the responsibility of ferrying relatives from the airport or railway station in my second-hand Fiat, while he moved around on a scooter. On a late winter evening, my car broke down a mere kilometre from MS's clinic, which was a good twelve kilometres from our home. I rang him up and asked him to come urgently with a mechanic.

'Where will I get a mechanic at this hour?' he said.

'But we have to do something. I am stranded at Shadipur Depot, which you know is not a nice place for a lady to be stranded in.' Night fell early in winter months and a dense shroud of smog added to the danger.

'I cannot leave the clinic,' he said and put the phone down. I never thought that there was any scope for MS getting more despicable than he already was, but he managed to prove me wrong. Why, any stranger would help a lady in such a predicament and he wasn't bothered about his own wife!

I rang my sister to enlist the help of *her* husband, but he was in South Delhi on business and would take a long time to come. I had half a mind to leave the car and go home by a three-wheeler, but the loss would be mine, in case it was stolen. Mustering courage, I looked for and finally found a mechanic in the lane behind the shops. There were no streetlights there, and it was pitch-black. A resigned recklessness, a fatalism would wash over me whenever MS landed me in such a situation. If my husband was not concerned about the welfare of his own wife, why should I bother? Luckily, nothing untoward happened and within 45 minutes, my car was roadworthy again.

Circumstances had forced me to forge a new personality. I learnt to manage affairs that women usually depended upon their husbands for, be it banking, insurance, and income tax. All major decisions concerning my practice, I made on my own, be it new equipment for the clinic or an attachment to a hospital. I learnt to take my car for repairs to the local mechanic whenever necessary and got used to being ogled at by black-faced mechanics for ladies did not go to garages in those days. I had come a long way from the timid girl who could not go to the college bathroom alone.

37

Was this all there was to life? Were hard work, ingratitude, and disharmony my lot? Was I not entitled to love, companionship, care, or compassion? Despite evidence to the contrary, I dared to sow the seed of hope in the harsh unyielding soil of reality. A hostile sun desiccated it still further. Just when I thought I could bear it no longer, the seasons turned. Clouds gathered in my heart, rained from my eyes, giving birth to little saplings of desire. I burned with a need to be needed.

My birthday dawned in the middle of May. Not a soul wished me. My husband forgot as usual, the children were with their grandparents at Mussoorie, and cards from my parents and siblings hadn't reached me yet. Was there no one on this earth who was happy that I was born? Cold was the company of an empty house in the heat of summer. Waves of self-pity washed over me. To stem the tears that threatened to spill, I opened a cupboard, flung out the clothes, and set about tidying it with meticulous care. My idea of a birthday was a weekend away from the maddening crowd. If for some reason that was not possible—to be woken in the morning with a kiss and flowers, receive a gorgeous sari or a small piece of jewellery, go out for a movie and dinner, and finally to bed, replete in my beloved's arms. Simple enough pleasures that most married couples indulged in. And here I was, cleaning a cockroach-infested cupboard for want of anything better to do.

Rajan Bhardwaj couldn't have chosen a more opportune moment to re-enter my life. It was a year since I had banished him for misbehaving. At any other time, I would not have tolerated his presence. Today I could forgive him murder. To think that of all the people in my life, he was the only one who remembered my birthday! My heart overflowed with gratitude. I sat amidst the heap of crumpled clothes, grinning from ear to ear. With feminine vanity, to my hand flew my unruly curls. Close on his heels, came his driver carrying a pot with a flowering jasmine. He remembered that I loved jasmines, but a plant! Never mind, it was the thought that mattered. A number of exotic potted plants followed. I was overwhelmed but that wasn't all. As a coup de grace, he pulled out a red velvet box. There was limit to what a woman would accept from a man who was not her husband (not that my husband gave me anything), and this was beyond limits. I refused to touch it.

'At least have a look.'

'What's the use? I will not accept it.'

He opened it to reveal a beautiful gold necklace, chunky, and ethnic.

'I am sorry, but no means no.'

'Don't worry, there are no strings attached. Here, let me put it around your neck.'

The man was incorrigible. He sure knew how to overdo things. Nevertheless, contact was resumed and we fell into the old routine of treatment spiced with audacious flirting. Perhaps I was partly to blame. It felt nice to be desired so. God knows how I craved attention, and it wasn't forthcoming from legitimate quarters.

What attracted me to my unlikely suitor was the fact that he was the complete antithesis of my husband. His generosity set MS's miserliness to a disadvantage. He was fearless while MS was a 'poor thing' who had to be looked after by the likes of me. He was daring while MS was cautious to a fault. Rajan caught the bull of life by the horns; MS skirted it. Most important of all, he made me feel *alive*.

A few days later, he came in a blue matador and said, 'I have brought it to my goddess for blessings.'

'I am no goddess. Moreover, what has my approval to do with it?'

'Just have a look,' he said. Inviting me to admire its interior, he whisked me away. My protests regarding the propriety of such a move fell on deaf ears. He was like a child showing off a new toy.

At a turn, he braked suddenly and my head hit the windshield.

'An earnest wish has been realised today,' he said.

'What, throwing me off balance?'

'That I've been trying to do unsuccessfully for years.'

'Then what?'

'I longed to have you by my side while I drove.'

Before I could think of an answer, he stopped on a lonely stretch of road and said, 'I will be honoured if you drive.'

'But I couldn't. It's too cumbersome. I've never . . .'

'O yes, you can. I'm with you, *phiker* (worry) not.'

Strangely reassured, I got into the driver's seat. After wobbling for a while, I got the hang of it. It was as if I had driven a matador all my life. The wind in my hair, the smooth black road slipping beneath me, an attractive, adoring man by my side was a great turn on. Every fibre of my being was tinglingly alive. All of a sudden, he threw back his head and laughed. His teeth flashed like lightning on his bronzed face. He was enjoying himself thoroughly. To my surprise, I realised that so was I. The speed, laced with guilt and fear, was a heady cocktail.

'Let's go to Badkal Lake,' he broke into my thoughts.

'Well, let me see,' I said, shockingly playing the tease.

'You'll really come?' he was wild with joy.

'Sorry, no.'

'Why? Don't you trust me?'

'I can trust you with my life, but not with my virtue. Let's go back before my reputation is soiled for no reason.'

Left to him he would have gladly provided the reason. By now, guilt had weighed down the exhilaration and I worried that my absence may have been noticed. Going downhill was much more difficult. I asked him to change places with me, but the very devil was in him. The vehicle lurched and tilted precariously. It would have overturned had he not gripped the steering wheel in time. I almost clutched his sleeve in fear, but even when my life depended upon it, propriety came in the way of holding on to a man who was not my husband.

'This could have been the end of both of us,' I said aloud.

'Like in the movie "Silsila",' he said gleefully, totally unafraid.

'We don't even have the excuse of love like Amitabh and Rekha.'

'Speak for yourself.' He grinned.

Repeated attempts at AIH (artificial insemination husband) failed on account of Rajan's poor sperm count. He had given up his philandering ways but no baby ensued. Each time his wife had her periods, he would go into a fit of depression. God knows I was doing my level best. Tentatively, I suggested artificial insemination donor (AID). He bristled like a porcupine and left the clinic in a huff. The heavens had indeed been cruel to him and hung him halfway—taking away the faculty of reproduction while retaining hope. My heart went out to him.

38

He is like a cobra, fascinating and lethal. He has the cunning of a fox, the hide of an elephant and the grace of a panther; the body of an Adonis, and the heart of a child. I am drawn to him against my better judgement. I know him to be a liar, a cheat, a rogue, and a rake, and yet I cannot bring myself to dislike him. I hate it when he acts fresh, and hate it still more when he doesn't. I have no intention of giving in to him, and yet I thrive on his need for me. I am outraged at his audacity and yet am thrilled by the liberties he takes. My rebuffs deter him not one whit. I like his daring and perseverance. Most importantly, I like him because he desires me as no other man ever did. He is the enigma called Rajan.

It's exhilarating to walk on the edge of a cliff. He is as determined to push me over as I am not to fall. The battle has been raging for years, yet neither side is ready to concede defeat. I am content to let matters continue so indefinitely but he will settle for nothing less than victory or death. At this point of time, if someone had told me that I would succumb to lust one day, I would have slapped that person's face. Why, I still fancied myself in love with Rajiv Mehra, and I still believed in the sanctity of marriage vows. All the same, it felt nice to be pursued by an attractive man. I had done with loving and rejections.

On his birthday, I wrote a poem for him. It was a noncommittal, unsigned document that wished him the best in life and the satisfaction of his heart's desire. In short, I prayed that God give him the child he longed for. The next day he rang up.

'If there is anything I can do for you, you have only to tell me,' he said with fervour. 'My heart, my soul, my life is at your disposal.'

'How can I take so much of your anatomy without giving anything in return?' I could have kicked myself for making such a provocative statement.

'But you can give me something.'

'My heart and body are pledged to another.'

'I want none of those.'

'Then what is it that you want?' I asked intrigued.

'You can give me your word?'

I did not answer.

'Hello, are you still there?'

'Yes,' I said slowly.

'If that is too much, can you give me a . . .'

'What?' I waited with bated breath.

'A thought.'

Thoughts I had given him in plenty, but I wasn't going to confess.

'What good will that do?'

'That is for me to decide.'

Fed up of the protracted, unrewarding treatment, his wife adopted her brother's newborn son. They invited us for the christening ceremony. Observing our reluctance for MS was not too keen, he insisted on picking us up. So it came about that on a beautiful February morning I found myself seated in the backseat of his car with his wife, while MS sat with him in front. We discussed the weather and politics like a couple of family friends. No one suspected the undercurrents of passion. I watched the muscles of his forearm ripple under his smooth brown skin as he drove. Occasionally, our eyes met in the rear view mirror and sparks would fly. His glance slid over me, thick and warm like honey. The string of sexual tension was pulled taut just short of snapping.

The party was in full swing. We blessed the little boy who had been christened Sonu. My husband filled his plate with snacks and sat glued to the cricket match on TV. Snehlata busied herself with the guests. Rajan took this opportunity to show me the additional floor they had recently built. On the wall of their bedroom was an enlarged photograph taken on their marriage anniversary. Even in the picture, his vibrant vitality contrasted vividly with her mousy dullness. He was a river in spate while she, a dirt water drain.

On the return journey, he drove with the speed of a bullock-cart. It was as if he was reluctant to let go. In the post-lunch somnolence, no one spoke. He put on a cassette. Amitabh Bachan's deep baritone echoed Rajan's thoughts.

'Main aur mere tanhai aksar ye baate karte hai, tum hoti toan ye hota tum hoti toan voh hota . . . kyon na dinuya ko bata dey mohabbat hai, mohabbat hai, mohabbat hai. (Me and my solitude often converse–if you were there this would happen, if you were there that would happen . . . why not tell the world we were in love, in love in love)'

If it was unbridled lust before, it was gentle romance while returning. It was uncanny how this male animal struck an answering cord in my heart. Back home, reason reasserted itself. Away from the sheer force of his physical presence, the delirium subsided. I steered the foaming horses of temptation to conformation by the stinging whip of conscience. Yet it was but a battle won. The war still raged on. This was not love, not even lust, but something infinitely more lethal. Tidal waves of passion broke against the rock of resistance. How long could opposing forces remain in a state of flux? One of them *had* to give way and it has been seen that water eventually erodes rock.

I felt it was best to avoid him. If I could only tide over time till our impending European tour, I would be free of him. I had much to occupy my mind, but he remained at the back of it like a shadow on the wall. I tried to dispel all thoughts of him and almost succeeded. After all, who was he—an upstart, trying to gain entry into the upper echelons of society, through the back door, in a backhanded manner. He was common and coarse, a type I positively detested. I was well rid of his disturbing influence.

On the day of our departure, I busied myself with the last minute packing. The June sun sent in waves of shimmering heat. The doorbell rang, and Rajan Bhardwaj stood on the threshold. His sexuality smote me afresh. My resolve came crumbling down though I managed to keep a cool exterior.

'I have come to wish you bon voyage.'

'Thank you.'

I stood at the door barring his entrance. He pretended not to get the message and asked.

'Can I have a glass of water?'

Ashamed of my rudeness, I let him in.

'I have brought you a farewell present.'

'I'm sorry, I cannot accept anything from you.'

He opened the box to reveal a fine gold chain. He *did* have the knack of converting pleasure instantly into rage. As he extended the box towards me I flung it away. The bathroom door was ajar and the chain slipped irretrievably into the Indian toilet! Before we could react, my husband arrived. After exchanging pleasantries, he went to the bedroom to rest in preparation of the long night of travel ahead. Within five minutes, he was snoring, oblivious to the high drama being enacted in the adjoining room.

'I'm sorry, I'm so very sorry, but you shouldn't have provoked me so.' I apologised.

'It doesn't matter, forget it.'

The silence between us crackled with electricity.

'I have a request to make,' he said after a while.

'What?'

'I would like to shake hands with you.'

'But, but . . .' I sputtered. Till now whatever interaction I had had with him was verbal.

'It will cost you nothing and give me immense pleasure. Everyone does it where you are going.'

'I do not cease to be an Indian because I am going abroad.'

'Please.'

'No.'

'I refuse to budge till you shake hands with me,' he said.

Making himself comfortable on the sofa, he began flipping through the pages of a magazine. I walked into the bedroom and lay down by my husband. I looked at his sleeping form with loathing. I needed him to save me from temptation, and he slept on unconcerned. The audacity of one man and the indifference of the other were driving me mad. Acutely aware of the intruder, I could not rest. Fifteen minutes passed with excruciating slowness. What if my husband woke up and found him still there? I hated him for making me feel guilty without reason. Unable to bear the tension any longer, I got up. After all, what was there in a handshake? Might as well get it over and done with. Hadn't I shaken hands with people before, but Rajan did not belong to the strata of society that believed in handshakes. I got up, walked up to him and held out my hand. Within a fraction of a second it was engulfed in his huge paw. To my horror, he wouldn't let go. With slow deliberation he raised it to his lips. It was the first kiss a man other than my husband had given me. The feel of his lips on the back of my hand stayed with me throughout the tour.

39

Though Rajan accepted Sonu, he still longed for a child of his own flesh and blood. On my return, he asked me to resume treatment.

'You will have to abide by the rules I set,' I said sternly.

'What are they?'

'You have to maintain the dignity of the doctor-patient relationship.'

'Yes, ma'am.'

'You will talk and behave decorously.'

'Yes, ma'am.'

'You will not try to touch me on any pretext.'

'Can I look at you?' he asked, shaking with silent laughter.

I hated him for making a farce of the whole thing, and flung a paperweight at him, which he deftly avoided. My rules and regulations mattered not a whit. I smiled, unable to help myself. Despite his flirtatious behaviour, I knew that if I were in trouble, he was the one person I could depend upon.

Whenever I appeared distracted, Rajan would say, 'You have only to tell me of your problems to get rid of them.'

This time I said, '*You* are my problem. If only I could get rid of you.'

'You could shoot me,' he said. Unbuckling his revolver, he laid it on the table.

'Please be serious for once.'

'I am in dead earnest.'

'You profess to love me?'

'I cannot help it.'

'You know that your feelings are not reciprocated.'

'It doesn't make any difference.'

'Why don't you go elsewhere for treatment? As for your "love", can't you love me silently from afar without trying to wreck my life? Promise, you will never see me again.'

'Don't ask the impossible out of me.'

'Surely you would not like to disgrace me?'

'I promise,' he said and left without a backward glance.

Where was the relief I ought to feel? It hurt me to hurt him who loved me as I had always dreamt of being loved. Well, the love of a lifetime had come too late from quarters I did not appreciate. I knew that I had done the right thing in sending him away, but did not feel noble or good about it.

Now that I had banished him from my life, a lingering fondness remained. Like of a dead person, I retained only the happy memories. I forgot his annoying persistence and lack of sophistication. I remembered the selfless devotion, the eagerness to please. Though I knew I would get over it in time I missed his attention for whatever it was worth.

Rajan was back exactly a fortnight later! The blood froze in my veins even as my eyes blazed with fury.

'Why have you come?'

'You do not know how I passed these 14 days; I did not shave, I did not work. I stationed myself at the turn of the road to catch a glimpse of you as you drove past. I cannot live without you. Do what you want with me.'

With a resigned sigh, I let him back into my life. The treatment was but an excuse to see me. I did my best to maintain a dignified distance. Desperate to regain entry into my private domain, he brought gifts in lieu of medical fees and followed me up the stairs to deposit the packets on the table.

'You look beautiful today.'

'Thank you.'

'Blue suits you.'

'Thank you once again.'

We had almost reached the landing when he rapped me playfully on my rump! Horrified, I swung around and slapped him on his face.

'This is one bit of insolence I can never forgive,' I said softly between clenched teeth. This frightened him more than any frank display of anger would have. He slunk away.

It took a long time for the palpitations to stop. He was coarse and common. This was what comes of leading the likes of him on. Was there no difference between the sluts he pursued and me? Perhaps he did not think so. Otherwise, he would not have taken such liberties with my person.

Rajan kept his distance this time and I missed him not at all. I had outrage to sustain me. As a fitting finale, the expensive plants he had given me shrivelled up. Viciously, I planted cacti in the empty ceramic pots. At least, they did not demand the attention I could not give. At least, they were honest about their motives, prickly or otherwise. Little did I know that even the thorniest cacti, flower once in a lifetime.

40

Indignation could sustain me only for so long. At last it dawned upon me that it was his very audacity that drew me to him. His daring, plus the sexuality he exuded was an irresistible combination. If I needed an extramarital affair to enliven my drab existence, I could have encouraged any of my suave admirers, but they left me cold. Rajan evoked hungers that I did not know could exist in a human form.

The tables had been neatly turned. Till now he had been the supplicant, while I bestowed or refused favours like a queen. Now that he was lost to me, I realised that Rajan was one in a million. It took me years to see the uncut gem beneath the brazen exterior and I liked what I saw. Now that he had stopped pestering me, I wanted him back. He was not one to be cowed down by my anger, then why did he keep away? I was willing to forgive him his irritating persistence if only he would persist. I realised that the Rajiv Mehra I had loved all these years was but a shadow. As with Ashley in 'Gone With The Wind', I attributed to him qualities he did not possess. Rajan was the Rhett Butler of my life who loved me despite my faults, who made no effort to hide his own, but the realisation came too late. Days coalesced into months and not a sign of him. I was miserable.

Strange are the quirks of human nature. He who revolted me became desirable the moment he made himself unattainable. At last, swallowing my pride I rang him up.

'Hello?' It was the well-remembered voice.

'Hello,' I said eagerly.

There was an ominous click. In spite of myself, I tried to make excuses for him. One never knew with these Delhi phones. They had a habit of disconnecting in the middle of a conversation. I was fooling no one, but gave myself an excuse to ring up again. Once again, I dialled his number. The click at the other end had the finality of doom. I could not even pretend any longer.

'So this is how he must have felt when I snubbed him,' I thought dully. I remembered once he had brought fresh flowers with the dew still on them and laid them at my feet. I had trampled on them viciously.

'How can you be so cruel?' he had asked in a tear-laden voice.

'Serves you right for coveting another man's wife?' I had declared self-righteously.

Now that I was willing, he would have none of me. His indifference was a bed of brambles on which I lay night after night. It cost me a lot to contain the pain in the crucible of my heart for an illegitimate pain had no right to spill from my eyes or sighs. I maintained a façade of normalcy but the demons within gave me no respite. What if Rajan found someone more amenable to his overtures? Where would I be then? Why, at my rightful place, by my lawfully wedded husband; but that was poor consolation. It was unbearable to think that he was fed up of me now that I had acknowledged to myself my need of him.

Time blunted the sharp edges of my grief. Tumultuous streams emptied into the placid lake of loss. Barely had I come to terms with my predicament when he churned the still waters again. At Diwali, he drove to my gate, unloaded a quantity of presents in the hands of my astonished servant and disappeared! That he had come to my doorstep and my eyes could not feast upon him was more than I could bear. If I had known, I'd have run down the stairs barefooted, pounded his chest, and asked him why he tormented me so, but I already knew the answer. It was revenge, sweet revenge for the times I had rebuffed him.

That he still cared for me was obvious. Why then this feigned indifference? Perhaps his pride had been wounded. It was up to me to overlook his little vengeances and make peace with him again. The least I could do was to thank him for the gifts.

This time, he returned my greetings amicably.

'Thank you.'

'Mention not,' he said. I couldn't help smiling.

'Why didn't you talk with me when I rang you up?' I had vowed never to ask him and here I was doing just that.

'You set the rules.'

'What do you mean?'

'I was never to contact you again.' This had never deterred him earlier but I let it pass.

'Did you miss me?' I asked softly.

'Every single day, I waited at the crossing beneath the bridge to catch a glimpse as you sped past to the polyclinc. You were wearing a black sari yesterday, weren't you?'

'Yes.' My heart was singing. 'Can you forgive me for not forgiving you?'

'*What!*' He was incredulous. Where was the haughty doctor who looked down her nose at the likes of him?

'Diwali is the time to sort out differences. Let's clear the air between us,' I said.

'Yes.'

'Can you come to my house today?'

'What time?'

'Around 4 p.m., if it suits you.'

'Yes, if you will offer me a cup of tea.'

'Sure.' I was jubilant.

There was a sun on my horizon again. I barely ate a morsel for there were hungers other than the stomach that needed to be appeased. My body was 'want' personified. Time seemed to limp forward on paralysed legs, but four o'clock came and went without Rajan. Minutes stretched to hours and hours to eternity. Despair sucked on my legs like quicksand, even as desire was held aloft by stays of hope. To these vacillating emotions was added a horrifying third—fear. He did have a penchant for driving fast. What if he had met with an accident? What if he lay broken and bleeding in a hospital or worse, still in a mortuary? It was a thought too terrible to contemplate. By six o'clock, I had to know. Pride and propriety be damned. The different grades of hell he had pushed me through! Little did I know that worse was to follow!

Raju picked up the receiver at the first ring. After identifying my voice, he told the office boy, 'Tell her that Sahib has gone out.'

Reeling with shock, I put down the phone. The bastard! It needed the mind of a devil to stoop so low. I had rejected him because I genuinely believed it wasn't right for a married woman to respond to the overtures of a married man. There was nothing personal about it. Now when I had succumbed to temptation I had been honest enough to admit it, and this was what I got in return. Perhaps my just desserts, as some would say.

Tears poured like boiling acid down my cheeks. I could have gladly murdered him even if I had to grieve over his dead body for the rest of my life. Suddenly, the irony of the situation struck me and I burst out laughing. Here I was crying my eyes out when I should be thanking my stars for saving me from adultery!

41

Life would have continued in the same vein, had it not been for the accident of accidents. I had a galore of mishaps ever since I married. If my husband was a nervous driver, I was trifle too confident. I had barely learnt to drive when I took a carload of relatives to a funeral. We almost had our own *kiryakaram* (funeral rites). I was naïve enough to believe that people in Delhi follow traffic rules. As I was on the highway, I thought I had the right of the way. The motorist who charged in from a side did not think so and a collision was inevitable. No one was injured, the damage to the car wasn't extensive, but the foul words mouthed by the offender shook me badly. It would have been the end of my driving career had there been one person in my car who could drive. Perforce, I had to take the wheel again. So what, if I drove at ten kilometres an hour in second gear to the sound of *waheguru, waheguru* (invocation of the Sikh gurus) chanted by my terrified passengers?

As for my husband, he was an expert at unloading us from his scooter at the most inopportune moment. Karan was 5 years old and stood in front. I rode pillion while Simar, a mere infant, reposed in my arms. Without ceremony, my posterior was dislodged from the rear of the vehicle. Even at this juncture, the maternal instinct was stronger than that of survival. Though I skinned my nose, knees, and elbows, I cushioned Simar in my arms and covered him with the arch of my body. He escaped unhurt, much to the surprise of onlookers.

Another time we were riding home after a movie, when the back wheel of our scooter decided to disengage. Off it went on its solitary sojourn through the heavy traffic. There was screech of metal against the tarmac, and we fell. On seeing our wheel wobble, the kindly driver of the vehicle behind us took care to shield us from the speeding traffic, thus saving our lives.

All this took place before we bought the car. On that crisp, December afternoon, it was sheer thrift that prompted us to take the scooter in place of the Fiat. There was a cousin's wedding at Ashoka Hotel. Jeeju had come from Chandigarh and my in-laws from Mussoorie. As MS had some house calls to make, it was decided that we follow later. Along the lovely stretch of the ridge we sped, on his scooter. Near Buddha Jayanti Park, the front tyre burst without warning. We flew through the air to our deaths, or so I presumed. 'Rajan will never know that I love him' was the last thought that came to my mind before I lost consciousness.

When I regained consciousness, I took some time to get my bearings. My spouse had fallen on his face. His turban was askew, his topknot loose and lopsided. His specs were broken and blood poured from his forehead into his eyes and mouth, staining his teeth. He looked more like a Red Indian than an Indian. I crawled up to him and stemmed the flow of blood with a handkerchief. A Good Samaritan escorted us to a government-aided hospital. We were still too dazed to speak; all that mattered was that we were alive and our children were not orphaned.

The causality of the hospital was dim and dirty, with an indifferent nurse on duty. After informing the doctor, she continued her interrupted phone call instead of attending to our injuries. Such then was the plight of the unknown patient. My husband lay on the only bed available, while I shivered on the hard bench.

The resident, a girl still wet behind the ears, attended to my husband's wounds. Her canary yellow dress hurt my eye and I turned away. The dizziness was killing me. What if there was a slow leak inside my skull and I lost some of my faculties? If at all I had to pay with some handicap, I prayed, 'Please God let it be my legs; not my eyes, not my hands, for I would be finished both as a doctor and a writer.' I would be as good as dead without them, but I had hit the ground on my occiput wherein lodged the centre for sight. Though my eyes were open, the light began to flicker. I rubbed my eyes but the unmistakable flicker persisted. I feared the worst. Much to my relief, I learnt that the tube light was at fault and not my vision. At this, I began giggling and wouldn't stop. Reaction had set in.

It turned out that though my husband looked frightful, his injuries were superficial. Now it was his turn to occupy the uncomfortable bench while I shifted to the solitary bed. As it was a Sunday, no neurologist was available, and I was subjected to the inadequate ministrations of the resident. Meanwhile, the entire horde of relatives rushed to the hospital. My father-in-law burst into tears and demanded why his precious son sat on the cold bench while I luxuriated on the bed. He sure had his priorities right. I had to explain apologetically that we had just exchanged places.

Back home, a strange phenomenon occurred. All the admirers I had shaken off came crowding back. Jeeju became presumptive all over again. As I rested in the darkened room, I felt a cool hand on my unsuspecting brow. I got up with a start. MS had gone to the toilet and Jeeju utilised the opportunity to show his concern. I was too weak to protest.

Dr Raman was summoned to give me a neurological checkup. He too professed to have a soft corner for me. The confession had put an end to a profitable business relationship. Now, he was examining me from head to toe in a manner that made me realise that a medical checkup could be turned into a sensuous experience, if the doctor willed it so. He slid his hand up my arm to push the loose sleeve of my gown away and take my BP. He rubbed the balls of his fingers over my head to look for bumps or external injury. He held my ankles and tested my soles for planter reflex. He lifted my gown up to my knees for the knee jerk. In short, with full permission of my husband, in full view of the family, he felt me all over.

Uncleji rushed to our bedside the moment he heard the news. As behoved an elder, he did a *sarvarna* of Rs 100/- and gave it to the servant. He told me that he asked God to debit any good he had done in life and credit it towards my well-being! I was strangely touched. To think that sometime back I had almost brought about *his* death. I had told him explicitly what I thought of lecherous old men panting after women young enough to be their daughters. That night he suffered a massive heart attack and he laid the blame squarely upon me. Within a matter of days, he had shrivelled up into a harmless shell of the original. The frail and shrunken version of Uncleji posed no threat to me, or so I thought till time proved me wrong.

The concern of so many people gave me no joy whatsoever. The one person I wanted to comfort me did not come. Yet I was being unreasonable. How was he to know? That very night, a patient was wheeled in my nursing home with haemorrhagic shock due to an incomplete abortion. My head was woolly and my feet wobbly, but her need was greater than mine. With an effort, I came down the stairs, evacuated the retained products of conception, and saved her life. It was 10 p.m. by the time everything was in control. Wearily, I laid my head on the table of my empty clinic and closed my eyes. I felt a hand on my shoulder. Instinctively, I knew that it was Rajan. A strange calm descended into my soul—as if quarrelling twilight birds had found a niche on the bough of my heart and quietened all at once.

42

A strange recklessness swept over me like a high velocity wind, ripping apart the barriers of caution and conformation. My perspective changed after my brush with death. I realised that I had spent a lifetime in self-denial. It was the honour of my father, my husband, my family that came first. I grew corns standing on the pedestal of glorified womanhood and longed to step down. Of what use was self-sacrifice when it gave not the promised exultation? Let others be noble for a change and obtain the solace that so eluded me.

The accident had given me a jolt in more ways than one. Life was short and unpredictable. From now on, I was going to live every moment for myself. I knew that I would have to pay the price with the currency of pain, but it would be worth it. Till now, I had borne the pain without the preceding pleasure. I would etch the lines of fate on my palm myself, and if things went awry, I was prepared to face the consequences. When it was time for retribution I would beg for mercy neither from man nor God.

I had been too near death to be complacent about life. There developed in me a ravenous hunger for the hungers of life. Strange thoughts began crowding my mind.

'What if I had died with so many lives yet unlived?'

'What if Rajan had died before me?' I would have spent a lifetime regretting my redundant virtue.

Once, perhaps a lifetime ago, I had told Rajan to exercise restrain for the sake of society.

'What has society ever given us that we should pay heed to it?' he had asked.

'Nothing, but it has the power to take away everything.'

'Then I'll take you beyond the confines of society.'

'Unfortunately, no such place exists on the face of this earth. Moreover, we'd tire of each other in two days flat; we are too volatile for peaceful co-existence,' I said to dispel the desire that hung thick like fog between us.

'Who wants peace at this point of life? Let there be devouring desires and insatiable hungers.'

By the sublte change in my demneanor, he sensed that I was ready to give in but resisted out of habit, and said, 'It was meant to be. Accept the inevitable.' I kept quiet.

When I thought I was dying, my last thoughts were of him. By some strange telepathy at that very moment, he pushed away his lunch and told his mother, 'Doctor sahib *ko kuch ho gaya hai* (something has happened to Doctor).'

'My premonition forced me to come to you, otherwise how could I have known?'

Now that I was receptive, Raju began to woo me in earnest. The seven years long blow hot, blow cold relationship was heading towards a thundering climax. There were declarations of love and eulogising of virtues. He would go over my features one by one as if I was a statue, and not a woman of flesh and blood. He loved the way my nose crinkled when I laughed, the way I pushed my irrepressible curls from my face. Most of all he loved my mouth—the one part of my anatomy I was conscious about. If for nothing else, I could love him for that.

He also revealed some startlingly embarrassing fetishes. Over a period of time, he had hoarded various articles from my place, precious to him because they belonged to me. They included a letterhead from an old prescription pad, a pen, tube roses that had fallen from my hair, and a photograph that had been kissed beyond recognition. Most shocking of all was a bra! A beige-coloured lacy affair, which I had thought that the washerwoman had filched! He used it to masturbate whenever a semen sample was required to impregnate his wife. It now reposed in his locker.

On his birthday, I gave him a small 14-karat gold heart in a mother of pearl case I had bought from England.

'This will also be stored with the rest?' I asked.

'I will wear it proudly on a chain. *This* has been given, not robbed,' he said.

Holding my shoulders, he brought his face down on mine. Startled, I turned away and the kiss landed on my cheek. Not one to give up, he held my chin, brought my face in alignment with his and kissed me full on the mouth. I did not know that a kiss could feel so good. Though the pleasure was intense, guilt reared its ugly head. I pushed him away, my face flushed with shame and anger.

'No! Please, no.'

'How beautiful you look when angry,' he said. 'Your cheeks blaze, your eyes flash fire.'

'This is not right.' Years of conditioning could not be brushed away with one kiss. 'My body belongs to my husband; over the rest I have no control.'

His pupils dilated.

'That means your heart is mine . . . I dare not hope.'

'So you see, you are still the gainer,' I said softly.

'I could have whisked you away in 7 days flat, but I waited for 7 years because I wanted you to want me as much as I wanted you.'

I could kill him for rubbing it in, yet it was true. Conflicting emotions wracked my form. It was not as easy as I thought to override a moral upbringing. With tears gliding down my cheeks I beseeched,

'I have not the strength to resist anymore. Seven long years I tried but you were like a vulture bidding your time. Please go before irreparable harm is done.' He spun on his heels and left without a backward glance.

He was the only man besides my husband whose lips had branded mine, and there was no denying the fact that it felt wonderful. I stood in front of the mirror like a silly adolescent, to see if I looked any different. My eyes were luminous, my cheeks pink, and my lips full and red. A faint tingling lingered on my cheek where his clipped moustache had brushed my soft skin. Snug, I slept that night between the mattress of memories and the eiderdown of dreams.

43

I was fed up of my old jalopy. She had a personality that did not get with mine. Wilful and defiant, she hated taking orders. Her windows wouldn't close, her doors wouldn't open, and once she flung her bonnet back on the windscreen as I sped down a flyover! Her horn would blow itself hoarse when in the mood, but plead laryngitis when I needed its services. One day a roaring in my ear startled me. I thought that a truck wanted me to give way, but the rear view mirror showed no vehicle behind me. It was my Italian lady chortling daintily. Her silencer had given way! And she sure did have the time to stand and stare, especially in the rain. She had only to see a puddle to stop right in the middle and gurgle happily. Her sense of humour was atrocious. Once, she let loose a mouse under my sari as I was driving; my screams could be heard down the road! The blatant hussy would wink outrageously at passing vehicles no matter how many times I got her headlights repaired. If a handsome Mercedes happened to pass by, her tyre would flatten with an exquisite sigh.

My Fiat was giving me more trouble than service. The number of times I was stranded far outnumbered the times she took me to my destination. She spent more time in the garage than my porch. Considering the number of parts that had been replaced, she should have been as good as new wine in an old bottle; but no, she was an arthritic old lady who gave herself airs. To cap it, she was a confirmed petroholic. Enough was enough! I would have to put sentimentality aside and buy a new vehicle. I coveted the toy cars called Marutis that plied the roads these days. I was determined to buy a brand new one. Never again would I be taken in by the good looks of second-hand goods. To think that I was impressed by Fiat's pearly grey lustre and the silver horse on her petrol cap. It turned out that that was all she had to recommend her.

A car was a necessity for a practising gynaecologist, but where was the money to buy a new one? Raju (with the change in attitude, Rajan endearingly became Raju in my thoughts) had bought a Maruti van recently and I asked him details of the purchase. He offered to help me clinch the deal. When I told him that I couldn't afford cash down payment he was surprised. We had yet to recover from our monetary losses. Raju tried to 'lend' me the money, but I would not hear of it. He rang up a few days later and said

'I have been thinking of what you said the other day.'

'Of all the things I said (mostly without thinking), which of them has captivated your mind?'

'I was thinking how best to solve your monetary problem?'

'We are not all that poor,' I retorted, stung to the quick. 'The last thing I want is your pity.'

'Don't get me wrong. I was thinking that we could enter into a partnership—I'll buy and sell property in your name and we'll share the profits.'

It was true that his *muh boli behan* Shashikala Bhardwaj's collaborated with him in this manner. Though Shashikala was the wife of a high-ranking official, she was not averse to the extra income on the side. A commission agent did have a bad reputation, not always without reason; I did not intend to become one and told him so.

'I am not a petty realtor. I sell farmlands and do not cheat the poor for the simple reason that only the rich can afford to buy farms. You know I am also a coloniser and many a poor have a roof over their heads because of me. And what about doctors? Don't they take commission for referrals?'

'*I* have never stooped so low.'

'Nor have I. I could do without derogatory remarks about my profession.'

'I am sorry, but how could you think that I would agree? Have I no self-respect?'

'Why can't you put aside that pride of yours and let me take care of you?'

If only I could. I wearied of being the man about the house. It would be bliss to rest my head on his chest and let him take over, but I also knew that I was a born fighter and would not be able to watch the battle from the sidelines for long. At best, Raju would be a strong ally and together we could have conquered the world. Nevertheless, it was nice to know that he cared.

I decided to buy the car in instalments. When I asked MS to accompany me to the finance company, he refused! Not for anything in this world would he miss his clinic. It was industry without enterprise, but, not even the birth of his son could pry him from his office during working hours. I couldn't very well shop for a car as for groceries. When Raju offered to help, MS agreed with alacrity. Not that I was complaining, but he *could* have displayed a wee bit of interest.

On a balmy February morning, Raju and I set off on 'Mission Maruti'. So intense was our awareness of each other that every bit of small talk had sexual overtones. Casually, he asked me my daily routine.

'I rise early and exercise for about 40 minutes.'

'What sort of exercises do you do?'

'The usual.'

'No I mean, do you prefer doing it standing or lying down?' he asked grinning wickedly.

'If you speak to me like this, I'll get down this very minute.'

'We have just started, don't get down so soon.' He continued in the same vein putting me off by his crudity. There was no such thing as a romantic prelude in his book of wooing.

'You know how we'll inaugurate your new car,' he said after a while.

'No, please enlighten me,' I asked scathingly.

'We will book a room in Sultanpur bird sanctuary. I'll lock the door and carry you to the . . .'

'Have you no compunction about coveting another's wife?'

'No. I have earned you after seven years of *tapasya* (penance).'

'*Tapasya* indeed!' I wished could be as amoral as him.

'We'll make love till you are sore and you beg for mercy. Till . . .'

'Shut up this very instant.'

'Then I'll massage your aching . . .'

I threatened to get out, but he paid no heed. By the time we reached the office at Daryaganj, I was breathless with the verbal foreplay. Thankfully, the tedious paperwork cooled our ardour considerably. By evening, I was the owner of a brand new car.

As we drove off into the sunset he said, 'Let's pretend for a while that we are man and wife.'

'No, I am happy the way we are.' Which husband worth his salt would woo his wife with such passion? I thought. Nevertheless, I was suffused with a rare contentment. I was acutely conscious of his arm stretched carelessly across the back of my seat. I gazed out of the window and espied the moon flung like a silver coin across the horizon.

'Look, look,' I said, showing him the wonder of the sun and the moon together in the same sky. The sudden movement loosened my bun and my hair cascaded in waves down my shoulders. He pulled on the natural ringlets and watched them recoil in fascination. I tossed my head to extract my hair from his grasp and knotted it hurriedly.

'Put your hand in mine,' he said, laying his hand palm upwards between us. I couldn't bring myself to do so.

'Please reach out for me this once. I can grab your hand any moment but I want *you* to touch me.'

Shyly, I put my hand in his. Our fingers interlocked and stayed thus for a while. Slowly, I raised our clasped hands, rubbed the back of his across my cheek and drew it to my lips. Incredulity, wonder, and ecstasy flitted across his face.

We took the car to Bangla Sahib Gurudwara for blessings. I cast furtive glances around, hating the stealth in the house of God. Yet it felt so right to wash our hands and feet together at the cleansing trough. We bought marigold garlands and *kada parsaad*. Together we bowed in front of the Guru Granth Sahib and stretched our hands in supplication. After this, we descended down the stairs for a perambulation around the holy tank. On the chequered marble floor, we walked bare feet to the silvery music of my anklets. At a secluded spot, we sat down and dipped our feet in the water. The wind played with my hair, the ripples with my toe rings, and Raju with my heart. There was a complete sense of belonging, of mutual trust even as we betrayed the trust of others. It was so easy to live in the present, as if there had been no past and never would be a future.

With a loving gesture, Raju took the *prasaad* from the leaf cup and raised it to my mouth. I did the same, and we fed each other till the cup was empty. With a shock, I realised that we hadn't eaten since morning. There were hungers greater than those of the stomach that clamoured for appeasement. Suddenly, he caught hold of my wet feet and declared.

'I swear in this place of worship that I will not rest until I make you mine.'

I was overwhelmed. I remembered another man at another time who would not rub the cold from my feet because it was beneath a man to do so. Raju recalled me to the present by a playful question.

'Did you for a moment think that I would give up?'

'No,' I said, suddenly shy. 'But never for a moment did I think that I would give in.'

'You had no choice.'

'I could not bear to hurt my husband or for that matter, your wife.'

'Sometimes, I feel it is criminal to violate such innocence.'

'Then why you do you tempt me?'

'Because I have crossed the point of no return?'

'And when did you cross that point?'

'The day I set eyes on you.' He was incorrigible! 'I swear it's true. When I first saw you, I was blinded by your *lashkara* (flash). It is as if someone had held a mirror in front of the sun. I knew nothing about you, your marital status, your personality, all I knew was that I would possess you one day.'

'And I harboured an intense dislike for your type.'

'And now here we are.'

'Yes.'

We sat silent for a while lost in thought. After a while he asked, 'Tell me, what did you ask for in there.'

'You tell me first.'

'Why, the obvious—that both of us remain together in this birth and in all births hereafter. What did you ask?'

'I asked for the strength not to betray the trust my family has reposed in me. If that were not possible, then forgiveness for what I am about to do.'

'So you have accepted the inevitable.'

My eyes filmed over and I averted my gaze. Why would God forgive me? It was like putting my hand in a crusher and expecting it to come out unscathed?

44

Love makes people do strange things. I found myself fasting on Shivratri because Raju worshipped Lord Shiva, and went to the local temple in the evening. Perhaps, I would find an answer to my dilemma there. I entered the alcove that housed the Shiv Mandir and poured milk over the *Shivling*—His big, black, stone phallus.

'Shiva,' I prayed ferverently, 'I sway like a pendulum between emotions and principles, reason and desire, society and self. Tell me should I choose my way, or the way of the world? Give me a sign.'

The Shivling continued dripping milk, Nandi the bull sat complacent, and the snake and moon that adorned the statue of Shiva batted not a lid. All that prevailed was a stony silence. From there, I entered the main temple to enlist the help of the remaining gods. I bowed in front of Sherawali Mata and quickly slunk away, ashamed to voice my desire in front of the virtuous virgin goddess. The orange-coloured monkey god Hanuman was a confirmed bachelor and would not understand my dilemma. Ramji stood resplendent with Sita and Laxman. He had the good fortune to marry his true love. How could he realise my torment? Ah! There was Krishna with his beloved Radha. She sat on his lap, their legs entwined. Coincidentally, Radha too was also older than Krishna and married to another, and yet the two are worshipped as eternal lovers. In front of these two I gave vent to my pain.

'Why is it that the passion you have for each other is glorified, while mortals have to pay for it? Tell me how do I get social sanction for a love such as yours?'

Oblivious to my entreaty, Krishna continued to gaze into the eyes of his consort. Was there no way out of my awful predicament? But then, what did I expect—cymbals and celebrations? As I turned to leave, a familiar voice called out. It was the *panditiyan* who had recently delivered at my nursing home.

'Doctor Sahib, what are you doing here?'

'It is Shivrati and I had kept a fast so I thought . . .'

'I see,' she said, though she couldn't quite see why a Sikh woman kept a Hindu fast. 'Here take some *prasaad*.'

She took me to the sanctum sanctorum and gave me holy water. She asked me to pass my hand over the holy flame and raise it to my eyes. She took the choicest of *prasaad* from the very feet of Lord Shiva and put it in my cupped palms. After this, she smeared my forehead with orange paste. My spirits lifted and my heart was singing. I had been granted permission for my unholy love from holy precincts!

Raju came a few days later and whisked me away. Some paperwork remained with the car dealer. The formalities took merely an hour. After that, he took me to Gauri Shanker Mandir at Chandini Chowk. Though my gurus had been 'appeased', we still needed the sanction of *his* gods. After buying an offering of rose garlands and sweetmeats, we entered the holy precincts. I was awestruck by the magnificence of the place—the sliver relief work on the walls, the statues of Gauri Shanker, and the enormous Shivling.

He held my hand and solemnly declared, '*Main apne isht devta ko saakshi maan kar tumhe apni patni sweekar karta hoon aur vachan deta hoon ki aajeevan, sukh main, dukh main tumhara saath nibhaoonga.* (As my patron god bears witness, I accept you as my wife and promise that I will stand by you in happiness and sorrow, as long as I live).

I knew that he meant every word. He filled the parting of my hair with vermilion. I felt more married to him than to my lawfully wedded husband. Later, when reason doused emotion, I asked myself, 'Why did we need this farce of a marriage to justify our impending fornication? It would hold no ground in the eyes of law and society. We couldn't wish our spouses away. Moreover, if we could break our original vows at the behest of our bodies, how long could we maintain the sanctity of *this* marriage?'

'Rosy, you think too much.' I gave myself a mental shake. 'Do not resist the inevitable.'

Now that the first hurdle had been crossed, the second question arose. Where do people with such 'marriages' go to consummate it? There was no precedent in our family and I had no one to compare notes with. Of one thing I was sure. It was not going to be in hotels or guesthouses. I shuddered at the prospect of a police raid. It certainly wouldn't be under a bougainvillea bush in Budha Jayanti Park where the caretakers took money for looking the other way and pried lovers apart at closing time!

It was seven o'clock by the time I reached home. The family was frantic with worry. I had never been away for so long without prior information. Those were not the days of cell phones, and there was no way they could contact me. My father-in-law was pacing up and down the driveway. My mother-in-law sat on the stone bench by the gate praying. My brother-in-law stood at the turn of the road looking out for me. The children were crying. MS rang up home every half an hour from his clinic. The floodgates of shame opened to submerge me. From the exaltation of fulfilled love, I was plunged into abysmal self-loathing. I had been through an entire gamut of emotions in a day, each as earth shattering as the next. With this all-consuming love came lies and deceit, so alien to my nature. I mumbled something about delay in paperwork and traffic jams.

It was so easy to deceive the trusting. That night, I clung to my husband as if my life depended on it. Perhaps it did. All was not lost yet.

'Hold me tight, don't let me go.' Every fibre of my being seemed to scream, but he did not heed my silent cry. He unclasped my clinging hands and turned the other way. In desperation, I shook him and said, 'I want to ask a question.'

'Yes, what is it?'

'If I ever commit a mistake will you forgive me?'

'Yes.'

'Even if it is a grave one?'

'Yes, but why do you ask? Have you done something?'

'No, nothing as yet.'

He did not bother to question me further. I was amazed by his lack of curiosity. I thought that sleep would vanish from his eyes, that he would sit up and take note of my extraordinary question. I wanted to hate him, to whip up a fury against him, to recollect all his past misdemeanours and hold them against him so that I could justify *my* misdeeds; but two wrongs never did make a right.

45

Now that we were 'married', Raju wanted to buy me a *mangal sutra* to proclaim my marital status. We left his car at the Red Fort parking lot and proceeded on a rickshaw through the congested lanes of Chandini Chowk. The rickety vehicle jostled through the throng. Sexual tension mounted with every jolt that threw us together. He bought me the *mangal sutra* and a pair of diamond tops from Dariba, the lane of goldsmiths. When I protested, he hissed, 'Act natural. Have you ever heard a wife telling her husband *not* to buy jewellery for her?'

At the parking lot, he led me to the rear seat and put the sacred ornament around my neck. I kissed it and raised it to my eyes. He made me wear the diamonds in my ears and instantly began extracting his pound of flesh. I felt like a bought woman. I was available for free, for love. Why did he think that I could not love him for himself? I longed to hold him to my breast and soothe his insecurities away. I wanted to tell him that our need was mutual, that he did not have to pay me to do what I wanted to do but I did none of those things.

Instead, shame goaded me into saying, 'You want the returns so soon?' It hurt him as I knew it would. Out of this hurt was born the desire to hurt me as I had hurt him.

'Rs 25,000/- for a kiss? You must be joking.' I ended up feeling quite foolish. I was so used to giving that I did not know how to take gracefully. I leaned forward to offer my lips in reconciliation.

The window glasses were tainted and the parking lot vacant. Before I knew it my blouse was open and his mouth fastened on my breast. I put my tongue in his ear and probed deep inside, sending shivers of ecstasy down his form. Gradually, I was pushed back till I lay supine on the seat, his weight upon me. For a second, I held him tight, revelling in our togetherness. He was aroused beyond measure, so was I. When he lifted my sari to end the delicious agony, something snapped within me. I pushed him away, opened the door of the car and rushed out.

With one stride, he caught up with me, held my upper arm and herding me to the centre of the back seat, got in after me. In one swift motion he lifted my sari, locked my left knee with his right one and held both my wrists in one hand. Having immobilized me, he proceeded to put one finger then two deep inside till I ended up loving what I had been forced to do. In and out went the fingers slowly, then rapidly till I gasped with pleasure.

'Is this the same woman who said that she'd rather give up her life than her honour?' he asked, but I was beyond caring.

I was in an agony of excitement that I never knew existed on the face of this earth. I do not remember when he released one of my hands and drew it towards him. So consumed was I by sensation that nothing else registered. Just when I thought that I could bear it no longer, he withdrew.

'Now you will know how it feels to be taken thus far and left high and dry.'

Before the impact of his words could sink in, there was a knock on the window. I dared not turn to look.

'Shall I call the police?' said it was the parking attendant.

Raju got out and silenced him with a hundred rupees note. I snapped out of the sexual haze and perceived things in their right perspective. How could have I allowed myself to be manipulated by a ruthless crook? How could I *love* a man I did not *like*? The scene with the parking attendant was too horrible to contemplate.

'For the first time in my life I could not meet someone in the eye.' I sobbed hiding my face with my hands as Raju manoeuvred the car through the thickening evening traffic.

'It was nothing. You think too much.'

I was amazed at his utter lack of perception. If he didn't understand what killed me while I still breathed, how did I expect him to understand anything else about me? How I hated him, the vengeful, sex-obsessed bastard! Ever since I had given in to him there had been assaults on my psyche hitherto unknown. Like a yo-yo, I swung from heights of rapture to canyons of humiliation. I was filled with loathing so intense that I could not bear to sit next to him a moment longer. Flinging his jewellery at him, I got down at the next red light. He couldn't possibly forsake his vehicle to follow me. Before the lights turned green, I had hired a three-wheeler and disappeared from sight.

I felt weighed down by the sins of the world. My body felt soiled and sticky. I longed to soak myself in a warm bath to cleanse myself of him. I took off my clothes and stood naked in front of the bathroom mirror and was aghast at what I saw. My skin was blotched black and blue by love marks. My nipples were raw, red, and erect. I touched them briefly to feel their exquisite soreness. Suddenly, I smiled through my tears. I forgot that he was a wicked vindictive bastard who thought nothing of using sex to take revenge from a lady. I revelled in being his whore!

Later, when the phone rang, I knew it was him.

'Hello,' I said in a hoarse whisper.

'Who's speaking?' He hadn't recognised my voice on account of the tears in it.

'Your prize bitch!'

'Don't say that. You are my wife.'

'Cut the crap and tell me why have you phoned?'

'To find out if you have reached home safely.'

'Well I have, now leave me alone.'

'Why did you throw the sacred *mangal sutra* on my face?'

'Because you did not honour it.'

'What did I do?' Could a man be that obtuse? Didn't he realise the enormity of my degradation? I kept quiet.

'If you don't tell me I will not be able to sleep tonight.'

'That's your problem.'

'I'll die if you don't tell me.'

'Then die.'

'Do you hate me that much?'

'You will die but once. I die again and again because of you.'

'I have something to confess.'

'Don't bother. It's not going to make any difference.'

As was his habit, he continued as if I hadn't spoken, 'I am feeling shy . . .'

'You and shy!' I was incredulous.

'Actually, I had already spent myself when you touched me there.'

I could barely control my laughter. So that was what was bothering him. The scene with the parking attendant mattered not a whit. He thought that the size of his manhood put me off, and I had broken off with him on that account! Men! Men were such megalomaniacs, such children.

46

While for Raju it was the culmination of a seven years pursuit, for me, it was the beginning of the thaw. Though he was impatient for consummation, I wanted to tread cautiously. As in the ghazal sung by Jagjit Singh, *'Idhar toan jadli, jaldi hai, udhar ahista, ahista, ahista'* (This side it is hurry, hurry while on the other slowly, slowly, slowly.)

Raju too began to see things from my perspective and indulged me with a bit of romantic wooing. For obvious reasons, we would go to the less frequented parts of Delhi. Malai Mandir, in RK Puram was a beautifully carved grey stone structure atop a hill. As the gods rest in the afternoon, we knew that the sanctum sanctorum would be closed and there would hardly be anyone around. Up the numerous steps, we went to admire the epics sculpted on stone and pray. I prayed that God grant him a child he so desired. He prayed that I suffer at least 1/100th of what he had suffered on my account! As he cupped his hand to drink the holy water, some of it trickled down through his fingers. I gathered the precious drops in the hollow of my palm and raised them to my lips.

'I will never forget this moment as long as I live.' he said, visibly moved.

At times, he was a mischievous little boy. As I drove towards him for another rendezvous, on another day, my car got stranded in a herd of sheep. The insolent goatherd stood under a tree smoking a bidi! I marched up to him and gave him a piece of my mind. He pointed to a wall without saying a word. Hidden behind it was Raju, grinning wickedly. He had actually paid the fellow to do this to me!

In our wanderings along the outskirts of Delhi, we came upon an untouched expanse of water. I expressed a desire to explore it, so down a precarious dirt road we went. We had chanced upon a veritable jewel. It was a huge lake fringed by a dense keekar forest. Time and trees stood frozen as if in a photograph. Short and erect, most trees spread their branches like green parasols. Others bent obliquely while yet others stretched horizontally to taste the life-giving waters. The trunks were rough; the branches thorny and the tiny leaves wore the new green of spring. As I inhaled deeply of the silvery silence, the call of a peacock rent the air. Soon enough, one appeared trailing his brilliant plumage, and not so brilliant harem.

Like one woman showing off her jewels to another, Nature unfolded her treasures in front of my appreciative eyes. There were water birds in shallow marshes, with wings the size of small sails; in the pasture beyond grazed mares with foals. Shoals of fish swam in the transparent waters. Temple bells chimed in the village beyond. I was overwhelmed with such unspoilt beauty in a city as desecrated as Delhi. Even as I was lost in the wonder of nature, Raju stared at me in wonder. The serenity of a cloud-spattered sky, the sensual touch of the breeze affected him not at all. His life had revolved around materialistic gains and it surprised him to learn that pleasure could come without a price. He remains indebted to me for acquainting him with natural beauty that had always been there for him.

For quite some time, this remained our private haven. We would go there for rejuvenation and sustenance whenever the futility of our relationship tore me apart. On full moon nights, we'd watch the moonbeams polish the lake into a sheet of silver. I cried on the day Delhi tourism took over. *Our* lake was now called Balesha Lake. Workers descended upon it with a vengeance, mauling it in the name of beautification. Trees were chopped and embankments built. Kayaks raked its virgin breast with oars. The water birds took fight and peacocks retreated farther into the woods. Gone was the enchanting disarray, and with it a sense of belonging. It wasn't our lake anymore.

Sensing my affinity to water, Raju took me Ram Ghat on the banks of the Jamuna. There was a full body of water here. The sun was lovingly warm and the wind, teasingly chill. Gossamer clouds draped the sky like a stole. On shimmering sands, oyster shells gaped like plundered jewel boxes. Canopied snails left silvery trails. A path darted through the reeds like a snake. On a rickety boat, we cleaved through waters that resisted cleaving, past a sugarcane field pat in the middle of the river. The Jamuna would reclaim its legacy in the monsoons. Till then, the locals ploughed these denuded pieces of land. A little while later, we reached a veritable paradise, a natural water garden. Pink lotuses with yellow hearts rose on slender stems out of the Jamuna. Large green leaves floated like plates on its surface. On these, sat little birds, devouring a sumptuous meal of insects. Raju began plucking the beautiful flowers thinking that it would please me.

'Don't.' I begged. He was surprised at the pain in my voice. We had a lot to learn about each other.

One day, we encountered a barbed wire fence around this area, too. A high security official building was coming up and the monster of development swallowed another bit of heaven. Farther down the river, we went and crossed over to the other side over the Pontoon Bridge built on bobbing boats. Here sat vendors with watermelons harvested from these very banks. Mounds of green coconuts lay on the sand to quench the thirst of passersby. We chose the biggest one and drank its sweet water through two straws, our heads touching like the silly teenyboppers. So what if we were on the wrong side of thirty, the mantle of age slid away whenever we were together. We shelled water chestnuts and ate the tasteless, succulent white flesh. We played with kittens, and fluffy, yellow chicks. We climbed on boulders strewn along the ridge and espied a tiny mandir. It was manned by a foreigner turned ascetic who found peace in remaining unwashed and unkempt. His burnt, bare torso and matted blonde hair aroused my curiosity but I knew Raju would not approve of my probing the unlikely god man for his story, which I knew would be interesting. Raju, the high caste Brahmin, also took me to places that verged on the bizarre. He showed me the tomb of a hermit who had buried himself alive near Nigambodh ghat! He took me to Mauni Baba who hadn't spoken a word for nine years. Sickly pale, with tangled hair and a sandalwood caste mark on his forehead, he sat cross-legged in a dark cave in the womb of the earth. I shuddered when Raju begged him to bless our union! At another place, he showed me boys between 4-14 years who never sat down once they had learnt to stand up! They even slept while standing! To be trained to behave in such a manner, their bottoms had been whipped raw. The object of such torture was to attract those whose faith earned their keeper his livelihood! We saw wild-eyed women visited by the 'mata', who went in a trance every Tuesday at the local mandir. With open hair and rolling eyes, they writhed and slithered on the polished floor. Raju's eyes shone with religious fervour as he showed me all this. It was my turn to stare at him in amazement. Unbridgeable was the chasm between his way of thinking and mine.

47

The continual proximity, the unbearable sexual tension was taking its toll. Raju talked in his sleep and perhaps let the cat out of the bag for his wife was waspish without reason. He dared not question her lest he learn what he did not want to learn. She starved herself to punish him and asked him to kill her because she was nothing but a living corpse.

When his mother asked her the reason for her unreasonable behaviour she said, 'I want to die. I am of no use to anyone. I cannot give you the heir you long for' for she thought that a child of his own would release him from my clutches and bind him to her.

The old woman brought her son and daughter-in-law to me.

'Look at Raju's bloodshot eyes. Look at Snehlata pallor. Help us doctor,' she pleaded.

I looked at them in mute agony. They were asking redemption from their executioner. I was as helpless as they were, caught in the web of our entwined destiny from which there was no escape.

'What do you want me to do?' I asked, wetting my lips.

'I ask you with folded hands to give them a child.'

If only I could. That very moment I struck a deal with God. I would restart treatment with a vengeance. I had bought a laparoscope recently and would put into use the latest technology. If I succeeded, I would give up Raju. It would not do bring a child in this world only to snatch away the father.

If I failed, he was meant to be mine. Time would prove to be the final test.

It was with apprehension that I performed the laparoscopy, for keyhole surgery was a relatively new procedure. Despite my fears, it went off without a hitch. There was nothing obviously wrong with Snehlata. As his adopted son, Sonu was alone, Raju dropped his mother home and returned to his wife who was recovering from anaesthesia and would be discharged by evening.

I usually ate a solitary lunch. The children weren't expected till 4 p.m. and MS did not come home in the afternoons. Even as I contemplated warming last night's leftovers, the doorbell rang. Raju stood on the threshold, his arms full. The rich aroma of *sambar* filled the air. I watched him lay the food on the table and latch the door. Predator and prey stood face to face.

'Where do you stare at me like a lamb at a butcher?'

'I can't, I really can't.'

'You won't have to do a thing.'

'But, but . . .' I sought to buy time.

'We'll bypass the preliminaries today to break your reserve.'

Such cold-blooded calculations! Yet, left to me, we would never consummate our infidelity.

'Won't love do? I love you more than anyone else on earth. I really do.'

'I want to possess you completely.'

'But I'll never be able to do it,' I said not vehemently enough.

He manoeuvred me to the bed, sat me down on the edge and arranged two pillows behind me.

'How thoughtful,' I thought.

Thoughtful my foot! In one swift motion he pushed me backwards, raised my sari and jackknifed my legs. I was taken completely by surprise. Before I could react, he was standing between my legs trying to stuff his barely tumescent organ in!

'Contract your vaginal muscles, contract them damn you.' He urged, and I didn't know how to do so!

This was ridiculous—the rapist enlisting the help of the raped! Was this what I had staked my honour for? A half-hearted attempt by a half-erect penis! Years of trying to get me laid climaxed into an anticlimax! He hadn't been able to move me at all. For that matter, he hadn't moved much himself!

All the manoeuvring and boasting had come to this? It was much too funny for words. We laughed till our stomachs ached and tears ran down our cheeks. We laughed till we could laugh no more. We tried to turn our attention to food, but the *dosas* had turned limp and soggy reminding us of something similar and we dissolved into laughter once again. In fact, the *idlis* we ate with *sambar* and coconut *chutney* gave us far more satiety than the over-hyped, much-anticipated non-act had given us.

48

The image of a ladies' man that Rajan had carefully cultivated was but a ploy to entangle me in his web. Perhaps subconsciously, I wanted to be taken by a real man. I now learnt that he had never known any woman besides his wife. Though it had ceased to matter, I believed him, not because I was naïve but because he had a congenital penile defect called hypospadias. This was his secret shame. He dared not expose his deformed organ to anyone for fear of ridicule. Though I did not recoil in horror when he laid bare his vulnerability, I was ill-equipped to handle him sexually. The foreskin was pushed back and the mucosa of the glans had hardened into skin. As skin required greater friction, he needed a lot of time and innovation to reach a climax and I did not have the know-how. It was on this account that our earlier sexual encounters were disappointing. Perseverance paid, and we ended up using the condition to our advantage.

A wife I had been for fourteen years, a mother for thirteen; but a woman, I became at the ripe old age of thirty-five! I did not know that the body could give so much pleasure. Never had the flesh been loved and pampered so. Like a new convert, I went overboard and gave myself up to sheer sensuality. Morality and reason were banished from the happy space of hedonism where I gave myself up to physical gratification. The year passed in a sexual haze—sexual awakenings and sexual raptures, sexual rages and sexual jealousies. There were ecstasies beyond belief, and agonies beyond endurance. Passion took hold of me like a virulent virus and in the rigours of this fever, I convulsed. To think I could have lived and died without experiencing such bliss!

The Ultimate

The soaring of happiness,
Like powerful winged birds,
A cataract of pleasure
Cascading over flesh.
The agonised clamouring,
The striving, the straining,
The exquisite torture,
The tormenting clasp;
Grim determined pursuit,
As if battling for life.
Like two wild animals
In lethal combat.
Reaching for the intangible
Tantalizingly out of reach.
Faces curiously contorted
As if in pain,
The building of pressures
The rapturous convulsions.
The languorous stupor
The gratification intense,
A bounty greater than this
Can Nature bestow?

Raju patiently untangled the web of my inhibitions. Like water hyacinths, they had clogged the pool of my sexuality, making ripples of any sort impossible. He was the founder, propagator, and follower of the cult of the cunt. If my eyes and mouth had drawn him to me initially, it was this part of my anatomy that kept him riveted by my side. According to him, it was something to live for, and die for! It was not an idle boast for he did get occasion to stake his life for me. He had never seen anything quite like it before. I dared not ask how many he had seen to make comparisons. As a gynaecologist, fingering women's vaginas was a part of my job. Till now, I viewed the female sexual organs clinically—as a passage for procreation, rather than recreation. I even thought of the private parts in medical terms. It never occurred to me to observe them for beauty or to compare them with mine. I hated Raju for putting such ideas in my mind.

Each day, Raju marvelled afresh at my innocence and I at his expertise. He had an unbelievable libido and incredible staying powers. In due course, I became his mate in the true sense of the word. With this all-consuming love, came a cloying possessiveness. I resented the presence of other women in his life. Though he professed to be 'pure', his sex appeal enticed women like the silver strings of a spider's web. In order to hurt him as he hurt me, I told him about *my* admirers—Jeeju, Uncle, and Dr Ramani, with whom I had done precious little. It was gratifying to learn by his darkened countenance and bloodshot eyes that my arrow had struck home. Passionate outbursts, thunderous jealousies, massive quarrels that turned physical at times, became a pattern with us. Our love was not the soothing, restful type between two people at peace with each other. It was the gathering and lowering of rain clouds, the deluge followed by snatched moments of tranquillity till the next cloud burst.

At times, there occurred lucid intervals in this hypnotic state and my conscience wouldn't let me enjoy the manna from heaven. I made half-hearted attempts to get out of the well of deceit; but the walls were slippery and my will not strong enough. Not only was I living a colossal lie, I resorted to a number of little lies to sustain the big one. Lies begot lies faster than flies hatched flies. Truthful by nature, I hated the deceitful person I had become.

When guilt raised its ugly head I'd ask him, 'How can we build our happiness on the misery of others?'

'It was meant to be,' he said simply.

'I quail at the thought of a scandal. I suffer both ways—with you, without you. Let's retrace our steps before all is lost.'

'I'd rather die than give you up,' he said, shutting my mouth with a kiss and the straw of resistance would be swept away by the mighty river of passion.

An unlikely fallout of this attachment was a spate of love poems from my pen, that found instant acceptance in various magazines and widespread readership. This prompted Raju to say, 'From now on every sentence *I* utter will also be in verse.'

'What could be worse?' I shuddered in mock horror.

Laughter welled and escaped from our throats as if let loose after years of captivity. Little did we know that we would have to pay the price of every little joy a thousand times over.

49

Bit by bit the wonder of another human unfolded itself. I learnt about Raju's likes and dislikes, his fears and phobias, hopes and ambitions. All that he symbolised—courage, conviction, daring, and intrepidity impressed. I loved his altruistic bent of mind for he went out of the way to help a pigeon entangled in electric wires, or a boy run over by a bus. So what if I was educated in convents? He had been educated in the classroom of life and learnt lessons that no school could ever teach. He was a self-made man, and that I thought was something to be proud of. I marvelled at his unabashed sexuality. The greatest compliment he could pay to a woman was to desire her. He made no distinction between love and lust; perhaps, there *was* no difference. Intellectuals like me indulged in unnecessary hair splitting. My love for Rajiv Mehra had been purely emotional, the sex I had with my husband was physical, while with Raju, there was a union of heart, mind, body, and soul. It did not matter which way we worked out our equations as long as the result was the same.

I also realised that there was more to Raju than the persuasive lover who would not take no for an answer. His hurt, little boy look belied a ruthless personality. He had seen the world far too closely to trust it implicitly. Early in life, he learnt that nothing was for free. He had a way of rubbing in favours with the subtlety of a truck horn that irritated me. Yet he was a softie at heart and broke down easily. Tears looked so incongruous on his manly frame that my heart broke the first time I saw him cry. When this threatened to become a pattern, I resorted to stinging barbs that dried his eyes faster than words of solace would have done.

Before I knew it, he had alienated me from my friends and family. I hardly noted this cold-blooded segregation, for my sun rose and set with Raju. I did what he said because I loved him. What aggravated was that he did nothing I wanted him to do until I learnt to bargain. There would be conversations like, 'I'll put *sindhoor* (vermillon) in the parting of my hair, if you wear a *kada* (steel bangle that Sikhs wear) on your right wrist.'

It was a strange barter between two people supposedly in love with each other, but love, I learnt, was curiously akin to war—a thrilling, nerve-tingling war where differences dissolved in the melting heat of mating bodies.

At times, I woke up to the fact that Raju was not a nice man to know. He wasn't someone I would have cultivated had I been in the right frame of mind, yet my dependence on him was complete. I dared not call my attachment by any other name than love, for it was demeaning to confess, even to myself that it was sheer sex appeal that I had succumbed to!

Problems arose when the sex appeal he exuded had a similar effect on other women. His presence made virginal women uncomfortable, post-menopausal women lively, and those in the reproductive age group respond unwittingly. It was an attraction that proved lethal, at least, in one case. Raju would frequent a police station for the SHO (Station House officer) was his friend. His assistant, sub-inspector Sonia—a pretty girl with short hair and hazel eyes—sat in the anteroom, and would wish him whenever he walked past her to his friend's room. It was an open secret that she serviced her boss.

That fateful afternoon, Sonia overheard their 'man to man' conversation, learnt that Rajan took a long time to come, and instantaneously fell in lust with him! She, who had no problem in attracting males, who took sexual harassment as an occupational hazard, was amazed at Rajan's lack of response to her overtures. He was newly and totally involved with me and had eyes for no other, which she found out by following him one day. When she berated him for choosing an 'old cow' over the 'slender doe' she thought she was, he gave her such a dressing down that she walked out of her third floor balcony in an inebriated state that evening, and fell to her doom. Whether it was an accident or suicide, no one will know. I was badly shaken by the incident.

Raju got all the poems I had written for him published privately without my knowledge as my birthday gift. The gesture would have been sweet if he hadn't brought the female owner of the printing house along with the poems! He charmed his way into her life, promising her the world; once his business with her was over, he dumped her. This was his modus operandi and it had yet to fail. I remembered that he had used similar tactics with me too, in the initial stages. When the situation threatened to get out of control, he confessed everything to me with that little boy look of his.

Keeping me in a perpetual state of jealously was another ploy he used to keep me hooked. It had worked beautifully till now, but I had had enough.

'Why did you encourage her in the first place?' I fumed.

'I wanted her to do the best for your book.'

'It's either her or me.' I gave him an ultimatum.

'All I do is for you.'

'I could do without a threesome.'

'I have tried my best to shake her off but she refuses to let go.'

'You leave that to me.'

It took but one anonymous call to her husband to get her off his back.

The most persistent of all was Anjana, the daughter of a prominent politician. As Rajan dealt in farmlands, he dealt with the ultra rich. She had recently bought a large tract of agricultural land and Rajan had clinched the deal. She liked both the profession and the realtor, and worked out a business deal with him. With her highflying contacts, she would supply the customers, Rajan the land, and the profits would be shared. He visualised himself a multimillionaire in a year's time. What he had not reckoned with was the fact that she wanted him to service her, for husband (no stud himself) was busy at his stud farm, and she needed him to supply a fillip to her jaded sex life. When she tired of him, she would pass him on to her friends for that was how these high society women whiled away their time. This hurt his pride as nothing else could, and he vowed never to work with her again. He went one last time to her residence to settle accounts. She led him to the bedroom and shut the door as the sum was huge, and she did not want servants prying.

She turned, ostensibly to open her safe for the cash instead, opened her blouse to expose her breasts, and begged him to quench her desire.

Taking her arms off his neck, he said, 'I despise the likes of you. You are no better than a bitch on heat.'

'I'll make you pay for this, you bastard,' she screamed, insane with thwarted desire.

He spun on his heels and left. As far as he was concerned, their association was over but she was a woman scorned. She baited him with the money she owed him and lucrative land deals, but he did not respond. She hired a detective to follow him and discovered me.

'High society, wealth, youth, and beauty beckon and you spurn all for *her*!'

'It only shows that she has got something that you don't,' he retorted.

By this time, I was suffering from a massive inferiority complex and asked him the same question.

'What we have between us is exquisitely precious. For Anjana and her likes, I am but a plaything to be used and discarded. As for the money, if it is in my *kismet* I'll earn it somehow, certainly not as a gigolo!'

A few days later, she rang me up and with the arrogance born of wealth and asked me to quote a price to free Raju. I put down the receiver without answering.

By now, I was fed up of his harem and the havoc they wrought in my life. Why did he charm his way into their lives and then dump them, making himself irresistible? He was made like that and I had to accept him as the way he was, he implied in not so many words. Well, two could play the game. I encouraged the men interested in me to give him a dose of his own medicine. Insane with jealousy, he promised that I would have no reason to complain, provided I gave him none. The ploy worked beautifully. I gloated in triumph. It was sheer survival.

50

Biographies of great men make interesting reading, but lives of ordinary mortals are no less absorbing. They are the stuff that novels are made of. Keenly interested in what went into the making of Rajan Bhardwaj, I encouraged him to talk about himself. The more I learnt, the more I marvelled at the colossal difference in our upbringing. Yet, it was destined that our lives be intertwined hereafter.

In the village of Kotputli in Rajasthan, two generations ago, there lived a learned head priest. Though highly honoured by the prince, he was an unhappy man having buried eleven children in as many years—all stillborn. Insane with grief, he was digging a grave to bury himself alive when a wandering ascetic chanced to pass by. On hearing his tale of woe, the ascetic gave him a *kavandal* (wooden bowl) filled with holy water that he was asked to sprinkle around his house, and bury the vessel under the threshold. He did as told and was rewarded with a son Kishan.

Though Kishan was an ascetic at heart, he married Kunti, a young girl from Sunderpura (a tiny village in Rajasthan) to fulfil his duty towards his family. Within a year of her marriage, she conceived much to the joy of all concerned. At term, as was the custom, Kunti went to her maternal home to deliver. On a cold winter night, in the dark recesses of their crumbling old *haveli*, she lay in labour. A kerosene lamp cast eerie shadows on the wall. A tight knot of women huddled around the hapless Kunti, bonded by the feminine business of childbirth. Having done their bit, men were now redundant; in awe of the very vaginas they had lusted for not so very long ago.

Kunti's eyes were glazed with pain—a pain she never knew existed on the face of this earth. She squat on a pair of bricks. One woman supported her back; another loosened her plait for it was believed that open hair facilitated delivery. Yet another fed her milk, heavily laced with almonds and *ghee*. The vaginal effluence was collected in the *tasla* (iron basin) beneath her, filled with sand. Another *tasla* filled with ripe wheat was kept on the threshold as a symbol of fecundity. The air was thick with the cloying smell of blood and amniotic fluid. The baby was taking an inordinately long time to emerge. With each contraction there rose a chorus, 'Push, push, push hard.'

Kunti pushed till her face was red and her jugulars stood out. Beads of sweat glistened on her brow even as the other women shivered under their shawls. The midwife put her hand on the top of her protruding belly and gave violent little jerks with each pain. Everything in her book had been tried and yet no baby emerged. When hope was all but abandoned, and it was thought that Kunti would die in childbirth, she gave a final thrust and out slipped the baby slick with slime. It was 4 a.m., the blackest hour before dawn. The lamp sputtered and died leaving the room in total darkness. Feminine hands fondled the genitals of the newborn and exclaimed.

'It's a boy! It's a boy.'

There rose in Kunti's breast a glorious surge of maternal love and the pride of giving birth to a son. Her joy was short-lived though. By the light of dawn, it was discovered that his penis was curiously deformed. The bulbous tip was splayed open like the hood of a cobra. The foreskin was wrinkled and bunched up at the junction of the shaft and the glans. The urinary orifice opened not at the tip but at the underside of the junction. She woke up her mother, and the two slapped their foreheads in despair. Horror squeezed the blood from of their hearts. What if the eunuchs got an inkling of her sexually-malformed child? They would take him away forcibly. The mother and daughter had no parameter to judge the exact nature of the defect, for Raju was no eunuch. He was a normal male with a penile defect that could be repaired by plastic surgery, but how were they to know? Instead, they kept his genitalia covered. Women sniggered at Kunti's fancy city ways, for village children roamed naked almost till adolescence, but Kunti did not rise to the bait. She had the future of her child at stake. After a while, she joined her husband in Delhi, leaving Raju in the care of her mother, Raju's naani, till they could afford to keep him.

Naani was married at the age of 8, started childbearing by 16, and was widowed at 21. The third child was born after her husband's death. He succumbed to TB condemning her to a life of celibacy. As a mother of three young children, she was lucky not to be burnt alive on her husband's pyre. This was usually the fate of childless widows, especially if her husband had property that her relatives coveted. Those who survived their husband's death but lost their children later, were called *dhakans* (witches) and lynched to death. Though no such horror befell Naani, being a young widow and a comely one at that, she was forced to remain within the haveli, lest she fall prey to the advances of lecherous men. Over the years, her sons grew up and took up jobs in distant cities. Little Raju was now her companion-cum-guardian. On him she showered all her repressed love.

Naani lived in mortal fear of inadvertent exposure of Raju's genitalia. She made him promise not to pee in the open. She told him stories of lizards that turned into crocodiles at night, instilling in him the fear of darkness and ghosts so that he never ventured out alone. In short, she took every care that the eunuchs did not kidnap him. As Raju grew older, he realised that his sex organs were different; and ashamed of the fact, did not take part in competitions like 'Who'll pee the farthest?' that the other boys indulged in.

Life in the village was hard but happy. The children would get up early to follow the cowherd as he took the cattle to graze. With *taslas* over their heads, they would aim straw arrows on dung heaps to stake their claim. Rajan would bag the maximum number of steaming mounds and run home happily with a full *tasla*. Naani used a part of the precious heap to plaster the floor. The rest, she patted into dung cakes and dried on the roof and walls. These were used as fuel in the monsoons, when firewood was scarce. The extra pats were sold at Rs 2 a cart. Besides this, there was grass to be cut for the cow, firewood to be gathered, and green berries to be plucked from thorny shrubs. By the time he was done, Raju would be ravenously hungry and gobble thick stale *rotis* with homemade butter and pickled berries, washing them down with gallons of buttermilk.

The village air, the hard work, and healthy appetite laid the foundations of an excellent constitution. The only time he succumbed to any form of disease was when he had an attack of measles, but the cure proved worse than the disease. In a bid to soothe his itch one night, Naani rushed to the kitchen to get some ash. As all earthen pots looked the same in the dark, Naani grabbed a handful of red chilli powder and rubbed it over his sore body. He screamed and ran out, ready to jump into the well.

Though Raju went to the village school, his heart was not in his studies. Most of his time was spent at the wrestling ground honing his skills on the newly-turned earth, till he finally became a champion wrestler and weight lifter. It fell upon Naani to foment his aches and bruises—every night.

Life revolved around their 'engleesh' cow. Raju fed and watered her. Naani milked her and sold the milk, butter, and *ghee* to the village folk. It was also Raju's duty to get the cow mated. The price of one mating with a stud bull was two and half kilograms of jaggery. As Raju led the cow to the cowherd's, he ate most of it on the way. The cowherd's wife was churning buttermilk in a large earthenware pot. Arms, covered with white bangles up to the armpits, whipped the thick creamy fluid. Her multi-hued silver lined *lehanga* (Indian long skirt) rode high up her legs. A thin, muslin veil covered her head and face. Through it shone her silver head ornament, the *borla*.

She peered at him with kohl-lined eyes, weighed the proffered jaggery expertly in her hand, smiled to herself, but said nothing. Together they watched the bull trying ineffectively to mount the cow. After a while, she got up in exasperation, held the bull's organ in her hand, and inserted it expertly inside the cow.

While fornicating animals were nothing out of the ordinary for this rural kid, dealing with amorous adults was proving to be difficult. He dreaded the visits of his Maamas (mother's brothers), who came with their wives. A pair of lustier females he had yet to see. While their husbands gossiped with their mother late into the night, the wives, denied their conjugal bliss, tried to make do with the little boy! Short of raping him, they did everything else. The elder one pinched his bottom and buried his head in her bosom. Even as he struggled to break free, she pulled down his shorts and dipped her hand in ghee to massage his 'circumcised' penis. As Naani was not to be disturbed when her sons came visiting, he ran to his younger aunt. She held a mirror in her hand and asked Raju to help her pretty herself for she had a rendezvous with her husband that night. He painted her lips, lined her eyes with kajal, adjusted the *borla* on her forehead and tied the string of her bodice. As a reward, she swirled her 52 yards *lehnga* and buried him under it!

Years later, when Raju visited them as a young man, he bent to touch her feet out of respect. She looked at him through her veil and winked! He stepped back startled. That evening, while serving dinner she whispered,

'If you had winked back, I'd have known that you were ready for a lay.' And he knew that she was only half joking.

51

Infrequent matings with his fertile wife Kunti, lead to the birth of three offspring—a son, Rajan, and two daughters. After that, Kishen abandoned his family to become a temple priest. People held him in great esteem for, like his father, he was a learned Sanskrit scholar. He subsisted on the offerings made by devotees, which was precious little. This was bitterly resented by Rajan for he considered such income no better than alms. He could not look up to a father who felt no responsibility towards his family. As a result, Raju had to grow up before time. Kunti, however, bore her husband no grudge for the desertion. She felt that he was a holy man above worldly affairs and it was an honour to be his wife. She added to the family kitty by selling the milk and *ghee* of their cow, like her mother had done back in her village Sunderpura.

Schooling in the city was something of a shock to the gauche country bumpkin. Not only was Rajan older than his classmates, he was also big for his age. They made fun of his accent, his mannerism, and the lunch he brought to school— thick *chapattis* with fat green chilies pickled in rye. Could he ever forget the worn-out khaki shorts that gave way at the bottom? His mother patched it up, but his butt remained the butt of their jokes. So deep was his embarrassment that he did not go to school till he saved enough money selling newspapers to buy a pair of second-hand shorts.

Another sensation Rajan was familiar with was hunger. He never seemed to get enough to eat. He befriended a Sikh boy so that he could accompany him to the Gurudwara, and eat to his fill the *langar* (free food) served in the holy precincts. Despite being a high caste Brahmin, he shared the lunch of a Muslim class fellow, much to his mother's horror; but hunger made strange table-fellows. He also ran errands for the local sweets vendor for the surplus buttermilk and left over embers that he took home to warm their miserable winters.

Diwali in Delhi was like none he had seen in the village. From behind the bars of his window and poverty, he watched people exchange sweetmeats and laughter. With houses and faces lit up, they personified the festival of lights. Best of all were the crackers he could not afford. He craned his neck to watch the rockets zoom into the sky and explode into a bunch of stars. The sparklers, flowerpots, cartwheels and bombs, made him gasp in wonder. He stayed awake till late into the night, admiring the astonishing display. When he was reasonably sure that the streets were deserted, he prowled amidst the ashes like a stray dog, scavenging quite a treasure. With a few half-burnt sparklers, a couple of *anars* (flowerpots), and a number of bombs that hadn't gone off, he set off to celebrate his solitary Diwali.

Down the street, he ran with a fiery sparkler in each hand; shouting with joy gone berserk, '*Holi ayee re, holi ayee hai!* (holi has come, holi has come)'

A passing drunk reminded him that it was the festival of lights, not colours. With tears streaming down his face, he made a promise to himself on that moonless night: he would become so rich that never again would he have steal a few moments of light and joy. Years later, when Raju blew up thousands in smoke every Diwali, I had no inkling of the desperation that prompted such wasteful expenditure.

Rajan was impressed by his lavish lifestyle of a coloniser named Bhagat, and envisaged such a life for himself. One day, Bhagat accosted Rajan on his way to school.

'I have cut a colony on a fine piece of land. Ask your teachers if they are interested in buying property at throwaway rates.' He did not really expect any response, but spoke out of habit. Bhagat had not reckoned with the intensity of the boy. By evening, Rajan had the entire staff wanting to buy a plot! He gave Rajan Rs 200/- for his pains. It was far less than what he deserved, but for Rajan, it was a windfall. He bought a Romer wristwatch for Rs 42/- and a transistor from super bazaar worth Rs 75/-. The boy, who had flapped his way to school in cheap plastic chappals and patched up knickers, became quite a dandy. By the time he was in the tenth standard, Rajan became a school dropout (though business was one of the reasons) and was employed full time with Bhagat. He learnt much more in the school of life than he ever could in stuffy classrooms.

While Bhagat's son lazed around, Rajan worked hard. Whatever the weather, whatever the time, he did not hesitate to take customers to the site and convince them that they were getting the deal of a lifetime. Business picked up steadily. Though Rajan was underpaid, he did not mind, for he was learning the trade. In his heart, Bhagat took the place of the father he so despised. A father who thought that the parental duty began and ended by siring Rajan and his two sisters; whose only contribution had been a sprinkling of semen—as he overheard his mother say in a rare moment of bitterness. Out of respect, Rajan took to calling Bhagat *Chacha* (father's younger brother). A customer impressed by the boy's earnestness told Bhagat, 'Your nephew is very enterprising.'

'Nephew?'

'Rajan.'

'That upstart! He is just a paid servant.'

That was the last day Rajan worked for anyone in his life.

With a chair under the shade of a tree, he opened shop. On the slimy terrains of human greed, he stumbled and rose again. He saw the underbelly of human nature and learnt lessons that he never forgot. He kept a low margin of profit and did not cheat his customers. In a short time, he had built up a large clientele. People began to trust him. His word was signature enough; transactions worth lakhs were finalised with just a rupee as token money. After a while, he acquired a licence and became a coloniser himself. He donated generously to charitable institutions and acquired power and position as head of various organisations. He gave large amounts for Ram Lila celebrations and was made the chief guest each year; the very Ram Lila he used to act in as a lad. His files, oiled with bribes, moved smoothly on the rusty rails of bureaucracy, for he kept high-ranking officials, the police, and politicians happy. The one motivating force in those early days had been his rage against Bhagat. He undersold property to get even with him. After all, he had nothing to lose. People deserted the established dealer for this fool of a fellow who sold land at throwaway prices. If Rajan did not profit, Bhagat lost all, on account of his complacency and a good-for-nothing son. Even as an employee, Rajan had dealt directly with the customers, making contacts that stood him in good stead now. In due course, Rajan bought Bhagat's office and felt vindicated when he occupied as master the very office he had left in disgrace not so very long ago.

52

Rajan grew up to be a healthy, virile young man. He took great care of his body. Armed with a *lota* (small round metal vessel), a bottle of oil, and his super bazaar transistor, he set off for the fields each morning. After his ablutions, he would strip to his underwear and massage his body, then loosen the string of his drawers to rub oil over his genitals with masturbatory pleasure. After this, he did push-ups till sweat poured down in streams despite the chill in the air.

In the early sixties, Najafgarh was a rural area. There were green wheat fields as far as the eyes could see. Phoola, a 15-year-old girl, climbed to her rooftop to take in the fresh morning air, took in Rajan's near naked body and fell in lust with him. Every morning, she would wake up early to observe his magnificent physique.

One day, Phoola's mother summoned Rajan to shift the heavy stone grinder to the courtyard so that she could grind wheat in the mellow sun. Phoola rushed out to 'help' him. Putting her hands over his, she whispered, 'You are coming to Reena's wedding? I will be waiting for you.'

Rajan was flattered by her attention. He was young, the juices of life welled up in his lithe body, and it felt good to be alive. Matters came to a head at the wedding. Feet tapped to the beat of the dholak; songs rent the air. While the others flopped down exhausted one by one, 15-year-old Phoola and 17-year-old Rajan danced throughout the night, scandalising the orthodox community. He was severely reprimanded by his mother, whom he called Jiji (elder sister, as from childhood he had heard her brothers call her) for associating with that shameless low-caste hussy.

She ended her tirade by stating, 'If you are ready for marriage, I'll find a demure Brahmin bride for you.'

This only served to whet his desire for the buxom girl. Dusshera was around the corner and teenagers were busy rehearsing for Ram Lila in the smoky months of September and October. During the ten days preceding the festival, people would hurry through dinner and rush to Ram Lila grounds. They'd watch the characters of Ramayana come down to in the guise of these actors and relive the entire epic. Months of practice went into the preparation. Rajan delighted in taking part. Being a devout Brahmin, Jiji was glad that her son was playing the part of the Lord Rama. Rama the obedient son, the just ruler, the conqueror of evil, would descend amongst mortals for ten days. On Dusshera, he would demolish Ravana and rescue his beloved wife from the clutches of the ten-headed demon. Thousands would watch as Rama aimed a burning arrow at the effigy of Ravana. There would be a collective gasp, as the demon king went up in flames and crackers burst in his belly.

What Jiji did not know was that Phoola was playing Sita, Rama's consort. In *Kalyug*, there was a new twist to the immortal tale. Rama (Rajan) watched Ravana (a boy called Mohan) fall in love with Sita (Phoola), Rama's wife. So far it was as in the epic. The two even had a fist fight over her. What was unthinkable was that though Sita was in love with Rama, she was not averse to the attentions of Ravana. During one rehearsal, Rajan saw Mohan elbow her breasts. Instead of slapping him hard (as he expected her to do), she smiled coyly. Rajan spat on the floor and walked out.

Sorry for her flirtatious behaviour, Phoola ran after Rajan to beg forgiveness but he cut her out of his life altogether.

Meanwhile, worried about their daughter's uncontained sexuality, Phoola's parents arranged a match for her. She was kept under house arrest till the date of her marriage. All she could manage was a frantic phone call.

'Let's run away and get married,' she whispered in a voice hoarse with desperation.

'I would be glad to do so if I only knew who you were,' said Rajan gallantly.

'It's me Phoola, your Phoola! My marriage has been fixed to another, but I love *you*.'

'My mother would never allow an inter-caste marriage,' he said, and put the receiver down.

What he said was true but if he really wanted to marry her, nothing would have deterred him. No woman who allowed her breasts to be caressed by another while she professed to be in love with him could be his wife.

A year later, when she returned to her maternal home for a holiday, she stopped by at his shop and announced, 'The least you can do is to have an affair with *me*!'

'Why Phoola, you haven't changed at all,' he said mightily amused.

She pouted and flounced off in offence when he refused her generous offer.

The next girl in his life was Neelam. Their affair began with a pencil. The master was dictating notes, and Rajan's pencil broke. The new girl in class gave him a sweet smile and a neatly sharpened pencil.

Rajan was bowled over by her gentle ways and good breeding. Though he was only too aware of his frayed collars and gauche ways, he could not keep away from her. He took to walking her home after school. She radiated a goodness that enveloped him. To please her, he stopped punctuating his sentences with swearwords and stopped behaving aggressively. She was drawn to his gallantry and eagerness to please. The situation was too idyllic to last. Shanker, a classmate of Neelam's social stature, was trying to woo her in vain. To shake off the upstart who shadowed her, he announced that his watch was stolen and he suspected Rajan! Rajan was too stunned to retaliate.

'So now we have a thief in class,' said the teacher. 'It is a serious matter. The headmaster shall hear of it.'

'But, sir, I have not taken the watch,' began Rajan, only to be rapped sharply on the knuckles by a ruler.

At the headmaster's office, injustice was meted out without a trial and Rajan was condemned. His ears were punched and his pockets searched as if he was a common criminal. The entire school watched his degradation. He would have borne all had not Neelam whispered in reproach, 'Rajan, how could you?'

He swung on his heels and walked away.

As he reached the school gate, Shanker's father, the village headman, strode in. The headmaster rushed out in unctuous welcome. Something snapped in Rajan. He picked up a brick and flung it at the headmaster saying, 'You bastard, you boot licker, you swine.'

Needless to say, he was rusticated. The false allegation and its aftermath left an indelible mark on Rajan's psyche. He became hard and ruthless, and a loner. Days on an end he sat under the peepal, throwing stones into the pond. One evening, as he desultorily indulged in this pastime, he felt a hand on his shoulder. It was Neelam.

'Please forgive me,' she beseeched.

'What makes you come now?'

'Shanker's watch fell out of his pocket today.'

'You didn't believe me then. It does not matter now,' he said bitterly.

'I am sorry, I'm really very sorry.'

'Leave me alone.'

He never forgave Neelam for not believing in him. Soon after, she was married to a wealthy businessman and shifted to another city. Their paths crossed but once. The wheel of fortune had turned a full circle. While Rajan prospered, her husband faced bankruptcy. Unable to cut his losses, he took to drinking and wife-bashing. Rajan held himself responsible for her plight and bailed him out with an anonymous cheque.

53

Now that Rajan was 20 and well settled, his mother set out to find a bride for him. She selected Snehlata, a girl from a poor Brahmin family. Her father owned a tiny wheat mill in the trans-Jamuna area. The mill occupied the front of their two-room tenement while the entire family, which consisted of a wife, three daughters, and a son, occupied the room at the back. Food was cooked in a tin shed behind the house. The kitchen also served as the bathroom when not in use. The toilets were communal, away from the house. Jiji fixed the alliance without Rajan's knowledge or consent. He was livid. Having attained a status in society as a coloniser with a shop of his own, Rajan dreamt of making a good marriage with a girl who would supply education and breeding, the two things his money could not buy. His mother thought otherwise.

Traditionally, he was not allowed to see his fiancée before marriage, but posing as the 'boy's' cousin, he entered forbidden territory. Snehlata, he found to his horror, was a short-statured, mousy girl with stained teeth and a sallow complexion. Not a single redeeming feature did she have! Had his mother gone blind? Did she have so low an opinion of him that she thought that *this* girl was the ideal mate for her only son? Something was terribly wrong somewhere. He had to convince Jiji that he couldn't possibly spend the rest of his life with this female.

'Jiji,' he began conversationally, as his mother served him dinner that night. 'What did you see in Snehlata that made you decide she is the girl for me?'

'She comes from a pure, high class Brahmin family.'

'So do a lot of other girls.'

'She is industrious and homely.'

'And . . .'

'And she can cook, sew, and keep house.'

'And . . .'

'And she does not squint or limp.'

'What about the dowry?' he asked after a pause.

'I did not ask for anything. God had given us more than enough and the poor fellow has two more daughters to marry.'

'What is this, a marriage, or charity? Tell me, is she too beautiful to let go? Do her looks make up for her lack of dowry?'

Jiji did not answer. She continued to ladle curry in his plate quite unnecessarily.

'You haven't answered me,' he hissed through clenched teeth.

'She's okay.'

'*You lie!*' He got up abruptly upsetting his dinner plate.

'I mean she is not bad looking.' Jiji was on the defensive, suddenly afraid of her own son.

'She is positively plain,' Rajan stated categorically.

'How can you say that?'

'I sent my friend . . . what the heck, I went to see her myself.'

'You, you went to your in-laws before marriage!' Jiji was appalled. On firmer grounds now, the authority of a mother over son restored. She said, 'How could you?'

'Cut the crap and listen carefully. I am not sorry that I went there. Break off this alliance at once.'

'I will do nothing of that sort.'

'Oh yes, you will.'

'I have given my word of honour.'

'I care two hoots for your word of honour. I will not marry her and that's that.'

Days rolled by. Neither would relent. The good-for-nothing father was busy ringing temple bells, oblivious to the high drama being enacted at home. As a last resort, Jiji threatened suicide on the railway tracks.

'Two can play the game,' replied Rajan coldly, but when she bent down to touch *his* feet, he realised the futility of his resistance.

'You pay the price of my milk just this once. I'll never ask anything of you again all my life,' she said, spreading her sari *pallu* as if for alms.

In answer, he put his head on her ample bosom and sobbed uncontrollably.

'Jiji!' he cried 'Do you have such a low opinion of my worth that you chose *her* for me?'

Jiji said nothing but let her tears mingle with his. How could she tell her beloved son that after one look at his deformed penis any right thinking girl would bolt. Only a plain one with plainer prospects and the bait of a dowry-less wedding could be made to stay. It was simple market sense. One had to make concessions for defective goods.

Snehlata entered her husband's house as a demure bride on a wet July afternoon. With *alta*-lined feet, she pushed over a pot of grain before crossing the threshold of her new home. A threshold she would cross only on the bier after her death. Such was the permanence of a Hindu wedding.

The *Suhaag Raat* was a debacle where the roles were reversed. Rajan fumbled for an inordinately long time without getting anywhere. Exasperated, the 16-year-old bride pushed him down and sat on top of him! Elated at having consummated the marriage before Snehlata discovered his abnormality, Rajan did not notice that she did not bleed at first penetration. That this utterly uninteresting female could be anything but a virgin did not occur to him. Later, when the battles in bed began, he'd ask, 'Why didn't you bleed on the first night?'

'Some women don't.'

'And pray, why don't they? Don't they have a hymen?'

'Yes they do, but it ruptures at the time of menarche.' It was a falsehood but how was he to know? As he was digesting this piece of information, she said, 'Speak for yourself. How come your organ is different?'

'How do you know it's different? Have you seen a naked man before?' he countered. She had a brain if nothing else, and was quick to reply, 'Little boys run around naked all the time.' This shut him up.

If the physical defect was all they had to cope with, they would have managed somehow. It was discovered that Rajan could not ejaculate. Entire nights were spent trying to milk a rigid erection. The wife experienced multiple orgasms and wasn't complaining, but his mother was. Of what use was a daughter-in-law if she had to do the household chores herself as before? This one slept throughout the day. Tired of her mother-in-law's admonishing, Snehlata retaliated, 'Why don't you tell your son to stop pestering me? I am sick and tired of his nocturnal activities.'

This shut the old woman up. She had feared that Rajan was impotent, but the voluptuous stretching of the wife in the morning had proved that he was man enough to satisfy her. What had happened now?

Appraisal of situation subdued the older woman and her reprimands lost their sting. Snehlata held Rajan's defect as a whip over mother and son. And did she use it to her advantage! The power she wielded was enough to make the other wives in the neighbourhood wonder what her husband saw in her? Though they were prettier, had brought handsome dowries, *their* husbands did not dance to their tunes.

Then it happened. After a year of relentless effort, Rajan ejaculated. The solving of one problem, led to the unveiling of another. Now that satisfactory sex had been established, where was pregnancy that ought to follow?

There followed endless rounds of hospitals during which Snehlata was found to be normal, while Rajan had a low sperm count. He was damned twice over. Snehlata's power was now complete. She made Rajan 'loan' money to her father with which he bought a new house. It was never returned. She asked him to 'contribute' towards her sisters' marriages; he dared not refuse, though it was against the very grain of Indian culture. A chauvinistic Indian male, Rajan felt castrated by Snehlata. He *had* to father a child to regain his position as the master of the house.

54

Rajan's dreams of marrying culture and education had been shattered, but he was not one to be cowed down for long. He began cultivating people with good breeding and social status. Opportunity knocked at his door one morning in the form of a high-ranking bureaucrat—Mr PK Bhardwaj. As they belonged to the same caste and state, an instant rapport was established. Rajan became a part of their family within a month. One would wonder why a person of Mr Bhardwaj's stature would want to cultivate the likes of Rajan. There were his ill begotten gains to be adjusted in land and inquiries revealed that Rajan was a reputed and honest property dealer.

A peculiar phenomenon is observed in orthodox society where mixing of sexes was taboo. A brother-sister relationship is established between people who are not related by blood. Though it remains platonic most of the times, it could also serve as a cover for 'incestuous' behaviour. Mrs Shashikala Bhardwaj had lost her brother in an accident, and Rajan replaced him readily enough. Shashikala was years older than Rajan and dominated him in the guise of an elder sister. Now that PK became his Jijaji (brother in law), Raju stopped taking commission in land deals. Over the years, their capital increased many times over on account of Rajan's enterprise. In return, he gained what he had craved—an entry ticket into high society.

Rajan used his contact with them, and their contacts, to his advantage. Dropping PK's name in business transactions helped. They became a status symbol that he flaunted. It was a symbiotic relationship, wherein his money bought their position. While Rajan spent lavishly on their family, Jijaji helped him bypass bureaucracy, get a licensed revolver, an early *'darshan'* at the Vaishno Devi shrine.

Shashikala was pretty in a vampish sort of way, and quite vain. She was an MA in psychology, which impressed her barely lettered 'brother'. So taken up was Rajan with his 'sister' that he neglected his work to humour her. With her husband at work and the children in boarding schools, she used Rajan to fill the void in her life. They went on outings in the name of religion to Hanuman Mandir, Bhairon Mandir or Kalka Devi Mandir. At least that was the pretext. There were *gol guppas* to be eaten, purses and sandals to be bought. There were bumpy rickshaw rides where sisterly breasts accidentally brushed brotherly elbows. There was affectionate running of fingers through Rajan's hair, and there was much holding of hands. If someone were to hint that this was flirtatious behaviour, they would be outraged for *their* conscience was clear.

Shashikala soon realised that the way to Rajan's heart was through his stomach. She prepared *dahibahllas, shahi paneer* or mushrooms in cream sauce for him, and would be amply rewarded with gifts that ranged varied from vats of pickle to handspun silk saris. It was strictly a 'sibling' affair. Jijaji was too busy to join them and Snehlata was never included, lest she object to her husband's lavish spending. Not that Rajan was keen to take her anywhere. With her bad breath, stained teeth, and homely face, Snehlata was an embarrassment to him.

When I came into the scene, Shashikala's jealousy was beyond the realms of sisterly love. She felt as if I had dethroned her. Instead of visits to Hanuman Mandir with her, it was to the Jamuna with me. Instead of flooding her with gifts, he smothered me in them. Instead of helping her while away her time, he barely had time for her. Redundant and usurped Shashikala went berserk. Oblivious to her state of mind, Raju decided to acquaint the two most important women in his life with each other. This was to ensure her support for us when the world turned hostile. How naïve could a man be? When he suggested a meeting, she exclaimed outraged, 'Don't you dare bring that bitch to my house!'

'But, Behenji . . .'

'You fool, you poor, besotted fool. Don't you realise that she is only after your money? Once she's done with you, she'll discard you like a banana peel.'

She refused to accept that Raju was the one pursuing me and attributed to me vices I did not know I possessed. She told him categorically that I would be the cause of his downfall. Desperate to pry us apart, she even offered to get him a virgin Brahmin wife if he was so dissatisfied with the present one! When he refused to accept her 'offer', she screamed with impotent rage, 'I'll destroy that bloody bitch, if it's the last thing I do.' But Raju sorted her out in no time. He knew far too many of their secrets which could jeopardize her husband's career *and*, land him in jail!

She tried to lure him back with mouth-watering delicacies she knew he could not resist. He ended up aggravating her by saying that he would come with me or not at all. It was my turn to get angry. How dare he suggest such a thing when I had no desire to cultivate her acquaintance? The woman disgusted me, though I understood her insane jealousy. In desperation, she joined hands with Snehlata, the woman she had loathed all along. After all, they had a common enemy.

Now, Raju was nothing if not perverse by nature. Without my knowledge, he decided to invest all he had in my name to see if I left him afterwards. He asked Jijaji and Behanji to return the money he had given them for safekeeping. They obliged, though it was quite a bother going to the various hideouts for the same. Raju had made a similar request a few years back to test their integrity. They thought that he was doing the same again, would panic in a day or two and return the vast sum like the last time. It was the biggest mistake they ever made.

Oblivious to the above goings on, I stood on the terrace on a winter afternoon. Raju's car stopped at my gate. Opening the boot, he pulled out a huge sack.

'Don't you dare bring it up,' I said but he paid no heed.

My heart sank for I remembered the last time he had brought such sacks to my place. He had gone to a village to discuss the sale of an agricultural land with a zamindar and unloaded a truck of vegetables in my house! Spinach and radish, carrots and cauliflower, beans and cabbage, overflowed. Tomatoes and the onions rolled into the drawing room and bounced down the stairs. He left me stranded in a veritable vegetable market! I had a tough time explaining the harvest to my husband.

I waited on top of the stairs with a heaving chest. With a hand on my hip and the other pointing to the door I said, 'If you think I'll . . .'

He shut my mouth with his, pulled open the string that bound the mouth of the sack and turned it upside down. Out flowed lacs and lacs of rupees!

'What the hell . . .?'

'This is all yours.'

'I'm fed up of your pranks.'

He had a habit of ignoring what the other person was saying and continued his one-sided conversation.

'I've always fantasized about making love on a bed of rupees.'

'You disgust me. Collect your loot and scoot.'

'This is for you.'

'I will have none of your ill-gotten gains.'

He pouted in offence.

'Every single rupee has been earned by the sweat of my brow.'

'More likely, by the gift of the gab.'

'What?'

'Nothing that you'll understand.'

In a nutshell, he told me what transpired between him and Behanji as a result of which his life's earning lay at my feet.

'No, thank you,' I replied. 'The sweat of *my* brow earns more than enough for me.'

'What shall I do with it?'

'You should have asked me before bringing it over. Why don't you buy land?' advised the doctor to one who dealt in land. 'No one can rob it and the rate will appreciate with the passage of time.'

A month later, he kidnapped me for a picnic on a farm. Acres upon acres of golden mustard rippled as far as the eyes could see. On a dirt road, we drove through the fields filled with the fresh green of young wheat, bordered by eucalyptus that stood erect like sentinels on guard. Past water chestnuts in ponds, peacocks on trees we went inhaling the fragrance of freshly tilled earth. We stopped beneath a banyan tree at sundown, watching the rays set the mustard field on fire. Replete with the simple joys of nature, I sighed in contentment. He waved his hand with a flourish of a king, put a sheaf of papers in my hand, and exclaimed 'This is all yours.' He exclaimed.

I burst into tears.

'How dare you put my name in jeopardy? How will I explain this to my family and the taxman?' I wailed, handing the papers back to him. Raju was jubilant! Behanji had been proved wrong; I was not after his money after all.

For all his lack of formal education, Rajan was smarter than Behanji and me put together. He had killed not two but three birds with one stone. He had extracted his money from a hostile Behanji, showed me how much he loved me by buying land in my name and he kept the papers with him so that the land was not really mine. I had a sneaking suspicion that he had merely used my name to avoid the taxman. Behanji went berserk. She thought that I had manipulated him, and behaved as if I had snatched what was rightfully hers. She visited the site every week while I had seen it only that once. It became her life's ambition to retrieve it. This was ridiculous. As far as I was concerned, it wasn't mine to give. I had made an enemy for no earthly reason. Before she could plan her next move, calamity struck. Her husband was caught red-handed taking a bribe! It made headlines in all national dailies. He was suspended and asked to vacate the official premises. She, who reaped the benefits of his position, had to share his disgrace. We had cut off from them when he was still a powerful force to reckon with, therefore Raju could not be called a rat that deserted a sinking ship.

55

Raju's father succumbed to a heart attack. I went to offer condolences. Jiji wailed surrounded by women. Snehlata shed silent tears in a corner. Raju was nowhere to be seen. Even as I was wondering where he was, a little boy came up to tell me that Raju was suffering from mild chest pain and wanted me to examine him. He led me to a room upstairs. Alarmed, I climbed up the stairs to find him staring tearlessly at the wall. With a dry sob, he reached out, clung to me and broke down. Before I knew it, he was kissing me, his father's body not yet cold downstairs! I understood his need for solace and did not push him away.

Some days later, he expressed a desire to open a charitable hospital in his father's name. Jiji was filled with pride and told him to go right ahead. Naturally, I was asked to run the place. I insisted that it would be on a partnership basis. I had become so accustomed to autonomy that it was difficult working for someone even if that someone was Raju. It seemed a viable business proposition too, but the price of land had skyrocketed and all that we could afford was a flat. Raju had used up his money for the agricultural land, and I was still repaying the loans we had taken for the nursing home. So a flat was bought jointly in his mother's name and mine. Raju paid two thirds of the money and I paid one third, as I was the sole working partner. I also bought the hospital furniture and equipment. My husband neither approved nor disapproved.

We inaugurated our joint venture by making love on the bare floor. We had fun doing up the place. Painters, carpenters, and electricians invaded the premises. Every evening we converged to the flat, to observe the progress made, pay the workers, and finally to make love. Raju insisting on choosing my writing table; I agreed indulgently. Much later I learnt that, as in all things else, he had an ulterior motive. The table he got was a wooden one with the front completely covered because I had a habit of crossing my legs due to which my sari rode up a bit. He did not want people see my ankle and calf, a form of voyeurism he had indulged in as a patient's husband!

On the day of the inauguration, as was his desire, I wore what he had bought, right from the flowers in my hair to my sandals. The Mayor was called to cut the ribbon. The entire neighbourhood was invited. No one came from Mussoorie. They were appalled at the very idea. Their daughter-in-law, a partner of that upstart! How could MS have allowed it? After welcoming the Mayor with a bouquet, I found it difficult getting down from the dais on unaccustomed high-heels. As I hesitated, my husband held one hand and Raju the other, to help me down. The scene was frozen for posterity in a photograph taken by Uncle. In a crowd of a hundred odd people, Raju had eyes only for me and he did not like what he saw—Uncle clicking my photographs, Dr Raman monopolising my conversation and I, smiling happily at both of them. Raju showed his displeasure by not touching a morsel of the lavish repast. I had yet to learn of his pathological possessiveness and did not understand his sudden change of mood. I was unhappy because he was unhappy, somehow on my account. Little did I know that a silent war had been declared between the three men, and I was the bone of contention!

After the function, we stayed back to settle accounts and fight. It was our first major quarrel, and upsetting to say the least. He accused me of leading them on. I was furious at such insinuations. I rued the day I had told him about their interest in me. *I* had never responded to their overtures. I had Raju and needed no other. I told him so categorically but he refused to believe me.

'How can I convince you that I do not care for them?' I asked in teary-eyed misery.

'Promise that you will never speak to them again,' he said, driving a hard bargain.

'But how can I? Dr Raman is a colleague. He admits patients in my nursing home.'

'He can take them elsewhere.'

'Now you are being unreasonable. How do I tell him to go away?'

'What about Uncle?'

'He is just a family friend.'

'You forget that you told me a different story.'

'Well, he does show an extraordinary interest in me.'

'And you?'

'Surely you expect to have better taste than that? He is so ugly, and old, and has a grandson my son's age.'

'Perhaps his riches interest you.'

There was a pistol shot crack as my hand struck his cheek.

'Who gave you the right to hold such an inquiry?' I said, my eyes blazing fire. 'How dare you cast aspersions on my character? If you think I am of that sort, you are welcome to end this affair and good riddance. Both men are gentlemen, which is more than I can say for you.'

This stung him as no other barb would. As I knew it would. I wanted to hurt him as badly as he hurt me. He was suddenly contrite. He promised never to doubt me, but it would make him happy if I had no further connection with these two men. Could I do it for his sake, he added slyly. Appalled at having struck him, I played right into his hands. After all, their attention was merely an ego boost and I could stop interacting with them, if it gave my beloved peace.

'I'll try,' I said, wanting to make amends. 'Give me some time.'

'You are much too innocent for this world. Men understand men better. I can tell you that these two are up to no good.'

How right he was! When my husband buckled under the weight of adversity, I was a creeper without a prop ready to latch on to the first support I got. In retrospect, I'm glad that it was Raju, for the others were out for an affair on the sly after which I would have ended up despising myself.

I had not reckoned with the fury of men scorned. I was easy enough game until that 'uncouth villager' came into the picture, or so they thought. Instead of accepting polite rebuttals, they redoubled their efforts to woo me. Dr Raman referred female patients to me by the dozen. Besides playing on my business sense, he came often on the pretext of visiting the patients he had admitted. He opened a clinic of his own and wanted me to sit there as the gynae expert! As for Uncle, he declared that he would convert his palatial house into a nursing home for me and have his initials intertwined with mine on the board! I was horrified at the prospect.

Raju saw that I was making no headway in getting them off my back and decided to take matters in his own hands. I looked at him with admiration and respect. He may be a rustic, but he sure knew how to protect his woman, which was more than I could say of MS. He accosted the doctor and returned from the meeting stunned. Raman had proclaimed that *I* was a woman of loose morals and cautioned *him* to beware of me! I was appalled at the salacious tales they wove. My eyes filled with tears of frustration.

'It is his word against mine.' I sobbed. 'Even Sita could not prove her virtue to Ram, how do you expect me to? I swear that you are the first person who has touched me besides my husband, and if you don't believe me, there is nothing I can do about it.' He gathered me to his arms and kissed my tears away.

'Of course, I believe you, my precious.'

Much, much later, I learnt that *he* made up such stories so that I would distance myself from those he wanted me distanced! Never was a human more at the mercy of another than I was at his. It was up to him to make or mar me for life. It was my misfortune that he chose to do the latter.

56

Tempestuous and tortuous was the path of our love, fraught with hateful partings and tearful reconciliations. Peaking ecstasies alternated with abysmal misery. Added to this was the guilt that would not let me enjoy what I had risked so much for. Flighty conversations, clandestine kisses, quick embraces, and the stealth all this required turned me into a nervous wreck. It was agony that we suffered in the pursuit of ecstasy, but the lethal attraction that defied reason held us enthralled. Meanwhile, Uncleji and Dr Raman were unfinished businesses. When the latter crossed my path one day, he lamented.

'I hardly get to see you these days.'

'I have been busy with the building of the new clinic.'

'Busy with the building, or the builder?'

I gave him a withering look, but my heart was hammering. The next time, he actually ventured into the clinic and passed another snide remark.

'Where is your bodyguard today?' The 'bodyguard' came barging in that very moment and waited in ominous silence till the discomfited doctor left.

'That man will not step in my clinic again. Understood?'

'So it's your clinic already?'

'Don't evade the issue.'

'I will not take orders from you.'

'Why did he come here? You are not encouraging him, are you?'

'How dare you hold such an inquest? Do you think I am that stupid? Why would I entertain *my* men friends in *your* clinic?'

As before, he was immediately contrite. Though his propensity for possessiveness and suspicion boded ill for the future, matters were settled for now.

Hardly had we got over this bump in the roller coaster ride we had boarded in the name of love when Uncle brought with him his brand of high drama. He came over to give me the photographs and videotape of the opening ceremony. I thanked him and wanted to know the expense incurred.

'You are insulting me,' he retorted. 'This is my present for the opening of your new clinic.'

'The clinic isn't mine alone, I'll have to a give a copy to Mr Bhardwaj.'

'I am nobody's servant. If he wants copies, he can bloody well make them himself.'

I was surprised at his vehemence.

'Let's watch the video now,' he requested.

As we settled in front of the TV, the phone rang. It was Raju.

'Are you free? I'd like to come over.'

'No.' Like a blundering fool, I told him that Uncle and I were watching the video of the inauguration.

'Tell him to go away this very instant.' It was preposterous.

'How can I? It would be bad manners.'

'Manners! You speak of manners when it's a matter of life and death for me.'

He banged the phone down. I was angry with Raju for reading the worst in any situation. There was a tempest in my heart, and I couldn't appreciate Uncle's handiwork as much as he would have liked me to.

'That is one person I detest,' said Uncle, though I had not told him who was on the line.

'But why?' I asked surprised. 'You hardly know each other.'

'You hate some people instinctively just as you like others without reason.'

I was troubled with a sense of impending doom. When the doorbell rang, my worst fears was confirmed. Raju arrived with wife in tow. He had dragged her along for the sake of propriety.

Without preamble he announced, 'As I am 50 per cent partner, I am entitled to pay my share. Even you can't stop me,' he said looking pointedly at me.

'Can't you be a bit more courteous?' I said.

'I am the epitome of politeness. I cannot take charity in my father's name.'

'I don't know you,' said Uncle. 'This is entirely between Doctor Sahib and me.'

'But it isn't.'

'I have given her the video tape, not you.'

'But the place is in my father's name. Please take the money.'

'I'll take it later—from her.'

'There is no dearth of photographers in Delhi. It's just that she gave you her word . . .'

'I did nothing of that sort,' I interjected quickly.

'What made you think that I am a photographer? I am a very successful businessman. By God's grace, I earn so much that seven generations after me need not work for a living,' said Uncle.

Observing his darkening countenance, I told Raju, 'I've got the original; we'll make your copy later.'

'No. I want to give him the money now.'

'In that case, my price is ten thousand rupees,' declared Uncle, incensed.

Raju threw a wad of 100 rupee notes on the table and announced, 'Take it.'

Uncle looked as if he would burst an artery.

'I'll put in another ten thousand, and donate it to the clinic.'

'I haven't taken a paisa from anyone, and I am certainly not going to take it from you,' said Raju.

I watched the scene flabbergasted. The two were fighting over me! A woman married to neither of them! How did I manage to land myself in such a situation?

Raju took me inside, bunched the front of my dress in his fist and hissed, 'It's either him or me.'

'You of course.'

'It did not seem so by the way you were siding with him.'

'He is nothing to me.'

'Then prove it by giving him the money in front of me.'

Like a puppet, I did as he bade. Uncle refused to touch it. Dragging his hapless wife along, Raju left. She had not uttered a word.

'What does he think he is?' said Uncle after he left. 'Making so much of noise over that stupid flat? Why, I could build a hospital for you and install the latest medical equipment and . . .'

'No thanks,' I said sharply.

That night Snehlata rang up.

'Doctor Sahib, I have lost the will to live. I want to die. Please help me.'

My heart lurched. I wasn't up to handling so many assaults on my psyche at the same time. If this was my state, I could well imagine what she was going through.

'How can you even think of such a thing?' I said, appalled at the harm I had done her.

'There is nothing left for me . . .'

'You must fight for your rights.'

She put the receiver down.

When Raju came the next day, his eyes were bloodshot and his chin stubbled. His lower lip quivered and tears trembled on his lids. He knew no peace and gave me no peace. He would have us fight over Uncle. With tact, I steered the conversation to his wife. I was anxious to learn what had transpired after they left.

In bits and pieces I learnt that by now Snehlata had more or less accepted our affair as an unpalatable fact of life. True, she lost the sway she had over him (for all I knew he was with me to spite her) but the alternative was worse. There wasn't much choice for an uneducated Indian woman who was socially, financially, and sexually dependent upon her husband. She did not fancy going back to her parent's place as a deserted wife and serve her brother's family as an unpaid servant for the rest of her life. So she tried making the best of the situation. What she resented was his making a public display of it. The scene with Uncle had been intolerable.

'Why do you have to make a fool of yourself over that bitch?' she had asked. 'God knows how many she is servicing besides that old fool.'

'I can't help myself,' he said dejectedly.

'Then I'll tell her to lay off,' said Snehlata. 'She can have her pick while I have only you.'

'If you ever confront her, you'll be sorry for it.'

I did not tell him that she had already talked with me.

'Fine. Why should I fight over you? What have you given me that you'll give her?' she said in a bid to regain her power. This enraged him so that he slapped her!

I interrupted his monologue.

'Tell her,' I said with a dry sob, 'that you have given me everything I've ever wanted—dishonour, degradation, doom, and damnation. Not for anything in the world would I exchange these priceless gifts.'

57

I hadn't forgotten my promise to myself. With all the medical expertise and equipment at my disposal, I endeavoured to get Snehlata pregnant. I was deeply ashamed of what I had done to her. If she conceived, I would leave Raju no matter what it cost me. It would never do to bring a child into this world only to rob him of his father. This would be the final test.

Now that laparoscopy was found to be normal, I wanted to restart artificially insemination with the husband's semen. When I examined Raju's sample under the microscope, I exclaimed, 'But there are hardly any sperms.'

Everyone outside the thin partition heard! I could have bitten my tongue off for uttering such a loose remark. Raju never forgave me.

On their next visit, a strange thing happened. Raju, Snehlata, and Jiji accosted me separately and wanted me to inseminate Snehlata with a donor's semen, without the knowledge of the other two. Jiji wanted to see her son happy at all costs, Snehlata thought that she would get her wayward husband back if she could mother 'his' child, while Raju wanted the slur on his manhood erased. Each of them made me promise not to tell the others. I was in a dilemma. As per medical ethics, husband and wife have to give a joint consent for the same. I made a slight compromise here. I asked them each sign separately on the consent form and began the treatment. I was willing to bet that they would carry the secret to their graves, each for a different reason.

On the day of the artificial insemination donor (AID), Raju was deeply depressed; it was a poison he had to swallow for the sake of his self-esteem. I knew that the birth of the child would not end his agony but perpetuate it. He would hold the child one moment and fling him away the next; gaze at him in wonderment or wonder whose offspring was he? Yet, he must go ahead because to be called a *namard* (impotent) was a fate far worse than this. I was pained by his pain, and offered to throw the offending sample away.

'*No!*' he exclaimed vehemently. 'You do not understand. Snehlata holds my deficiency as a sword over me. I will be under her thumb forever if I don't give her a child.'

I kept quiet. He wanted consolation not abandonment of the procedure. I ran my fingers through his hair as he sobbed on my lap. I yearned with every fibre of my being to bear him a child. At that moment, I was ready to take on the world for the joy of seeing him hold his own child in his arms.

With time, his pain decreased considerably. He came to terms with AID by likening it to a blood transfusion. I did not have the heart to tell him that sperms carried the genes of the donor with them, unlike blood. The next time I was to inseminate Snehlata with the donor's sample, a perverse desire made Raju want to watch the procedure. Ordinarily, I would have refused such a request from a patient's husband but Raju was Raju, and I was putty in his hands. Not only did he enter the examination room, the nurse was asked to stay out. She had only to hold the speculum, which Raju volunteered to do. In those days, semen was not prepared and washed in the laboratories as it is done now. As a result, it was to be deposited in the upper part of the vagina and not in the uterus. To show off, I inserted a bit in the cervical canal. Snehlata moaned in pain and collapsed! I was horror-struck! The nurse was called in and emergency measures were adopted. What if she died? Nothing would justify the liberties I had taken with protocol.

What was the husband doing inside?

Why was the nurse sent out?

Why did I insert the unprepared semen in the cervix?

There would be a hundred such questions to which I had no answer. The love angle would be revealed and there was no way that we could prove that we had not eliminated her intentionally. I died a thousand deaths in the few seconds Snehlata failed to respond to resuscitative measures. After what proved to be the longest minute of my life, she stirred. I could have kissed the soles of her feet for not dying on me. God knows I had no intention of hurting a single hair of her head. I had harmed her enough already.

After three cycles of hope and despair, Snehlata finally conceived! The family was ecstatic. I sat rigid as if carved of stone, a smile of congratulation frozen on my face. Jiji touched my feet in gratitude. Raju picked me up and swirled me around in jubilation, while Snehlata beamed with joy.

The next day, I told Raju about the pact I had made with Heaven. It was over between us, I told him. He tried to take me in his arm but I pushed him away.

'It isn't fair on anyone, especially on the unborn child. You will not touch me ever again. Understood?' The finality of my tone made him keep his distance.

I accepted the unbearable abstinence as a form of penance. My only consolation was that my husband was spared the knowledge of my infidelity, and for that I was mighty grateful. Two months later, Raju brought a profusely bleeding Snehlata to my clinic. She was in the process of aborting, and I had to evacuate the uterus immediately. When I came out of the operation theatre, Raju was grinning from ear to ear.

'What is there to be so happy about?' I asked.

'It's the best thing that could have happened.' He put his thumb and forefinger under his tongue and whistled like a schoolboy.

'I don't understand,' I said, shaking my head in bewilderment.

'My purpose has been solved. It has been proved beyond doubt that I can father a child. *She* was unable to hold the child in her womb. I can thumb my nose at Snehlata now. Thank God for the abortion. It would have been torture watching another man's child grow up in my house. *Most important of all, I have got you back.*' He tore off my clothes with urgent familiarity and I offered no resistance.

58

Our joint venture gave us a legitimate excuse to spend our mornings together. Patients were few and we encouraged such a situation, for the clinic was but a cover for our nefarious activities. I had also transferred one of my nurses, Usha, to this place. On alternate mornings, Raju would drop in after clinic hours. While Usha sat on guard, we locked ourselves inside to satiate our bodily hungers. By this time, we were old lovers comfortable with each other's bodies. Though the time and atmosphere was not conducive to lovemaking, we had no choice.

The most shameful part of the entire exercise was not being able to look Usha in the eye. It was demeaning to be at the mercy of a mere employee. To ensure that she kept her mouth shut, Raju took to giving her presents in cash and kind but however much we appeased her, she always held the upper hand. The inevitable happened. Usha's blackmailing progressed from the subtle to the blatant, with alarming speed. Matters came to such a pass that the presents Raju bought for her were more expensive than those he bought for me! If she hadn't been so thin, black, and ugly, I would have almost thought that he was two-timing me with her.

With the passage of time, her insolence grew. She got away with a lot of things, which I would not tolerate in a subordinate under ordinary circumstances. She took to making overseas calls to her boyfriend in Saudi Arabia from my landline, and dared me to stop her. She started a practice of her own behind my back, using up my stock of medicines, and I dared not question her. I was amazed at the transformation in that timid female. Gone was the diffidence, the eagerness to please.

She had total autonomy. She had a flat with a cooler, fridge, and TV to herself, which was more than could be said of any other person of her status. She was also privy to the most shameful secret of her boss and *that* made all the difference. She gave a daily commentary about our affairs to the nurses at my place so that I lost respect with them. They made snide remarks and sniggered behind my back. I could not scold them even for legitimate reasons, lest they utter words I could not bear to hear. I was never more ashamed of myself.

It was becoming more and more difficult to live with each other, without each other, yet the raging fires of passion devoured me. To call it love would be slander. There was nothing noble about it. It did not uplift or exalt. It was a thirst that had to be quenched again and again, a need that plunged me into the depths of depravity and deceit. It managed to convert a virtuous, upright lady into a two-timing bitch who thought nothing of cuckolding her husband. Raju was an addiction I could not rid myself of. I knew him to be a bully, a moral coward and yet, I could not do without him. He took advantage of my dependence on him, but I ceased to care. Just because we had exchanged garlands at the mandir, he made demands of me that a husband would of a wife, till in exasperation, I exploded.

'Make me your wife in the eyes of law and society, then exercise your rights.'

'Do you really want that?'

'More than anything on this earth.'

Raju had a thoughtful look in his eye but kept quiet. If only I could curl up and die.

'I'm sorry to have put you in such an embarrassing position.' I hastened to make amends. 'Do not pay heed to what I have said.'

'I would be honoured to take you as my wife. They don't make the likes of you anymore.' I blushed becomingly. 'What is it that you see in me?' he asked.

'That I have yet to decipher. Perhaps I am stark raving mad, perhaps I am a masochist who enjoys being tormented.'

'Okay, tell me what you dislike in me.'

'There is a list—your suspicious, possessive, dominating and jealous nature for instance, but worst of all, is the gifts you shower on me. They make me feel more like a mistress than a beloved. Why do you demean me so?'

'To remember me by when I am dead and gone.'

'What do you mean?'

'Don't you realise the gravity of the situation? Your husband, father, and father-in-law could get me killed any day. That is why I call you *meri maut* (the death of me).'

'They could kill me too.'

'No, they won't. You are the goose that lays the golden eggs. Besides, they need you to bring up the children.'

'They lynch a woman to death for adultery in Arab countries,' I said, shuddering. What a mess I had landed myself into. If I only knew where it would end.

Little did I know that the day of reckoning was around the corner. Oblivious to the time, Raju and I were in the midst of a petty quarrel one afternoon when in walked MS!

'*Namaste*, Doctor Sahib,' Raju said.

Ignoring him, MS held me by the upper arm, dragged me out, and said, 'Have you any idea what time is it?' I was too terrified to resist.

Had MS come an hour earlier, he would have found us behind locked doors! I could stand the deceit no longer. Anything was better than the guilt that sat on my chest like a boulder. I decided to confess, whatever the consequences.

Back home, I stood by the door for a quick escape if he turned violent and said,

'I have something to tell you.'

'What?'

My heart thrashed like a captive bird in my breast, but I forced myself to continue.

'I am in love with someone else, and I want a divorce.'

He sat rigid as a statue, moving not a muscle. I stood petrified, unable to utter another word. A twitch appeared on his left lip and his mouth began to work soundlessly.

A while later he asked with great effort, 'Who is it?'

I would have thought that it was obvious. Much later I learnt that he used to surreptitiously read my dairies and found out that I had a soft corner for Rajiv Mehra.

'Does it matter?'

'I'd like to know.'

'The important thing is that I want a divorce.'

'Let's talk it over rationally.'

'There's nothing to talk about. I want to opt out, that's all.'

'You have been led astray. Your virtue has been without blemish all these years. A forty days *chalia* to the gurudwara will absolve you of your trespasses and all will be well again.'

I was flummoxed! Of all the reactions, this was the most unexpected. A *chalia*, goodness! Was it so easy? I complied, but visiting the gurudwara for forty days at a stretch failed to remove unchaste thoughts from my mind. I still hankered after Raju, and still wanted a divorce.

'Think of the family honour,' said MS.

'I can't help myself.'

'How can you forget your duty towards your family?'

'If you had done *your* duty to me, we wouldn't have landed in this predicament.'

'What about the children?'

'I'll take them with me.'

'You think we'll allow you to do so?

'I can support them.'

'As if to say, *they* will want to go with you.'

'We'll cross that bridge when we come to it.'

'I'll jump off the terrace and commit suicide.'

'You always did take the easy way out. What if you don't die? I refuse to act as nursemaid for a coward for the rest of my life.'

'Let's start afresh. I am willing to forgive and forget.'

'I do not want your forgiveness. I want my freedom.' At this, he broke down and cried like a child. I felt terrible doing this to him, but each time I showed signs of giving in, Raju drove away the flimsy clouds of remorse by the force of his personality.

As the days passed, there occurred a dramatic change in MS. He began doing all the things I had wanted him to do, ever since we got married. He remembered my likes and dislikes, my birthday, and our marriage anniversary. He looked after me when I fell ill and got me all the things I liked to eat. In short, he tried to kill me with kindness and almost succeeded. I knew that he could not indefinitely behave contrary to his nature, but he was making a desperate attempt. He even added my name to the property papers!

It took me awhile to realise that MS was slowly but surely turning my children against me, for he took care to perform his acts of goodness in front of them putting me at a disadvantage. The kids wondered why Mama was being so nasty when Papa was doing all he could to please her. They did not realise that the harsh, unresponsive woman they saw now, was what their father had made of a caring, loyal, wife. The times he had been cruel, insensitive, and indifferent occurred when they were too small to understand. The times he had gambled away our earnings and put me in front of wolves in men's clothing, happened when they were young. How were they to know that this rejection was a response to all that?

My children were more important to me than anything else in the world. Their hostility was killing me. So, bit by bit, I began to tell Karan about the atrocities his father committed against me. He was in the 10th standard and seemed mature for his age.

I was preparing him for the eventual separation, divorce, and remarriage. Before I could tell him all, thanks to my in-laws, my infidelity became an open secret and everything boomeranged. Karan became disrespectful, rude, and aggressive. He never forgave me for poisoning his mind against his father when I was the culprit all along. Simar clamped up.

59

When MS saw that he was getting nowhere with me, he decided to enlist the help of my parents. I was alarmed. My mother was a heart patient and such revelations could worsen her condition.

'We are mature adults, why can't we sort out our problems without involving others?' I asked.

'You refuse to listen to reason. Which other husband would forgive such a lapse? Instead of falling at my feet in remorse, you remain obstinate.'

'I cannot live a lie.'

'What lie? Our marriage is an irrefutable fact of life.'

'It isn't.'

'If you insist on being so adamant, I'm left with no alternative . . .'

'If something happens to my mother, I'll never forgive you.'

'Then mend your ways.'

'What about your parents?' I flared, stung to the quick. 'Were they not involved in arranging this ill-fated union? Don't they need to be consulted?'

'They are at Mussoorie. We'll leave them out of this for the time being. If your parents drive some sense into you, they need not even know.'

'I told you that I can't bear to live with you any longer.'

'*Haramzadi, randi; ma piya ne kutti nu mere gale pa ditta* (bastard, whore, your parents have thrust a bitch upon me),' he spat out the words.

I stared at him in shocked silence. Strangely, what hurt was the fact that he had belittled my parents when it was not their fault. They had given him a jewel beyond compare. They didn't make girls like that anymore—loyal, docile, industrious, and undemanding. If I was a bitch now, he was as much to blame as I was.

'If this is what you really think of me, why insist on my staying here?'

'If you go out with the oaf again, I'll break your legs. You have made life hell for me.'

'All the more reason to let me go,' I replied obstinately.

He looked as if he would burst an artery. Herding me into the car, he took me to my parents' place. Surprisingly, my mother's heart did not buckle. She beat her forehead in despair and bemoaned her lot. She asked me why hadn't I died at birth and spared them this. I wanted to ask her 'why did she give birth to me, I would have been spared the ordeal of living this life' but dared not. My father shrivelled into an old man in front of my eyes. I could not bear to see his broken pride.

'I have reached the end of the road,' said Daddy. 'I would not think twice before gunning down that bastard,' after which he broke down and sobbed like a child. I felt awful at letting him down. I was almost persuaded into forgoing personal happiness once again for him.

Dear Father

Once again I sacrifice desire,
At the altar of your honour for,
I cannot bear to see you bend under
The weight of my indiscretion.
Tentatively,
I had emerged from under the
Dismal umbrella of conformation,
To let the sun,

Thaw the ice within.
But happiness got
At the cost of yours,
I cannot savour.
Once again, I withdraw into
The shell of compromise.
I would if I could pluck,
My wayward heart
To wipe the stricken look
From your face but
Please,
Don't shut yourself
From me now,
Specially now,
When I need you
More than ever.

I wished I could have spared my parents this pain in their old age. It was unreasonable to expect acceptance, but I needed their support. It was unbearable that they spurn me in my hour of need. They were partly to blame. After all it was an arranged marriage. If only they had chosen a husband I could look up to, I wouldn't be in the predicament I found myself today. Early in my marriage, people would wonder what my father saw in MS that he chose him for me. I had looks, culture, education and breeding. I even earned more than him. Now, when I forsook him for another, everyone thought that I had found an intellectual superior. They were appalled at my taste but how could I explain that I did not choose Rajan, *he* chose me and wore down my resistance.

My parents went through the entire spectrum from wanting to kill Raju, to fearing for my life. They advised me to leave both the men and go abroad. Away from distracting influences, I could pursue my academic career. I was sorely tempted, but the question of my children arose. On no account could I forsake them. I asked Daddy to help me with the divorce and let me live with my kids in his house.

'I have neither the desire nor the means to look after you at this stage of my life,' he said. Fair enough, but I was hurt nevertheless. I would have paid for my keep. It was social security and emotional anchor that I needed. Most unhappily married Indian women are spurned by their own parents and have nowhere else to go. No wonder they take their own lives.

Though I did not contemplate suicide, I was assailed by doubts. My was heart riddled with quills of guilt. Not a single religion endorsed my behaviour. Not a single person lauded my action. Surely, all could not be wrong? I was never more ashamed of myself. How could I put self before society, the demands of the flesh before family? Was it that awful to crave bodily fulfilment? Was it just sexual satiety that Raju gave me; if so, was it right to give up all for such a shameful necessity?

Years later, I came across an article that put to rest this guilt of mine. To quote an authority on human behaviour,

> *'Only the most wilful blindness can obscure the fact that sexual intimacy is a sensitive, key relationship of human existence, central to family life, community welfare, and the development of human personality. Human beings define themselves in a substantial way through their intimate sexual relationship with others.'*

It was daunting to learn that the health of a people depended to a large extent on its sexual health.

Moreover was MS totally without blemish? He had taken his father's advice rather seriously and treated me like his *pair di jutti* (footwear) lest I get swollen headed and 'sit on *his* head'! Sometime later, another apt pearl of wisdom came my way that did not improve the situation but made me understand it better. It read:

> *Most men aren't smart enough to realize that the higher you elevate your woman, the less available she is for other men. When you break her down, you make her accessible to anyone she thinks will treat her better.*

60

MS's family descended to the plains in winter and learnt of the disastrous development in our relationship. At MS's insistence, they pretended that nothing was amiss but had no qualms about turning my sons against me. I could forgive them anything but this, especially when my husband wanted me for reasons best known to him. My father-in-law drilled into their impressionable minds that I was a whore, who their father, in the goodness of his heart, was willing to keep! The poor things tried their best to defend me. Unaware of such goings on, I put down Karan's rebellious behaviour to the adolescent hormonal surge. How was I to know that he harboured a burning resentment against me?

When MS failed in forcing me to do as he wished, he told my mother to take her wayward daughter back. Oblivious of what transpired, I was summoned to her house. As soon as she opened the door she asked, 'Where is your suitcase?'

'Which suitcase?'

'Aren't you coming to stay here?'

'Why should I come to stay here?'

'Didn't MS tell you anything?'

'No. What happened?'

'He wants us to take you back.'

'No way.' Daddy called from inside. 'Tell her to go back to where she came from and sort out her problems herself.' Indeed! When *he* initiated my problems by marrying me off to a person I had nothing in common with. 'Why do people match religion, caste, horoscopes, social status when they arrange their children's marriages, when compatibility is the one thing that is required for a happy marriage.

What on earth was going on? I had been thrown out of my own house, and refused shelter in my father's home without my knowledge! I drove right back and dared my coward of a husband to tell me to get lost. After all, I had paid more than half the money in building the premises we lived in. Though nothing concrete came out of this incident, I wisened up on a lot of things. For one, I knew where I stood in the general scheme of things. The guilt of having shamed my parents in their old age decreased considerably. No one was bothered about *my* pain. They had washed their hands off me when I needed them most.

Adding insult to injury, Daddy handed the keys of their house to my younger sister when they went abroad (they gave it to me during their earlier trips), lest I use it for my nefarious activities. If this wasn't degradation enough, they persuaded my brother and his wife—who had come to India for a conference—not to leave his infant son with me! Did they think that I ceased to be a good mother, a competent doctor, and an upright human being, because I had ceased live a lie? They had written me off completely.

Shattered Reflections

Like a streak of lightning,
Forbidden love, split the
Fragile mirror of my life
Into two,
Creating a fissure that
Distorted images
Beyond recognition.
A grotesque reflection
Stares back at me,

Is it mine?
Terror stricken
I raise my hands
To touch my face,
To my relief,
It feels the same.
But this is no hall of mirrors
In a country fair where,
Variations in contour are
A source of fantastic fun.
This is real life and
The monstrosity reflected
Is me, as the world sees me.
And
The claustrophobic closeting
With warped images is forever.
However much, I may be appalled
At the misinterpretation,
I have to live with the fact
That the chasm between the truth
And their perception of truth
Is as insurmountable as the crack
In the mirror is irreparable.

Mummy was of the opinion that even if I washed MS's feet for the rest of my life I would not be able to repay his goodness.

'What goodness?'

'Despite your involvement with that oaf, he wants to keep you?'

'That's exactly the point. Why does he want to keep me?'

'Such impudence when you should be thankful that your life has been spared.'

At other times, she'd try a softer approach.

'Sacrifice is but another name for womanhood. Live for others.'

She was a fine one to speak when she had lived her life exactly as she pleased without caring for *her* parents' feelings. Half my years were spent being groomed for life, and the other half I had to deny myself to live for others. I had neatly been tricked out of living! Why didn't she understand that there were forces beyond me that shaped my behaviour? The wheel of fortune turned relentlessly caring not for the feelings of mothers and daughters. My grandmother had hurt her parents by creating a situation, which led to her being thrown out of her husband's house. Mummy pained her mother by marrying into the very family, her mother had been expelled from in disgrace and now, I ended up shaming *my* mother. We were all victims of our destiny.

Finally, she conceded defeat asking but one concession of me.

'If you want that man so badly, at least be discreet about it.' I flinched at the way she put it. Indiscretion was perhaps a personality flaw, but dishonesty certainly wasn't.

When I kept obstinately quiet, she said, 'At least do not deny your husband his conjugal rights.'

'When he denied me mine all my married life?'

'What do you mean?'

'I have never had an org—You know what I am trying to say. Can you imagine how it feels to be called to his side of the bed when the lord and master is in the mood, for a brief unsatisfactory encounter, and be told to go back to my side after it was over? I would lie awake shivering under my cold quilt while satiated and warm, he snored blissfully.'

She had no answer to that.

'Even now, I know you'll take his side and say that he cannot help it, but what about a loving kiss, a cosy cuddle, a back rub? How about looking after me when I am ill or taking me on a vacation or buying me a present? Give me one reason why should I forgo every wifely right and take up all the responsibilities? Tell me how can an unhappy woman form the base of a happy family life?'

Weighed down by resentful relatives, hostile children, suspicious husbands, and oppressive lovers, I had lost twenty-three kilograms! From a pleasantly plump woman with a glowing complexion, I had been reduced to skin and bone. I needed to get away and decided to take up my brother's offer and visit Muscat. Perhaps from that distance I would be able to observe matters in their right perspective.

Muscat was beautiful in a stark sort of a way. Waves of water met waves of sand on shimmering shores. Bare mountain ridges, undulated like the spinal column of an ancient monster. The sea had more shades of blue than I had ever seen together in one expanse of water. There were boat rides through natural arches sculpted out of rocks. There was shopping to be done at modern malls and local souks. There were men who wore flowing white tunics called dish-dash, and women surprisingly emancipated for a Muslim country. There were dates to be devoured and seafood to relish. In short, it was everything a vacation ought to be but for one thing. My brother and his wife sent me weeping to bed every night after heated arguments. They would contradict everything I said and put me at a disadvantage.

At times, I'd lash out in retaliation, only to be told, 'The trouble with you, Rosy, is that you can't take criticism.'

'And you,' I retorted, 'know only how to criticise.' This offended them no end, but I was fed up of their 'holier than thou' attitude. This made me vow to keep away from those who 'had only my good at heart'. After all, I was grown up enough to accept the responsibility of my actions.

61

I returned from my vacation as confused as ever. At home, MS wasn't sitting idle. With cold-blooded calculation, he planned a two-pronged attack. While he put up a public front of an ideal father and husband, he set out in an underhand manner to wreck vengeance. He tapped my telephone and had me shadowed. Raju was bombarded by anonymous calls. He was accosted by couple of sardars at a traffic light. One of them held a knife at his belly and said, 'This is but a warning. We'll not have a Hindu preying upon our womenfolk.'

The duo sauntered away, leaving Raju quaking with fear. This served to deter him only for so long. He had to prove to me, and more importantly to himself, that he was no coward. As he drove to the flat for our next rendezvous, a jeep came out from the side and banged into his car! A murderous rage goaded him to follow them at breakneck speed. The jeep managed to escape while he was booked for speeding! Terrified at the turn of events, I implored him to keep away.

'You are worth dying for!' he declared.

It wasn't as if he was intrepid. The threats gave him sleepless nights, but he was determined to see the war to its end.

'Let's meet away from the flat for a while.' I suggested, but, I needed a legitimate excuse to get out of the house. Opportunity came my way when I had to discuss the emerging AIDS scenario in India with an authority on the subject at AIIMS, for an article I was writing. We decided to meet at the Moti Bagh Gurudwara. On that overcast August morning, a mammoth rally blocked the main road and traffic was diverted to a narrow lane, leading to a traffic jam. As if this was not trouble enough, the skies opened up and poured their wrath upon hapless humans. Stranded vehicles dotted the waterlogged stretch of road. I reached our point of rendezvous three hours late. There was no Raju was waiting for me. No one in his right senses would venture out in such weather. Three wretched beings were the only ones about on that dismal day. A madwoman washing herself in the same rainwater puddle she had urinated in, a sow trying to shake back to life an offspring run over by a car, and me—a miserable woman past her prime, scanning the bleak rain-veiled horizon for a lover who stood her up.

By the time I finished surveying the gloomy scene, I was completely drenched. My sari clung to me legs like a live thing. Wet hair and tears blinded me. Irrationally, I had staked our future on this rendezvous. If inclement weather deterred him, how could I expect him weather the vagaries of life with me? Defeated, I climbed the marble steps of the gurudwara and prostrated in front of the *guru granth sahib*. There I lay in my solitary sorrow, sobbing unabashedly. Having expended my grief, I got up wearily and came out to find Raju at the foot of the stairs! His clothes were plastered to his body, his hair to his head, and water ran in rivulets down his face. The few hours we had lost and found each other had been a journey to hell and back.

We rushed to the sanctuary of my car. The warmth of the blower, the rain at the window, the wonder of togetherness, was all the heaven we needed. A long while later, I drove him to his car parked some distance away. To our horror, it had been smashed beyond repair! The sardars (we took to calling them S) rang up to inform him that this was but a foretaste of what was to come if he did not pay heed to their warnings. Next time, it would be his head they would crush in place of the car!

After this, I insisted that we never meet again. What was the use of putting his life in jeopardy for a relationship that had no future? Like that beautiful song by Sahir

'Voh afsana jise anjaam tak, laana na ho mumkin,
Use ek khoobsoorat mod dekar, bhoolna behatar.'

(After giving it a beautiful turn, it is only right to forget a story that has no dénouement).

I was surprised at his reaction. He accused me of joining up with my husband and abandoning him! A few days later, I agreed to meet him one last time to get it past his thick skull that I was leaving him for his own sake. His eyes were blood shot and there were dark circles under them. Terror had bred insomnia, irritability, and a low temper threshold. He feared a violent death; he feared that I would desert him, and could not decide which was worse.

, *'Main kutte ki maut nahin marna chahata* (I do not want to die the death of a dog),' he said. His vulnerability smote my heart.

'Which is exactly why, I insist that we never meet again,' I replied.

At this he caught me by the upper arms and shook me till my teeth rattled. His fingers left bruises on my skin. The moment his grip slackened, my hand sprung out like a cobra and stung his cheek. Fear of death and the fear of losing each other had reduced us to this. With tears coursing down his cheeks, he clung to me.

'I can take on the world as long as you are with me.'

'Even if I am the "death of you" as you once said.'

'Yes. Life isn't worth living without you.'

So I promised eternal fidelity to our infidelity, but a sense of impending doom prevailed. Any Sardar (and me a Sardarni) hovering near me would evoke terror. If this was my state, I could well imagine what Raju was going through. He was the one being threatened and attacked; *his* property was being vandalized.

Though Raju risked his life each time he came to see me, we could not enjoy each other's company. Fear laced with sorrow became an integral part of our love. Unwittingly, MS cemented our relationship further. After all that we had gone through, it was unthinkable that we could ever part.

62

Though I became adept at sailing with my feet in two boats, Raju tired of pitching his tent at crossroads. He insisted that we decide one way or the other. I agreed to tread the path less trodden with him, but there were certain preconditions. I would never stay with him as a mistress or a second wife. I needed social and legal sanction to make our private union public. Secondly, I would not leave my kids till they were grown up enough to fend for themselves. He would have to act keeping these two things in mind.

However hard we tried, our respective spouses refused to divorce us. Despite our infidelity, they stood to gain by our presence. Desperation prompted Raju to scourge the courts of law till he found an alternative. Legal divorce could be obtained by illegal means at an exorbitant price. It was like getting a valid driving licence without knowing how to drive, or a false birth certificate. As long as there were corrupt officials in government offices, everything was possible. Like the above documents, the divorce papers too would stand scrutinty in any court of law.

Raju brushed aside any qualms I had about the morality of such proceedings. I allowed myself to go along, as these papers would not make any difference to our lives, yet. The kids were small and I would stay in my own home till they grew up. There would be no major upheaval.

I insisted that Raju go through the divorce first. Though I loved him to distraction, I hadn't learnt to trust him. He agreed reluctantly and after a while, he showed me the papers. When my turn came, I was taken to court and exposed to yet another seamy side of life. Our lawyer took us to one of the numerous little cubicles that led off the corridor. It was nothing like the courtrooms I had seen in movies. There were hard wooden benches on which no one sat. Lawyers and clients crowded around a large nondescript table as the judge disposed of their cases perfunctorily. When my turn, I answered glibly for I had been briefed by the lawyer and knew precisely what to say. The judge knew that I was lying; I knew that he knew, but all was fair in the courts of justice. For a hefty fee, the lawyer had made it as authentic as any genuine case. Preceding the final verdict, entries of previous hearings had already been made in the court register. Before I knew it, I had been granted divorce on the grounds of desertion, even as I continued living in the same house with MS!

Where was the freedom I ought to feel? It was like declaring victory over your opponent without a war! I had insisted on a legal divorce, not a legal deception. Yet, with our spouses playing dogs in the manger, what alternative did we have? It was a step, albeit a dubious one towards our goal of togetherness. It called for a celebration, which we decided to club with Raju's birthday, which fell a few days later.

'For all you know it may be my last birthday,' said Raju morosely.

'They only want to frighten you away. You are a sitting duck. The S would have trained their guns on you long back if they wanted to. Stop brooding, and tell me what you want for a birthday present.'

'Will you promise to give me what I ask?'

'Yes, if it is within my means.'

'It doesn't cost money.'

'Now don't ask for something stupid like a kiss or a promise.'

'No, it isn't that.'

'What is it then?'

'I spied a priceless jewel on your person the other day.'
'What *is* it?'

He whispered something in my ear. A thrill of shock and pleasure coursed through me. Was there such a lover on the face of this earth? He wanted my first white pubic hair! Though I blushed bashfully, I was inordinately pleased. Ever since my fortieth birthday, I had experienced a diminishing sense of self-worth. Though I had no reason to doubt Raju, the fear of losing him to a younger female always lurked at the back of my mind. This served to reiterate my faith in him.

On the D day I waited with a loving heart, and his birthday present. I waited with a cake and bouquet. And I waited and waited. He turned up three hours late, gave me a perfunctory kiss, and rushed out entirely forgetting the precious present! The S were after him like a pack of wolves, but he was determined to have a glimpse of me on his special day. I understood what it must have cost him to defy them, but I was disappointed nevertheless. In a fit of pique I mowed down the entire crop, birthday present and all!

Meanwhile Usha, the nurse, had turned into a Frankenstein of our own making. She demanded thousands of rupees as 'loan'! I had had enough of her and refused outright. She retaliated by standing outside the flat and broadcasting to all and sundry the activities that took place within. Vile, vicious, and vengeful, she informed those willing to listen that we forced her to act as guard against her will! What else did this star-crossed love have in store for me? For every smile, I paid with a thousand tears.

All that Raju could babble was, 'I'll kill her, I'll kill that bloody bitch if it is the last thing I'll do on this earth.' As if to say, it would serve any purpose. The damage was done. Though a thousand eyes bored my back, I brazened it to my car with my head held high.

MS learnt about the public proclamation of his wife's indiscretion through sources of his own. When he confronted me, I was too shaken up to put a false front. Once again he surprised me with his reaction. Instead of a 'Serves you right' stance, he accompanied me to our neighbours, told them that Raju was like a family member, and Usha was trying to defame us because we had chucked her out. I added my mite by telling them that she had spread sordid tales about them too. According to her, Mrs Matthews, our right hand neighbour, had a son from her husband's friend and the lady on our left solicited customers for her teenage daughter! It seemed that no one was chaste in the neighbourhood. These accusations (true or false I could not care less) made their hackles rise and put them on the defensive. It was unanimously agreed that Usha was a bad sort, and I was well rid of her.

63

MS almost shamed me into relenting by his act of nobility. I needed little persuasion to lower the flag of revolt, but Raju held it aloft by the sheer force of his personality. He was like the Bhramaputra in spate and I, but a straw on its surface. There was little that could be done to rescue me from its furious flow. Nevertheless, war had been declared between the two men. I was no longer a wife who needed to be restored to her rightful place. I wasn't even a beloved, desired above all else. I was a trophy—a symbol of victory coveted by these two. My wishes counted not at all. It would matter not a whit to them if I were to stand up and announce that I wanted neither of them. Matters had gone beyond me.

Raju risked his life and sanity for me. MS harmed his person and property, even as he wore the injured air of a wronged husband. These underhand tactics alienated MS as nothing else could. My skin crawled at his touch. I wondered how could he want to sleep with me at this juncture? Raju had stopped bedding his wife a few months back. He said that it was sacrilege to cohabit with her after the exalted experience with me. Thwarted desire almost made her rape him one night.

MS had reduced the love of my life into a sordid extramarital affair. I retaliated by putting an end to the intra-marital one. I shifted sheet and pillow into the children's room, publicly announcing the rift between us. It was intolerable for a man who set great store by appearances. I hadn't reckoned with the children though.

'Go back to you own room,' ordered Karan.

'You keep out of this. If I am intruding upon your privacy, I'll sleep in the drawing room but I will not go back. Understood?'

My in-laws were using the guestroom during their winter sojourn here. Mataji threatened to go on a hunger strike. She even tried to drag me back to my room, trailing streaks of blood on my arm with her nails. I reminded her of the words she had uttered at Karan's birth, 'I gave you my son, you give me mine.'

'Take back your son with my blessings,' I said.

Papaji insisted that I touch my husband's feet and beg forgiveness. 'My foot!' I declared. In retaliation, he smote me where it hurt most.

'Who will marry the children of a whore?'

MS continued to pretend that he was the aggrieved party. When I confronted him with evidence, he pleaded ignorance. According to him, *he* was being bombarded by phone calls that gave him an hour-by-hour account of our exploits. *He* was the one being prosecuted, and not that cunning bastard who has played on my emotions to gain sympathy.

At her end, Snehlata wasn't sitting idle. She tried to poison her husband by putting small doses of copper sulphate in his morning *lassi*. He got the blue drugs tested in a laboratory, after which, he stopped eating anything cooked by her. But she hadn't done with him yet. One summer night, Raju was pouring diesel into the generator during load shedding. On the pretext of showing him a light, she threw the candle in the can and backed away! Within moments, he was engulfed in flames. I reached the hospital to a hideously unrecognisable Raju. His lips were swollen, his ears singed, his hands skinned, and his left leg was a quivering mass of denuded flesh. Compassion further flavoured the cocktail of our star-crossed love.

It was around this time that *I* began receiving intimidating phone calls. It was my turn to uphold the banner of love with intrepidity. Ignoring the threats, I visited him at the hospital again and again. Stones were pelted on my car. There was deep dent on the side of my Maruti as it stood innocuously in the parking lot, but I could not forsake Raju in his hour of need.

He made a slow recovery over a period of time. Once he was well enough to come to me, the attacks were again doubled. The physical and psychological harassment began to take its toll. In desperation, we decided to run away. He resigned from all the honourable posts he held, and wound up affairs. I took out my jewellery from the locker and packed my bags. Thoughts of the dishonour, disgrace, and scandal, I put firmly from my mind. I *had* to get away whatever the cost. Even death was preferable to the fear of death that stood like the chariot of Yama in the backyard of our minds.

I backed out at the last moment. The mother in me won over the woman hands down. My children were dearer to me than life, and not for anything in the world could I forsake them. Being a man, a childless one at that, Raju could never understand. I told him that my maternal instincts were an irrefutable fact of my life and he was free to leave me if he wished. To his credit, he respected my decision and abided by it.

'If it is destined that we stay here and weather it out, so be it,' he said resignedly and I loved him all the more for it.

However much I loved them, I could not protect my children from the disharmony at home. Fed up of it all, Karan asked, 'Why don't you go away?'

'Because of you both,' I replied, a statement he misinterpreted in a manner that shocked me. He thought that Simar and he were millstones around my neck! He was going through a crisis of his own. His girl friend had ditched him; his best friend betrayed him, and his mother resented his very existence for he came in the way of her ill-gotten pleasures. No one on earth wanted him. In a bid to end his life, he consumed calmpose tablets. The number was far below the lethal dose, but I was badly shaken. It was unnerving to think that Karan was unhappy enough to attempt suicide.

The loving, lovable Karan metamorphosed into a Karan I did not recognise. He was rude and rebellious; blatantly defiant, daring me to restrain him. He used my predicament as a whip over me. It was either lend me your car or get lost with it. He had the audacity to order me out of my own house! To think I had fought like a tigress to regain his custody from his grandmother. I was reduced to a quivering mass of misery. Tears hovered on my lids like washings on a clothesline, yet fearful of ridicule, I dare not let them spill. Was there a woman on earth as unhappy as I was? I had lost out on both worlds. Had I forsaken the only bit of happiness life had offered to be tortured by a chit of a boy sprung from my own womb?

64

The clinic remained closed for the month. Time enough for the 'Usha generated' rumours to die down. My husband insisted that we sell the place. It was the least I owed him for helping me out of a sticky situation. I could not see how I could refuse. Providence intervened in the form of Jiji. She wouldn't hear of shutting down a hospital opened in the name of her departed husband. She vowed by his photograph hung there that the place would run as long as she was alive. As I owned only half the flat, I couldn't sell it till she agreed. As disposing it off was out of question, we decided to convert it into a polyclinic. With a doctor in every room, where would there be the time or the opportunity for us to mess around? This seemed to satisfy MS, and he gave in reluctantly. We were grateful for the reprieve. The polyclinic flourished and we did manage to steal a few moments of togetherness.

Having burnt our fingers with a nurse, we decided to keep a male attendant this time. Jasbir was handsome and intelligent, quick and efficient, and in a short while we grew to love him like a son. Insidiously, we got entangled in his affairs. There was a property dispute between his father and their neighbours, which resulted in much stick wielding and skull splitting. The police demanded Rs. 20,000/- to look the other way. With his clout, Raju managed to settle the matter amicably without monetary loss. As Jasbir hero-worshipped Raju, we thought that he could not turn into another Usha. Little did we know then that he had already made a duplicate key of the cash drawer, though he was smart enough to appropriate small amounts of money at a time.

He wore expensive clothes and rode a scooter. He was fond of good living and he *did* seem to live beyond his means, but we thought that his doting father sent him the money and left it at that. Trouble began when he fell in love with a girl above his social status. Her parents refused his marriage proposal. After all his thieving (of which we were yet unaware), Jasbir had no qualms about enlisting our help. As uniting lovers was something close to my heart, I urged Raju to help. Raju told the girl's parents that she would lack nothing in life as long as he lived. As Jasbir was like a son, Raju would set up a business for him in due course. They relented and Jasbir brought his bride home. Little did we know, we had let in a serpent. They had the audacity to use the one room we had kept for ourselves instead of the quarters we had given him. I caught on when I saw his coat hanging from a peg in our room!

Meanwhile, telephonic tapping and surveillance by MS's goons continued unabated. It is amazing, given the time, what a human being can get used to. Not very long ago, the very thought of someone overhearing our conversation horrified me. Now, we punctuated every sentence with '*I love you*' to incense MS. We made false plans to mislead him. We had mock quarrels, which led him to believe that we had broken up. At home front, though volcanoes erupted beneath the marital sea, surface calm was maintained at all costs, for MS willed it so.

Raju was trying to get around our tormentors by offering to buy them off. At last, one of them nibbled the bait and double-crossed MS. Startling were the facts revealed. After my confession, MS had broken down at the local gurudwara and appealed to the fanaticism of terrorists who had taken refuge there. Thus began a reign of terror. The S staged a multipronged attack. Besides threats to Raju's person and property, they reduced him to a pauper by relentless extortion. Within a matter of months, they had relieved him of his last paisa. He began borrowing to buy a few more days of life and finally, had to mortgage his office. When the S realised that he had nothing left, they began using him to do their dirty work. To put the police off scent, they travelled in his Tata Sumo to the various other locales to extort other hapless humans, stuffing in his vehicle sacks filled with money, which they needed for their nefarious activities. Sometimes there were kilos of gold jewellery that they sold at Dariba. As they gave him no time to earn his livelihood, Raju was reduced to borrowing from me off and on.

When I informed my family what my 'all suffering' husband was up to, I was amazed to learn that no one believed me! My parents said that Raju was fooling me. Even for a moment, if they believed what I said was true, it only increased their respect for MS. He was not a spineless sissy after all! My sister laughed at my naiveté.

'Can't you see that this is but a ruse to extract money from you?'

Doubts assailed me. After all what proof did I have? For all I knew, Raju was making up the entire story to entice me. Hadn't MS done the same? Trust my fate to fall in the trap of mercenary men. I remembered the blood-curdling phone calls, the attacks on my person and car. Could he have hired people to terrorise me? Now that mistrust had wormed its way in my mind, I realised that it was not very difficult for Raju to do so. I could not bear a second betrayal and pestered Raju to give me definitive proof. He looked offended, but I was adamant.

After weeks of trying, the double-crossing S taped for us a telephonic conversation for a steep price of Rs 11000! The information gained was worth every single paisa paid. My father-in-law, whom I had recently pulled back from the brink of death, was at that this very moment plotting against me! On the tape I heard him tell them to break Raju's legs so that he would be bed ridden for at least a year.

'Why don't you stop your daughter-in-law from going to the flat? That will solve all your problems,' said the S.

'I can't.'

'Why?'

'For reasons I cannot tell you.' The bastard needed me to look after him and dared not antagonise me.

There were abuses directed towards my parents for foisting a slut upon them. By the time I came to the end of the cassette, my blood was boiling. How could Papaji do this to me at a time when his life depended upon my ministrations? The only currency he had paid me with, was flattery, and now this stab in the back. I could not tolerate the sight of him. I told MS that it was high time *he* looked after his father, but Papaji decided to faint in the toilet when MS was away. Once again, the doctor in me came to the fore and I resuscitated the despicable fellow. Had the shoe been on his foot, he would have surely let me die. Soon enough, he was fit to go back to Mussoorie.

On the eve of his departure, Papaji sat by me and began, 'I wonder if I will live long enough to come back next year.'

'Papaji don't say that.' I mouthed words I was expected to. He had been saying the same thing for years and turned up like a bad coin every year.

'As a daughter, mind you not as a daughter-in-law, I want to ask something of you.'

'When did you ever treat me like a daughter?' I would have liked to ask but kept mum.

'You have saved my life not once, but twice. I can never repay what you have done. Just do one more thing so that I die in peace.'

I waited for him to continue.

'Now, that your life is almost over, renounce the pleasures of life.' Indeed! He was nearing 90 and was not averse to pinching the breasts of my female help! He still wanted the best life had to offer, in terms of food and fruit. Before I could say anything he continued, 'Think of your children, their mental state when they learn of your activities from outsiders?'

I could keep quiet no longer. Words spilled out like hot lava.

'When we have people like you in the family, what need do we have of outsiders?'

'What do you mean?'

'My children have stopped going to Mussoorie because you have been instigating them against me. You told Karan that his mother was a *kanjari* (whore).'

'I never said such a thing.'

'You lie. He did not know the meaning of the word and asked me! I can forgive you anything but this. How could you turn my children against me *and* flatter me when you need my services?'

'*Meri chiti daadi da kuch te khayal kar. Ke kara, main phansi chad javan* (Have some respect for my white beard. What should I do, hang myself)?'

'You are the one who started it. Now that the veneer of an ideal father-in-law/daughter-in-law relationship has been cast aside, let's speak our minds for a change.'

'Okay, tell me what do you want?'

'I want to divorce your son. Get him a new bride so that he does not buckle under.'

There was a stunned silence. All the poison within him gushed out.

'*Eh to oh gal hui na, jhak maarke gu khaana.*' I did not know the exact meaning of these words, but I got the general drift. At last, I was learning exactly what he thought of me. 'You are no better than a bitch on heat with a bunch of street dogs sniffing her. If it is a dog you want, why not my son? At least he is faithful.'

'If I am a bitch, your son is not dog enough for me. He is a weakling and I am fed up of being the man in the house. I am fed up of taking care of you, knowing full well that you hate my guts and have to put up with me for your own needs.'

315

'What is it that you are so proud of—your beauty, or the fact that you earn more than my son? Neither money nor beauty will stay forever.'

'I know. But I also know that I cannot turn to *your* son or *his* family for support when I lose them.'

'At this age you want a divorce!' He was incredulous.

'You know that MS and I haven't been living as husband and wife for years.'

'In that case why did you marry him?'

'I didn't. *You* arranged the match.'

'You want to divorce him for that bastard. Tell me, why hasn't he divorced his wife as yet? Do you intend staying the hole he lives in with his wife—his bed in the centre and each of you on either side?'

I did not have to listen to this. I got up and left. Realising that it was against his interests to antagonise me, he hobbled after me, apologising profusely.

'I know exactly why you ask forgiveness. The son you so canvass for is no good either as a doctor or a caretaker, and you need me.'

Incensed beyond measure he screamed, 'You *are* all what I said you are and more.'

'Then why apologise?' I said sweetly and walked out.

65

Seema Aunty was the only relative on MS's side with whom I could connect. She was his maternal uncle, Jogi Mama's wife. There was an age difference of 30 years between us, yet we functioned on the same wavelength. During our walks in late winter afternoons, I would tell her my secret sorrows and she would sympathise. A little problem had cropped up. My signatures were required at the Tasildaar's office, in connection with the agricultural land Raju had bought on my name. As the farm was some distance away, it was impossible to absent myself from my house for such a long period of time. With Seema Aunty's consent, I planned a picnic with her and the kids to which no one could object. We picked up Raju and Jasbir on the way.

For a city-bred woman, a day in rural India was bliss. Young wheat, barely a span high, glittered green in the sunlight. A large peepal fanned over the village pond. Eucalyptus trees stood tall and fair, huddled aloof like the foreigners they were. Mustard in flower shimmered like a sea of gold as far as the eye could see. This was my domain, at least on paper. I took the dark earth in my hand, and inhaled deeply of its rich aroma.

The children were excited. They exclaimed at the fish in the pond, the peacocks on trees. They rode a camel, shrieking delightedly with every lurch. A keen wind, a penetrating look from a loved one, brought an unusual flush to my cheeks. We rattled down the dirt road on a tractor that after an initial hesitancy, I was soon driving. The official formalities over, we returned to our farm's caretaker's home to devour *sarson ka saag*, *makki ki roti* topped with melting pats of white butter. This was washed down with thick creamy buttermilk. Dessert was jaggery, and fresh fruits. They gave me a bottle of honey to take home. Like Cinderella, I overstayed my time. MS learnt about our little outing from his sources (the S), and I had a hell of a lot to pay at home. What hurt most was Seema Aunty's perfidy. She got out of the sticky situation by pretending that she did not know that Raju was coming along!

Soon after, a scandal shook the foundation of the Anand family. MS's second maternal uncle Gopal Mama, a 75-year-old widower, was caught trying to molest a 10-year-old girl at his general store! The entire colony was in an uproar. His house was pelted with stones and shoes. People shouted derogatory slogans, blackened his face, and would have lynched him to death had it not been for the police who took him in custody. Protests continued unabated. Pamphlets were distributed highlighting the despicable act. His shop was boycotted. My mother-in-law could not look anyone in the eye, though loyally she pretended it was a false story being spread by his enemies. His brother, the respected Professor Jogi (Seema Aunty's husband), hid his head in shame.

With petty vindictiveness, I got a perverse pleasure in thumbing my nose figuratively at my in-laws. There were people in their family who behaved in a manner far worse than mine. When I gave Raju this juicy bit of information, he was thoughtful. He was on backslapping terms with the magistrate in charge of Gopal Mama's case and was naïve enough to believe that if he helped, I would be handed over to him on a silver platter. As far as I was concerned, that odious old man deserved to remain behind bars; but when I saw Jogi Mama's dejected face, I relented. Tentatively, I told him that Raju could help, as he knew the magistrate. Jogi Mama agreed with alacrity, but I laid down two conditions. Firstly, on no account would I be directly involved. Secondly, the matter would be kept a secret from the rest of the family. So it came to pass that Professor Jogi accompanied Raju to the magistrate's office, got the necessary papers sanctioned, and freed his wayward brother from the police station. He was all praise for Raju and I glowed with happiness.

Ever since I had linked my fate with Raju, we had become a two-people industry on which a host of people subsisted. It was Jasbir's turn to exploit us now. I had taken to hoarding whatever extra I got by way of presents in the flat so that at some future date I could set up house with Raju. Little did I know that I was tempting Jasbir! He had borrowed the imported camera I had kept there, for his engagement ceremony. When he did not ask for it at his wedding, I thought that they had hired professional photographers for the occasion. Little did I know that he had stolen it and had no need to borrow it! Matters came to a head when Raju told me to keep Rs 80,000/- in the almirah for a day. It was advance payment for a property deal. When he asked for it the next day, the money gone! No lock was broken and yet the money was gone; gone were the valuables I had stored— camera, quilts, crystal, and crockery!

Raju made me go over the story meticulously over and over again till finally it dawned upon me that I was the prime suspect! According to him, if Jasbir had been the culprit, he would have run away with the loot instead of watching Raju cross-examine me! It was the worst blow anyone had ever dealt me. Raju had a duplicate key to the room but never for a moment did I think that he had appropriated the expensive goods I had stored there. Even if he really believed that I could stoop so low, how could he humiliate me in front of a servant? I wished I had never set eyes on this ogre. I had an overwhelming desire to take the revolver from the holster at his hip and shoot him.

'I will have to sell this house,' stated Raju, for it would be a reminder of the 'great betrayal'.

'Have you forgotten that I own half the place?'

'I don't care,' he hissed through clenched teeth.

My heart hardened into a block of concrete. I vowed that I would buy a home of my own from which no father, husband, lover, or son could throw me out.

The different kinds of hell he had pushed me through! I was amazed that I was still retained my sanity despite the mental atrocities. Though I could not stand the sight of him, I needed him to find the culprit. I couldn't enlist my husband's help to get me out of *this* mess. So despite an intense loathing for the man, I went with him to lodge a FIR at the police station. Immediately afterwards, he was called away to his village to attend a funeral. The police descended upon the clinic in swarms, and interrogated me as if I was the culprit instead of the victim. What proof did I have that I owned the things that I claimed were robbed? Did I have receipts of purchase? So on and so forth they tortured me, till I rued the day we had lodged the FIR. Finally, Raju returned and put pressure on the SHO (station house officer) from contacts higher up. The very policemen who harassed me a few days ago now fawned over me; not that they did anything to find the thief. I was disgusted with the entire lot. When we had almost given up hope of retrieving our goods or catching the thief, help came from unexpected quarters. The S who had been double-crossing both sides asked Raju if we had fired Jasbir.

'No, why do you ask?'

'He made innumerable trips on his scooter with his wife, lugging luggage from this place. So I thought that they were shifting.'

Everything fell in place. Raju strode in and pummelled the despicable fellow with blows. Jasbir begged for mercy, but Raju was like a man possessed. Finally, Jasbir confessed to the crime and offered to retrieve the goods and money from a hideout at his village. Raju suggested that he keep his wife's jewellery with us as collateral till he got our things back. While we waited for Jasbir's brother to bring the jewellery, Raju called his mother over. Jiji, accustomed to managing a household without a husband, was a tough woman. Once the jewellery arrived, Raju took it to a jeweller for evaluation. It was as we had suspected—merely gold plated silver stuff! This time, Jiji reached forward and slapped Jasbir hard. Catching hold of his hair, she banged his head against the wall again and again.

Meanwhile, Raju worked out a plan that seemed feasible—he would use Jasbir as a collateral. Locking him up in one of the rooms at the flat, he made Jiji sit on guard and went with Jasbir's brother to their village in my car, for his vehicle had broken down. I returned home, lest MS gets suspicious and told him that my car was at the garage for repairs.

At 6 p.m., I got a frantic call from Jiji. Jasbir had unlocked the door from inside with a duplicate key, pushed her aside and fled! I told her not to panic for I would be reaching in five minutes. As my car was with Raju, I begged Jogi Mama for his. Now Jogi Mama's battered old Fiat was dearer to him than his wife, and he would allow no one else to drive it. As he owed me a favour, he agreed to drive me to the flat.

While Jogi Mama waited in the car, I rushed to Jiji to calm her and apprise the police about the latest developments. As I picked up the phone, I remembered the diaries I kept here, in which I had chronicled my life story. If the police got hold of them, to the case of robbery, would be added the angle of illicit love. Quickly, I emptied a suitcase and dumped all the books in the flat in it. Where was the time to sort them? As I lugged the load towards the car, Jogi Maama drove off leaving me stranded in the middle of the road! I couldn't believe my eyes! How could he do this to me after all I had done for him? The coward did not want to get implicated in a police case. I hired a rickshaw and took it home. In the confusion, I forgot to contact the police.

After behaving so abominably, Professor Jogi had no qualms about sending Gopal Mama to me to pursue his case. What right had he to demand favours from his sister's daughter-in-law's lover, especially when he had ditched her when *she* needed him? Before I could tell him to sort out his brother's problems himself, Gopal Mama ended the sordid tale by bleeding to death from a stress ulcer.

As of now, I returned to the flat to find Jiji in the throes of an anginal attack. It was the last thing I needed at the moment. I gave her sublingual sorbitrate and sat vigil by her side till Raju returned—empty-handed. We apprised him about the dramatic turn of events. He was glad we hadn't contacted the police, adding grimly, that he would handle the matter his way.

From the SHO, we learnt that Jasbir had bribed a SI to intimidate me into taking back the FIR. No wonder they had been so nasty to me! Now that the tables had turned, they tripped over themselves to help us—at our cost. We paid for the petrol and for the bottle of whisky they needed at the end of the day. After days of futile search, the police decided to take Jasbir's wife in custody. Jasbir got the information through his informer in the police force (which was what we intended anyway), and surrendered. He was put in police remand and given 'treatment' he was not likely to forget.

On being told that Jasbir had confessed in police custody, Jasbir's wife agreed to co-operate. It was a calculated move and paid dividends. Out of the haystack emerged crystal glasses, filigreed silver, foreign lingerie, a food processor, and a host of other articles. I was so grateful to the police for recovering my things that I vowed to reward them amply when all this was over. How was I to know that they would appropriate half the recovered goods without my permission? As for the money, we spent Rs 50,000/- to get back our 80,000/-! The only good that came out it was that Raju was made an SPO (special police officer) for helping the police to catch a thief.

After going through all this together, it was impossible to stick to my original plan of cutting off from Raju. Jasbir had demanded total attention. I hardly had the time to nurse my grudge, but I neither forgot nor forgave. He apologised over and over again, but I was relentless. Though the police and public lauded him, he was miserable. The one person whose appreciation mattered loathed him. I was determined never to throw my lot with a man ever again. If he wanted any contact with me it would be on my terms. First and foremost, I needed to buy a flat of my own. How could he understand that it was not a roof and four walls that I craved? It was my belief in myself that needed reiteration. Never again would I exist as some man's daughter, mother, wife, or beloved. I was an individual in my own right and the house would be a symbol of my identity.

When Raju realised that I was determined, he suggested that I buy his mother out of this very flat. I would be saved of the liability of an unoccupied flat in a distant area and our heirs would be saved the hassle of fighting over a property owned jointly by sworn enemies. The advice made sound sense, for I had only a small amount to invest. It was better to buy out Jiji than buy a tiny flat in some godforsaken place to prove a point.

Finally, I was the proud owner of my own property. I was happier than I had been in the past, happy enough to forgive Raju. From now on, he would come to meet me in *my* house, on my terms. The knowledge that I could throw him out if I wanted to was gratifying. As I crossed the threshold of my own home the first time, I bent down to smear its dust upon my forehead.

66

Karan returned from the United States (he had gone there for a job interview) a changed person—aloof and alienated. He was to join in a month's time, and considered America an escape from the horrors of home and the mother who perpetuated them. It was as if he was bidding his time till he could thumb his nose at me. Now that he had become self-reliant, he could show his true feelings. My heart was laden with loss.

He poured all the poison he harboured against me into my sister's ears, saying that being on his own in the US, he had time to reflect; and told her how much he hated me. He had done all the horrible things he did, purposely to punish me. I was devastated. I was nothing but a miserable failure. I had failed as a daughter, wife, and mother. I was a source of shame for my parents, an embarrassment to my siblings; I had dishonoured my in-laws and pained my husband. I could not earn the love and respect of my children. I spread unhappiness all around and found no happiness myself.

I had learnt to live with the pain of causing pain to my loved ones but, unbearable was the hatred of my son. I writhed in agony and yet dared not reveal my anguish, lest I be exposed to ridicule. After sleepless nights and tortured days, I decided to write him a letter. I *had* to know where I stood in his scheme of things. If I was a nightmare he wished to forget, so be it. Even loss of hope was bearable to hoping against hope. If on the other hand he had matured enough to understand why I did what I did, I might be able to salvage relationship dearer to me than life itself. With the desperation of a gambler I sat down and wrote:

Dearest Karan,

I was shocked at the venom you spewed, appalled by the colossal lack of communication that exists between us; most of all, I was deeply pained to learn of your hurt and hate, revulsion and rejection, from a third person—ten years too late. Each accusation is like a nail driven deep into my heart. You said that:

- *I poisoned your mind against your father.*
- *I thought you were a millstone around my neck.*
- *Your tears dried up in the 10th class.*
- *You attempted suicide.*
- *How could I choose someone like him?*
- *I eat your father's food, live in his house, and go about with another.*
- *You hate me for making you chose sides—you chose Papa; and Simar, me.*
- *You are glad to get out of here and may not even return for the holidays. I may burn in hell for all you care.*
- *I have put you off marriage completely.*
- *You had been horrid to me to punish me for destroying your childhood and last but not the least of all,*
- *May God never give anyone such a mother!*

My poor tortured baby. If only I could hide you in my womb and save you from the sufferings of this world, from me. How can I explain to you that, <u>I have ceased being a wife, not a mother</u>; that I can never stop being a mother even if I wanted to, even if you did not want me? You think that both come as a package deal and this accounts for your unbearable hostility.

How can I explain that despite the colossal differences between your father and me, I stayed put so that you would not have to make choices? It seems as if the entire exercise has been futile. I have failed miserably to protect you from the disharmony between us. That somehow you felt guilty for having forced me to stay back. If it weren't for you I would be somewhere far away enjoying my illegitimate pleasures. As I have told you, I love you and Simar beyond anyone else on this earth, beyond myself. You two are the only good that I have got out of this marriage, and not for anything in the world would I have it any other way. Just pause to think for a moment, what could I have gained by staying back—nothing. All I wanted was to give—give my beloved children my love, care, attention, affection, and of course, my worldly possessions. I had so much to give yet I was sorry to learn you opted for so little—just materialistic gains—to finance your trip to the US. A mother's prayers and blessings mattered not at all. You hated me enough to hurt me, but had no qualms about taking my help when your father failed as a provider. It did not matter for all I have—money, jewellery, and property, is for you two. In fact, I was glad that you needed me. All I wanted in return was a kind word, an affectionate gesture, which would have made all the difference to a woman who has got no happiness from any quarter. If you feel that you owe me nothing in terms of love, respect, and loyalty, fine—I am too proud to beg for them.

As for the drying up of tears, let me tell you about mine. Four men in my life provoked torrential tears and paradoxically they were the ones responsible for drying them. In childhood I suffered from a massive Electra complex yet was the least loved of all. I did well in studies, braved Mummy's wrath to impress Daddy, but to no avail. Maybe because, even then, I did not take injustice lying down and questioned his autocratic behaviour. This was taken as answering back, and Daddy would tell Mummy time and again to 'snub her', which made me lock myself up in the bathroom and cry my eyes out.

Another thing my parents could not accept was the unpalatable truths I uttered. I was called 'Harish Chandra ki aulaad' in such a derogatory manner that I was made to feel honesty was a vice instead of a virtue. 'Shut your bloody trap' was another of Daddy's favourite admonishes.

Now too, I could have had my cake and eaten it too, but I did not want to make a cuckold of your father and have people laughing at him behind his back. It took a lot of courage to confess that I was involved with another man and wanted to opt out. I expected him to

- *Kill me.*
- *Throw me out.*
- *Give me a divorce.*

Instead he

- *Refused a divorce.*
- *Threatened suicide.*
- *Took me to godmen and for a* chalia; *and the brightest move of all,*
- *Tried to kill me with kindness.*

He suddenly became all that I had ever wanted him to be. More importantly, he took care to perform all his good deeds in front of you two, putting me at a disadvantage. Never in my life was he the husband I could look up to. In everything I surged ahead of him—education, income, breeding, even things like driving a car, swimming, etc. I got him out of the financial mess he landed himself in, by repaying his colossal debts even as he betrayed the one thing that existed between us—trust. The times he showed neither compassion nor care during illnesses, the times he did not protect me from the amorous advances of other men, the time he bashed me up, the time he let his mother take you away, leaving me heartbroken—occurred when you were too small to understand. I bore all and protected his eggshell ego because I understood that he was trying to

*get the better of his inferiority complex by subjugating me.
I would cry copious tears in those days. Your father would
turn away in disgust and order me to stop the 'dramebaazi'.
I grew a shell around my heart and for years afterwards,
my eyes became dry wells.*

*Then came Rajan Bhardwaj, bringing with him tears
of shame and sorrow, dishonour, and disaster. Believe me,
he did not break our marriage. As there was nothing left
in the marriage when he entered the scene (I have diaries
to vouch for it), I was easy prey for any predator. Fed up of
loving and rejection, I was desperate for someone to restore
my sense of self-worth. It was a salve to my bruised heart
to have someone so desperately in need of me. And let me
tell you, I did not choose him. He chose me. I would have
opted for Rajiv Mehra (a colleague at AIIMS), had my
parents allowed me to do so. It was Rajan Bhardwaj who
pursued me relentlessly in spite of repeated rejections. Like
you, I was disgusted by the sight of him, but he would not
take no for an answer. I complained about him to your
father, but as usual, it was of no use. I tired of resisting,
and finally succumbed. For every little smile in this star-
crossed relationship, I paid with a thousand tears. I cried
till I could cry no more. Yet, despite of the havoc it caused,
I have no regrets for true love is a rare commodity. I pray
that you and Simar too get someone who loves you above
all else—preferably within the bonds of marriage.*

*Perhaps someday you will reconsider your denial of
a long-lasting marital relationship. Why have you to look
only at Papa and me to sour your outlook? So many happily
married couples exist in our family, and all around you.
Surely you cannot have such a tubular vision. It serves
no purpose, taking things so much to heart. Everyone is a
victim of his circumstances. It is up to us to rise above the
negative and latch on to the positive.*

*I definitely did not intend to poison your mind against
your father. I only wanted to let you know why I rebuffed
his advances, for I was being shown in a bad light. I also
told you that he has been a good father and you should*

never to disrespect him, which you had likened to the statuary warning on a cigarette carton!

I read books on child psychology and learnt that an atmosphere of hostility was far more detrimental to the psyche of a child than a non-messy divorce. I also read that it was wiser to discuss the separation with the children, and to prepare them for it. That was what I was trying to do. I would have told you the rest in due course, but matters spiralled out of control and you learnt all in a manner that turned you against me forever.

Whatever I did in those days boomeranged. In order to acquaint you with my future partner, I sent you with him to buy CDs from Palika bazaar, which you construed as a bribe!

When the divorce did not materialize, I did not abandon you and run away. On rational reflection I realised that it was for the best, for sooner or later, the question of child custody would arise. It was unbearable that any child of mine stand in court and makes choices; most of all, I could not bear it that you do not chose me. I decided to wait till you were old enough to decide. But how old was old enough? When does mothering stop, if it ever stops at all during a mother's lifetime?

As for 'she eats my father's food . . .' Let me tell you that, I am the only female in your father's entire clan who earns. I invested more than your father did in the house we live in. I pay for the washing of your his clothes, the polishing of his boots, the cleaning of his car, the pressing of his clothes, the gas for his food, and I pay the servant who cooks it. Surely, that costs more than the money he spends on my food. Your paternal grandparents can't bear the sight of each other, other females in his family carry secrets in their hearts darker than mine (which I will not divulge), yet have no qualms about subsisting on their husband's income; then why this cruel, unwarranted barb?

As for your suicide attempt, I am ashamed of myself for raising such a weakling. You buckle under the first onslaught. Karan, this is just the beginning. There is a galore of failures, frustrations, and rejections awaiting you or, for that matter, everyone else on this earth, and it is terribly easy to give in. Learn to be a survivor come what may.

*You are fourth male in my life to evoke torrential tears, and nowadays the only one. You have hurt me the most because I love you best of all. Ever since your birth, your affection has been at a premium. I have cried inconsolably on account of the enforced separation in your infancy. Your accident aged me by ten years, and now this intolerable hostility. As a result, my love for you has been laced with possessiveness, jealousy, and insecurity. On your side it has never been unconditional and complete like Simar's. It was always **Maasi** who was prettier, **Daadima** whom you loved 51 per cent and me, 49 per cent. Mind you, all this occurred when I was a normal loving mother who hadn't fallen from her pedestal. You would hide from me to kiss and hug Daadima, as if you were guilty lovers though she smugly showed off your preference for her. I remember an incidence trivial in itself but one that made a deep impact on me. I had half jokingly told Maasi that first you were your grandmother's, then you would be your wife's, bypassing me altogether. You had snorted and said **'abhi se** (from now). The look that passed between the two of you twisted a knife in my heart. Something died within me that day and I gave up trying. It was never so with Simar. I did not have to contest for his affection simply because I knew that there was no need to. He was my son first and foremost, everything else afterwards.*

Remember the time you tried to throw me out of my own house? Like a vulnerable fool I grovelled in front a chit of a boy who played God. All this served to reiterate the fact that in a few years from now, when you are independent and self-sufficient you would fly the nest and I would remain where I was—bereft, lonely, and at crossroads forever.

God forbid that I ever become indifferent to your indifference, for then I will cease to be a mother. I can forgive, and in due course forget. What amazes me is that *you have allowed emotional insults to grow into festering wounds. You were smart enough to use the situation to your advantage though. Undermining my authority as a mother, you held my predicament as a whip over me and I uttered not a word. You will be pleased to know that that you **have** punished me and I hurt badly. Judge me, condemn me, but after a fair trial. Even a common criminal is entitled to one.*

Now that you are poised to take flight; now that you are on the brink of a bright future in a faraway country, do you intend to leave with a sense of relief, cynical, hardened, cruel, and harsh with all positive emotions entombed alive? Or would you like to clear the air, forgive, and forget? Would you accept me with all my faults? I offer no excuses for I have none. I have done what I thought was right in the circumstances. Either way, let me know where I stand. I will respect your wishes and abide by them.

*Remove all trace of my existence from your life if you will (I see that you have not put any picture of mine in your bag). I will try to adjust even if it took me the rest of my life. I stake no claim on you as a mother. I will not trouble you with my problems, perhaps even with my demise—for according to you, they will be my just desserts. As of now, you will be glad to know that I suffer as no mother ever should—a suffering I would not wish upon an enemy. Yet it is human nature to hope and the sole glimmer of hope that remains is exposure to Western culture to which, as far as it suits **you**, you have taken to, like a fish to water. Perhaps your horizons will widen, your outlook will alter, and you will realise that what I have done was, after all, was no big deal—I acknowledged my incompatibility with your father and tried to opt out. With time, you might understand that I too, was entitled to a place under the sun. Till then, where ever you go my estranged son, my prayers and blessings go with you.*

Love,
Mama

331

When I gave it to Karan, I felt it was not a letter but my fate that he held in his hands. After he went through it, he touched my feet and begged forgiveness. I held him to my heart and covered his faces with kisses. All was well with my world again.

67

Of late life had become a placid pool, and I was thankful for the calm. I was available for my children and for Raju and MS did not have to face public humiliation, which was all that mattered to him. I was content to let matters drift along, but Raju was the type who created rapids where there were none. He insisted upon a court marriage. I tried to tell him that there were many like us who lived parallel lives, but to no avail. He was tired of having me in bits and pieces. He wanted to set up home with me, to make leisurely love at night and wake up with me in the morning. He wanted me to play hostess to his colleagues, travel with me, and see the world through my eyes. In short, he wanted me as a wife in the proper sense of the word.

I tried to reason him out of it. Our lives were full of uncertainties. The S continued to be a real threat. He had to drop all business affairs and do what they demanded of him whenever he was summoned. His partners did not take kindly to his mysterious disappearances, suspecting that he was double-crossing them. The last time he was forced to act chauffeur to the S, they were stranded in the Gujrat floods. Food and water were at a premium, and all shelters submerged. They spent a week on the roof of the matador with a decomposing body inside, for the oldest S died of gastroenteritis, and the body could not be disposed of, till the waters receded. Raju returned from that trip badly shaken. He wanted me to come away with him, but I told him that as long as I stayed with MS, we were safe. The moment I stepped out, we would be dead meat.

'You call this living?' he said dramatically. 'Better to die together than to live like this.' Such a foolish romanticism did not warrant an answer.

Another reason we could not leave was that, thanks to the S, he was up to his ears in debt. How could he leave without returning the money to those who had helped him in his hour of need? What would we subsist on if I left my work too? This was not some teenage love story; we had to be practical.

'I have a few pieces of land still left that I can sell. This will solve all our monetary problems.'

'What about MS?' I asked.

He harassed Raju relentlessly calling him a eunuch—I heard it myself taped on Raju's cell phone. It hurt Raju as it was meant to hurt and there were tears in his eyes. I told him to retaliate by saying, 'Shame on you for your wife prefers a eunuch to you.' At this he laughed happily like a child and the taunt troubled him no more. I did wonder though, how MS got to know about his defect. Maybe, MS was taunting him for not fathering a child.

Last but not the least, there was the question of my children. They were not settled as yet, and there was no way I could ditch them at this point of time. Coming to think of it, I wondered, what was cut off point? Perhaps when I was old and ailing, and needed them more than they needed me. They would not want me then, but neither would anyone else.

Once the S saw that there was nothing further to gain, they were willing to 'forgive' us. But there were conditions attached. Raju had to go for a *chalia* for forty days to Bangla Sahib Gurudwara. So the high caste Brahmin went to a Sikh place of worship for 40 days at a stretch. After he had finished, they told him that this *chalia* was invalid because he did not abstain from sex in those 40 days. There was no such precondition for a *chalia*, but who were we to argue with the might of the

S? Another 40 days went by and we did not even see each other, lest the S decree that this chalia too, was a failure. When we finally met, it was as if we were meeting after 40 years. This time, his fault lay in the fact that he did not go to the gurudwara on the 41st day for *shukrana* (thanksgiving). How on earth was he to know? Never one for ritualistic religion I did not know either. The third time around everything went according to their satisfaction, but they weren't done with us yet. As a final form of penance, they insisted that both of us visit the ten historical gurudwaras of Delhi after 8 p.m. I had to wear a wrought iron pendant as an identity tag! So if it was the Majnu Ka Tila on the banks of the Jamuna one night, it was Nanaksar atop a hill on another. To Sheesh Ganj, Bangla Sahib, Rakab Ganj, Nanak Pio, Tikana Sahib, Bala Sahib, and Moti Bagh gurudwaras we went. Most embarrassing of all was a visit to the local gurudwara with him, in place of my husband. The pendant felt like a dog collar and I had an eerie feeling of being watched by unseen eyes. Though it was difficult to get out of the house at this time of the night, I managed somehow because our lives depended on it.

At last, we were free of the fanatics. The impossible had been accomplished. The least we owed each other was a marriage. Never mind the financial constraints. It wasn't as if I was running away from my practice. Moreover, Raju was a healthy adult male with an astute business sense. With the sword of Damocles removed from over his head, he could concentrate on earning for our future. Of course, public declaration of the ceremony would have to wait till the children were settled. He wanted it nevertheless. I asked myself was there anyone one else with whom I would like to spend the rest of my life? No. After all, there must be something in a relationship for it to mature from black to grey hair. He made me feel loved and cherished, young and desirable. Though he had inflicted immeasurable pain, he had also taken me to the acme of joy. It was flattering to be so desired. Moreover, I tired of resisting and as usual, he wore me down. The month's notice was given. As I was reluctant to enter the dingy portals of the courtroom again, the court person came home, and we signed the papers in our flat. It was on the same date we had acknowledged each other as husband and wife at Gauri Shankar Mandir, twelve years ago. It saved us the expense of buying two anniversary presents each year!

I was sorely disappointed with the wedding present. I felt as if I had a done him a favour by marrying him (after all he was the persistent one), and deserved the Kohinoor! He who had been so generous as a lover gave me a mere silk sari on the most important day of our lives. It has been rightly said that all lovers are different, while all husbands are the same. Suddenly, I was ashamed of my avarice. Why, *I* was behaving like a wife already. As a beloved, I was reluctant to accept expensive gifts and now as a wife of a few minutes, I *expected* him to spend lavishly on me, that too when I knew that his finances were in sorry straits.

Did I feel any different as a wife vis-a-vis a mistress? No, because the marriage was a nonevent of no import—a surreptitious, illegally conducted legal affair, like the divorce years ago. As far as I was concerned, official bindings had ceased to matter. I had agreed for a civil marriage mainly to humour Raju. Of all the corny reasons to get married, this was the corniest. His insecurity had goaded him to insist on it. How could I explain to him that there was no binding the heart? If for some reason this union failed, the real me would be light years away, and the marriage certificate would remain what it was—a piece of paper.

68

Never for a moment did I think that Raju would pocket me with the marriage certificate and forget all about me. I was but a loose end that had to be tied before he went on with life; ostensibly, to earn for our future. It took me a year to understand that he had no further use for me. I was but a trophy he had bagged. To think that the chief reason for marrying him was that he was the only one on this earth who loved me for myself! Perhaps he did; hadn't he risked his life, fortune, and sanity for me?

Suddenly, the lure of lucre became more alluring. If it were another woman, I would have understood, but money? I could not fight. Wealth became his new mistress. He began talking in terms of corores! Instead of being pleased, I was afraid and unhappy. No one could earn so much by fair means. I told him to be wary of his new partners lest he land in trouble, but there was no reasoning with him. The goddess Laxmi had finally showered her blessing on him and he was not going to spurn her bounty.

Overnight, he became an industrialist. His lifestyle improved. He wore designer clothes and sunglasses. If lunch was at Hyatt, dinner was at Taj. His tastes had improved with his company. His partners even tried replacing the ageing female in his life by foreign whores in luxury suites. He refused, saying, 'You may be one of the richest men in India, but you are poorer than me in one respect. You have never known true love. If you had experienced what I have experienced, you wouldn't be dangling female flesh in front to me. And I do not

337

need your help to get the services of a whore however high class!' Raju had retorted.

I glowed with happiness when he recounted such conversations to me, and there would be a resurgence of the old love. This tided me over the next week or so. Then the euphoria would die down and I'd ask myself, 'So what if he is not seeing other women? He isn't seeing me either.'

I missed the old Raju who would spend hours talking with me. I used to admonish him for taking so much of my time and ruining my practice.

'Why can't you work like normal men?' Little did I know that he would throw this sentence on my face, now when I craved attention?

'You were the one who insisted that I work like normal men.'

'You swing from one extreme to the other. Either you stifle by your continual presence, or you remove yourself altogether. This is not how normal men behave.'

'But I am doing all this for you.'

'At what cost?'

'I promise you that the moment I reach a target of 100 corores, I'll quit.'

'100 corores! Whatever will we do with that much money?'

'I know the pinch of poverty and the shame of being in debt. Now when I have got the opportunity to make money, why shouldn't I?'

'But your travails have sifted fair weather friends from real ones. If you remember correctly, I did not ditch you when you were bankrupt though probably, I'll be the first woman in the world to leave a man for his money.'

I needed a mere half an hour of telephonic conversation to update each other on daily events, but he was too busy to give me thirty minutes of his day. When I complained, he'd hand me an expensive gift. Agreed that his presents were classy and elegant these days, but it was degrading to accept them in his stead. Of what use was a diamond pendant if he wasn't around to appreciate it? Money had become as much as an addiction with him, as he had become with me. He refused to accept the fact that he had started taking me for granted, and I hadn't the guile to play hard to get. The original repulsion was real and the present affection was genuine. What was the use of trying to retain a man by artifice? I hated the whining, weeping nag I had been reduced to.

All the living we did together was in a weekly 2 hours interlude. Life had to be fitted in that much time. We quarrelled, cried, aired grievances, laughed, updated each other on our affairs, and made love all at the same time. It was a highly unsatisfactory state of affairs, but with which I had to contend because *he* willed it so. I desperately needed an emotional connect, but he was never there for me.

The love in my heart was not a jungle tree that could sustain itself. It was a hothouse plant that needed constant tending. If I could not tolerate neglect from a husband whom I did not love, one can imagine the agony I went through at being neglected by the man I loved. I befriended a scientist during my morning walks and the editor of a poetry magazine who had published a few of my poems. When I told Raju about them during the course of a conversation, he demanded that I give up these innocuous friendships. It was preposterous. Now that I had time to contemplate, I was amazed at what I had given up for his sake. I was determined to resist him this time. To think, that he had been attracted to me because I was educated, cultured, and modern. Once he had me entrenched in his gilded prison, he proceeded to convert me into a veiled village woman. It was galling to toe his line and be dumped for my pains. Flashes of my old personality began to resurface.

'Don't ever make the mistake of thinking that you have me in your clutches by that joke of a marriage. It makes not a whit of difference. Once I cease loving you, no bit of paper is going to bind me. Understood?'

Now that I had shown some spirit, I became the wild mare he had to harness. He wooed me like a princess and humoured the incorrigible romantic in me. He took me to our old haunts. We held hands and smiled into each other's eyes. I rested my head against his chest and listened to the reassuring beat of his heart. Such were the moments I existed for. But these interludes were few and far between, like lampposts in the dark and dreary road of life, and the cycle of neglect and tears would start all over again.

I tried to pick up life from where I had left it before I had met the tornado called Rajan. I resumed my writing and got a good response. I was no longer in a rush to depart from my hospital, and re-established contact with my colleagues. I swam, walked my dog and almost succeeded in reclaiming my soul from Raju's clutches. Then his business partner would be called away on a personal matter; with time to spare, Raju would expect me to drop everything and rush into his arms. I resented this bitterly. It was as if I existed in a state of limbo in his absence, and he had only to snap his fingers to bring me back to life. He was one conceited bastard who had me where he wanted me, and what's more, knew it. I'd be dishonest if I said that I did not enjoy our time together, oases as they were, in the arid desert of my life.

Little did I know that there would come a time when, I'd prefer the monotony of the desert to upheavals of episodic ecstasy.

69

Word came from Mussoorie that Mataji was ill. Bahabiji, her elder daughter-in-law, could not cope and sent her to Delhi. I was shocked to see the formidable matron reduced to this—her hair was sticky with grime, there was mildew on her artificial teeth, and her private parts were excoriated and raw. She was totally incontinent and recognised no one. That the domineering woman so fond of good living could come to such a pass was unbelievable.

She had suffered serious setbacks due to diabetes previously, but this time it was the irreversible hold of Alzheimer. Though her present was obscure, she recounted in minute detail events that occurred 50 years ago. She wept over *her* mother's death with fresh grief and remembered with renewed relish the fritters she had eaten at Sapphire Hotel 25 years ago. Her ramblings brought water either to one's eyes or mouth. She worried about imaginary babies and called out to people long dead and gone. She was agitated and comatose in turns. She attacked those who looked after her. I bore her kicks and slaps stoically for she knew not what she did.

They had put her on sedatives in Mussoorie to calm her down. The result was disastrous. She would be found lying unconscious on the floor wallowing in her own excreta, she who, unlike her husband, was scrupulously clean. Appalled at Mataji's state, her daughter, who had come to look her up, rang up to ask if she could bring her to Delhi. After all, MS was doctor and son rolled into one. To her shock, he refused stating that she would not tolerate the Delhi heat! His excuse was inexcusable and the two quarrelled bitterly. I had no inkling of what transpired between brother and sister. Bhabiji had made it amply clear that she was not up to looking after the invalid. In desperation, the daughter rang me up at a time when she knew that MS would be at his clinic for she could see her mother suffer so.

'But of course. Of what use are doctors in the family if we cannot look after our own?' I said.

'I knew, I knew you would not refuse.' She gushed with overwhelming gratitude. She could never forgive Bhabiji for neglecting her mother. Not that Mataji had ever behaved like a mother to either of us. I do not recollect being the recipient of a single kind word or gesture from her. Whenever she visited Delhi, there were presents for her son and grandsons but nothing for me. Dry fruits bought by Papaji from Khari Baoli would be eaten on the sly. Fresh fruits *my* husband bought were hidden in the cupboard! I wondered how she could swallow edibles stolen from the mouths of her grandchildren. Did she not choke on them? Even at her age, she wanted expensive clothes and footwear while I had to make do with the old. MS would soothe my ruffled feathers by saying that she was illiterate and did not know better, while I was intelligent enough to avoid wasteful expenditure. Indeed! Most of all, I could never forgive or forget the way she alienated my firstborn from me but, this was not the time for dwelling on grievances or wrecking vengeance upon her.

It struck me that kindness to daughters-in-law is an investment that stands one in good stead when the power equation alters, as it does eventually. As the saying goes 'be good to people on your way up; you may need them on your way down', but at the height of power, people tend to think that they are invincible and commit atrocities that the sufferer is not likely to forget. I had no desire to increase her sufferings for I was genuinely sorry to see the state she had been reduced to. With proper nursing care, we had her sparklingly clean in a matter of days. There was nothing anyone could do about her deteriorating mental condition though. As Mataji gained strength, some of her faculties returned. She reverted to her old ways. A confirmed diabetic, she craved sweetmeats, and made the servant get them for her on the sly. She wanted new clothes and slippers, and worried about her things being robbed. She blamed the sweeper for stealing her money—this when she was brought in a semi-comatose state and had no cash on her. She thought that I was keeping her here by force and demanded that she be sent back to Mussoorie. Exasperated, I said, 'Mataji, if people in Mussoorie could look after you, they wouldn't have sent you here. What have I to gain by keeping you here?'

She took to sitting in the lounge, beating her breast and complaining to all and sundry how badly I was treating her even as she urinated on the sofa! I would have become a nervous wreck had I not decided to forget that I was her daughter-in-law. From now on, I would treat her like a patient and steer clear of the emotional aspect. Even here I encountered opposition. She did exactly what the doctor told her not to do. Proud and independent as ever, she refused the bedpan and walked to the toilet alone. The inevitable happened—she fell, and broke her femur! It was the worst thing to have happened to a woman of 86. She was shifted to the Intensive Care Unit (ICU) of a nearby hospital. Obstinate as ever, she was the only patient who pulled out all her tubes. Her limbs had to be tied to restrain her. As her haemoglobin was low, blood transfusion was required. Once again, her beloved son backed out. Karan was abroad and her less loved grandson Simar donated blood for her. I had nothing against *my* son donating blood, but why couldn't MS, *her* son? As if this was not shameful enough, he made *me* to pay the hospital bills—for his pocket, as usual, was empty.

Back home, nursing care had to be redoubled to prevent bedsores. I doubled my nurses' salary for the extra burden on them. MS had neither time nor money for his mother. The nurses and I had a gruelling time managing her. She would pull out the Ryles tube again and again till her nose was reduced to a bloody pulp. She managed to pull out the urinary catheter, the inflated bulb notwithstanding! Repeated re-insertions led to severe urinary tract infection. As a result she developed high-grade fever with rigours and intractable vomiting that plastered her hair and made us gag. It would have been kinder to let her die, but I could not dream of withholding treatment. Appalled at her miserable state, her sisters sprinkled holy water on her for an easy exit of her soul and my father-in-law kept an *akhand path* for *deh mukti* (three days continuous reading of the gur granth sahib for the release of her soul), but she held on to life with unbelievable tenacity. I watched the proceedings with tears in my eyes and hoped that when my time came, I would take leave gracefully before my near and dear ones prayed for *my* death.

Mataji took to making patterns on the wall with her shit (a new art form?) and throwing it on whoever ventured near. It collected under her nails, which in her agitated state, she would not let us cut. From where did she get the strength to resist us, I could not fathom? One day, I was helping the nurses clean her up, for they could not control her on their own. As I tried to turn her against her will to clean the faeces smeared on her back and thighs, she spewed forth the choicest epithets.

'Whore. Bitch, slut. I hope you rot in hell. *Tainu kod paye, keede pain* (may you get leprosy, may you be maggot ridden). I know what sort of night duties you do. I know all! You have opened a prostitution den here. You lie on your buttocks under ten men.'

These were not the ramblings of a sick mind. This was what she really thought of me. Dementia had ripped apart the curtain of social restrain. I was badly shaken. Did she not understand that she was totally at my mercy? Of her entire clan, I was the only one who was looking after her and this was what I got for my efforts!

Angered beyond measure I screamed, 'If I am that hateful to you why have you come to me?'

'Because we have spent money on you.'

'What money?' I asked surprised.

'Money on your marriage, you bitch. Go away.'

'Why don't *you* go back to where you came from?'

'This is not your father's house.'

'It is not *your* father's house, either. Can't you understand I am only trying to help?'

'Smear the shit on her face,' she told the sisters.

I tried to restrain her, but she had the strength of a demon in her frail body. Continuing her tirade she said, 'Whore, bitch, I curse you from the bottom of my heart. *Tera beda gark ho* (may the ship of your life sink).'

I had had enough.

'You must have done something far worse than me to find the ship of *your* life is such sorry straits,' I retorted stung to the quick.

'This is but a temporary phase. I will recover soon enough.' she retorted.

'You are totally at the mercy of someone you hate. Don't you understand that I am looking after you despite all? Give me one reason, why should I?'

What a family. I had been married into! Papaji was sickeningly sweet when he needed me, but had no qualms about stabbing me in my back. MS maintained the veneer of normalcy no matter what, because it suited him to utilise my services and money. Now it was Mataji's turn to exploit me. Did they not have an iota of self-respect?

Why was I, a right thinking, intelligent being, allowing myself to be manipulated so? Why didn't I run before I lost my sanity? Even as I asked myself the question, I knew the answer. Subconsciously, it was penance for the wrong I had done my husband, but I had had enough. Trembling with rage, I marched upstairs and confronted Papaji.

'You insisted on coming to Delhi at a time when I had my hands full with Mataji, saying that 'I too have a duty towards my wife'. Why don't you stop warming your bed and do what you have supposedly come to do?' But he did nothing of that sort. He had come to Delhi because he was afraid of dying in the bitter Mussoorie winter. He had no intention of wobbling down the stairs to care for a wife he never liked, and risk breaking a leg. Sure enough as summer replaced winter, he returned to the hills leaving her behind.

Day after day I watched the sick woman fade away. Her heavy breasts were reduced to mere nipples. Her full abdomen scalloped into a scaphoid and her right leg, a broken stick, lying any which way due to her non-healing hip fracture. Her eyes were sunken, her cheeks hollow, and every rib could be counted on her chest. She had been reduced to a skin-covered skeleton, and yet she breathed. I marvelled at her will to live despite all.

She had nightmares about demons coming for her and would try to ward them off with her claw-like hands. She raked my arms with her nails and resisted all that was good for her. She continued to spew a volley of swearwords that had not existed in her conscious vocabulary, but her abuses had lost their sting for she cursed everyone in sight. She thought the nurses were seducing her doddering 90-year-old husband for his money; the sweeper was robbing her, and the servant was trying to murder her! She cursed her husband for dallying with other women (which he must have done in his heydays), her sons for deserting her, her sisters and daughter for neglecting her.

At times such as these, she would cling to me and beseech, 'You are the only one who has stood by me. Promise that you will never leave me.' And with tears streaming down my face I'd promise to remain by her side.

During sporadic lucid intervals, she would ask me to tell the loved ones who had forsaken her to pretend that she was already dead and come for she sorely missed them. At other times she would ask me not to inform them of her death; what use would they be to her after she died.

'I'll get up from my funeral pyre and strangulate them if they come after my death when they neglect me now.' She would scream in impotent rage, and I would pity her. The very people on whom she had showered love (and gifts in cash and kind) had abandoned her now that she was of no use to them.

After 2 years of insidious, tortured wasting, she finally gave up the ghost. Of her huge family of husband, children, grandchildren, and great-grandchildren, not a soul was by her side. The nurse who came to sponge her in the morning found that she breathed no more.

70

I became reconciled to the fact that Raju was busy earning for our future and could not give me the attention he gave before. Instead of consigning the time so gained to boredom, I put its untold wealth to good use. There was a rewarding life beyond Raju, and I learned to reap its serene riches.

Matters came to such a pass that I began to resent his calls, considering all he rang up to say was, 'I love you, my darling wife, God bless you.' And expect me to say in return, 'I love you, my darling husband, God bless you.' It was the last sentence we were supposed to utter every night, after exchanging news about our day. Our interaction had so diminished that more often than not, this was the only sentences we uttered during the entire day. It ceased to have any meaning as far as I was concerned. What rankled was that, at times he used it as an effective tool to shut me up mid-sentence! I began to wonder at the futility of such a relationship and wrote:

What Does One Do?

What does one do?
When lovers become
Husband and wife,
Without the
Bondage of marriage?
When passions
Refuse to ignite,
Like an ageing car

On winter mornings.
When pulsations slow down,
In time-hardened arteries.
When the reservoir of love
Has sprung a leak,
And emotions seep out.
When the cataract of proximity,
Obscures clarity of vision.
When love has come and gone
Like a virulent attack of small pox,
Leaving indelible scars behind.
Do you
Cling together for old time's sake,
Or, go while the going is good?

As I was not up to offering resistance to the brick wall called Raju, I allowed myself to drift along. Then something happened, trivial in itself, but which altered my perception of our relationship. Raju had bought a new car and was given a complimentary dinner coupon for two at Vasant Intercontinental by the car company. He offered to take me, knowing full well that I could not go out with him at night.

'Then I will tear up the coupons,' he said loyally, which I thought was a waste. At night he rang me up on my landline to hurriedly exchange the standard dénouement but I had something of import to tell him.

'Can't it wait till tomorrow?' he asked.

'Why, are you busy?'

'I am in a meeting. Moreover, I am ringing up from my cell phone and the battery is low.'

'Okay.' My heart was heavy.

'Say it quickly.'

'I love you, my darling husband, God bless you.' I stated parrot-like. As I was putting the receiver down, I heard an operator say, 'Vasant Intercontinental' on a parallel line.

I felt myself grow cold all over. It wasn't an important meeting and he was not ringing up from his cell phone. He was availing of the free dinner coupons at the five-star hotel with God knows who? If this was the place I held in his life, I might as well exit gracefully. I was nothing but a sparsely used sexual toilet.

Oblivious of the havoc he had brought, Raju rang up a few days later to fix up a rendezvous.

'I cannot come.'

'I'll come nevertheless and wait for you.' This was one form of emotional blackmailing I had succumbed to in the past. I would not be bulldozed into submission anymore.

'As you like.' I was noncommittal.

He did not heed the quiet desperation in my voice. He still thought that he had but snap his fingers for me to come running. Well, he was in for a nasty surprise this time. An hour later he rang up to ask incredulously, 'Are you held up in an emergency case?'

'No.'

'Then why haven't you come?'

'Because I told you I wouldn't.'

'I have a surprise for you.'

'So what's new?' I refused to nibble the bait.

He begged and bullied, ordered and cajoled, but nothing would induce me to go.

Unable to bear the rejection, he turned belligerent and began berating me in the foulest language.

'I don't have to listen to this . . .'

He was immediately contrite. 'I'm sorry. Please don't put the phone down.'

'Okay,' I said resignedly. 'What is it that you wanted to tell me besides making a prestige issue of calling me over?'

'I told you that I have a surprise for you.'

'I am fed up of your surprises.'

'But why aren't you coming?'

'Because I don't want to,' I replied stubbornly. 'Strangely, one who stood me up time and again cannot stand being stood up once.'

'You are not coming on purpose, I always had a reason.'

'Like the one at Vasant Intercontinental?' I taunted.

'I'll explain . . .'

'Don't you lie your way out of this one.' If there was something I hated more than his petty fibs, it was his pretending that he hadn't uttered them.

'Please come and see what I have brought?'

'I am not in the least bit interested.'

'I have got a briefcase full of 500 rupee notes. It is for sending Simar abroad for higher studies.'

He knew that my children were my weakness and this was something I would not be able to resist. I was furious.

'How dare you try to bribe me? As for his studying abroad, it was but a passing fancy. I know how to live within my means.'

'Well, the offer is open. Come.'

'No.'

'Then you'll never see my face again,' he said, getting desperate.

'Who wants to?' I could be as ruthless as him when I chose.

'You know how desperately I love you.' He changed tactics.

'You have a fine way of showing it.'

'Everywhere I go, I buy things for you.'

'I do not care for them anymore.'

If anything, they made me feel like the retired concubine of a benefactor, who threw an occasional trinket my way for old times' sake. In the early days of his newfound riches, he tried to rub his generosity in my face. Throwing the gift back at him I had said, 'You would have given them to any whore who pleasured you.'

I forgot that I wasn't baiting a gentleman, but an uncouth villager, who gave the lady as good as he got. He had laughed at my face.

'I can get the best hooker in town for one-tenth the amount and would not have to put up with her tantrums either. As for the pleasure, isn't it mutual?' At which he had burst into laughter and I into tears. I wondered whether our feelings for each other was really love. There raged between us a constant war for supremacy. Anyway, I had won this battle. It was one of my few victories and I gloated over it.

71

Though MS had not pressed for his conjugal rights earlier, he now started making passes at me. He would brush my breasts accidentally when he passed by. He tried sleeping in the bed next to me. He even bought a gold bracelet for our marriage anniversary which was a big deal considering his miserliness, and tried to kiss me. I ought to have been flattered at having two men vie for my affections, but I was not.

The next time I met Raju, I was stupid enough to complain to a jealous lover that a husband was demanding his conjugal rights! He went ballistic, and nothing I said soothed his ruffled feathers. To distract him I changed the topic.

'You know the money you were offering for Simar. I have discovered a course in Europe that costs twenty-five lacs. It is cheaper than . . .'

'Why don't you ask MS for it?'

I relapsed into a stunned silence. I knew jealousy was provocation enough to say hurtful things, but this was one blow my self-respect would not take. He had humiliated me en number of times and I had forgiven him; but when it spilled on to my children, I could not take it. Why, I could sell the flat and send my son abroad this very instant. It was only because Raju had been so persistent that I had presumed, and now this totally unwarranted rebuff. He tried to make amends in the only way he could. Firstly, by denying that he had ever said such a reprehensible thing; then pretending that I had misinterpreted it, and finally, by apologising and offering to bear the entire cost of Simar's education. Disgusted, I walked away.

A few days later, his wife fell seriously ill. When I asked him if he had taken her to the doctor he said, 'Why should I? What is she to me?'

My jealousy notwithstanding, I felt a pang for the sick woman and an enduring contempt for Raju. He could have taken her to the hospital on humanitarian grounds, but he wanted to rub in the fact that he had detached himself completely from her, and expected me to do the same with my husband. The next day, he sent his driver to me on an errand. I asked after Snehlata's health.

'Sir got her admitted to the hospital. She is better now,' he said.

'Oh!'

If he could lie to me about such a small thing, God knows what else he was lying to me about. For all I knew he was still sleeping with her after alienating me from my husband. Why, in the initial days he had bribed my servant to confirm whether I had actually shifted to another room. He was nothing but a despicable rat who deserved to be shot. The next time we met, I felt cheap confronting him, but I wanted to see how he would extricate himself from this one. At first, he blatantly denied it but when I glared at him disbelievingly he said, 'I was going that way and gave her a lift to the hospital.'

'Then why pretend that you have washed your hands off her especially when you insist that I keep away from MS?'

'How do I know that you have kept yourself from him?'

'As if to say you don't? Only a mind as diabolical as yours can stoop so low as to bribe my servant to spy on me.'

Within minutes, the fight snowballed into proportions beyond control. Grievances were brought out of closets and aired. Long forgotten files clicked open in the computers of our minds, escalating altercations. At one point in time he lost control, wrapped his hand around my throat and squeezed!

Then, horrified at what he had done, he covered my face with kisses, trying to pass off the attempted strangulation as a joke. A funny sense of humour he had. I howled and I keened; I sobbed and I cried. I rocked back and forth, calling out to my mother. Raju clutched my feet and washed them with tears of repentance but I had had enough. Enough of abuse, abasement and atrocities to last me a lifetime. He vowed to make amends for the rest of his life, but I was beyond him, beyond us.

Something snapped within, never to be mended again. Perhaps it was the leash that chained me to him. I escaped from the clutches of his cloying attention and cunning captivity. Relief washed over me like rain on desert sands. Released of the resentment and rancour, desire and disappointment, hurt and humiliation his 'love' had spawned, my spirits soared like a bunch of helium balloons –wind-buoyed dancing specks of colour in vast open skies.

It has been said that the loss of someone you love is not the greatest loss a person suffers; losing yourself in that person and forgetting that you are special too, is your greatest loss. Long had I been enslaved to one who did not value my worth. Now that I had broken free, I experienced the exhilaration of liberty. Never again would I endure so much for the love of a man. It simply wasn't worth the price I had to pay.

I fled to the sanctuary of the mountains, to lose myself in their vastness so that my puny pains and pleasures mattered no more. Before I knew it, I found myself in a bus headed towards Hemkunt Sahib in the Himalayas. It was one of the holiest places of pilgrimage for the Sikhs, but I found God in the eternity of the mountains. In the arduous climb and rarified air, in melting glaciers and dripping forests, in rising mists and lowering clouds, in the sheer, stark faces of multi-hued rocks. I found Him in waterfalls hurtling down heights into rivers that surged through gorges and frothed on boulders. In the rainbow hued spray that shone in the sun. In the wild flowers that draped the hill slopes with sheets of colour; in

Brahma Kamals—lotuses that grew on rock instead of water. Tranquillity, an emotion that had deserted me during my 'Rajan Bhardwaj' years, now descended into my soul like a homing bird and folded its wings to stay.

After days of clinging precariously to mountain sides on a thin ribbon of a road, we reached the base of the shrine, for that was as far as a vehicle could go. The rest of the arduous climb, the pilgrims covered on ponies and then on foot, quenching their thirst with crystal clear waters of tiny falls that trickled down mountain clefts. After crossing a slippery glacier, we reached our destination—the clear cold spring nestled amongst seven mountain peaks (*sapt shringi*), where the gurudwara was situated. Guru Gobind Singhji had meditated here in his previous birth. It is said that even now, the gods bathe in this pool at night. No wonder the Himalayas are called the abode of the gods. Every inch of this exalted range is steeped in mythology. I gazed in awe at the untamable immensity of these gigantic ridges, and captured their incredible beauty in my soul. I felt big enough to encircle them in my arms, and small enough to merge in a snow flake. Instinctively, I knew that from now on, I had to look inwards for the peace I craved. I needed nothing. I needed no one. Raju and their ilk were shadows receding into a fading past.

> From gardens to wastelands to a vacuum sterile,
> From pain to numbness to complete anaesthesia,
> From reason to confusion to absence of thought,
> From desire to apathy to lack of want
> From action to reaction, to passive acceptance
> From animation to automation to inertia
> Have I attained Nirvana or death?

Epilogue

After years of acrimonious matrimony, we have settled into amiable incompatibility. Acute antipathies have been reduced to chronic irritants that I have learnt to live with. The mess I made of life or the mess that life made of me has been sorted out more or less. After thrashing about or being thrashed about, emotions have finally latched on to sense and the froth of futile rebellion has subsided. Passions, like red-hot lava, have run their tumultuous course and the bubbling volcano now lies dormant.

The children for whom I had put my life on hold have gone to distant lands to live lives of their own. Not that I have any regrets on that score; the one mission I had in life was to bring them up to the best of my ability. Whether I have succeeded or not, is for them to decide. As of now, I am content with their weekly phone calls, the only form of contact we have.

Living exclusively with the man I resented all my life is not proving as difficult as I had anticipated. It is strangely comforting to have another human in the vicinity. Quite like a lonely walker in failing light is reassured by the mere presence of another person in the park. Despite our differences, I would be lost without him, for though the situation is not idyllic, I have much to be grateful for. Meals are not eaten alone, I have an escort for social events, a man to deal with troublesome servants and I do not sleep in an empty house at night. Mostly, he does his thing, and I do mine without impinging upon each other's space. In fact, space is all that we give each other these days, except perhaps for company to Sunday movies. We share a house, household chores, and expenses as roommates do. Despite the turbulent waters that have flowed under (sometimes over) the bridge, living with a person for forty years has become a habit that is hard to break. There is no sharing of confidences, desires, or fears, no cuddling up to each other in bed, but that never was in our marriage. We *do* talk, but of mundane things like a leaking faucet, an atrocious electricity bill, an upcoming wedding in the extended family, and we still have our spats—chiefly over money. I argue just to make a point, for I understand that his stinginess is a personality flaw that cannot be rectified. All said and done, I am not unhappy. As I read somewhere, a successful marriage is not about happiness but stability and stability is what we have achieved, if nothing else.

Most fires have burnt out. I still enjoy my profession, but the enthusiasm has waned. I 'like to' swim and dance when it was 'love to' swim and dance earlier. The one thing that lingers is a lust for travel, for I long to see the beauty of the entire world before I take my leave of it. Physical fires that enslaved me to another, burn no more; and I do not miss them. I now devote my time and energies to more productive pursuits. The sole passion, vital and vibrant, that sustains me these days is my love for the written word, a passion I hope to retain till my dying day.

As my mother used to say, *'kashmakash hai zindagi sukh mey padna maut hai* (life is a struggle, peace is akin to death), so it is with me. Even as I marvelled at the remarkable adaptability of the human nature, even as I felt that I was done with the highs and lows and looked forward to enjoying my hard-earned contentment in the mellow evening of my existence, there arose in the trajectory of my life a horrendous hurdle. Cancer struck; but that is another story for another time.

~Amrinder Bajaj

Printed in the United States
By Bookmasters